P9-DMF-861

Advance Praise for
The Longings of Wayward Girls

"Brown tells a wonderfully suspenseful and eerie story as she goes back and forth between Sadie's childhood and her adult life, and the result is a novel full of mysteries, surprises, and the best kinds of psychological revelations."

—Margot Livesey, *New York Times* bestselling author of *The Flight of Gemma Hardy*

"Nothing is as it seems in this psychologically complex story of girls gone missing and mothers who stray. Karen Brown deftly alternates between two generations of parallel drama in a neighborhood of facades and gentle menace. I stayed awake far too late with the rich tension of wondering whether she'd bring her characters in for a safe landing."

—Nichole Bernier, author of *The Unfinished Work of Elizabeth D.*

"A heart-stopping novel of suspense that's as intelligent as it is compelling, as beautiful as it is disturbing. Brown's skill, empathy and sensitivity make this debut stand apart, and stand out. The astute observations, evocative atmosphere and bone-chilling scenes make for a moving, provocative read. A star is born."

—M.J. Rose, internationally bestselling author

"Brown intricately weaves together past and present, demonstrating how casual acts of childhood cruelty can linger well into a seemingly stable adult life. But Brown is also a uniquely talented writer, capable of teasing out poignant commonalities between her protagonist's teen and middle-aged selves. A beautifully written, unbearably tense debut novel."

—Holly Goddard Jones, author of *The Next Time You See Me*

"An absorbing novel about the misgivings and shortcomings of domestic life, about the confusing intersection of glamour, lust, and self-destruction, and about a woman haunted by a long-ago act of girlhood cruelty."

—Susanna Daniel, author of *Stiltsville* and *Sea Creatures*

"Through pitch-perfect details and an eloquent voice, Karen Brown delivers a suspenseful and memorable debut. Moving effortlessly between the late 1970s and the present-day, Brown explores what harm may come should we choose to follow the path laid down by those who came before us."

—Lori Roy, author of *Bent Road*

"In the time between playing with Barbies and puffing on stolen cigarettes, girls' games can turn dangerous—and sometimes fall far over the line. In *The Longings of Wayward Girls,* the past returns to plague the present with a vengeance that can cost a woman her husband and children. Brown's haunting prose sets the mood for the heartbreaking choices made by mothers and daughters."

—Randy Susan Meyers, international bestselling author of *The Murderer's Daughters* and *The Comfort of Lies*

"Delicate and beautiful, but with the spark and charge of a psychological thriller . . . Brown writes like an angel, but the shadows of past ghosts linger on every page. I could not put this compelling novel down."

—Jennifer Gilmore, author of *The Mothers*

"Lost and missing children haunt the pages of *The Longings of Wayward Girls,* a story rich with astute and poignant detail. This is compelling, read-all-day drama."

—Maryanne O'Hara, author of *Cascade*

ALSO BY KAREN BROWN

Pins & Needles: Stories

Little Sinners and Other Stories

THE LONGINGS
of
WAYWARD GIRLS

A Novel

KAREN BROWN

WASHINGTON SQUARE PRESS
New York   London   Toronto   Sydney   New Delhi

Washington Square Press
A Division of Simon & Schuster, Inc.
1230 Avenue of the Americas
New York, NY 10020

This book is a work of fiction. Any references to historical events, real people, or real places are used fictitiously. Other names, characters, places, and events are products of the author's imagination, and any resemblance to actual events or places or persons, living or dead, is entirely coincidental.

Copyright © 2013 by Karen Brown

"Reeling in the Years." Words and Music by Walter Becker and Donald Fagen. Copyright © 1972, 1973 UNIVERSAL MUSIC CORP. and RED GIANT, INC. Copyrights Renewed. All Rights Controlled and Administered by UNIVERSAL MUSIC CORP. All Rights Reserved. Used by Permission. Reprinted by permission of Hal Leonard Corporation.

By Tennessee Williams, from THE NIGHT OF THE IGUANA, copyright © 1961 by The University of the South. Reprinted by permission of New Directions Publishing Corp.

"Cecilia." Copyright © 1969 Paul Simon. Used by permission of the Publisher: Paul Simon Music.

Excerpt from "Young" from ALL MY PRETTY ONES by Anne Sexton © 1962 by Anne Sexton, renewed 1990 by Linda G. Sexton. Reprinted by permission of Houghton Mifflin Harcourt Publishing Company. All rights reserved. Reprinted by permission of SLL/Sterling Lord Literistic, Inc. Copyright by Anne Sexton.

All rights reserved, including the right to reproduce this book or portions thereof in any form whatsoever. For information address Washington Square Press Subsidiary Rights Department, 1230 Avenue of the Americas, New York, NY 10020.

First Washington Square Press trade paperback edition July 2013

WASHINGTON SQUARE PRESS and colophon are registered trademarks of Simon & Schuster, Inc.

For information about special discounts for bulk purchases, please contact Simon & Schuster Special Sales at 1-866-506-1949 or business@simonandschuster.com.

The Simon & Schuster Speakers Bureau can bring authors to your live event. For more information or to book an event contact the Simon & Schuster Speakers Bureau at 1-866-248-3049 or visit our website at www.simonspeakers.com.

Designed by Kyoko Watanabe

Manufactured in the United States of America

10 9 8 7 6 5 4 3 2 1

Library of Congress Cataloging-in-Publication Data

Brown, Karen, 1960–
   The longings of wayward girls : a novel / Karen Brown. — First Washington Square Press trade paperback edition.
       pages cm
   1. Women—Connecticut—Fiction. 2. Secrets—Fiction. 3. Psychological fiction. 4. Suspense fiction. I. Title.
   PS3602.R7213L66 2013
   813'.6—dc23
                                                                    2012044427

ISBN 978-1-4767-2491-1
ISBN 978-1-4767-2493-5 (ebook)

For Valerie and Dianne,
and for our parents.

. . . it was summer
as long as I could remember,
I lay on the lawn at night,
clover wrinkling under me,
the wise stars bedding over me,
my mother's window a funnel
of yellow heat running out, . . .

—Anne Sexton, "Young"

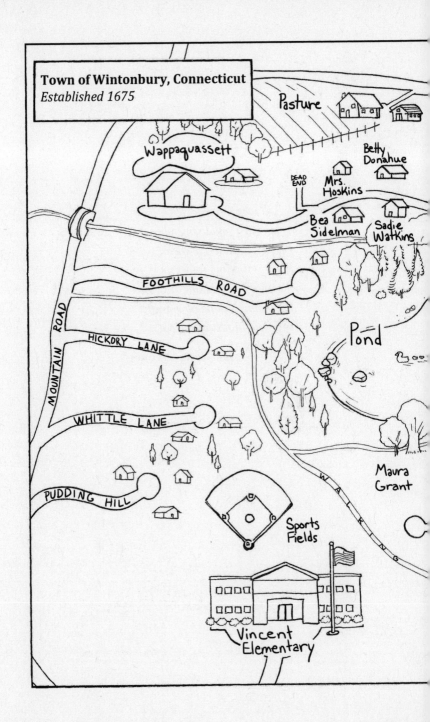

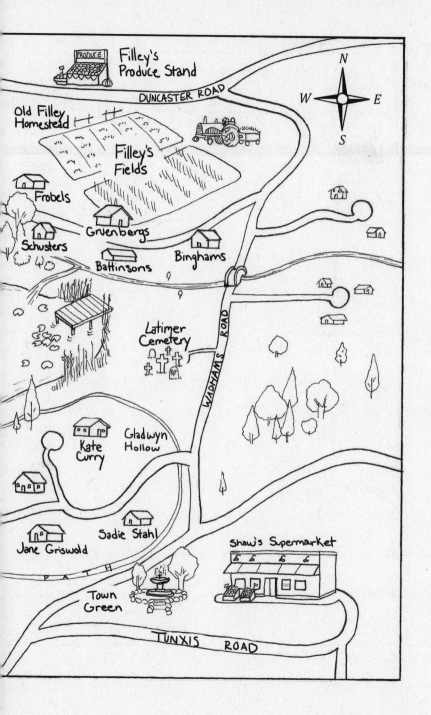

PART ONE

THE SEARCH CONTINUES FOR MISSING NINE-YEAR-OLD

Wintonbury—June 14, 1974

Nine-year-old Laura Loomis, missing now since late Thursday, never went into the woods surrounding her house alone, according to her mother. The afternoon of her disappearance Mrs. Loomis had taken Laura and a friend to the Wampanoag club pool. They'd gotten ice cream at the concession stand. Mrs. Loomis said she dropped Laura at a friend's house down the street from theirs, and she was to return home by dinnertime. Laura was last seen walking toward her home on Hickory Lane at 4:30 P.M. She is described by her mother as 4 feet, 8 inches, blond with blue eyes, and wearing a shirt with a rainbow, blue shorts, and blue sneakers. The search continued today, with firefighters from Bloomfield and Windsor sweeping the wooded and often swampy area surrounding the neighborhood. No clues have been found, and police are not ruling out the possibility that foul play may have been involved in the child's disappearance.

May 5, 1979

SADIE WASN'T A BAD GIRL. WHEN SHE WAS LITTLE SHE played church, flattening soft bread into disks, singing the hymns from stolen paper missals: *Our Fathers chained in prisons dark, were still in heart and conscience free, how sweet would be their children's fate, if they like them, could die for Thee.* She set up carnivals and lemonade stands, collected pennies for UNICEF on Halloween. She bought a tree to be planted in her name in a forest purged by fire. She included everyone in her neighborhood games, even the irritating younger siblings, even the girl, Sally Frobel, who was clearly a boy, and the boy, Larry Schuster, who was clearly schizophrenic. They were cast in roles like the frog in her production of *The Frog Prince* or the dead boy in her Haunted Woods. She understood, perfectly, what was expected of her—and still, when it came to Francie Bingham, none of this applied. She was feral, unequivocally vicious, like a girl raised by the mountain lions that occasionally slunk out of the wilderness of Massacoe State Forest, between the swing sets and the lawn furniture, into the tended backyards of her neighborhood.

It was May when it all started, and the seventeen-year cicada nymphs (genus *Magicicada*) emerged from the soil to shed their skins on window screens, in shrubs and trees, and unfold their new wings. The air was still sharp and the forsythia waved its long arms of bright flowers. The bluets opened on the pasture hillsides like white carpets. The apple blossoms

3

dropped petals onto the dark ground like snow. Sadie Watkins was twelve, nearly thirteen, and she and her friend Betty Donahue had begun stealing their mothers' Salems and Virginia Slims, hiding them in clever places in their bedrooms. Sadie had taken off one brass finial and slipped the cigarettes into her curtain rod. At prearranged times they'd retrieve them to smoke in the woods, but one day they put on the clothes from Sadie's basement first: her mother's pleated plaid boarding school skirt, a cocktail dress. They put on her old winter coats, alligator pumps, and black patent-leather sling-backs. They went out walking in the woods behind Sadie's house, pretending they were someone else. They were too old for dress-up—this was their last fling. They put on the clothes and assumed other personalities with accents.

"Blimey, this is a steep path, I say."

"Where are we headed? Isn't that the clearing, darling?"

Two years before, when Sadie had been ten, she'd devised the game of Old-Fashioned-Days House. They'd studied Connecticut history in school that spring, and she'd created a diorama in a shoe box—a scene from the Pequot War that dramatized the Pequot abduction of two girl colonists in a miniature canoe she made out of white birch bark. Her teacher's mention of the girls' kidnapping had been the one vivid thing among the names, dates, and details of the lesson, and Sadie knew it had to do with the shadow of Laura Loomis, who had been a year older than Sadie when she disappeared, a girl who resembled her so closely everyone thought they were sisters. In school, Sadie often imagined the empty seat in the sixth-grade classroom that would have been Laura's. At home, she scrutinized the photo of their Brownie troop lined up on the school blacktop, she and Laura posing at either end like copies of each other—never destined to be friends. For her diorama she'd drawn the girls on the white cardboard that slipped out of her father's new shirts, their faces etched with terror as they glanced back to their cabin on the shore, their blond hair blowing long and loose behind them. Her teacher had raised her eyebrows at the scene but couldn't deny her the grade of E for "Excellent" she taped onto the back.

Sadie had been intrigued by the strife of the colonists—cooking over an open fire, fetching water, growing corn in rocky soil, the threat of animals and untrustworthy Pequots and Narragansetts. She admired the women for accomplishing their daily tasks in long skirts. If they were going to play Old-Fashioned-Days House, she told Betty, they had to dress the part. Sadie's mother, who had grown up a poor girl with a single mother in New York City, often returned there now to shop lavishly and had the best cast-off clothes—Chanel, Halston, Diane von Furstenberg, evening gowns in satin and chiffon, strapless, layered with tulle, brocaded and beaded, dresses they slipped on over their flowered panties. The gowns dragged the ground, and they had to diaper-pin them around the waist to get them to fit. They held the skirts in their hands and became Colonial women picking their way across Sadie's muddy backyard.

By that time their parents' mandate that they stay out of the woods was heedlessly ignored, even though the tragedy of the Loomis girl—who'd lived on a street that did not connect to theirs—was fresh and the questions surrounding her fate still unanswered. The woods had always been a place of imaginative games, the source of legends passed down from their grandparents, who as children might have encountered the old Leatherman, a kindly beggar fed by townspeople who lived his entire life outdoors. The girls wandered the woods behind Sadie's house in the long dresses, mindless of any threat. They hiked up to the old Latimer cemetery to place flowers on the children's graves, adopting the names on the stones for themselves: Prudence, Electa, Rebekah, Abigail. They used paths the boys had begun to tame and trample riding their bikes, pulling wagons loaded with stolen plywood intended for forts. When fall arrived and it grew cold, they used Sadie's basement as their house. Sadie had the little kids bring in large stones, and they stacked them against the wall into the semblance of a fireplace. They had tarnished sterling candelabra, and they stole candles from Sadie's dining room buffet, matches from the kitchen drawer. They learned to knit, and they sat beside the pretend fire in their dresses, their needles clicking, the pipes rushing water overhead. They'd play out the story of Snow White and Rose Red. From upstairs would come the smell of a roast in the oven.

The last time they'd played the game had been that winter when Sadie was ten, on a gray day threatening more snow, the old snow still on the ground. The game had begun to lose its allure, and the participants had dwindled to Sadie; her best friend, Betty; and that day, Francie Bingham, who'd come to Sadie's front door to drop off her mother's Avon brochures. In a rare move Sadie's mother called Sadie up from the basement and told her to let Francie play. When Sadie widened her eyes and protested, her mother reminded her of how little she asked of her, of her comfortable house, her multitude of friends.

"Some children aren't as lucky," her mother said. She wore a nearly floor-length red dress, a gold necklace. Her hair was long and blond, and once Sadie had overheard her teachers talking about her at school.

They'd been in the cafeteria last year during the chaos of a rain-day pickup, and Sadie had missed her bus. Her mother had driven up to school to get her, had walked into the cafeteria and been spotted by the two teachers—one of them Sadie's teacher, Mrs. Susskey, reviled by the students, and the other her young intern.

"Oh, she's like Julie Christie in *Doctor Zhivago,*" the intern said.

Mrs. Susskey glanced over to where Sadie's mother was making her way through the crowd of children, heading in their direction. Neither teacher knew she was there for Sadie.

"More like Sharon Tate in *Valley of the Dolls*," the older one said, her voice filled with resentment.

By the time Sadie's mother had reached them and taken Sadie by the hand the older woman's face had reddened and become blotchy with her mistake. "You didn't tell us this was your mother, Sadie," she said, her voice falsely sweetened, and for the rest of that year, even though Sadie couldn't really interpret the woman's comment, she'd lived in fear of her retaliation.

Standing in the dining room, with Francie Bingham waiting, hopeful, in the foyer, Sadie worried her mother would launch into the lesson of her own childhood—her forced attendance at St. John Villa Academy, a Catholic boarding school for girls, with its stern nuns and cold tile dormitory walls. But instead her mother glared at her and told her she would lose her television privilege if Francie wasn't included. So, Francie, two years Sadie's junior, was allowed to be the younger sister, a role that required she remove her glasses and attend to Sadie and Betty like a maid. They'd been knitting, but Sadie had grown tired of it. "Let's pretend our husbands are out hunting."

Betty always followed Sadie's lead. "Oh, I do hope they stick to the paths, Electa," she said.

Francie Bingham eyed them both. She wore a Halston gown—black sleeveless crepe bodice, chiffon skirt decorated with a spray of pale-colored leaves. Her chest was freckled, and she shivered and tugged her shawl in tighter. Earlier, she had argued and won the dress from Sadie, who'd chosen it first and given in when Francie said she would just go home.

"They know the woods well enough, I daresay," Sadie said.

Their needles clicked. The basement was dim. The candles flickered.

"You should set the table, sister," Betty told Francie.

"We don't yet know what they'll be bringing," Francie said.

"Methinks they will bring something," Sadie said. "Unless they are lost!"

Sadie dropped her knitting—a square of green wool that would never amount to anything—took the candelabra, and stood in front of the sliding glass doors that opened out onto the backyard. It was dusk, and the shadows thickened in the trees. The ground was white, pitted with footprints from the day before when they'd gone sledding and come in the sliding basement door to take off their boots. Brambles dotted with hard, bright berries edged the woods, their barklike stems gray and tangled. "We should go look for them, Rebekah," Sadie said.

Francie gasped. "Out? Into the wilderness?"

Betty jumped up. "I'll get our wraps."

These consisted of Sadie's mother's old coats, smelling of mothballs—camel's hair, tweed, herringbone. They slid the door and the cold air hit their faces, filled with the scent of fires stoked with newspaper and kindling. Spires of smoke marked the sky. Sadie took the candelabra, and she and Betty stepped across the frozen yard, their dresses and coats dragging. Francie remained by the basement doors. Sadie turned to look at her.

"Why aren't you coming, sister?"

Francie's face was pinched. Her resolve to follow the parents' rule made Sadie and Betty all the more aware of it. "We can't," she said.

"Our husbands may need our help!" Betty said.

Sadie knew that either prospect—going into the woods or staying in the dank basement alone—was terrifying to Francie, her hesitation a ploy to prevent them from going, and she turned to continue across the yard.

"Never mind her," Sadie said. "She can stay behind and tend the fire."

At this, Francie quickly relented, and the three girls headed into the woods, the main path leading up, the smaller paths heading off into an overgrowth of young saplings, and birch, and hemlocks shagged and heavy with snow. Their breath came out in clouds. They wore the pumps in patent leather, snakeskin, and pink satin, the toes stuffed with tissue. The incline proved difficult to manage. The candles flickered and went out. From this vantage spot the lights in the Hamlet Hill houses glowed yellow—desk lamps in bedrooms upstairs where kids did homework, sconces in carpeted stairwells, chandeliers in dining rooms, brass Stiffel lamps in living rooms and dens where fathers read the remaining bits of the Sunday paper and watched football on television, bathroom lights flicking on and then off after some child examined her pimple in the mirror, garage lights where mothers sought a screwdriver to fix a loose high chair. The houses were spacious, made with cedar shingles and painted clapboards and bricks, surrounded by landscaped beds of juniper and rhododendron. Their yards met each other in rolling hills and dips, occasionally marked by lines of shrubs or pine or forsythia. The kitchen windows were steamed up from cooking. The girls could see Mrs. Battinson opening cabinets, taking down plates. They saw the Schuster boys watching television on the couch. Sadie's house was dark save the one dim bulb over the stove.

"I think I see our husbands," Betty said.

"That is them, isn't it?" Francie said. She cupped her hand to her mouth and called out into the woods. "Halloooo!"

Sadie stifled a laugh and glanced at Betty. It wasn't proper to break character. "Oh, be silent and still," she chastised. "What if it's a bear!"

Francie squinted without her glasses. "Is something coming?"

Sadie looked out into the woods, through the brambles, past the big hemlock. There was someone there, a shape, waiting, not moving forward. "It's a stump," she said. "Part of an old tree, likely that one hit by lightning a few summers nigh." She kept her eyes on the shape. It wasn't a bear. She felt something tense in her, a quickening she would feel only a few times later: when she lost control of the car she was driving at seventeen; when she felt the sharp stab, then the dull slip of her first miscarriage at twenty-six.

The tree stump moved then. It took a step and a branch snapped. The girls huddled together, a bundle of fabric. The shape—not a tree, not a bear—seemed to be moving in their direction. Sadie, clear headed, clever, whispered, "Methinks we should head back." Betty's hand tightened on hers. Sadie stared, transfixed, at the moving shape. It lumbered, not in a bear way, but in a tall-man way. She thought, *Pequot*, but didn't dare say it. She felt the specter of Laura Loomis urging her to run. Betty tugged her down the path. "Move, move, move," she said. Francie saw the two of them moving away from her, and she turned to follow them and tripped. The man in the woods wore a camouflage jacket, a brown, broad-brimmed hat.

"Why doesn't he call to us?" Francie said, her voice bright with alarm. "Why is he walking this way?"

They could hear his footsteps now in the frozen snow, the crack of branches in his path.

Sadie felt the fear rise. She was the first to kick off her pumps and run, and Betty and Francie followed, all of them running, the silent man somewhere behind them. They reached Sadie's backyard and the sliding glass door, crying now, panicked. They got inside and locked the door and continued on up the basement stairs, and then up the stairs to the second story, where they flung themselves onto Sadie's bed,

Francie repeating, "I told you, I told you." Her mother came to the door and knocked.

"Girls," she said. "What's going on?"

Sadie glared at Francie, who seemed on the verge of telling. "Nothing," she said. "We're just playing."

"We're sorry, Mrs. Watkins," Betty said. Her face was smeared with tears, but now she was laughing, giggling. Sadie's mother made an exasperated sound on the other side of the door.

"Be good," she said. They heard the ice in her glass and then her footsteps retreating down the carpeted hall.

The hems of the dresses were torn, snagged with brambles, filled with snow that melted onto Sadie's bedroom floor. Their feet were raw and red and Sadie gave them pairs of the woolen socks she wore ice-skating. They were afraid to go back down into the basement for their clothes, but then Sadie went, flipped on all the lights, and grabbed everything, her anger canceling out her fear. In the light from the overhead bulb the basement world was transformed: the old couch with its doilies and torn upholstery; the warped drop-leaf table and mismatched chairs; the books, their spines broken and boards faded. They had dropped the candelabra on the path, left the shoes somewhere up there, too. When the snow finally came—a big storm that had them home from school for three days—she imagined these things buried under the weight of it, and then later, in the spring, when everything melted, she would picture moss growing over the shoes, the pink satin becoming part of the ferns, the pokeweed, the green world inhabited by salamanders and cottontails and the occasional snake. She would remind herself to look for the items they'd left on the path but become distracted by other things—the romance novel she was writing (*The Governess*), guitar lessons at the community center ("Greensleeves," "I'm Leaving on a Jet Plane"), a job as a mother's helper (i.e., indentured servant). Two years passed in this way, and she forgot about the game, about Francie, the difference in their ages making her too young to bother with.

At least until that May, when, bored and nostalgic, Sadie and Betty once again donned the old dresses and slipped out the basement door. They stayed off the main path and picked their way through the woods, by then a familiar place composed of young and old trees. A brook ran through it parallel to the houses, filled with brownish-looking foam that may have been the result of the DDT misted over them each summer. The planes would drone overhead while their parents sipped whiskey sours, and the children lay on their backs in front-yard grass like unsuspecting sacrifices.

"Oh, lovely, I've gotten my shoe wet," Sadie said.

"Look at that, the hem of your skirt is muddy."

"Jesus, Mary, and Joseph."

They walked along the brook's bank, and Sadie slid down the side in her high-heeled shoes and toppled into the water. The brook wasn't very deep, but it was fast-moving, its bottom a variety of smooth stones, and Sadie struggled to stand. Betty watched from the bank, strands of her long, chestnut-colored hair covering her face, doubled over laughing with her hand between her legs. Pee streamed down onto the trampled jack-in-the-pulpit, wetting her chiffon skirt, probably dribbling into her pumps. Sadie felt the icy water soak into her coat. They were too busy laughing and peeing to notice anyone nearby. If it had been a boy they'd have been embarrassed. But it was only Francie, with her doughy cheeks, and her intelligent eyes dark behind her glasses. She looked at them laughing, and Sadie sensed a sort of yearning in her face. But her watching only made them laugh harder.

"You're going to catch something from that water," Francie said matter-of-factly.

When they'd first met Francie in elementary school, she

had been consigned to the kindergarten playground. She'd carried a blue leather pocketbook and was always alone. Drawn to her oddness, Sadie and Betty often broke the rules to sneak over to talk to her.

"What's in your pocketbook?" Sadie would say.

Francie's lips would tighten with wariness. "None of your business." Her hair was cut short in the pixie style mothers foisted on girls too young to have sense enough to refuse. Francie was thinner then, dollish looking, the tortoiseshell glasses heavy on her face. Sadie and Betty laughed at nearly everything she said, most of it mimicked from a grown-up and strange coming from her mouth.

"Why can't you just be nice and show us?" Sadie said.

Francie knew that she *should* be nice, and she *did* like the attention. Finally, one day she undid the snap of the pocketbook and opened it up. The girls looked into its depths. There was a small change purse, the kind they made during the summers in recreation craft class when they were little—an imitation leather heart, stitched together with plastic thread. Hers was blue to match her pocketbook. She also had a handkerchief, a tiny pink one, and a bottle of Tinkerbell perfume. Sadie reached her hand in quickly and grabbed the change purse before Francie could snap the pocketbook shut. Francie's face hardened like Sadie's mother's would when Sadie forgot to make her bed.

"Give it back," she said.

"I'm not taking it," Sadie said, dancing off a ways. "I'm just looking. I'll give it back in a minute." She opened it up and looked inside. Francie had quite a bit of change in the purse—silver, not all pennies. Sadie and Betty glanced at each other. This would buy a few packs of gum, or the little round tin of candies they loved, La Vie Pastillines, in raspberry or lemon. So they talked Francie into giving them the money. They would bring her a tin of the candy, they said. For weeks after, Francie would stand at the low fence that separated the playgrounds, small and resolute, waiting for them. That, too, had become a game. "She's there, she's there again," Betty would say. They became practiced at avoiding her, except for those rare times she showed up at the door of one of their houses and their mothers told them to include her.

Sadie climbed out of the brook and stood dripping on the bank.

"Why are you wearing dress-up clothes?" Francie asked.

Sadie would admit later that the question annoyed her. For a moment, standing there in the wet coat, she felt as if she and Francie had switched places, and Francie had become the older girl entitled to make disparaging comments. If Francie hadn't seen Sadie fall into the brook, if she hadn't asked about the dress-up clothes, spring would have simply progressed into summer, and nothing of the business would have ever transpired. Maybe Sadie would have seen her riding her purple bike in lazy circles at the end of the street, but that shapeless figure of her wobbling on her Schwinn, those annoying plastic streamers spraying from each handlebar grip, wouldn't have prompted it. While Francie's appearance at the brook that day was purely accidental, Sadie's desire for revenge was not, and the plan to retaliate sprang from her surprise at the younger girl's ability to guess at her own shameful longing for childhood.

"Go away," Sadie said. "We're meeting someone and we don't want you around."

She took out the cigarette she'd hidden in her coat pocket. Only a bit of it was wet, and she straightened it out and lit it up. She held the lighter up to Betty, who took out her own cigarette and leaned in to the flame.

Francie's eyes widened. "Who are you meeting?" She took a careful step closer, pretending their smoking wasn't anything out of the ordinary.

Sadie put her hands on her hips. Her coat opened, revealing the shape of her new breasts beneath the dress's bodice. "A boy," she said.

They held the cigarettes out in the vees of their fingers.

"What boy?" Francie asked, suddenly wary.

"Hezekiah," Sadie said. "You don't know him."

Hezekiah, a name she'd seen on an old cemetery stone, one used for the husbands in their games (*Hezekiah, dearest, bring home a nice fat rabbit for stew*).

"He lives on the farm there, over the hill," Betty said, catching on quickly, flipping her long hair back over her shoulder.

Francie's eyes narrowed to where Betty pointed beyond Foothills Road, to the rise of Filley Farm's pasture. Francie had been young when Laura Loomis disappeared, but Sadie felt sure that like all children in the neighborhood, she'd been warned. In the intervening years they'd reclaimed the woods and pastures—the parents' vigilance, and the punishment for infractions, had lessened. The curving asphalt streets that cut through the countryside, their slate roofs and storm doors, their porch lights and decorative landscaping, were, to the parents, all reassuring aspects of safety. Instead, Sadie knew Francie was remembering that winter day and the man in the woods, the crunch of his footsteps, his anonymous menace.

"How do you know him?" Francie asked.

"We found his letter," Sadie said.

"A *letter*?" Francie asked, well aware that this was something mailed from one house to another with the proper postage. A letter had requirements they mastered in penmanship class: *heading, salutation, body, complimentary close, signature.* Sometimes, a *postscript.* A note was hastily scribbled, passed between popular girls in the dull hour of American history. And then Sadie told her it was none of her business. "Isn't that your mother calling?" she said. "Are you supposed to be here?" She and Betty continued on through the woods, taking the path along the brook. They could hear Francie behind them, following them, wanting to believe what they told her was true.

Sadie knew that this was typical human behavior. She remembered the UFOs that circled the neighborhood one summer evening, flashes of silver and iridescent violet panning across the night sky, bringing them out of their houses to marvel—parents with cocktails and cigarettes, children in cotton pajamas, everyone poised on their own wide sweep of perfect grass. Francie crept behind them and they pretended they didn't notice her. They put out their cigarettes on a rock, and they saw her bend down and retrieve the butts, like evidence or talismans. She followed them up to the next road, and then to the dead end where a strip of old barbed wire separated their neighborhood from the farmer's field, where beyond the asphalt curb Queen Anne's lace bloomed and twirled its white head, and cows lowed and hoofed through muddy grass, around stones covered with lichen. There at the foot of the cedar post was one of these stones, and Sadie pretended to lift it, to pocket something in her mother's heavy coat that she carried slung over her arm. Francie took it all in at a distance, her white face round with pleasure, while they pretended they didn't see her.

Years later, Sadie would not be able to say what made them revel in deceit. She might have blamed it on something pagan and impish, the fields and woods surrounding them a sort of pastoral landscape. There was the farmer riding his tractor; the newly planted corn emerging to shake its tassels, all pleasant and bountiful; the smell of manure seeping through window screens into kitchens and bedrooms, awakening in them a sort of misplaced disgust. But mostly, it was easy, because Sadie wanted the deceit to be true. She wanted there to be some mysterious boy—some Hezekiah—who had been watching her, in love with her from a distance. She'd imagine that out beyond the bay window, on the street that wound higher up the hill than hers, a boy with sweet wispy hair and lips that were always half smiling was watching. He saw her walk up the driveway to catch the school bus. He saw through the new spring growth of foxglove and pokeweed and fern, through those bright little shoots on the elms. From the fallow fields, white-sprayed with bluets, she could almost hear his sigh, his gentle breathing, and smell his sweat—coppery, the mineral smell of turned earth.

September 22, 2002

SADIE FIRST SEES HIM ON A WET SEPTEMBER EVENING, not long after she lost her baby—a stillborn girl. She has a cold, and the damp and the falling leaves all compound her sorrow. He is a boy she knows from childhood, now a man filling his truck at the local gas station. The few streets of their old neighborhood that wound together were built on his family's farmland. He lived in a midcentury modern house at the top of Sadie's road. It was fieldstone and glass, built by a famous Harvard architect and reached by a long curving drive with iron gates at its entrance. On the gatepost was a plaque that announced the place, ceremoniously, as Wappaquassett. Sadie finds the adopted Algonquian place names in town ironic—Mashamoquet, Susquetonscut, Quinnatisset; "big fish place," "place of red ledges," "little long river." The early settlers of the 1670s may have well understood their meaning, but they now signify parks and country clubs and shopping plazas. Despite this, the name on the Filleys' gatepost has always seemed authentic to her—"place covered with rush matting"—as if the land was named and rightfully given over to Filley ancestors by the original inhabitants. The grounds of Wappaquassett included a barn and an in-ground swimming pool, the only one in the neighborhood of 1960s Colonials and split ranches.

Sadie watches the man at the pump in front of her, gassing up an old truck, and remembers him as a swaggering boy, rakish, tall, dressed in wrinkled khakis, his private-school tie always askew. She tries to convince herself he was just an older boy who smoked cigarettes, who kept himself at a remove that only made him seem alluring. But she cannot deny the way her heartbeat steps up when she recognizes him, the romantic hero of all her childhood games. He is taller, broader, yet as he reaches back to replace the nozzle she notices his old fluid way of moving, the shake of his head to clear his eyes of his hair, still the same shaggy brown and long over his collar. As she watches he looks up and sees her, his face registering shock, and then a confusion that he struggles to hide. She waves, and he seems to collect himself and calls her by her old name: "Well hello there, little Sadie Watkins." He tips his head back and laughs, something she senses with disappointment is forced. They stand under the awning in the bright fluorescence, and nod and smile.

"You thought I was Laura Loomis," she says.

Through the years Sadie has lived with this misapprehension. As a child with her mother people would spot her and call the town police, and Officer Crombie would appear in the Youth Centre children's store, rolling his eyes. It incensed Sadie's mother to have her daughter confused with a missing girl, but Sadie had read the newspaper articles and imagined being the object of the steady, enduring love the Loomises revealed for their lost daughter. Lately, new age-progression images have appeared in the paper, and Sadie is once again scrutinized, accosted by strangers. Saying "I'm not Laura Loomis" has become second nature.

But Ray seems more confused by her admission. "Who?"

Sadie laughs. "I thought you may have mistaken me for someone else."

Ray's smile seems pasted on. "Actually, Sadie Watkins, you look a lot like your mother."

She is flooded with memory—a bright rush of images that

occur beyond her control: Ray Filley and her mother at the Filleys' pool that last summer, her mother laughing, and Ray dipping his head to speak to her, a gesture so intimate Sadie, as a child, felt compelled to look away.

"It's Stahl now," she says, hoping her voice won't betray her.

She never moved out of Wintonbury. She stayed and married and he left, and occasionally she'd hear from other people about things he'd done, or places he'd been, his life a blur of activity at a distance from her. Until she saw him just now she had nearly forgotten him.

His recent return makes him a stranger to the town, an outsider who would have no way of knowing about the baby she just lost. For the first time in weeks she doesn't have to endure looks of sympathy. Instead, they laugh about the town and its history of assorted characters: the drunk, Waldo, who can still be spotted pedaling his ancient bike through the center; the teenagers who race their cars along the stretch of road between the tobacco fields; the priest, a volunteer fireman who took young boys for rides in his car with the light flashing, who was finally accused of molesting them. She leans back against the door of her car. He says her name, "Sadie Watkins," for no particular reason, and she says his, "Ray Filley," as if he's been conjured up by the words on her tongue. He jokes about how he feels he's caught in a time warp. "Even the old Tunxis Players troupe is still together," he says.

Sadie smiles hesitantly. "Oh, sure. What play are they doing now?"

"*Cat on a Hot Tin Roof,*" Ray says. He waggles his eyebrows, and his smile widens.

"That's an old one," Sadie tells him. "Nineteen fifties old!" They have narrowly skirted the topic of her mother, but then she cannot help herself. "My mother was in that play."

She watches his face closely but sees he will not acknowledge her, even though she's always suspected he had a crush on her.

"So, a revival!" He does his laugh again, his teeth bright in the fluorescence.

No one is around. The gas station is on the corner of Jerome and Park, next to the library, the Masonic hall. Moths flit about the streetlights. There's a smell of wood burning, and Sadie is transported back to teenage parties on nights like these—the passing of a bottle around the bonfire, some boy's arm heavy on her shoulder. The road is quiet and empty, and their voices are too-sharp and high against the emptiness. Ray pulls out a pack of cigarettes and offers her one. "I quit," she says. "A long time ago." He must see her rings, notice the SUV with the elementary school magnet stuck to the side. She knows she should tell him about her children—Max, four, and Sylvia, seven; about her husband, Craig; the three of them waiting at home for the ice cream that sits, melting, on the passenger seat. But she is suddenly embarrassed by this evidence of who she's turned out to be. She is thrown back to a time when she expected to be so much more.

"What have you been up to?" she asks him.

Ray shrugs. He gives her that lopsided grin. "Same old thing. Music."

He joined a band she'd never heard of and went off to make records and tour after graduating from prep school. Her memories of Ray end then. She hated high school, was lost, a faceless person in the beige hallways. Every moment of her time there focused on clever schemes of escape—forged notes from the nurse to cover skipped classes; day trips with older boyfriends to Newport, Rhode Island, or driving around in their cars drinking; having sex in their boyhood bedrooms, all of them stuck, somehow, within the grid of the town—mechanics, shop workers, lightning rod installers. And then she got out and tried college to appease her father—three se-

mesters of courses at a staid women's college, in large lecture
halls where she once again felt overwhelmed by nameless-
ness, where the girls all knew each other, and where her ability to memorize the details of hundreds of slides of art, and
construct and support an eloquent thesis, brought her excellent grades but no appreciation of her own achievement. She
hated it too much to stay, eventually getting a job at Lord &
Taylor, selling men's accessories behind a counter—scarves
and gloves and beautiful wallets. Across the shining aisle the
women in cosmetics stood like mannequins with their garish
faces. She had to carry her personal items into the store in a
clear plastic tote and at the end of the day pass through the
security exit like a thief. Once she met Craig the promise of a
new life took over, with its babies to tend, its house—swatches
of fabric, paint samples, like the dollhouse she'd decorated as a
child, spending hours sewing miniature curtains cut from her
mother's discarded cocktail dresses.

"It's been a long time," Ray says then. "Twenty years?"

Sadie admits it might be longer. "What are you doing
back?"

Ray stares at her. He says his father has died, and Sadie realizes she has been cocooned in her own grief, that she has not
read a newspaper or left the house for anything but errands in
weeks. Ray tells her he's staying at Wappaquassett, where Beth
still lives with their mother. He says that they want him to
take over the farm and the store, and Sadie tries to remember
the last time she stopped at Filley's, Ray's father always so kind
to her—giving the children apples, tiny pumpkins, putting
extra ears of corn in the bag, adding a Christmas wreath for
free when they bought their tree.

"I'm so sorry," she says. She puts her hand to her chest.

Ray stares at her again. She cannot fathom what he's thinking. He reaches out his hand and brushes a piece of her hair
from her face, gently, tenderly. She smells the cigarette, the

gasoline. Later that evening, folding the children's clothes, stacking them in small piles, loading the dishwasher, locking the doors of her house, the street outside shining and black from rain, the neighbor's porch lights halos on the front walks, she thinks of his hand moving toward her face, the way he looked at her, and it's as if something dormant has sprung from the ordered dignity of her married life.

June 12, 1979

IN HAMLET HILL THE FRONT LAWNS WERE THE SITE OF baseball games and freeze tag, the grass threadbare, littered with bikes, gloves, Popsicle sticks. Sadie Watkins was an only child, the smartest of the neighborhood girls and the responsible one asked that summer to house-sit for Mrs. Sidelman, who planned to vacation at her cottage on the Connecticut shore. Sadie's mother vehemently refused to allow Sadie to do it, making up some excuse about its being too much responsibility, but then her father intervened, and Sadie was permitted to accept. On the last day of school in June, Sadie was given a key, which she kept in her jewelry box, and every morning she let herself into Mrs. Sidelman's shake-shingled Colonial, checked her houseplants, and fed the cats that appeared on Mrs. Sidelman's slate terrace after they slunk, primitive and bony, beneath the barbed wire separating Filley Farm's pastures from the tended backyards across the street. In the evening she returned and flipped on the outdoor lights, and retrieved the mail. In the afternoons she watered the annuals in the concrete planters. The damp soil gave off a smell she liked—one she remembered from spring and crawling behind the shrubs in front of her house as a child, where lily of the valley grew, little bells on delicate stalks. As a young girl, Sadie imagined small people, like those from *The Borrowers,* crawling out from inside the crack of the concrete foundation and sitting with a book under the bell-shaped flowers.

24

Her parents were notorious arguers, their shouting blooming on summer days through window screens, spilling out in tantalizing bits into the neighborhood. Sadie noticed that when she entered the room the drama of the moment faded, the heated conversation ceased, and so it was in her interest to become small and invisible, to wedge herself behind things, to flatten and slip beneath the bed, to make hideouts, to spy on everyone.

"Like a rodent," her father had said once, his shoes tamping down the carpet.

Hiding in the pantry, Sadie would eavesdrop on her mother's phone calls. Clare Watkins was an actress. She joined the community theater group, the Tunxis Players, when Sadie was a baby, and performed each season—Evelyn in *Guest in the House,* Elvira in *Blithe Spirit,* Laura in *The Glass Menagerie,* Raina in *Arms and the Man,* Hannah in *The Night of the Iguana.* Sadie grew up with her mother in various roles, and she was always confused about who she was at any given moment. Brooding actress? Shy cripple? Crazed seductress? Was her mother actually afraid of birds, or was it a character from a play? Sadie would lean up against the pantry shelves filled with Tang and Bisquick, with boxes of sweetened breakfast cereal, and hear her mother's voice soften in a new way, begging the caller to *Stop!* and giggling like a girl being teased. All of this was disconcerting, but none of it as terrible as the times Sadie overheard her mother discuss her with one of her friends.

"Sadie's so serious," she'd said once. "Where did she come from? I think the nurses gave me the wrong baby in the hospital."

Inside the pantry Sadie nodded slightly in agreement. She had always felt she didn't belong to her parents—that perhaps she was a changeling exchanged by elves for her mother's real daughter. Somewhere in a leafy glade a sunny, talkative, guileless girl was dancing and singing like Ann-Margret in *Bye Bye Birdie*. Other times she would imagine that it was she, not Laura Loomis, who had been destined to disappear, that there was a secret world into which Laura had slipped, like the girls in the books she read (*Jessamy, Time at the Top*) who step into a closet or ride an elevator and are transported to another time and place where they are someone else—a girl in a large family, who is able to solve a mystery.

Sadie grew to depend on her visits to Mrs. Sidelman's that summer. She could escape there on the pretense of "doing her job," let herself into the empty house, and then sit for hours in the living room reading, the dust motes and the warmth of the sun through the front window soothing. Mrs. Sidelman's library was composed of Book-of-the-Month Club selections from the forties and fifties, and secondhand books with faded inscriptions: *To Maureen, my little concubine, forever, Simon.* Sadie immersed herself in *The Catcher in the Rye, Appointment in Samarra, The Sheltering Sky,* the smell of the pages one she recognized from the town library, which she would come to learn later was a combination of chemical compounds formed from the disintegration of glue and paper and ink. She turned the yellowed pages carefully. She imagined where the books had been, who had read them, whose pencil had created the marginalia. Sometimes she slipped into the kitchen and found food to eat—saltines with butter, a jar of sweet pickles.

Each day she explored more of the house, venturing upstairs to lie on Mrs. Sidelman's children's abandoned beds like Goldilocks. From the master bedroom window she could see into Filley Farm's pasture, and sometimes Ray Filley himself with his dogs, the dogs running loose and fast between the pines. Sadie had always been conscious of Ray Filley, casting him as pretend characters in scenarios she'd dream up—as a British intelligence officer during World War II or a surly cowboy on a California ranch. But that summer she sat and watched him clap his hands for his dogs, brush his hair back, and imagined inviting him into Mrs. Sidelman's house. What they might do, or talk about, was always open to speculation, changing from day to day. Sometimes, after Ray disappeared, his younger sister, Beth, would appear. Laura Loomis had been Beth Filley's best friend, and after Laura went missing Beth was taken out of public school and enrolled, like Ray, in private, as if that would prevent her from going missing, too. Sadie watched Beth, small and spry, follow secretly behind Ray, and she marveled that Beth moved so fearlessly through the pastures and woods alone. Sadie quickly ducked back from the window when she saw her, as if Beth's boldness revealed her as some sort of magical being with the ability to spot her.

One afternoon, Sadie investigated Mrs. Sidelman's break-front, her desk, the kitchen cupboards. She knew that every-one had secrets: a diary hidden under a floorboard, a notebook of poems written in fading ink, a hatbox filled with high school mementos. Finally, slipped beneath a soft pile of sweaters in a cedar chest she found an old playbill: *Billy Rose's Aquacade, New York World's Fair 1939,* a swimming exposition starring Eleanor Holm and Johnny Weismuller. Eleanor posed in a white bathing suit and high heels. She had her head thrown back, her mouth open and laughing, her hair curling around her pale shoulders. Had Mrs. Sidelman gone to the fair and seen the show? Had it been a momentous occasion for her? It was a large booklet, and Sadie flipped through it quickly and a small packet of letters fell out. They were addressed to Bea Brownmiller, postmarked 1947. Sadie set the packet of let-ters aside. There were no marks in the playbill until the back, after the ads for Kern's Frankfurters, Chesterfield cigarettes, and Pabst Blue Ribbon beer, where the cast of the show was listed and a name was underlined with a careful hand: Bea Brownmiller. Sadie knew Mrs. Sidelman's first name was Bea from her mail retrieval. She looked at the name, listed under

"Aquafemmes." Mrs. Sidelman had been in the show, along-side girls named Constance Constant and Loretta Orleta, girls who performed at Billy Rose's nightclub the Diamond Horseshoe.

Sadie turned to the letters, opening each one carefully. The writer had used a fountain pen, and the ink on the thin paper in the fading light in Mrs. Sidelman's bedroom rendered the handwriting difficult to translate, but all of the letters were written by the same man, who signed his name *Bud*. The letters were short, each filling only one page. Sadie could make out phrases that told how much the man missed Bea, longed for her, and imagined the smell of her perfume. He mentioned *that time at the club, cherry blossoms,* and a *rooftop*. He wrote about songs: *Remember "I've Got You Under My Skin"?* Sadie imagined these were all clear signs of love—Bea and Bud. She put the letters away for another day.

October 16, 2002

S ADIE REALIZES THAT UNLIKE HER PREVIOUS MISCAR-
riages the loss of this baby, carried nearly to term, cannot
be a private grief she nurses over a glass of wine. She
can't hide her loss from the neighborhood women she's spotted leaving for school drop-offs, who cast sorrowful glances
toward her house and who send her the same covered dishes
and casseroles in sympathy that they would have prepared
had she been busy with a new baby. At the hospital the grief
counselor, a young woman in a narrow skirt and heels, visited
her with pamphlets. Sadie sat on the bed in her maternity
clothes, her feet in thick socks, her full breasts leaving her
feeling inexplicably empty.

"Would you like someone to take down the baby things
before you go home?" the counselor asked.

Sadie was affronted and assured her she would do that
herself. But once she was home she found she preferred to
leave the baby's room intact: crib, changing table, songbird
mobile, the small blanket monogrammed with an "L." *Lily*.
Now she winds the mobile, stares into the crib. She would be
two months old, and cooing, she thinks, and catches herself
sliding into some dark place.

She decides she must make sure she is too busy to remember the things that make her unhappy, but she has no
real skills, no education, and the idea of returning to Lord
& Taylor, a job she quit to start a family, is out of the ques-

tion. Instead she remembers the years after her first miscarriage, before Sylvia was born, when she volunteered with
the Wintonbury Historical Society. She calls up the director and agrees to meet a woman named Harriet at the same
Congregational church where Max attends preschool. That
morning she dresses in a skirt and blouse, an outfit she last
wore before her pregnancy, to Sylvia's school Christmas pag-
eant. Sadie is tall and has always been curvaceous, but the
skirt, she discovers with a swooning feeling, is too tight. The
blouse gapes at its pearl buttons. She leaves the skirt's clasp
undone, the blouse untucked to cover it. She wants to laugh
at herself, dressing up like her mother, who wore beautiful clothes every day—wool skirts, pressed white blouses,
gold earrings, and lipstick. She always knew her mother was
different, but now she realizes that difference was a certain
glamour—a movie-star quality. She glances beyond the bedroom window to the trees waving their bright leaves, and it
occurs to her, with a jolt, that the anniversary of her mother's
death has come and gone without her usual mental ritual of
acknowledgment.

Downstairs, Craig is in his shirtsleeves, his tie loose, his
face smoothly shaven and pink, as if he's come from a brac-
ing walk. The children, who sit at the kitchen table with their
bowls of cereal, cease their chatter and cast confused glances
up at Sadie in her outfit, waiting for an explanation. Sadie
feels, suddenly, as if she is wearing a costume.

"Why aren't you wearing comfy clothes?" Sylvia asks.
Sadie's clothing has lately consisted of cotton sweatpants and
T-shirts, jeans and pullover sweaters.

"I'm going to work," she says.

Craig opens the refrigerator and turns to look at her. He
nods, so careful, lately, that Sadie suspects he has read all of
the grief counselor's pamphlets. "Okay," he says. "Okay."

"I'm going to be a part-time historian."

Max smiles because she is smiling. She feels her face tight with the effort to be cheery.

"How will I get home from school?" Sylvia asks.

Max's smile fades. "And me?" he says. Sadie sees his eyes fill with tears.

Sadie knows they are remembering when she was in the hospital and Craig appeared—a glaring irregularity—at their respective schools to pick them up. She is exhausted, suddenly, from the effort of waylaying their fears.

"I'll only be gone a *little* while," she tells them. "I'll pick both of you up at the usual time!"

Craig exhales and closes the refrigerator door without retrieving anything.

"I'm glad for you," he says. "Sounds like a nice distraction."

He leans in to kiss her as he knots his tie, his breath tinged with the mint of his toothpaste. Sadie suspects Craig and the grief counselor of colluding against her. She feels the urge to slap him, to let him know how feeble this volunteering adventure will be in the face of the things she cannot forget and the things she's forgotten to remember. She and her mother have shared the same age for the last year, but now Sadie, at thirty-six, has moved into a space of time her mother never inhabited. There are no longer marked paths to avoid.

Sadie loads the children into her SUV and backs out of the driveway. It is a crisp fall day. The sun slips through the trees surrounding Gladwyn Hollow, a neighborhood of Capes and Colonials and imitation saltboxes, all built within the last five years. The front yards are still only grass and shrubs. Behind the houses on either side stretch the woods, where the trees bend and wave and toss their leaves to blow in eddies down the street and fill the lawns with color. After she drops Sylvia at the elementary school, Sadie takes Max to the Congregational church in the center of town on the green. His classroom is warm with children's bodies, and the teacher looks up and sees her in the doorway and then pretends she hasn't, as if she has seen as well the shadow presence of Lily in her carrier at Sadie's side and is awkward with sadness for her. Max joins a group of playing children, casting only one quick, doleful glance back.

Sadie climbs the stairs to the church offices, expecting to be of help stapling or photocopying the historical society newsletters. Harriet greets her, a small, energetic woman with gray hair like a cap and bright eyes below her bangs. She announces they are going to go through the church death records and then visit the old Latimer cemetery and match the names with those on the stones. Sadie realizes that Harriet, like Ray, knows nothing of her loss, and she accepts the projected task quietly, with trepidation. *This is how you face your fears,* she thinks. The church records are on heavy, crumbling paper, the ink blood-colored and difficult to decipher:

> *Elisabeth Cadwell, daughter of Matthew died 3 Nov 1764, in her 15th year, "She dropped down dead almost in an Instant at Dinner."*
>
> *Sarah Burr, wife of Samuel died 25 Feb 1806, age 76, after a long state of derangement.*
>
> *Isaac Eggleston, died 2 Oct 1811, age 67, "in consequence of the tearing off of his fingers in a Cyder Mill."*
>
> *Abigail Gillett, daughter of Jonathan died 25 Feb 1752, age 5 years 11 months, 5 days, drowned (buried in coffin with brother, Stephen).*
>
> *Stephen Gillett, son of Jonathan died 25 Feb 1752, age 3 yr. 8 mo., drowned (buried in coffin with sister, Abigail).*

They spend the first morning writing down the family names, the ages and years, in notebooks. Sadie immerses herself in the work, the copying and matching of names from the church records. She fills pages with rough family trees that chart the demise of generations—Bigelows, Prossers, Cadwells, Burrs—and before long she must leave to pick up the children. She's enjoyed Harriet's company. They've made tea, taken their warm cups into the little records office, and chatted about the early town families. As Sadie leaves, Harriet catches her in the hallway and hands her a book—the diary of Mary Vial Holyoke, who lived in New England during the eighteenth century.

"You seem so interested in the period," she says. "This will give you a more personal feeling than the church records."

Sadie is uncharacteristically moved, and grateful. When she gets home she sets the book on her bedside table, and that night she thumbs through the entries—all of them spare and focused on chores and company—until she reaches one about Mary's daughter:

> *Jan. 8, 1764. First wore my new Cloth riding hood.*
> *9. My Daughter Polly first confined with the quinsy. Took a vomit.*
> *10. Nabby Cloutman watch'd with her.*
> *11. Very ill. Molly Molton watched.*
> *12. Zilla Symonds watched.*
> *13. My Dear Polly Died. Sister Prissy came.*
> *14. Buried.*

Craig climbs into bed, the frame groaning under his weight. In the past, they've laughed at the bed, an antique threatening collapse, but tonight the noise fills her with despair.

"What's that you're reading?" he asks. He fluffs his pillows, leans on his arm to look at the book's spine. "An old one."

Sadie closes the diary quickly. "Boring," she says.

When Craig reaches to take her in his arms she sighs. She expects he will initiate the conversation they always have of "We'll try again," but this time he does not. He rubs her shoulder instead and, with his mouth a grim little line, settles away from her on his own side of the bed.

She tries to imagine the sleeping forms of her children, the way the house protects them from the wind that picks up in the trees, but she cannot avoid imagining Lily in her crib in the room that still awaits her, the owl nightlight on the dresser, the birds she pasted to the pale walls caught in mid-flight or perched on a branch. The image of the baby in the crib is so real that Sadie must restrain herself from going to the room to check. For hours she is left lying awake, listening, waiting, feeling the small aches of her body, the strange noise of her heart in her chest.

The next day she drives with Harriet to the cemetery. They leave Harriet's Saturn parked along the road's shoulder and trek up through the woods with their steno pads, their ball-point pens. There was once a road leading here, Harriet explains, but eventually trees grew through, and the creeper and fern filled it in, and then everyone forgot about it.

"The housing developments were built around it," Harriet says.

The woods have changed, the paths Sadie remembers from childhood are gone, but they reach the little clearing and the clusters of graves. The stones are slanted, or toppled over, or crumbling one into the next so that portions are just a patch of rubble. All the leaves settle around them, and their brilliant color shifts overhead like a living ceiling. She knows if she continues past the cemetery, up the rise of pasture to the line of trees, she will see down into Hamlet Hill, the neighborhood where she grew up. She tells none of this to Harriet.

As she moves through the cemetery she has to brush the debris from the stones to read them, and she walks among them until she comes to one, still upright: *Emely Filley, wife of*

Abijah, died November 10, 1748, age 15 years. She remembers the ghost story of Emely Filley from her childhood. It was Beth Filley, Ray's sister, who told it to her one summer afternoon when they were little. Sadie's mother and Patsy Filley were friends, and Sadie would often be taken to the house with her mother as a playmate for Beth. They would be told to go up to Beth's room—a large, carpeted space with wide windows, shelves of dolls in costumes of foreign countries, and a brightly painted carousel horse in the corner. Beth never participated in anything the neighborhood kids organized. Since Laura Loomis's disappearance she would stand at a distance or clop by on her horse, as if they didn't exist, as if her mother had told her not to play with them. Sadie assumed she had her own friends from private school and they did things only with each other, in places Sadie didn't know about.

Still, Beth never complained about having to entertain her. She was clever and talkative, and she and Sadie spent hours lying on the white carpet playing backgammon. Beth would go on at length about her brother, Ray, and their plans to travel the world together—to charter a boat and sail the Galápagos Islands; to visit Mount Kelimutu in Indonesia, the volcano with different-colored crater lakes; the Guanajuato mummy museum in Mexico.

"We have a map," Beth would say, as if Sadie didn't believe her. "Want to see it?" And she would rummage in a drawer and pull out a much-folded map of the world, dotted with Magic Marker. Sadie felt a little sorry for her, suspecting, even then, that nothing of her dreams would transpire. When asked about Laura Loomis, Beth was uncharacteristically quiet.

"She should have come to *my* house that day—I invited her," Beth said matter-of-factly. "She might still be here if she had."

Sadie remembers those afternoons, the times that she would catch Beth staring at her, an unreadable look on her face. "What?" Sadie would ask. "What?" Beth would say, as if she hadn't been staring. These were the only times Sadie's likeness to Laura made her uncomfortable. Sadie and Beth became *half friends*—what Sadie called friendships that didn't feel right but could not be denied.

She puts her hand on the stone marker and feels the pitted surface, the soft moss growing on its face. Emely Filley was one of Beth's ancestors, drowned in the pond on the old Filley Farm land, a ghost that the family claimed still haunted the old Filley house. Sadie's learned from the records that it was a common occurrence in those times. Drownings, accidents, spotted fever, consumption, derangement. These things were marked down by some deacon or clerk, brief details that any-one might question, and yet all that remains of the story of the dead person's life.

Sadie sits down beside the stone. Harriet has brought a kind of picnic lunch, and she notices Sadie sitting and asks her if she's hungry.

"Let me get the basket from the car," Harriet says.

"Oh, nothing for me," Sadie says. "I'm staking out a spot for myself."

Harriet's enthusiasm takes over. "You're in the Filley sec-tion," she says.

Sadie glances around her at the stones of Emely's siblings, her parents.

"I knew a few Filleys once," she says. She tries to laugh, but it comes out oddly, and Harriet's smile dims. She remembers Ray Filley at the Mobil station, the brush of his fingertips on her face. She hasn't seen him since.

"You're sure I can't get the basket? I've got sandwiches—deviled ham and sweet relish."

Sadie has no appetite. Food isn't on her list of necessities, but Harriet is the type for whom food is a cure for every ail-ment.

"I'm fine, thank you," Sadie says. "I'll just sort out the Filleys."

She pretends to take up her steno pad. She can't move. Neither the stone nor the church records tell Emely Filley's story, the one conveyed by Beth that summer day, her eyes sharp with fear and mischief—that Emely Filley lost her baby and her grief sent her to Mill Pond, compelled her to wade into the icy water. Buried with her, though it isn't marked on the stone, is the lost infant son. It surprises Sadie, how many babies died, how many are without markers. Still, despite Beth's story, she feels peaceful here in the little cemetery, hidden away from the road. She has a vague memory of the place from before, when she and her friends first discovered it, and they journeyed through the woods behind her house dressed in her mother's long gowns, their arms filled with apple blossoms. They saw the children's graves and pretended to be sad and grieving. Really, they weren't able to comprehend the loss of a child.

When Lily was born, quiet and still, she was no more prepared. Oh, why not Craig? she thought. Why couldn't it have been him? Easier to explain to Max and Sylvia, who waited at home for their sister. And yet there was Craig's face, as devastated as Sadie's, and she felt tortured with guilt, knowing that despite his sorrow he would have never wished it were her instead. Sylvia had drawn pictures for the baby. *To Lily,* she'd written on one. Someone—Craig, or his mother, who'd arrived out of the blue from Denver—had put the picture on the altar by the little casket. Sadie didn't want the casket, the service, the stone. But if she remembered about this place she would have chosen it over the new cemetery—never mind that no one has been buried here since 1823.

Harriet eventually wanders over.

"You've gotten these down then?" she asks.

Sadie hasn't written anything. She rises, slowly, leaning

on the stone for support. "You'll have to excuse me," she says, handing her the pen and the pad.

And then she walks off through the woods. Harriet calls her; she can hear the woman's voice, first quizzical, then the edge of panic in it. Sadie ignores her. She walks through the abandoned orchard and up the rise of land where the trees have grown together, and the way is clotted with saplings and fallen leaves. It takes her a long time to reach the crest that looks down into Hamlet Hill. There is her old house, a Dutch Colonial, looking much the same as it did years before, although a vine has gotten up the side of the garage and wound its way into the gutter. The back deck is peeling and sagging. The sliding glass doors into the basement are dark and cold looking. She walks down the woods, crosses the little brook, and goes through the side yard, where the pines have grown so tall they form a thick wall separating the yards.

From the front the house looks more in decline. The siding has come off—a strip of it sags up high near the roof. The maple tree seems dwarfed, and she realizes that it is a new tree, that the old one must have died and been replaced with a Japanese maple, the leaves a bright solid red and ugly to Sadie, who grew up with the sugar maple's brilliant gradations of color. Betty's house across the street seems to be in better shape. Sadie hasn't heard from Betty in years. She knows that her father got sick and sold the house, that he and Betty's mother moved to a retirement community near the shore. Betty and her siblings live scattered across the state. Every so often Sadie runs into one of them, and despite the way time erases the past, they still avert their eyes and pretend they don't know her, rather than try to come up with something to say to her.

Sadie feels urged to walk up to the front door of her old house and open it and walk inside. She imagines the interior unchanged—the wallpaper the same, the slate hall, the empty living room, the carpeted stairway. She stares up at her

house, half-expecting to see her mother peering out one of the
bedroom windows. She cannot decide where to go next. Up
the street is Bea Sidelman's, and farther, the Filleys' house,
Wappaquassett. She wonders if Ray Filley is still in town,
imagines him spread out on his childhood bed, and then she
remembers that Beth is living there as well. Sadie feels a vague
unease at the prospect of running into Beth, and she decides
to head down Hamlet Hill Road instead, past the Schusters',
the Battinsons', the Frobels', past Francie Bingham's house,
imagining each of them the way they were that last summer—
their freshly painted shutters, the potted geraniums, the smell
of the lawn sprinklers hitting the hot tar, the hazy time between afternoon and evening, the sound of children in the
yards playing Mother, May I?

She walks to the end where Hamlet Hill meets Wadhams
Road and continues down Wadhams until Craig, alerted by
Harriet, passes by in his car, searching for her. He pulls over
and flings his door open, approaches her on the road with a
look of incredulity, his arms out, his suit coat flapping. She
senses he is there to rescue her, though she is unsure what he
is saving her from, and she feels both relief and fury. Craig's
face is mapped with confusion and love, and she is reminded,
suddenly, of the time he approached her counter at Lord
& Taylor to ask her out. She was twenty-three, and Craig
had come into the store more than once, always alone. The
first time he was in men's, buying shirts, and she caught him
glancing up at her, sandy haired, smiling, his broad shoulders
pulling at the fabric of his suit. He came over to her counter
and said he needed a pair of gloves. A week later—a scarf. He
was an attorney at Travelers Insurance and seven years her
senior. The women in cosmetics told her to be careful.

"He probably has a wife at home," one said, her lips dark
and lush on her powdered face. "And kids," another piped in.
The two of them laughed at Sadie's horrified expression.

Craig was too old for her, she told them. A Yale graduate, a star debater, the kind of man Sadie might have been destined for had she lived her life differently, although she didn't tell them that. Her own father had been disappointed that she hadn't continued with college. "A store clerk?" he'd said, not bothering to mask his disdain. "That's what you want to do with your life?"

The Saturday afternoon Craig appeared again, Sadie was busy with a customer, and when another girl offered to help him he declined. He wandered into the men's department, pretending to sort through the ties as the customer Sadie was with, a young woman trying to pick out a gift for her father, asked to see one wallet after another. Finally, Craig sidled up beside the woman at the counter and smiled at her. "I really like that one," he said, beaming, pointing to the wallet in her hands, and the woman blushed and made her decision. After she left he asked Sadie to dinner, and all she could think about were the cosmetic ladies' warnings. She stared at him for so long that his face grew pale beneath his ruddy cheeks. She couldn't refuse him, not because she was too nice, but because she'd seen his desire for her in his eyes and craved more.

She climbs into the car on the road's shoulder and feels his anger wash off of him, charging the air. It is later than she thought. One of the neighbors has been asked to pick up the children from school.

"What were you thinking?" he says. "You frightened that woman."

Sadie tells him she's sorry, she is so very sorry. Still, she doesn't cry. She watches the roadside blur by, the houses altered by time, the pastures now threaded with fresh asphalt and dotted with newly constructed houses. Craig drives quickly on the narrow road, one hand clenching the wheel. His silence presses her against the car door. Sadie allows herself to be driven home, feeling displaced, as if she is one of the dead, returning as her own ghost.

That evening as she lies on her bed watching the shadows of the trees on the wall, Craig comes into the room and sits down on the edge of the mattress. He takes her hand in his, contrite.

"What about Girl Scouts?" he says quietly. "Why not volunteer to be a troop leader?"

Sadie rolls over and looks up at him. His face, pale, handsome in the half-light of the bedroom, is entirely sincere. "I was going to ask you if you were serious," she says. "But I'm disappointed to see that you are."

Craig is exasperated with her. It's the end of a long, trying day. Sadie tells him she is fine. "I like to be morose," she says. "It's better than feeling nothing."

"Not for the rest of us," Craig says, suddenly indignant. He gets up off the bed and goes downstairs and Sadie hears him throwing around pans, trying to cook dinner. She stays on the bed a while longer, listening to the sounds of her family below her—Max asking his father for more milk, Sylvia sliding her chair back, saying she will get it for him. She experiences the odd feeling of being absent from their lives, of being forgotten, and she stays listening until the darkness presses up against the windowpanes and she feels the chill of the room. She rolls over and gets up, and goes to the mirror above her dresser and turns on the lamp. Scattered on the dresser top are small gifts from the children—a white, sea-washed stone; a feather glued to a piece of construction paper; a heart drawn with crayon, and Max's shaky letters—*MOM*. Her baby is gone and now something is needed to fill the space where she would have been. She remembers Ray Filley, the way he looked at her, as if he saw something there she had forgotten existed. Her face in the lamplight isn't her mother's, but admittedly, he is right—it is a striking version of her. Sadie's cheeks are fleshed out, heavier from the pregnancy, but her eyes are her mother's same blue, her hair the same pale blond, worn long and waving past her shoulders, the way her mother used to wear hers. *Like a model in a hair color ad,* Sadie thinks, and laughs. She leans toward the mirror and is surprised to see that her smile looks entirely convincing. Then she goes down to the heat and light of the kitchen, to the children, who leap from their seats at the table and welcome her back as if she's been gone on vacation, to Craig, his sleeves rolled up, his face grim.

"I'm going to join the Tunxis Players," she says.

Craig claps his hands together. "Great!" he says. He looks down at the children. "Your mommy's going to be an actress!"

The children cheer as they always do for grand announcements. Sadie laughs and rolls her eyes at Craig, determined not to take it seriously, and he shrugs and gives her a hopeful look, as if he is willing to do whatever it takes. And somehow, for the next few months, that is how their life evolves—Sadie playing her role, and Craig playing along.

June 15, 1979

E VERY SUMMER REQUIRED SOME DIVERSION, AND
Sadie, inspired by Bea Brownmiller's intriguing
past, and in an unacknowledged attempt to impress
her mother, sat down to write a play titled *The Memory of the
Fleetfoot Sisters*. The play's debut was slated for July. It was
a musical, with original lyrics composed to the music-only
versions of already-popular songs from bygone eras. These
were songs Sadie found in a box set of records called *Music for
Your Every Mood,* organized into categories. ("In a Haunting
Mood," "In a Bewitching Mood," "In a Carefree Mood"),
with music from Dennis Wilson's Cocktail Piano with the
Rhythm Quintet and the Philharmonic "Pops" Orchestra.
Sadie wouldn't know the songs already had words until she
was a grown woman and heard "Love Me or Leave Me" sung
by Doris Day on the oldies station. She still remembered her
own version, performed by Betty's sister as Lottie, the unhappy shoe clerk: *Love me or leave me / Just leave me, or love me /
I'm in some trouble / Don't know what to do! / Give me the answer /
and keep me from feeling blue!*

Someone was assigned the role of starting up the music,
the record player hidden in the laundry room, the list of songs
taped to the wall, the speakers set up in the area of the stage,
and the wires snaked under the laundry room door. Each
cue was recorded as well—the girls broke into song and were
discovered by a talent scout, and like most musicals the tran-

43

sition from speaking line to song was awkward, made more so by the scratching sound of the needle on the record and the difficulty of lining it up exactly in the dim laundry room lighting.

Sadie had typed up the script on an old IBM Selectric her father had brought home from the office.

> SCENE: *An office in disarray. An old wooden desk sits in the corner. On the walls are posters of the Fleetfoot Sisters under spotlights, their arms looped together and singing in front of a microphone. The posters are peeling off the walls. Some are on the floor. There is a sense of neglect and of time having passed. An old man (OLD ROGER) shuffles into the room.*
>
> OLD ROGER.[*Scanning the posters*] I remember those days. Ah yes. The Fleetfoot Sisters were at the height of their fame. I'm the one who discovered them, you know. They weren't really sisters. Take this one, the shortest and sweetest of voice. Lottie. Yes, Lottie. She was working in a shoe store. And the most miserable girl you'd ever seen.

Sadie's father's secretary ran copies of the script, and then Sadie held the tryouts. No one really came for those. Everyone already knew who would play which roles. Sadie herself would play Old Roger, wearing one of her father's winter suits and a hat, and Jane, one of the discovered girls. Young Roger was the only role she couldn't cast. The boys would only participate in the annual Haunted Woods held every year at the end of the summer. Then they were always available to climb trees and glide bedsheets down strung fishing line at certain cues, to make howling noises, smear themselves in fake blood, and arise from cardboard-box graves. But they refused to play a talent agent who discovers the fabulous Fleetfoot sisters. Sadie cajoled them and attempted to bribe them. "You don't have to sing," she said. "You're just the guy who talks the girls into joining the troupe!" But there was little she could offer that they would consider. In the end she had to relinquish her role as Jane, the woman discovered singing out her open window as she washes her dishes, and play Young Roger. She did this for the play, she said.

"I'm willing to sacrifice to keep the play going."

And it was a sacrifice. She had already picked out the silver lamé dress her character would wear, one her mother had on in a photograph labeled *Officer's Club, 1971*. This went to Darlene, one of Betty's sisters, the only one who could fit into it properly. Another of Betty's sisters took Darlene's spot as Genevieve, the klutzy but brilliant singer of "The Man That Got Away." Practice was scheduled every day, and Sadie typed up a contract that everyone had to sign to commit to showing up on time. The performance would be held in three weeks. They met in her backyard, in the cool grass under the apple tree. Sadie always let them in the sliding glass doors, believing that the allure of being the stars of their own show, of performing in front of the neighborhood families and hearing their applause, was enough to keep everyone showing up. They practiced for a week in the larger half of Sadie's basement. They'd emerge in the humid afternoons to find the ice cream man had come and gone, the boys' baseball game had ended. Plastic kiddie pools dotted the yards, abandoned, filled with spiraling cut grass. First one of Betty's sisters, then another quit the play, the lure of their usual summer activities, the boys' planning of the Haunted Woods, too much to give up. And eventually Sadie retreated to Mrs. Sidelman's, to the books, the love letters, to the emptiness of the rooms. She felt the disappointment keenly, as if there was more at stake than just the play.

But then one morning, as she sat at Mrs. Sidelman's bedroom window watching for Ray Filley, she saw Francie Bingham make her way up the road toward the dead end on her bike. The Binghams' house was at the very bottom of the hill where the newer houses sat on flatter plots, with younger, less substantial trees. There the brook often overflowed its banks, seeped into the grass and thwarted Mr. Bingham's feeble attempts to maintain a lawn. How he spent his days was open to speculation. He had some type of hobby shop in his basement and maintained a vendor booth at the Eastern States Exposition. It was said that Mrs. Bingham worked in the high school cafeteria, although this was later proven to be false and unduly cruel information. There were three children—Francie had two younger brothers who looked the same and were thought to be twins, but this, too, was untrue. The Binghams didn't socialize with anyone in the neighborhood, and no visiting cars were seen parked in their driveway, the tarred surface already cracked and threaded with weeds. That they were different was acknowledged by the imposed distance the neighbors kept from the Bingham house. Children invited to play were told by their mothers that they had to clean the gerbil cage, or by fathers that they had to rake the leaves—as if the parents, operating as an orchestrated unit, sensed something amiss and invented reasons to prevent them from going there.

Francie didn't usually venture up the hill on her bike, so her appearance was suspicious. Sadie turned from one window to another to watch her, and then went into the guest bedroom to view her better. From here she could see past Mrs. Hoskins's house through a stand of sycamore. Francie pedaled furiously up the last bit of hill to the dead end. Sadie saw her red cheeks, her hair stuck to her forehead. She saw

Francie drop her bike and look about, as if to check if anyone was watching, then kneel down, lift the stone, and deposit something small and bright beneath it. Around Sadie the house became a vacuum of silence, and suddenly she felt her days there, like a stay in a sanatorium, were over.

March 22, 2003

THROUGH THE FALL AND INTO THE WINTER MONTHS, a time in which the boundaries of the world outside Sadie's house seem to narrow, when at night the cold descends and covers the neighborhood like a tight lid, Ray Filley begins appearing places. She thinks it is a coincidence at first—that it is a small town, and now he is back in it, and why shouldn't she run into him at Shaw's Supermarket buying steaks one evening in November, at the bank with his deposit slip one morning in January, at the post office in front of the stamp machine in February, the cold curling beneath her coat collar, the parking lot filled with slush? *Everyone has errands,* she thinks. They make light of these encounters, inquire about the appropriate holidays. Ray laughs and shows his bright teeth.

"You again!" he says, raising his arms in the air. He wears a plaid wool shirt and a hunting cap, and his long hair hangs out around the cap's flaps. Or he has on jeans and a leather coat and hiking boots. When he smiles his eyes crinkle up at the corners.

"I guess I'll see you over at Battinson's dry cleaners next," she says.

She doesn't ask him why he's still in town, how long he'll stay. He asks her nothing about her family, her life. Instead, they exist in a strange alter world in which nothing exists beyond the moment they share.

Then one afternoon in March Sadie tells him she's joined the Tunxis Players. The revelation feels overly personal, as if she's performing a kind of striptease. "We're doing *The Night of the Iguana*," she says. It is the play her mother was in that last summer. She sees his face and knows he remembers, but he only nods and says, "Well, well," and nothing more about it. He tells her he's moved back into the old Filley Farm homestead.

"My father was living there until he died," he explains when she seems surprised. "I like fixing up old houses," he adds.

When they separate, Sadie feels people eyeing them, as if the space they occupy gives off its own heat. She lets herself imagine that there is something otherworldly at work, that their accidental circling of each other might be attributed to some alignment of magnetic fields, to the start of a cycle of preordained events. But then Sadie sees his truck, an old Filley Farm work truck, idling in the Vincent Elementary School parking lot after play practice, and she knows that he's investigated the Tunxis Players' rehearsal schedule. She must now accept that her childhood longing for him has somehow been made manifest, that he has been seeking her out, tracking her movements about town. But for some reason she refuses to do so. She gets into her car and lingers, waiting for the other players to head home, watching the string of taillights disappear, and then she pulls up alongside him. Ray rolls down the window and she continues to pretend they have just bumped into each other. They say things that she mulls over later, trying to read into them.

"So the nightlife here is the same as ever," he says.

"Is that a good thing or a bad thing?"

He shrugs, but she sees a line of bewilderment between his eyes.

Sadie smiles ruefully. She imagines how it all looks to him,

A. C. Peterson's restaurant with its sprung booth cushions, its cracked Formica; the John Brown's lounge, still smelling of popcorn, the sons of the old regulars now hugging their beers at the bar. She imagines him walking into the bar, how they'd all wave at him and welcome him in and buy him rounds of drinks, their hands heavy on his back, his shoulders. Sadie and her husband have gone there with couples at night after dinners out, and new music comes out of the same jukebox in the dark corner. The men at the bar talk about the girls they used to date, the ones that got away. They all married local women, work in family businesses, for the insurance companies, like Sadie's husband, or in local town agencies—law enforcement, fire department, DPW. Some of them wear loosened ties, others have on work pants, boots, and flannel shirts. They are the Seckingers, the Battinsons, the Mayocks. Sadie knows that Ray has never fit in. She must admit she has never fit in herself.

For the next two weeks, when she emerges from play rehearsal, she finds Ray's truck parked in the school lot. Neither of them mentions why he is there, the pauses in the conversation in which neither of them speaks seeming natural and yet weighted with what they do not say. They look at each other, or he fidgets with something in his truck. The parking lot lights leave them partially in shadow, his expression difficult to read. And then, "I hear they're going to tear down the old Bascomb house on Terry Plains."

"They're going to have some sort of a ceremony before they do it."

"Will you be going to that?" he says.

Sadie feels like she is still in character from *The Night of the Iguana*—her part that of Hannah, a woman who keeps her emotions carefully in check. When she says, "Look at the time," it's as if he's entered the play with her, saying his own line on cue: "We seem to have wasted it pretty well."

Sadie drives home, up three hills, along a wide open field,

past houses set back from the road behind split-rail fences, to her own house in Gladwyn Hollow. She leaves the windows open so the cold air blows through. She did this as a teenager driving home, airing the smoke out of the car, out of her hair, so her father wouldn't smell it. She isn't sure what she is airing out now—the remnants of the words they spoke, the heightened tension, the scent of what she must confess is desire from her skin and clothing? She parks the car in the garage and steps into her house—warm and lamp-lit—and feels instantly caged. She drinks a glass of water at the sink. Craig will be upstairs in bed, reading something for work, the television on. The children will be asleep in their rooms, their faces lit by nightlights plugged into the wall sockets. In Lily's room the streetlight outside will leave a pale stripe across the crib's patterned sheet. Craig will glance up at her and smile when she comes in, and she worries he will set aside his work, and slide down alongside her in the bed, and smell something on her skin, some evidence of everything she hasn't been saying to Ray Filley in the parking lot.

She has just gotten used to the predictability, the imposed parameters of their meetings, when Ray appears one morning at the end of her street. She is taking the children to school. It's a Monday, and the children are unhappy about going. They have projects they began over the weekend—Sylvia's amusement park for her tiny dolls, and Max's block city where his Matchbox cars careen and park. They want to wake up and continue their play, and Sadie is as sorry and disgruntled as they are that they cannot. She remembers the worlds she used to create, the sadness she felt on Sunday evenings when she knew they would have to be abandoned. Her mother, too, hated Sundays, telling Sadie how as a child she dreaded the impending return to school, the ferry to Staten Island, the skies dark overhead. Still, when Sadie complained about going to school her mother refused to listen.

"You come home every afternoon," she said, her eyes wide, as if she were revisiting the lurching ferry, the closed-in smells of the dormitory. "You don't sleep in a room with twenty girls, and nuns patrolling the hallways, listening for any little noise."

Sadie ushers Max and Sylvia through the morning preparations with singing and happy bantering: Guess what I'm putting in your lunch today? A brownie! Who knows what day it is? It's Daddy's birthday! She writes little notes with colored markers and drops them in their lunch boxes. She loads them into the car. She puts in a tape of songs Max likes, ones that Sylvia sings along to, changing the names to their own the way Sadie did when Sylvia was small. *There's a hole in the bucket, dear Sylvia, dear Sylvia, there's a hole in the bucket, dear Sylvia, a hole.* She comes to the stop sign and Ray is there, parked on the side by the woods, near the rotting cedar posts of the barbed wire fence. *With what shall I mend it, dear Max, dear Max, with what shall I mend it, dear Max, with what?* The children sing; the taped music is tinny and ridiculous. Sadie realizes that even as an adult Ray still makes her feel like a child.

When she returns he is still there. She drives to her house, parks her car in the garage, and then walks back down the street. The lawns are muddy, the grass yellow and flattened. Soon the men will be out with their fertilizer spreaders, their pruners and mowers. She raps on Ray's window and he rolls it down and smiles at her. His eyes are green, the color of the truck. She feels a warmth rush down the length of her body, a weakness in her legs. "Get in," he says. Her skin feels hot. She gets into the truck and smells the dirt ground into the floor mats, a powdery whiff of old hair pomade. They have never been this close before, and she feels his proximity, a flash of gooseflesh on her arms and legs, senses the tension in his hand, which plays absently with the gearshift. He glances over at her and then away, fiddles with the knob on the radio. His silence is a pent-up one—she imagines he is holding his breath, waiting for something from her. She slides along the seat, leans against him, and takes his face in her hands. His cheeks are rough, unshaven. His eyes close, and she kisses him, listens to his groans of pleasure, her own sighs filling the cab, the seats making everything impossibly awkward. When Ray puts the truck in gear, his face flushed, she pulls away and opens the truck door.

"What are you doing?" he says.

"I'm getting out," she tells him. She slips out of the truck, into the spongy grass by the woods. She smells the damp, the snow melting. Her mouth feels bruised.

"So what was this? Just some *necking*? Are we in junior high?"

Sadie laughs at that. "Necking! Yes, that's what it was."

She wants to start at the beginning, to have what she never had from him. She wants kissing, and fondling, and the feeling of venturing into a forbidden place. She shuts the truck door and walks up the road in the direction of her house. Behind her she hears his truck pull away, and she feels elation and regret. She folds the laundry, empties the dishwasher, peers out her front window, waiting. It is nearly spring. The snow clings to the grass beneath the hedges. The sky fills with loose clouds. It is Craig's birthday, and she bakes a cake. Pre-occupied, she lets the layers overcook in the oven, but she hides them beneath the chocolate frosting and decides no one will be the wiser. She wraps the gift the children picked out at Sears—a cedar shoe-shine box, one Sadie told them was ex-actly like the one her own father had, and a necktie she chose at random, its colors muted and conventional. She creases the striped paper, tapes the edges. *Good enough,* she thinks, although she feels a nagging sense that these gifts are inadequate, that she doesn't even know what present Craig would like. She hasn't taken the time to ask, to think it over. She is usually a good gift-giver, and she feels a brief flash of guilt that she brushes off. She knows that after Lily's death, he would accept any gift from her and the children, and knowing this, she has chosen anything.

June 15, 1979

SADIE LEFT MRS. SIDELMAN'S IMMEDIATELY AFTER spotting Francie and went to Betty's house with her news, but Betty had to first do the dishes and sweep the kitchen floor, and then she and Sadie had to make a circuitous route of the neighborhood to shake her younger sister, who had traipsed out the door after them. The cicadas revved up in the trees, their sound an explosion of noise that followed them up to the dead end, where they discovered Francie's first letter. She'd written it on flowered stationery, the kind that parents give to children when they go to camp. *Dear Hezekiah,* it said. Reading on, the letter revealed aspects of her family life—her little brothers camping out in the hall closet, her mother sleeping all afternoon on the couch, her father and his woodworking hobby. *He carves puns out of wood,* she wrote. *Shoe tree, water gun, bookworm. He is now making a train track that one day will run through the entire house, upstairs and down.* They read the note in the upstairs bathroom at Sadie's house. This was the only room with a lock. They sat on the closed toilet lid, where they often sat together to read the *Playboys* her father had hidden in the vanity drawer. As little girls, they had mixed up potions in paper Dixie cups on the counter— toothpaste, shaving cream, Old Spice.

"The whole family is crazy," Betty said. Her eyes feigned shock beneath her bangs.

Sadie told her to wait a minute, and she slipped from

the bathroom and returned with a sheet of her mother's stationery—heavy, ivory-colored paper—and a pen.

"What is that?" Betty asked.

Sadie held the paper and pen out to her. "Tell her they sound *eccentric,*" Sadie said. "He doesn't care about her family, anyway. Say: *I find you incredibly intriguing. I want to know more about you.*"

Betty stared at the pen and paper, and hesitated. But they both knew she was the best at making up handwriting. Hadn't they spent one long winter day copying the slanted script off of old postcards and letters from Betty's grandmother?

"Come on, Hezekiah," Sadie said.

Betty took the paper and pen and grinned. "So what was that again?"

It was a weekday, and Sadie's father was at the office. Her mother was downstairs talking on the phone. Betty invented a handwriting that was part boy's messy cursive, part arthritic scrawl. She wanted to write *I think I love you.* They laughed until they cried at this, a Partridge Family lyric. Sadie finally decided it was too soon. "He has to woo her," she said, wondering, as she said it, where she'd ever heard of such a thing. They sprinkled Sadie's father's Old Spice on the envelope. They'd used one of his old *Playboys* to write on, May 1974, Marsha Kay in sheer bra and panties. And then they slipped out to the dead end, past boys building a go-cart out of plywood, past girls running through a sprinkler, their legs speckled with grass. No one knew where they were headed. No one followed them. They had their cigarettes, and after they left the note they lifted the barbed wire and kept walking through the field's tall grass, its black-eyed Susans, dame's rocket, and chicory, the kinds of flowers they used to bring back in damp fists to their mothers on their birthdays. They sat down in the middle of the field in the tall grass and no one could see them.

"She'll look today," Sadie said, predicting what would happen next.

She practiced smoke rings. In a year she would be caught with Ritchie Merrill, an older boy who drove a motorcycle, on the Schusters' bed while babysitting their eight-year-old. The news would spread, and she would become infamous in school, and she and Betty would no longer be friends. But that summer neither of them knew that this would happen. In their bliss they believed they were forever bound in their conspiracy against Francie. They would always press their foreheads together, and stare into each other's eyes, and know exactly what the other was thinking. It was the beginning of summer, and they could predict nothing more than what they'd come to expect from summers past: the possibility of days of endless letter-writing, and grape-flavored ice cubes, and gum-wrapper chains, and a new attraction to plan—their own Aquacade, where they would convince Beth Filley to let them use her pool and devise an elaborate swimming performance, all of them in matching suits, doing flips and headstands in the water, dreaming about being watched and applauded. They would have their stack of books from the library as they always did—*Flambards* and its sequel, *The Edge of the Cloud*. They expected that boys would continue to keep clear of them, that they'd find evidence of them—murdered robins riddled with silver BBs, muddy trails in the woods littered with potato chip bags, and soft drink cans, and trampled violets—but that they'd remain elusive as they always had. Sadie would form the basis of her knowledge about sex from Mrs. Sidelman's books, from the bits of the love letters she'd been able to read, the man, who did not seem to have ended up as Bea Brownmiller's husband, discussing the plumpness of her lips, the curve of her hip, the strangely intoxicating scent of chlorine in her hair.

April 3, 2003

RAY RETURNS THE NEXT DAY, AND THE ONE AFTER that, parking in the same place at the end of Sadie's street. She avoids him for a week, and then he stops coming, and she feels as if somewhere inside of her a space has been carved out. The day he comes back she walks down there, purposely passing the truck, letting herself feel the longing, drawing it out until he puts the truck in gear and drives alongside her.

"Going for a walk?" he says to her over the chug of the old truck's engine.

She won't look at him. She looks ahead, places her feet carefully on the pavement until the truck forces her to the side of the road, to the mud, to the brambles beginning to bloom.

"Stop it," she says through the passenger window. "Just stop it."

He looks at her from under the brim of his Filley Farm work cap. His eyes look startled, as if she's just given him a slap.

"I can't," he says. She notes the longing in his voice, and her heart swims. She takes hold of the passenger-door handle and tugs the door open and climbs in. He gathers her into his arms, his mouth wet and searching. They kiss on and on, and then he puts the truck in gear and this time she allows him to drive her away. They take the back road up the mountain, past Filley's gravel lot filled with sleek Mercedes, Audis, a Lexus.

Smoke billows out of the stone chimney. His father opened the produce store fifty years ago as a seasonal roadside stand. Now it's popular with the wealthy people who come over Avon Mountain to buy native corn, fresh eggs, or Christmas trees and mulled cider.

Ray has her pulled in tight under his arm. At the stop sign, he leans down to kiss her. *Like teenagers,* Sadie thinks, a little abashedly. He tells her that the manager, Ludlow, keeps the fire going in the hearth, and she tells him that people like that—stopping in for tea, or coffee, or fresh cider, sitting around that hearth with home-baked crumb cake. "I remember your father would come in and chat with everyone," she says.

Ray laughs and shifts the gears of the old truck with his left hand, removing it from the wheel to reach over so he doesn't have to let go of her. "Oh, yeah, fresh from the fields with his mud-splattered pants and chapped hands. The old New England farmer."

Sadie looks at him carefully. His voice is harsh, as if she has opened up some old wound. She leans up and kisses his neck. Each part of his body, she suspects, will be like a new territory.

"Get your pumpkins, get your yellow squash, peppers, beans, get your fresh eggs," he says in a barker's voice. "Now they're all ready for spring—the bulbs, Easter."

"Will you stay?" Sadie asks him.

She can't imagine that the life he's so far revealed to her—as a pampered prep school boy, or traveling to Aspen skiing, to Europe, or on the road with his band, playing gigs in dark rock clubs—has even remotely prepared him to run a store, much less a farm.

"It's like some kind of joke," Ray says, looking pained. Even the truck is his father's, one of the old faded green work trucks he insisted on driving everywhere. Ray tells her that when he flew in from Florida his sister, Beth, picked him up in it. "Oh, she thinks it's hysterical. 'It's your truck now,' she says."

Sadie shifts uneasily on the old vinyl seat, sits upright away from Ray and feels the springs beneath the upholstery. She hasn't yet considered Beth as part of this. She remembers her obsession with Ray and almost asks him if his sister is still following him around, but decides against it.

"How is Beth?" she asks, trying to be kind.

Ray laughs. "She teaches elementary school in Granby," he says. "If you can believe that."

Sadie finds this incredible, but she won't say so. She imagines one of her children, one of her friend's children even, assigned Beth as a teacher, and knows she would be uneasy without really knowing why. She's relieved Beth teaches a few towns away.

Ray tells her his parents divorced years ago, that his mother used to accuse his father of playing the "country bumpkin."

"He drank, too," Ray says. "There was that."

After the divorce, his father moved into the old Filley homestead, built by his own great-great-grandfather. He quit drinking, went to AA, and was sober, as far as anyone knew, until he died.

"I don't come back here often," Ray says. "But when I have the old place always seemed more like home than Wappaquassett." He says the name of the house he grew up in with a hint of distaste, and Sadie laughs. Ray laughs, too, and she slips back under his arm.

He drives down Duncaster Road, the woods on either side belonging to him, and then the fields where they grow the corn, the wildflowers women buy now in paper cones for fifteen dollars. He drives the truck over potholes, asphalt dislodged by tree roots. He pulls down a long, winding gravel drive lined with forsythia, to a rambling house made of trap rock. The house sits on a wide plot of open land, the woods encroaching in back. They sit in the truck and watch the wind knock the plaque by the front door (*Oliver Filley House, 1765*), watch it whip the forsythia's bright shoots against the blue sky.

When he gets out, Sadie follows him. She asks him how his father died, and Ray tells her it was a heart attack. They go into the house and Sadie smells the old plaster, the paint and sanded wood. She smells linseed oil. Ray pauses in the doorway to the kitchen and points to where Ludlow found his father when he didn't come into the store for two days in a row.

"Two days?" Sadie says.

Ray shrugs. "I guess no one checked in with him every day. I know I didn't monitor his life. I don't feel guilty about that."

They stand in the doorway to the kitchen where his father fell. Ray tells her that the day Beth picked him up at the airport and brought him to the house the soup was still in the pan, congealed and mottled with mold, the can on the counter.

"She didn't even clean up?" Sadie says.

"This place gives her the creeps," Ray replies.

The morning sun bounces off the chrome handles on the stove and the refrigerator. Ray turns to Sadie. "We used to come over here and play hide-and-seek when we were little." He tells her how Beth found a secret hiding spot behind a panel. One of those places in old houses that held stores for the Revolutionary War or escaping slaves. She called it her hidey spot. He points to the open, nearly empty room that Sadie imagines is the main living area, the chestnut floorboards wide and scarred. "There, beside the fireplace."

"What happened?" Sadie asks.

Ray smiles. "Old Grams and Gramps Filley used to tell us they had a ghost. When we were playing one day Beth got stuck in the hidey spot and just freaked out."

"Didn't anyone know she was there?" Sadie says.

Ray shakes his head. "My grandfather was dead by then. My grandmother never knew about it. We were little—Beth was probably about seven. I would have been nine. I had quit playing the game when I couldn't find her and gone outside."

The panel beside the fireplace is sealed up and painted and looks exactly like the one on the other side. Sadie imagines how Sylvia might crawl into such a place to hide, and then she tries not to think about Sylvia. Outside the wind picks up and rattles something against the house.

"How did she get out?" Sadie asks.

Ray tells her he heard Beth crying, and eventually, he figured out where the sound was coming from. "After that, it was our secret, me and Beth's."

Sadie remembers the glee Beth took in frightening her with the old house's ghost story, back when Laura Loomis had been missing only a year, and Sadie had mentioned, more than once during their backgammon marathons, her fear of what might have happened to her. "Beth never seemed like the type to scare easily," Sadie says.

Ray laughs. "Horseshit," he says. He laughs some more and crosses his arms. "I can't believe I just said that. My father used to say that."

Sadie smiles. She likes to see him laugh. She realizes she rarely saw him laugh when they were younger—he always seemed preoccupied, older than his years.

"It's my house now," Ray says. He takes Sadie in his arms. "And I always liked the ghost. I used to imagine it was like Georgie, in those books I read as a kid."

Sadie wants to remind him that the ghost is a woman, Emely Filley, but like many of the things she seems to recall so clearly, she decides not to bring it up, to let him know she remembers. He leans in and kisses her then, his hands moving along her waist, up over her breasts. He tugs her toward the stairs and then up, Sadie barely taking account of the rooms they pass, their doors opening off the long hallway, most of them empty. Ray takes off her clothes, keeping his mouth busy with hers. She feels his fingers, quick and desperate, working the buttons of her blouse, and she thrills at his desperation, the person she imagines she's become. He pushes her down onto a bed that has been slept in, the quilt hastily shoved back, the sheets wrinkled and smelling of him. She nestles in his arms, warm, safe, the house's timbers groaning like an old ship, the windowpanes, buffeted by the wind, banging in their frames. Outside, the crocuses peek from between the wall's fallen stones, the grass brightens, the leaves unfurl like little green cloths, all wet and wrung out. The smell of manure fills the fields. Ray tells her he remembers when she was a girl and would come swimming at the house. He says he used to like watching her.

"Watching me where?" she says. "In the pool?"

He says nothing for a moment. His hand keeps moving over her thigh.

"When?" she asks him. "How old was I?"

"I don't know," he says. "How old are you now?"

"You know how old I am," she says.

The bedroom is papered with pink peonies and wild roses. The sun filters through the old glass to fall pale on the wood floor, on the dust beneath the dressing table. This was once his grandparents' room, he tells her.

"I used to like watching you and your friends play your little games," he says.

His hand moves up along her waist, slips over her breast. She can't think clearly when he touches her. She forgets what she was saying, what word comes next. "Oh," is all that escapes. She wants to tell him she's loved him her whole life, dreamed of him, invented scenarios of the two of them together. But his mouth brushes hers, and words became secondary. She focuses on his lips, his tongue, his hands moving over her skin. She luxuriates in her ability to stretch out her limbs on cool sheets. She hears the wind outside, the birds' shrieks, the soft moans that slip from their mouths. Then she hears a disturbance downstairs. A chair being pulled out from under a table, a woman's voice:

"Ray!"

He slides off of her, stealthy, quick, exposing her body to the room's draft. He gathers his clothes from the end of the bed and glances back at her with his finger to his mouth. She sees his erection disappear inside his boxers.

"Beth, I'm up here, getting dressed," he calls. "I'll be right down."

Ray leaves the room and shuts the door, and Sadie props herself up in bed. Though they live in the same town, she hasn't seen Beth in years and tries to imagine her mischievous eyes, her small, pouting mouth, on the face of a grown woman. Sadie remembers how the teenage Beth always pretended things, so that you never knew what she really thought. Parts of their conversation come up the stairwell, and Sadie lies under the quilt on Ray's grandmother's bed, waiting, listening, trying to make it out. It feels just like when she was younger and tried to spy on Ray and Beth while they sat around their pool or walked the dogs down the street. Even then she could never quite understand much of anything they said, as if they spoke a foreign language, and listening only filled her with a dislocated longing.

"Did the ghost take a turn last night?" Beth says. "Any rattling in the attic? Footsteps on the stairs?"

"What do you want, Beth?" Ray says.

"Groaning? Moaning? Glowing shape in a long gown standing in the hall?"

"It's not a her," Ray says dully.

"Gramps said it was."

"We have no idea—he, she, it."

"That's disrespectful. Remember when Mommy used to freak when we referenced her in the third person and she was right in the room?"

Sadie hears nothing for a few moments.

"Are you sad?" Beth asks him. "You seem sad."

"What do you want? Why are you here?"

"I just came to see if you're ready to come home," Beth says.

"I'm not staying in that house with you and Mother," Ray says.

"Well, then I'm going to make you lunch, like I used to. Pickle sandwiches. A little gin and Coke. Remember gin and Cokes?"

"Sorry, I can't. I've got things to do."

"I thought we'd play Chinese checkers."

"You thought wrong."

"You sound mad."

Sadie cannot hear anything more between them, though she can feel the vibrations of their movements downstairs. Someone opens a window. Someone slides a chair along the floor. She scans the room for her clothes. She didn't pay attention to where he tossed them, and she sees them now draped over an upholstered chair in the corner. She slips from the bed, crosses the cold floorboards, and as she gathers her clothing, she notices a suitcase tucked behind the chair. It is covered in plaster dust. The clasps are mottled with rust. A vintage American Tourister. Sadie remembers the old commercials—a suitcase being thrown from a train, tossed around by a gorilla in a cage. She pauses. The suitcase is familiar—turquoise faux leather with metal trim, a 1970s suitcase like one in the set her mother had. She remembers the blue brocade taffeta lining, the satin pockets. She sets her clothes down and listens for Beth and Ray. She hears their voices far off, outside, down below her window. Maybe Ray has convinced Beth to leave and is walking her to her car. Although she knows she should respect Ray's privacy, she feels compelled to open the suitcase. She doesn't, for a moment, think she'll find anything inside, but when she lifts it to the bed she can hear its contents shifting. She wonders whether her mother loaned her suitcase to Ray's mother, Patsy. She hears Beth's and Ray's voices return, and she struggles with the stuck clasps. One of them is bent, as if it's been recently pried.

"Why won't you?" Beth says, whining like a child.

"I'm busy, Beth. I'm occupied. In the middle of something."

"Oh. I see. A groupie? Out-of-town something?"

Sadie hears a long pause and Ray's mumbled response.

"Is it a *local* something? That Donahue woman? The one that had twenty brothers and sisters?"

Sadie strains to listen. After that summer, Betty Donahue became someone she saw only in passing from a car window, from a distance at a high school party. Could Ray have slept with Betty in all of those intervening years? She feels an irrational rush of jealousy. Beth's voice is high-pitched. She rattles out names of other women from town, from her own neighborhood, ones Sadie sees at Park Ave. Pizza, Drug City, Shaw's Supermarket, pushing strollers down her street. Sadie, her heart thudding, wonders if Ray has somehow had sex with all of these women since he's been back. She stands in front of the suitcase, naked, and realizes that she doesn't really know Ray Filley. She's only seen him a few times as an adult, between his gigs. She remembers him stacking Christmas trees at the store, his hands in bright orange work gloves, his face bearded and different. She was with Craig and Sylvia, before Max was born, and pretended she didn't know him, convincing Craig she didn't like the trees, that they should look elsewhere. Once she saw him in line at the drugstore, wearing a wool cap, looking hungover.

Beth's voice comes bright, cajoling, up the stairwell. "Is she here now?"

Sadie sets the suitcase back behind the chair. She takes her clothing with her to the bed, but there is no time to put anything on. Beth's footsteps are quick on the stairs. Sadie hears Ray clambering after her, telling her to stop it, to come down, to leave it alone. Beth bursts into the room. Sadie can tell from the shock on her face that she didn't really believe she'd find anyone. Beth's brown hair is disheveled from the wind. She still wears her pink wool coat and gloves. Sadie notices that Beth's face is creased and aged, and she wonders, fleetingly, if she, too, looks as old. Beth freezes, one hand on the door.

"Oh," is all she says. "Oh well." Sadie watches Beth's old face deflate, like Max's does when he has hold of something and loses it—a toad, a ball, a crab on the end of a string tied around a mussel shell.

Ray doesn't say anything. Sadie can see the shadow of him in the hallway. Beth looks at Sadie in the bed and then turns, quickly, and brushes past Ray. She goes downstairs and the slam of the front door echoes up the stairwell.

Ray steps into the doorway. Sadie stares at him, unsure, the sight of the suitcase awakening a memory that is too distant to access quickly, one that blots out the shock of being discovered in Ray's bed, that diffuses the desire she felt for him.

"What will she do?" she asks. "Why did you let her come up here?"

"She won't do anything."

"She knows who I am."

Ray comes into the room and sits on the edge of the bed. He stares at her, his eyes softening. "Does she?" He puts his hand out and touches her face.

Sadie doesn't know if she is angry or not. Ray doesn't seem to think she needs to be.

Ray leans in and presses his mouth to her forehead, to her cheek, to her lips, parted in an effort to speak. Certainly Beth will tell other women, the way that women do. Sadie herself has done it, even told her husband gossip she's heard. Didn't it make her seem better than they were in his eyes? But Ray seems to think otherwise. Sadie wants to dress and leave, and he presses her back into the mattress. "She might come back," she says.

"Oh no," he says. "She's gone." He even laughs at her for worrying. "You don't know Beth."

And she doesn't know her. She doesn't know any of them, even herself. The bed smells of dust and roses, of Ray's scent, of her own body beneath the sheets. The suitcase stays hidden behind the overstuffed chair, and she pretends she knows nothing about it as Ray climbs back into bed with her. "Let's start over," he says, and the room fills with the sound of his tender encouragements, her shameless, joyful cries. She has no idea where any of this will lead, but she doesn't want to spoil it with the past.

PART TWO

SEARCH RESUMES TODAY FOR MISSING 9-YEAR-OLD

Wintonbury—June 15, 1974

A massive search for missing 9-year-old Laura Loomis was called off by state police Friday, but will resume at dawn today. The search by more than 800 volunteers was called off about 30 hours after the 9-year-old was last seen walking home from a friend's. Laura, daughter of Mr. and Mrs. Jonathan Loomis, was given permission to visit a friend who lived on her street. When she did not return by dinnertime, Mrs. Loomis became concerned and called the friend, who claimed Laura had left her house right at 4:30, as instructed by her mother. By this time Mr. Loomis, home from work, began a search of the neighborhood with his wife, both calling their daughter's name. State police were notified at 6:00 P.M., and volunteer firemen quickly began a search of the surrounding woods and fields, until dark, when a house-to-house search was conducted. No leads have developed, says State Police Lt. William Reed. "Foul play is not suspected," reports police spokesman Dan Fontaine, "but it has not been ruled out." Late Friday he said that state police are proceeding with the theory that the girl is "missing and lost."

June 12, 2003

I N GLADWYN HOLLOW THERE'S A WALKING PATH. SADIE
and the other women consider themselves lucky to have
such a thing, neatly paved with black tar like their drive-
ways, cutting between their houses, through their own safe,
scenic woods, circling the elementary school's playing field,
connecting one street with another, one neighborhood with
the next. It is the start of summer when Sadie and her next-
door neighbor Jane Griswold discover that someone has
veered off the path and made one of their own leading up a
wooded hill through wild blackberry and fern. Their children
clamor for the adventure of the new path. Jane hesitates. She
is shorter than Sadie, and athletic, her long reddish-brown
hair kept back in a messy knot. She parts the overgrowth and
peers up, and Sadie stands back with the children.

"Teenagers," Jane says. She looks at Sadie, and Sadie
knows what she means—teenagers ferreting out their secret
places to congregate, to do what they both remember doing
when they were that age. Jane says she'd feel obligated to put
a stop to what she found, and she doesn't want to be "Old
Mrs. Brunner with her mothball breath and cranky threats,"
who used to chase her and her childhood friends out of their
neighborhood woods.

"No," Sadie says. "Who wants that?" But she eyes the path
like a teenager herself, the trampled-down fern, the wild ginger, the canopy of trees. She dreams of that time, being free

of responsibility, having only herself and her own desires to satisfy.

"And we don't want to encourage the children to wander in the woods," Jane says. "I mean not with *this* area's history."

Sadie looks at Jane, surprised. "What do you think they'll find? Ghosts?" She doesn't mean to sound angry, but her voice is unnecessarily harsh.

Jane is equally surprised by Sadie's tone. "I mean we don't want them to get lost," she says calmly, using a voice Sadie suspects she uses when her husband finds his underwear drawer empty or one of her children is throwing a tantrum.

"Or run into a predator," Sadie says. "Or the Old Leatherman."

She is sorry, instantly, that she's let herself get carried away.

"Who?" Jane says. She eyes Sadie with barely masked irritation. The children stand by Sadie's side, gazing up at her.

Sadie laughs and tells the story of the Old Leatherman, how he walked a circuit of 365 miles every thirty-four days, and housewives knew the exact day to expect him, the exact hour and minute. "They gave him food, and he lived in caves," she said. "He wore clothes made of leather patches."

They move on down the walking path, and Sadie teaches the children the rhyme:

> *One misty, moisty morning,*
> *When cloudy was the weather,*
> *There I met an old man*
> *All clothed in leather*
>
> *All clothed in leather,*
> *With a cap under his chin.*
> *How do you do?*
> *And how do you do?*
> *And how do you do again?*

The children and Jane are pacified by Sadie's story, but Sadie is unsure why she responded so strangely to Jane's mention of the past. Maybe she is sensitive after years of being mistaken for Laura Loomis. Since she's become a mother she will sometimes wonder about Laura, the first girl who disappeared and was never found. But she won't ever let herself think about the other one. She blames Ray Filley, their shared history, for these twinges of memory she cannot control.

For weeks she's ignored Ray's truck parked at the end of her street, his eyes following her car with their plea. She pretends she doesn't see him in the Vincent school parking lot after her play rehearsal. After sleeping with him at the old house, Sadie longs to be with him again. But, of course, she cannot. She is mortified that Beth came upon her naked in his bed, and she doesn't trust her not to tell anyone. Once school is out she is busy all day with the children. They have trouble adjusting to the unstructured time, and they've quickly become bored, lonely for their school friends. Sylvia spends mornings chewing on her hair and watching television—old shows like *The Brady Bunch* and *I Dream of Jeannie*. Sadie is shocked to see Sylvia has inherited her old hair-chewing habit, and she tells her to stop, that it's disgusting, just like her mother once told her. Still, drawn to the familiar television episodes, she finds herself beside Sylvia on the couch, transported back to her own childhood. Max invents elaborate treasure hunts and whines until they leave the couch to conduct house-wide searches for small clues he's hidden in unusual places—inside the pocket of Craig's winter suit coat, beneath the iron dachshund doorstop. Gone are the days when children roamed the neighborhood, knocking on each other's doors, meeting up in backyards. Playdates must be arranged, but Sadie avoids scheduling them, suspecting she will have to come up with ways to entertain children other than her own.

She often goes up into her room to hide, to be alone. "We're bored," they cry up the stairs to her. "We have nothing to do."

Driven to distraction by their demands, Sadie decides one day to try the new path. She tells Max and Sylvia to leave their bikes where the path diverges, which happens to be the Currys' backyard, close to the slate patio and the carefully arranged cast-iron furniture. She takes the children's hands firmly in hers, even though Max protests that he can walk himself.

It is midday. The heat dissolves in the cool woods. The cicada sound lessens. Sadie allows Max to walk ahead with his sister, because as soon as they maneuver past the blackberry's thorns they discover well-trodden dirt that leads up the hillside, mossy and speckled with sunlight. This dirt path curves through saplings and shade fragrant with pine. The children sing the Old Leatherman rhyme. They come upon large rocks, boulders that appear to have tumbled down off a mountain that no longer exists, or emerged from the leaf-strewn floor of the woods like something from the core of the earth, and she lets them scramble on their surfaces, shows Sylvia how with a small stone she can etch her name and her brother's name boldly on the flat face. They walk for ten minutes—"No more than that," she tells Jane later. And just when she thinks she will turn around she sees sunlight up ahead and steps into a clearing—a flat sunny place filled with meadow grass and a pond. Jane is disbelieving.

"What sort of *pond*?" she asks.

Sadie smiles. "Fresh water," she tells her. "It's more like a swimming hole, fed by this beautiful running brook." She doesn't tell her the rest—how she remembered the pond the moment she came upon it, how the memory of it, fueled by the cicada sound, felt bright and terrible all at once.

That night as Sadie is serving the children dinner, Craig comes in from work and they begin to tell him about their discovery. He has loosened his tie. His face is red from the stress of the day, from irritation, Sadie thinks. Each day she prays that Beth Filley hasn't told anyone about what she saw, that someone hasn't invited Craig to lunch or pulled him aside in some quiet office to break the news to him. She tells the children to calm down—their voices are filled with excitement, Sylvia's especially. They rise in pitch and vie for attention. Who can tell it the best becomes a competition. Sylvia, older, with more of a vocabulary, wins out. Her father turns to her and holds his hand up, the look on his face vaguely threatening, and she is quiet. Sadie wonders how he has managed to train them to follow his every command, like puppies.

"One at a time," he says. He looks up at Sadie and smiles. *Look at these two,* his expression says. *These are ours.* The love in his face wrenches her heart.

"There's a pond," Sylvia says. "It's in a magic glade. And we are going to swim in it."

"And I can bring my float," Max says.

"And we can pretend no one can find us there," Sylvia says. "Because it's a fairy place, protected by their rings."

Craig gets a beer from the refrigerator and twists off the top. "Really?" he says.

He looks at Sadie and raises his eyebrows. She is about to let the children take credit for this imagined world but then Sylvia sees the look on her father's face. Like Jane, he thinks they are making it all up.

"Mommy says," Sylvia tells him defiantly.

"Yeah, Mommy told us," Max says.

He looks then to Sadie, his smile flat and questioning. "Really?" he says again.

"It's a beautiful spot," she says.

And Craig leans in and presses his lips to hers. "Sounds like fun," he says, and the topic is closed, and Sadie knows he believes she's loaded the children in the car and taken them to a new spot, Salmon Brook Park, or Barkhamsted, or one of the other approved swimming places in the area. She lets him believe this—the days with the children while he is at work are her own to fill, however she best sees fit.

In the morning she digs out the low folding beach chairs, stuffs a canvas tote with towels. Max takes his blue bucket and climbs into his stroller. Sylvia rides her bike. Jane sees her on the walking path and approaches her by the Currys' backyard just as Sadie parks the stroller and takes Max by the hand.

"Are you going to let them *swim*?" she asks. "Aren't there leeches and snakes?"

"It's so peaceful," Sadie says. "The birds flit around. The kids can splash in the brook and catch frogs. They can swim in the shallows."

Sadie admits she plans to swim herself, the water ice-cold and clear. "You can see the sandy bottom. The little fish."

Jane shakes her head at her, as if Sadie is making a mistake and she is sorry for her. Sadie smiles at Jane, and turns from her, and leads the children up the path. The pond reminds her of her favorite childhood books—the one about the girl who finds a key to a hidden garden, the one about the kids who find the old summer houses surrounding a lake that has since disappeared, Nancy Drew's mysterious hidden staircase, the moss-covered mansion, the message in the hollow oak. On the walk up to the pond, Sadie tells her children stories, and she feels as if some part of her that was lost is bubbling to the surface. At the pond, Sadie stretches her legs out in the trampled-down grass. The cicadas' whine becomes a comforting backdrop. Max splashes with his tube. Soon, she hears Jane's children rushing past her toward the water, and Jane and Maura Grant come across the grass to stand beside her. Sadie looks up at them, shielding her eyes.

"Holy shit," Jane says, finally convinced.

Sadie laughs. Already her arms and legs are suntanned, her smile serene. Jane and Maura open their chairs and settle down beside Sadie in the grass. Sadie worries that her lost baby and how she is holding up will be the topic of conversation. But it is not. Maura, her face wide and friendly, dotted with freckles, takes out a tube of sunscreen.

"I remember one time up in New Hampshire we found a place like this," she says. She begins to tell her story, one that involves herself as a teenager, a cooler of Heineken, and a boy who drove his father's BMW, who broke up with her and went on to Stanford. Jane launches into her own teenage story, and Sadie imagines Lily's flitting presence, almost walking now, splashing in the shallow brook water, her hair so fair it is white in the sunlight. She closes her eyes and remembers the smell of the bed in the old Filley house, the way Ray's hands moved over her skin.

June 20, 1979

CLARE WATKINS SPENT MANY SUMMER DAYS AT Wappaquassett, sitting around the pool with Ray and Beth's mother, Patsy. She'd have her scripts and her drink and her cigarettes. Sadie usually accompanied her to spend time with Beth, summers the only time they ever saw each other, since Beth attended private school. But that summer Sadie felt uncomfortable being dragged over, forced to be Beth's playmate. She'd managed to avoid going, until one afternoon her mother, in her bathing suit and sheer yellow blouse, insisted. She wore her sunglasses, even though they were standing in the kitchen.

"I don't really even know Beth Filley," Sadie said.

Clare Watkins seemed unmoved.

"Whose fault is that?" she said. "You might have spent more time with her during the school year instead of sneaking off with Betty, like you always do. Or ordering around your little minions."

Sadie felt a deep resentment well up. Her mother smiled at her sadly.

"Don't you want to spend the day with me?" she said.

When Sadie didn't reply her mother's mouth grew tight. "You have two minutes to put on your suit. Maybe that new one you insisted I buy you?"

In summers past, Sadie's mother would sometimes leave for Filley's without asking her to go. Sadie would wake up late or come in from outside and discover her mother had gone without her. She'd imagine her mother swimming with Beth, or telling one of her funny stories that always involved imitations of friends and neighbors. Deprived of the chance to be in her mother's company, Sadie would become disconsolate and mope around the house, waiting for her to return. She never ventured to Filley's alone; fearful her mother had left her behind for a reason, and alert to the possibility of being forgotten, Sadie made it a point to be in her mother's line of vision, to impress her however she could. Lately, though, as if a switch had been thrown, the roles were reversed—the more Sadie sought to avoid her mother, the more her mother demanded she spend time with her. She went up to her room and slipped on her bikini, thinking about how this situation would have pleased her last summer. She told herself that today would be just as it always was—that she and her mother would sit together in the lounge chair and judge Beth Filley's diving. That her mother would count to see how long Sadie and Beth could stay underwater.

Sadie and her mother took the car down their street to the next, through Wappaquassett's gated entrance and up the long curving driveway, a trip that took all of five minutes. Her mother had her drink in one hand and the steering wheel in the other. She drove her new Coupe de Ville, cranberry red with white leather interior, a car that floated along the narrow tar roads of the neighborhood. The car nosed up the driveway's incline to the top.

"You're going to hit that shrub," Sadie said.

Her mother said she would not, and then laughed when she did. "You were right," she said. "Smarty pants."

It used to be that when her mother hit various stationary objects—trees, mailboxes, a bike abandoned on a lawn—Sadie would laugh along with her. These things became secrets they kept from her father, from the owners of the objects, as if the objects weren't really of any consequence to their owners, or if they were, they shouldn't have been.

"It was an old mailbox," her mother would say. "Jim Frobel should have replaced that rusted thing a long time ago."

That day Sadie suddenly saw it all differently. "You should be more careful," she said as her mother realigned the car in the driveway and put the car in park.

She turned to Sadie and lifted her sunglasses. "Are you judging me?" Her eyes were pale blue and glassy, ringed with liner, heavy with mascara.

Sadie said she was not.

Her mother leaned in and kissed her on the forehead. Sadie smelled the lime and gin, felt the thickness of her lipstick, and she reached up and wiped it away. Her mother turned off the car and climbed out.

"Help me with all of this, would you?"

It was up to Sadie to carry her mother's silver mesh cigarette case; the copies of her script; her straw bag with sunscreen, extra limes, and the new *Cosmopolitan,* her Chanel No. 5 scenting everything with notes of jasmine. They went up the two levels of stone steps and Sadie's mother rang the bell. The door was large, constructed of oaken planks. It was Beth who came and pulled it open.

"Look who I brought," Sadie's mother said.

Beth gave a bright, false smile that she dropped as soon as Sadie's mother walked past. "Where's your mother?" Clare called out, the gold heels of her sandals echoing across the foyer.

"Outside," Beth told her. She sighed and shut the door. She was shorter than Sadie now. She had her dark hair cut neatly to her shoulders, and she wore what Sadie took to be a boy's oxford.

Beth stood looking Sadie up and down. "Look at you," Beth said quietly. "All *blossoming.*"

Sadie instantly wished she hadn't come. Gone was the soft-spoken, easygoing Beth of summers past. Sadie usually didn't feel comfortable in other people's houses. The color schemes were different; the air was charged with the smell of an unusual food, or a damp odor coming up from the basement, or the musty smell of the recently used vacuum. At Betty Donahue's house her younger sisters and brothers—all chestnut-haired and freckled, copies of each other—squabbled over who would watch what on television, over a ball they'd bounce in the driveway, the sound of it ringing against the blacktop and the aluminum siding. They fought over the Cap'n Crunch, their father's bottle of Pepsi, the last Hostess cupcake. They threw things and struck each other. They slammed doors and played radios too loud. The mess of Betty's house was something Sadie could never get used to: clothes strewn everywhere—clean piles, dirty heaps, lone socks behind the toilet, wet towels flung over the glass shower door, handprints, smears, torn screens, ashtrays filled to overflowing, highball glasses, saucers, wrappers, crumbs.

The Filleys' house was unlike any other house in the neighborhood. The sunlight came in from all sides through the huge windows and shone across the wood floors. The walls were museum white, and every surface was clean and clear of clutter except the den, which seemed as if it was the only room the family ever used. It was here that Beth led Sadie, into the dim, wood-paneled space where the blinds were closed, and the only light came from the television—an episode of *The Andy Griffith Show* was on. Beth sat down on the sectional couch and pulled a blanket up around her.

"When I have children I'm going to raise them like Andy Griffith does," Beth said, her voice sullen.

The episode was the one in which Opie kills a mother bird with his slingshot. He apologizes to his father when he is caught. *Sorry isn't enough,* Andy says. At this line Beth began to laugh. Andy opens Opie's window and tells him to listen to the baby birds crying out for their mother. *And she's not coming back,* he says. "I love this part," Beth said.

Sadie sat down on the end of the couch. "It seems cruel," she said warily.

Beth stopped laughing and in the television glow Sadie saw that she was crying. "It's so sad," she said. "Funny sad."

Sadie watched Beth wipe her cheeks. They sat there until the show was over, then Beth flung the blanket off of her and stood up. She went to the built-in cabinet, pulled out a backgammon set, and began setting it up.

"I suppose you're here for this," Beth said moodily. "You think you can finally beat me just because you've grown some breasts?"

Sadie wasn't sure how to respond. "I'll play if you want," she said.

Beth looked at her in the dim light. Then she closed the set and all the pieces fell into the case. "Forget it," she said. "You don't sound enthused."

Sadie heard someone shuffling past the doorway. "Be nice to the little neighborhood kids," Ray said. He stopped and leaned on the door frame. Sadie hadn't seen him up close in a long time. He was much taller than she had been able to tell from the distance of Mrs. Sidelman's window. His voice held a new quality—a sly tone that she hadn't recalled from the times he'd raise his hand in greeting passing by her house on his bike. She felt her face redden.

"Why don't you play with her?" Beth said, disgruntled. "She seems perfect for you and your new interests."

"What's perfect for me?"

"Oh, please," Beth said. "Don't think I didn't notice your new *love* interest."

"You don't need to worry about any interests of mine," Ray said, his voice suddenly harsh.

"Don't I?" Beth said. "Who else will worry about them? I'm all you have, you know."

Ray stared at Beth, annoyed. "What are you talking about?"

"I'm talking about covering for you the other day when the car mysteriously disappeared, or pretending I know where you are when I don't. It's exhausting." Beth crossed her arms and blew her hair off of her forehead. "It's practically unfair."

"What do you want, Beth? Money?"

Beth's eyes were still red from crying, but she looked ready to start again. "Really, Ray? That's all I get?"

"Well tell me what you want! I can't read minds."

Beth sighed, a small quavering sound that made her seem as pathetic as the nest of orphaned birds on the television show. She looked away, and Sadie saw her wipe at her tears.

"I just want my brother to myself," she said softly. "Like it used to be."

Ray rolled his eyes. "I'm going swimming."

Beth turned to him, her face a mask of unhappiness. "Exactly," she said. She threw her hands up.

As usual, Sadie listened to their banter, confused by all that was going unsaid. It was as if she had disappeared from the room. "I'd like to swim," she said.

Both Beth and Ray looked at her. "Of course you would," Beth said. "Go see what our sweet mothers are doing. Maybe you can offer to refresh their drinks."

Beth turned then and left the room, and Sadie heard her stomping up the stairs. She stopped once and yelled over the railing.

"Next time I'll just follow you when you leave for your little tryst. Won't that be a pretty mess?"

Ray stiffened with anger. "You don't know what you're talking about," he said. "If I find out you've followed me, that's it, Beth. I mean it."

Sadie heard Beth slam her bedroom door. She was in

the awkward position of an eavesdropper caught out in the open. She wasn't sure if she had done something wrong, if she should go after Beth and tap on her door and urge her to come out the way Betty did with her little sisters. But then Ray brushed past her and she felt the heat that had stricken her face travel the skin of her arm, down her body, all of her limbs suffused with it, and instead of checking on Beth she followed Ray out to the pool, out into the hazy sunlight. There was her mother, her head back in laughter, her script arranged in her lap, her long legs kicking out on the chaise. "Oh, Patsy, you are too much!" her mother said.

Ray moved slowly around the pool to the diving board. He shed his shirt, kicked off his scuffed boat shoes. Sadie went to a chair in the shade under an umbrella. Her mother read a line, and then Mrs. Filley read the next line, hamming it up, making Sadie's mother laugh.

"Patsy, you have to be serious," she said. "How will I ever learn my part?"

She lifted her drink to her lips, the ice sliding around, and then she placed it onto the brick patio.

"I'll start over," Mrs. Filley said. She deepened her voice to read the part of Shannon from *The Night of the Iguana*:

```
SHANNON: How'd you beat your blue devil?
HANNAH: I showed him that I could endure him
    and I made him respect my endurance.
SHANNON: How?
HANNAH: Just by, just by . . . enduring.
    Endurance is something that spooks and blue
    devils respect. And they respect all the
    tricks that panicky people use to outlast
    and outwit their panic.
SHANNON: Like poppy-seed tea?
HANNAH: Poppy-seed tea or rum-cocos or just
```

a few deep breaths. Anything, everything,
that we take to give them the slip, and so
to keep on going.

SHANNON: To where?

HANNAH: To somewhere like this, perhaps. This
verandah over the rain forest and the still-
water beach, after long, difficult travels.
And I don't mean just travels about the
world, the earth's surface. I mean . . .
subterranean travels, the . . . the journeys
that the spooked and bedeviled people
are forced to take through the . . . the
unlighted sides of their natures.

SHANNON: Don't tell me you have a dark side to
your nature.

HANNAH: I'm sure I don't have to tell a man as
experienced and knowledgeable as you, Mr.
Shannon, that everything has its shadowy
side?

"You're such a marvelous Deborah Kerr," Mrs. Filley
said.

Sadie's mother jiggled the ice in her glass. She stood up
and tugged down the back of her suit, and then slipped into
the pool and disappeared under the surface. Ray had already
climbed from the pool when her mother came up the ladder
out of the deep end.

"Let me read the guy's part," Ray said.

Mrs. Filley grinned. "Then I can be Maxine."

Sadie's mother walked, dripping, over to her towel. Her
suit was a white two-piece, her stomach flat and tan against
the fabric.

"Oh, let him do it, Clare," Mrs. Filley said.

"I can read, Clare," Ray said. He smirked. He leaned down

and grabbed the script, then reached for his mother's pack of cigarettes and shook one out.

"Just the opposite, honey, I'm making a small point out of a very large matter," he said.

Sadie saw her mother give the faintest hint of a smile, and then she was all business, lighting the cigarette, saying her lines. Afterward, Mrs. Filley went inside to refresh their drinks.

"You shouldn't smoke," Sadie's mother said.

"You're just an old New England spinster," Ray said. "What do you know?"

She smiled then, and Sadie watched her lean in very close to Ray's face. She wasn't sure if it was her mother leaning close, or Hannah Jelkes from Williams's play. Her mother kept her eyes open. Their lips were so close Sadie thought they might be kissing. And then she pulled away and said something to him, low and barely discernible to Sadie listening in—something about rehearsing more of the scene. "The basement door, darling," she said. "At the back of the house?" She said it all in a careless way, her face bland. And then Mrs. Filley came out with their drinks. "Here we go," she called, clacking over the brick patio in her mules.

"I think we're done with the script for today," Clare said quietly. She kept her gaze averted. She stretched back out on the chaise with a little satisfied smile. Ray rose and walked once again to the diving board, his suit low on his hips, his wet hair tossed back. Sadie's mother glanced over toward Sadie in the shade of the umbrella and she seemed startled, and then angry.

"Where is Beth?" she said. "Why aren't you swimming?"

Sadie was at a loss, unable to strip off her shorts and T-shirt to reveal her body in the new bikini. Where once her mother might have called to her to come to her, slide her legs over to make room for her on the chaise, there was only her mother's silent appraisal. Sadie watched her lean toward Patsy, holding her hand to her mouth to hide her words, as if she were passing on a secret Sadie could only imagine was about her. Patsy let out a hoot. "Now, you are too much, Clare!" Patsy said.

Ray's body hit the water, made a smooth arc, and glided just below the surface. Sadie rose and left the pool by the iron gate. She glanced up as she passed through and Beth was staring through the bedroom screen, her face intent and dark. Sadie went around to the front and started down the drive to the street. She could hear her mother calling to her.

"Oh, Sadie, don't take it so personally!"

She wondered how many other places she would discover where she no longer fit. The idea of it made her ache, a pang as physical as the phenomenon of Ray's closeness. She went to Mrs. Sidelman's and let herself in with the key she kept in her shorts pocket. The quiet of the house, the order of the books on the shelf, the hum of the refrigerator, all calmed her. She saw Betty cross the street and knock on the front door of Sadie's house next door, saw her turn to leave and wander back across the front lawn. Still, she didn't call out to her. She took a book from Mrs. Sidelman's shelf, *Rabbit, Run,* and opened it.

June 20, 2003

O NE JUNE EVENING DURING PLAY PRACTICE AT
Vincent Elementary School Sadie watches in surprise
as Ray Filley comes inside and sits in the back of the
auditorium. Mrs. Bennett, the stage manager, notices him and
waves.

"Oh, it's Ray Filley," she says from the stage. "Ray's given
us a generous donation. Isn't that right, Ted?"

Ray sits quietly in the back row. He lifts his hand in greeting but says nothing.

"We can't tell you how much we appreciate your support,"
Ted Whittle says. He beams, holding his two hands together
in front of him to show his indebtedness. Sadie is embarrassed to be among these people—too old for their parts,
overly theatrical, the women with their glasses on their noses,
the men with tufts of hair growing out of their ears. She isn't
the youngest in the group—there's the high school girl there
playing Charlotte. Still, she feels her face flush.

Two weeks before Craig surprised her—got a babysitter and
showed up at rehearsal. She saw him walk in and immediately
forgot lines and cues, bumbled through scenes, wooden and
distracted. Afterward, he greeted her awkwardly backstage with
an invitation to dinner, his suit coat thrown over his shoulder.

"You were great," he said. His smile was false, hesitant.

"You don't have to say that," she told him, furious with
embarrassment for them both.

They went to the restaurant, and Craig admitted he found it strange, seeing her up on the stage, pretending to be someone else.

"It's disconcerting," he said. "Watching you flirt with another man."

She had to assure him that she was playing a role. "And badly, I should add," she said. They agreed he wouldn't make any more surprise visits to play practices. She had too much wine at dinner, and driving home she fell asleep in the passenger seat, only to awaken, disoriented, and in a panic, after Craig had pulled the car into the garage and hit the automatic door, closing them in.

She thinks she will never be able to say her lines with Ray there but is surprised to find that his presence makes her performance better. She plays the role of Hannah—her mother's role that last summer—a woman full of pent-up emotion. Ray's eyes on her only make her more aware of her power. Ted Whittle, the director, is thrilled with her.

"You're luminescent," he says. His hair is gray and slicked back with some sort of cream. He wears wire-framed reading glasses. "You're a star, just like your mother."

Sadie understands that his praise is sincere, but she doesn't trust his opinion in the least. She isn't anything like her mother. These are washed-up people who dream of being stars themselves, who tried to make it on Broadway and failed, who take the train to New York and audition for commercials and never receive a part. They live, like Sadie and her husband, in neighborhoods of postwar Colonials and Capes, their dreams tucked safely away under gables and eaves, behind storm doors and screens. After rehearsal Sadie walks past Ray as if he is invisible. As she passes him he reaches out a hand and brushes his fingertips along her arm. She hears his soft little intake of breath. She is filled with desire but afraid, so she pretends to be impervious.

The Vincent school hallways smell of wintergreen paste, and oak tag, and tempera paint. The linoleum squares are worn. In the classrooms chairs are placed on top of desks, their painted metal legs chipped. The school reminds her of her innumerable childhood projects: the dioramas in shoe boxes, *Excellent!*s on mimeographed tests, the ribbon for the one-hundred-yard dash, spring recitals in which she sang "There Was an Old Woman Who Swallowed a Fly." Sadie experiences a strange, clutching longing and sees that the past is suddenly, unexpectedly, part of who she's become, despite her best efforts to forget it. Her eyes fill with tears. And Ray is beside her, his footsteps stealthy, his body warm. Everyone calls good night and floods the blacktop, the school doors clanging shut. No one thinks it unusual that she has stopped to thank their new benefactor. She and Ray linger in the hall. He looks into her face and his eyes darken.

"What's wrong?" he says.

Sadie wipes her eyes. "Nothing. I mean, I don't know."

Outside crickets cluster by the school's brick foundation.

Ted Whittle saunters past and holds the door for them. He has the key. Sadie doesn't want to leave the heat of the hallway, the little wooden doors with the teachers' names, but she and Ray follow Ted outside. There are extended thanks and good-byes. Ray explains that they are childhood friends, and Ted says, "I'll let you two catch up."

And that is it. He climbs into his Camry. He takes a long time adjusting his seat belt, the radio. The crickets chirp. The moon is out, the stars. The night is filled with muffled sounds. Sadie feels her heart race. She watches the Camry pull away.

"How can you do this to me?" Ray asks. His voice is anguished, his face pale.

Sadie tells him she is a married woman. She has children. His sister has seen them together. She doesn't mention the extraordinary feeling she has that she has stepped into a play of another sort.

"Goddamn it, I told you she doesn't care. She hasn't mentioned it at all."

They stand in the parking lot and he takes her in his arms.

"Don't, don't," Sadie says. She brushes him away and walks to her car. Ray follows and takes her arm. "I said *don't*," she shouts at him, wriggling free, fumbling with her keys, all the time hoping he will stop her. He takes her arms and turns her around and holds her pinned to the car. She doesn't try to flee. She looks up into his face. "Oh, let me go," she says. He leans down to kiss her and she turns her face away. He lets his head fall to her shoulder.

"Hold me tighter," she whispers. "*Tighter.*"

They crawl into the car together like lust-filled teenagers, and Sadie feels both aroused and absurd, as if the role in this play is not quite suited for her. She knows that she should stop at every moment she succumbs. They climb, kissing, into the back of the SUV to avoid the children's car seats. The fogged-over windows make it seem they are somewhere safe, beyond detection, that there isn't a main road nearby, upon which occasional cars pass on their way to Cumberland Farms for milk, their headlights flashing like a beacon across Ray's forehead, Sadie's breasts.

The next day she has marks from his fingertips—on her arms, her thighs. Her mouth feels bruised and raw. And yet it's as if she's been sparked to life, and she's become the protagonist of the latest erotic novel the neighborhood women pass around. Craig steps from the shower, his torso pink and clean, and she invites him back to bed, pulling him under the sheets, where she has removed her nightgown. The sex is furtive, silent, so as not to wake the children. Sadie feels less guilty, somehow, her conscience more clear, as if the sex with Craig cancels out the sex with Ray. After, Craig keeps his eyes on her as he dresses for work, his expression satisfied and happy. Sadie lounges beneath the sheet and listens as he waylays Max outside the door, taking him downstairs for breakfast so she can sleep. Instead she lies there, awake, awash in new guilt.

She told Ray last night that she could no longer meet him, but she doesn't know whether she means this or not, and she could tell by the way he looked at her that he knew she wasn't sure.

"This is leading nowhere," she said to emphasize her point.

"We make each other happy," Ray said. "Maybe it doesn't have to lead anywhere. What's wrong with just this?"

He grinned at her, looking the happiest she's ever seen him. She cannot say what is wrong with it, why she denies herself the happiness she feels with him. But, lying in bed after Craig has left, Sadie feels only abject and used.

Later that morning, she wears Craig's Brooks Brothers shirt as a cover-up at the pond. She still worries that her transgressions will have spread and sullied everything, that she cannot simply hide them like the physical marks on her skin, but no one behaves any differently toward her. The pond is her place, her discovery, and the women all look to her as their savior.

"If it weren't for Sadie," they say, "we'd be at the Wampanoag club pool, roasting on the concrete."

At all times of day, women tramp up and down the wooded path. Those with children who nap, those who have scheduled dentist appointments and music lessons drag back early, the children angry and crying. No one thinks the Currys will mind the women and children passing through their backyard, treading a path through their grass, noisy and boisterous. The Currys' son, Michael, is college-aged, off somewhere in

Europe, someone has said. Both Walt and Kate Curry work in Hartford—Walt in insurance, Kate as an attorney. Their house is a Colonial, one of the first built in the neighborhood. There are French doors leading out to the patio, and that morning Sadie saw Kate standing there wearing an apron and yellow plastic gloves, and smoking a cigarette. The door was cracked, and the smoke snaked out, a thin white cloud.

"I could smell it," Sadie tells Maura up at the pond. "She looked like my mother used to, standing there."

Maura and the women circling her in their lawn chairs know what she means—their mothers with their hairspray and L'Air du Temps, with their bold print dresses, everyone back then reaching into coat pockets and purses for their cigarettes the moment they came out of church—the church the only place they couldn't smoke. Sadie wonders why Kate would be home during the day.

"Maybe it was a maid," someone suggests.

Sadie says the woman's hair was done. She had on pearl earrings.

"Maybe she's working from home," Maura says.

Sadie thinks that is the most reasonable explanation.

"Or she could be taking a sick day," Jane says.

"To clean her toilets?" Maura says drily.

Sadie worries she will emerge that afternoon to order them off her property, and she suggests making another path. But the day wears on, and they forget about Kate. Most of the women have dinner planned—meat defrosting, vegetables already cut and placed in Tupperware—and so they linger. The children make a fort, towels draped over sticks. They build it on the sandy bank and play house, pretending to cook over a fire for their own imaginary families. Sadie has remembered the bug spray, so everyone stays, lounging by the pond, watching the water striders skate across the surface where it is still and deep.

Heading back, Sadie always feels what she's come to call the end-of-the-day sadness, a weightiness that arrives with summer. She is reminded of summers of her youth—the lawn cool in the mornings, the sun just coming up, and a breeze moving the drapes of her bedroom. Her father would have gotten up and gone to work. Her mother, at least in those early years, would be talking to her own mother on the phone, or watering zinnias, or absently stirring her coffee, the clink of the spoon inside the cup a sound she now makes herself. The whole day stretches before her, a luxury she feels each time she treads the path up to the pond, a spaciousness that depletes as the day draws to an end. As a child summer seemed interminable, but as an adult she knows otherwise. It is in this mood that Sadie and a group of women descend and emerge from the woods toting bags and towels and assorted toys, the children singing something from television. They step onto freshly mown grass and meet Kate Curry.

She wears a pair of shorts and a white sleeveless blouse. Her dark hair is pulled back in a neat ponytail. She still wears the pearl earrings. Kate is older than they are, a woman who's worn suits and argued cases in a courtroom—an intimidating presence. Around her eyes are the fine lines they notice on everyone but themselves—*Worry lines,* Sadie thinks. But Kate doesn't seem worried, only happy to see them. She smiles and waves and invites everyone inside. "For a snack," she says. And then she squats down in front of the children the way they tell you to do when you speak to them, and says, "You'd like a snack, wouldn't you? A Popsicle? An ice cream cup?"

Sadie thanks her but begs off. "So close to suppertime," she says.

But Kate must know the children will plead and make it impossible to drag them off. It isn't that Sadie doesn't want to go into her house, but that she has her mind set on getting home, on taking her burden of unspoken sadness back to her own crumb-littered counters, sagging couch cushions, to the Colonial woman's diary on her nightstand that she's had for months and still hasn't really read. But the children and Kate win out, and Sadie and the other women file through the French doors into Kate's spotless kitchen. The children are shown the den and the television, where they can sit with their ice cream. Kelsey Simons asks for a place to change the baby, and Kate shows her a downstairs guest room, and then after she is done the place to put the sodden diaper. Kate's house seems suddenly to fill. They sprawl at the kitchen table, and she offers them a drink. "Gin? Vodka?" Sadie laughs, even though she senses it would offset the end-of-the-day feeling. And then Maura pipes up, her broad face rosy from the sun. "I'll take whatever you've got."

Kate makes them Harvey Wallbangers, the recipe taken from her mother's old copy of *Come for Cocktails, Stay for Supper*. She brings the drinks to the table in tall glasses, and everyone laughs about them—a drink from their parents' day. The children come in and ask to play in the backyard, and Sadie sees that Max's face is sticky from the ice cream. She gets up for a paper towel but Kate is there first, and Sadie marvels that Max stands still for her, stiff and straight like a soldier, and lets her wipe his face. After the children have run out the back door, Maura shakes the ice in her glass as if to announce a change in subject.

"My mother-in-law asked me this morning if I loved her son," she says. "Can you believe it?"

Sadie says she cannot. She notices a tone in Maura's voice that she can sometimes detect in her evening phone calls—a brashness, as if she might do or say anything.

"What kind of question is that?" Jane says.

"Maybe she thinks you married him for his money, or his looks," Kate says. She stands leaning against the counter, a pitcher of the Harvey Wallbangers at the ready.

"Of course I married him for those things," Maura says. She laughs, and the other women, Kate included, laugh, too.

Sadie feels a stirring, a strange trepidation. "Those things," Jane says, shaking her head. She nudges Sadie, expecting her to agree, probably thinking of the story Sadie has told her of how she and Craig met: "The Ambitious Attorney Falls for the Lowly Department Store Clerk," she'd called it. But Sadie is thinking of Ray instead—his sloppy clothes, his mysterious life performing in bars and clubs. She remembers his soap smell. Last night in the Vincent Elementary School parking lot he begged her to promise a time and a place to meet again, his face lit with yearning.

"How will I get in touch with you?" he asked.

"Write me a letter," she said wistfully. She worries she's pushed things too far, that the present nudged up against the past will mean the last of Ray Filley, that she will have just her memories of the sex, of his fervent proclamations, to carry her over for the rest of her life, and she accepts this state of things, this limbo from which she believes she will never be released.

June 21, 1979

THE DAY AFTER SADIE AND HER MOTHER WENT TO the Filleys', Betty came to Sadie's house before breakfast, and they slipped off to the dead end. No one was up except old Mrs. Hoskins, who lived in the house at the end of the street. She came out and stood at the foot of her driveway in her bathrobe with her hands on her hips. "What are you doing over there?" she called in the warbling voice of old-time comedic actresses.

Sadie explained that they were working on a science project. "We're testing the rate of decay on varying thicknesses of paper," she said.

Mrs. Hoskins pulled her robe around her shoulders. Sadie could almost smell the mothballs, the lilac powder she fluffed between her breasts. Her hands were gnarled like the branches of her crabapple.

"It's summertime," Mrs. Hoskins said. "School's over." She made a noise as if she didn't believe them, and turned away and shuffled into her house. As a teenager, after Sadie and her father had moved away from the neighborhood, she would bring boys back to the dead end to have sex, and once she and the boy fell asleep in the car. The next morning old Mrs. Hoskins, still vigilant, came to the car window and rapped her bony fist. "You in there," she'd said. "Are you alive? Wake up!" She watched them scramble to rearrange their clothes, embarrassed by their bodies, as if what they had

97

done with them had nothing to do with the pale skin showing in the morning light, the sex a ritual, and empty after, like the one thing they'd hoped for had died, and they were dead along with it.

They went into the field to read the letter, and Betty asked Sadie where she'd been the day before.

"Just at the Filleys'," Sadie said.

Betty shaded her eyes. The sun was bright, the day already hot. Soon the cicadas would start up. "Was Beth there?"

"My mother made me go," Sadie said.

"Since when do you do what your mother tells you?" Betty asked, challenging her.

It was true. Sadie knew she'd relented and gone with her mother to the Filleys' at the prospect of seeing Ray. She'd wanted to wear the new bathing suit, had wanted him to see her wearing it. She hated her mother for how it had all ended up.

Yesterday, Sadie had heard her mother pull her long car into the garage and hit the back wall, crushing one of the trash cans. She heard her come into the house, the tap of her sandals on the kitchen floor. Sadie had expected her to seek her out and lecture her about how childish she'd been to leave the Filleys' that way, but her mother had gone into her room and closed the door. When her father came in from work he asked Sadie where she was.

"Asleep, I think," Sadie said.

It wasn't unusual for her mother to fall asleep after a day at the Filleys' pool. Her father stared off into the distance, as if something out the window had caught his attention. "Too much practicing," he said. "Eh?" He reached out as if to ruffle Sadie's hair or pat her head, but then thought better of it.

"We'll make our own supper," he said. He slipped off his suit coat and draped it over a chair. He pulled out a frying pan and eggs.

"My specialty," he said.

Sadie noticed he'd gained weight. Portly, she thought, not fat. She knew from photos of her father that as a young man he'd been narrow waisted, gallant. His hair had been cropped short. In one he'd worn a tweed sport coat. Beside him even her tall mother had seemed dwarfed, tucked tightly under his arm like a little girl. Now Sadie saw, for the first time, that her father was old, older than her mother, his hair thinning, his body going slack.

When the food was ready he told Sadie to see if her mother wanted anything to eat, and Sadie climbed the stairs, dreading the confrontation with her, wishing she would just stay asleep. She knocked on her mother's door. When Sadie was younger her mother would reply to her knock in a singsongy voice, "Come in!" She'd ask Sadie to climb onto the bed with her. They'd lie together in the dim light on the cool satin bedspread, and her mother would put an arm around her and ask her questions about her day. Sadie would smell the gin and lime, the chlorine, the leftover scent of her perfume. That evening, Sadie expected her mother's delayed anger. She was almost relieved when she didn't answer, as if the silence was the only punishment she would get. Back downstairs she told her father her mother was still resting, and her father paused with his fork.

"Did she say that?" he said.

Sadie shrugged. "She didn't say anything."

Her father had waited a moment before he put the food in his mouth. "Go in and ask her again," he said.

After, Sadie would believe that he'd known all along what would be discovered, but maybe, if Sadie went, there would be some reversal of fate, and the scene wouldn't be discovered at all. Sadie knocked again, and then opened the bedroom door. In the last bit of light through the window she saw the empty bed, and she crossed the room to the master bath. This room had been taken over by Sadie's mother—her father was resigned to the hall bathroom. Here her mother usually sat before her vanity and applied her makeup, her lotions, the compacts and powders and brushes spread over the surface of the counter, the room filled with the fumes of nail polish. Sadie went into her mother's bathroom only when her mother was gone. She'd sort through her tubes of lipstick, her perfume, peruse the bottles of pills her mother had lined up in the medicine cabinet, sometimes taking them out to touch them and look at their colors, always putting them back the way she found them. Her mother's bathroom was where Sadie found her that evening, curled up on the floor in her bathing suit, the gold sandals still strapped to her feet. The glare of the makeup mirror's bulbs, the cotton rug rucked up underneath her, the way her hair covered her face, all created a surreal tableau. She knew her mother hadn't simply fallen asleep. A pill bottle was out on top of the vanity, tipped on its side and empty, pills scattered bright and shiny on the tile floor.

Sadie felt her body freeze, as if caught in some spell. She willed herself to take a step back, then another, trying, she realized later, to remove herself from the sight of her mother on the floor. Once she reached the bedroom door she ran down the stairs. Her father needed only to glance up at her, and knew. He dropped his fork and rushed to the bedroom. Sadie listened to his footsteps pounding along the floor, his voice as he tried to rouse her mother and then on the bedroom phone extension, terse and emphatic. She heard a frantic scramble, a knocked-over lamp, the closet door sliding open. He came through the kitchen carrying her mother in his arms, moving with a speed Sadie had never seen before. He'd put a blanket around her, and as they passed Sadie, heading through the den toward the garage door, Sadie saw just a bit of her mother's face—the eyes rolled up, her cracked lipstick. He put her in the backseat of his car, and Sadie watched from the door to the garage as he backed out, his tires making a chirping sound at the end of the driveway, his face white behind the wheel. Sadie stood in the doorway, wholly forgotten.

There had been other times her mother had been taken to the hospital, although Sadie had never quite understood the reason as a child. Often her mother would be awake, though listless, and issuing orders.

"Call Charlene," she'd tell her father. Charlene was Betty's mother, and Sadie would be told to go to Betty's house, where she'd stay until her father came to get her. *Your mother had a case of nerves,* he'd say, or *Your mother is allergic to scallops.*

Even though Sadie knew she should go to Betty's this time, too, she did not. It was dark, and she needed to turn on Mrs. Sidelman's porch light. She went through the open garage up the driveway to the road and saw the shrubs along the house filled with fireflies, heard Mrs. Frobel putting her youngest to bed. She could sense the world beyond theirs alive with movement and activity—movie theaters and restaurants in Hartford, the intersections of their own small town filled with cars heading out to destinations Sadie could barely imagine—and into this world her father raced in his Lincoln Continental, her mother spread out on the backseat. Girls and boys met up in the town center, their cars all in a line and the windows rolled down. She pictured Ray Filley one day driving off into this world, his hand easy on a steering wheel, one tanned arm hanging out the window, his other around a girl. When she returned she saw her father's suit coat draped over his chair, his unfinished eggs, the two plates he'd set out for Sadie and her mother. Sadie cleaned up the kitchen. She went upstairs into her mother's bedroom, the charged air settled and calm in her mother's absence. She smoothed out the rug, picked up the spilled pills, and put them back with the few left in each container: Seconal, Nembutal, Valium, Benzedrine. In the bedroom she put the lamp back on the end table. It was too early to go to bed, and she felt keenly aware of being alone in the house. She remembered the horror story the girls all told about the babysitter and the man calling from the upstairs extension, "Have you checked the children?" She thought about Laura Loomis walking home from a friend's house, the approach of a strange car. Sadie went downstairs to sit by the phone in the kitchen. The night air came in through the open window, and with it came the sound of crickets, the throaty sound of the frogs. She'd fallen asleep at the kitchen table when the phone rang, her father reassuring her that her mother was resting comfortably.

"Too much sun today," her father said, his voice forcibly cheerful.

Sadie pictured her mother sleeping peacefully in a hospital bed, served sugar cookies and ginger ale by nurses. She felt disappointment that her mother wouldn't suffer any consequences for what she'd put them through, but then she knew, too, that she should feel relief that she was safe. All of this had built, by morning, into a nagging resentment.

Betty had run out of cigarettes, and Sadie claimed she had only been able to steal one, so they shared it, sweating and uncomfortable in the long grass, the insects whining in their ears. Really, Sadie had taken her mother's entire pack of Salems and hidden it at Mrs. Sidelman's.

"Maybe Beth would let me come over and swim, too," Betty said.

Sadie tried to guess whether Betty was being serious or not. "Maybe if your mother went over there."

Betty rolled her eyes. "Like that is ever going to happen," she said.

Sadie tried to imagine Betty's mother, Charlene, sitting by a pool without children hanging on to her arms, asking for food, or crying because they were struck by a sibling. She saw the incongruity of Charlene and Patsy's being friends. Even

Sadie's mother was only friendly with Charlene in a stingy, almost grudging, way. Later, Sadie will surmise that this was due to all that Charlene knew about Sadie's mother's hospital visits and her essential use as a babysitter.

"You're so lucky you have a mother like yours," Betty said.

"Let's just read the letter," Sadie said. "It's too hot to stay out here."

They'd exchanged letters every other day for the last week, and Francie's letters were growing longer, written in colored ink on lined notebook paper. She drew designs along the borders—swirling paisley, hearts and moons and stars and clusters of grapes. She filled the pages with clever stories about her family and her pet gerbils, Pierre and Marie.

> *Dear Hezekiah,*
>   *Today we had an adventure! Marie escaped and is currently unaccounted for. The king and queen are beside themselves thinking they will put a foot into a shoe where she is hiding and crush her. Oh, the plight of a lost gerbil is one we will never have to endure. So small! And the world so large!*

The farmer boy didn't need to write much to convince Francie he was real. He said he had chores on the farm, and he hunted and fished in the pond they'd seen when they went on explorations as children, choosing a swath of green hillside showing over the trees in the distance, and heading out with Scout canteens and peanut butter crackers. It didn't matter what they wrote back. Any sort of acknowledgment seemed enough to keep her writing. Sadie guessed that Francie had a fascination with Grimm's fairy tales. When she was punished for some small household infraction:

> *My bedroom is a tower, and I will forever watch the world from it. I am thrown into the dungeon and the blackness is*

*deep and desolate. The queen is asleep, as usual, cursed by
some evil incantation. She is on the sofa, or in my room on my
twin bed, always sleeping. When I try to waken her she startles
and stares: "Do as your father tells you," she says groggily.
Or: "Be good." The king says, "You're looking more like
your mother every day." I am trapped in this sleeping world,
disheartened; I picture you, writing from your sunny meadow,
waiting among the trees to retrieve my letter, and I have hope.*

Sadie always read the letters out loud, assuming her near-perfect Francie voice. That day she began to laugh, and then Betty began to laugh, and Sadie couldn't finish.

"What does she mean?" Betty asked, laughing. "Let me see."

"What does she ever mean?" Sadie said.

They both pictured Francie as a miniature of her mother—with her glasses and her mousy hair, her round cheeks and stocky frame—and they began laughing more. If their laughter came from some anxious place that saw, too, Francie's mother's escape into sleep, her inability to oversee her household, to care for her children, they couldn't articulate it. If they recognized the fear in the letters, they didn't acknowledge that Francie's drama intrigued them. Didn't the fairy tales they knew as children always supply a happy ending? Betty yanked the pages from Sadie's hands to read them herself, and one of the pages blew off over the grass. They shrieked and chased after it, but it became caught in an updraft, tugged away into the swampy marsh, and they let it go. They never imagined once during this time that Francie believed she knew who she was writing to, and if Betty noticed the details Sadie added that made Hezekiah seem more and more like Ray Filley—how he looked forward to duck hunting with his two Labrador retrievers in the fall, how he was getting a band together in his garage and letting his hair grow long—she never mentioned them.

They walked back through the field to the road and wandered down that, their bare feet stinging on the hot concrete.

"What do you want to do?" Sadie said.

She had never been at a loss for something to do summers before. A plan had always presented itself: some minor event provoked a mystery that needed to be solved, a book prompted her to re-create its scenes in games of house. As they approached Betty's, they saw a group of kids had gathered under the stand of hickories. They were arguing, and Betty's mother called to them to get along through an upstairs window screen. Betty's sister saw them approach and asked them to help plan the Haunted Woods. Sadie had already said she would not do it this year. It went without saying that they were too old, but she also held a grudge about *The Memory of the Fleetfoot Sisters,* the play they had all quit. She was reluctant to initiate anything else. The Aquacade would never happen unless she approached Beth, and after yesterday, last night, she doubted she would ever do that. Her desire to follow through with anything seemed to be failing her.

"Your house?" Betty said.

Sadie's house had always been the locus of invention, a Colonial with a traditional floor plan—slate entry, carpeted stairway, living room to the left, dining room to the right, kitchen, family room. Upstairs: four bedrooms and a landing with a wooden railing and turned wooden finials. The presence of so many empty bedrooms had never seemed unusual to Sadie until now. Had her parents planned to have more children? Had the plan somehow gone awry? The downstairs living room was also empty—a long open space awaiting redecoration, with wood floors, a large bay window at one end, and interesting acoustics. Here they rehearsed winter choral productions, Sadie and her friends standing in a semicircle, their reproduced music held aloft in their hands. Sadie's mother listened to their rendition of "We Three Kings" as she prepared lamb chops, as she boiled the water for the peas, the potatoes, her gin and tonic set on the Formica counter, her cigarette balanced in the plastic ashtray on the table.

Sadie and Betty went in through the front door to the living room. Her father had come in late the night before, his face slack with exhaustion, and stood in Sadie's bedroom doorway.

"She'll be home tomorrow afternoon," he said. "She's going to be fine."

Sadie had pretended to be asleep and only mumbled a small assent, and he'd stood there, watching her, wondering, maybe, if he should go in and make sure she was all right. But then he turned and sighed and went into his bedroom, and Sadie heard him climb slowly into bed with a soft groan.

In the living room, Sadie saw her old Barbie case set on top of a table that had become a catchall in the corner—bags from G. Fox filled with items for the League of Mercy, old board games that Sadie never played, a pile of clothing that needed ironing. The living room had always been the site of an elaborate doll neighborhood, each section of the room commandeered by a different girl, each house constructed of found items: upturned glasses for tables, a book or a shoe box for a bed, a wooden jewelry box with drawers for a bureau. Some girls, like Betty and Sadie, used their doll cases, filled with clothing hung on pink plastic hangers. Upright and opened, the case served as a ready-made closet, a partition, part of a wall of a house. Behind it the dolls ate, slept, read, and dreamed, put on tiny shoes and outfits whose flimsily sewn seams and snaps often tore. The dolls went to each other's houses and rang the bell.

"Hi, Midge! What are you doing today?"

"Oh, it's you, Barbie. I need a dress for the party tonight. I'm going shopping."

"What party?"

"Steffie's party, didn't you hear? Aren't *you* invited?"

The dolls had arguments that led to stomping off in a huff. Sadie was the best at this. "I need a drink!" she'd scream. She'd take her doll across the room and out into the slate hallway. Beyond the living room was another world, one in which the dolls might get lost and need to be sought. Sometimes it was a city, or a town with department stores and restaurants, but other times it was a wilderness—woods, dark paths, mountains. To move the dolls they were held about their legs and made to hop. This hopping/walking wasn't paid much attention. It was an accepted part of doll activity that included the inability to hold a glass or brush back hair, to make any expression other than the tiny half-smile of satisfaction. They were Barbie, Midge, Stacey, Steffie, and Skipper. They were blond, brunette, mod, popular, and fashionable. There was one boy, and no one wanted to use him. He was placed at work, a remote area, and they mostly forgot about him.

Seeing the cases abandoned there on the table, Sadie opened them up and took out the dolls. She and Betty sat on the floor by the open window, and beyond the cicada whine they could hear the occasional shouts of the boys on their bikes.

"Look, it's Beth," Sadie said. She took off Skipper's pink dress. "Oh no! I'm flat chested!"

Betty laughed uncertainly, and Sadie took out all of the dolls and stripped them of their clothes.

"We're nudists," Sadie said.

"Let's set up the house," Betty said.

Sadie had already propped open the case. She dragged the table over and told Betty to set up the downstairs apartment for Ken. "We live upstairs," Sadie said.

They propped up the boards from the games and used the old clothes as carpets and beds. The preparation of the houses took up the time until lunch. They stopped and made sandwiches in the kitchen, and brought them back to the living room. It was hot now, hotter than before. The dolls were lying out on the roof of their apartment in the sun.

"I don't know how I could ever have worn clothing in this heat," Sadie said.

"Oh, neither do I," Betty said.

"Ken is coming over tonight for drinks," Sadie said.

Ken, meanwhile, was lounging fully dressed in his apartment on the couch.

"What will you wear?" Betty asked, sitting her doll up.

"What a silly question," Sadie said. "Nothing, of course."

They returned to their apartment to get things ready. They set up the tiny dishes, pretended to fix a meal. They styled the dolls' hair. Sadie thought they should do their nails with real nail polish. She slipped upstairs and took a bottle from her mother's bathroom, trying not to think about the way she'd looked on the floor, running back down the stairs as if she were being chased. They were doing the dolls' tiny nails carefully, taking turns, when Sadie heard the garage door open, and her father came in, and then her mother, the same gold sandals tapping across the kitchen floor. She dropped the doll and put the cap on the polish. She jumped up and Betty, seeing her face, did the same. They slipped through the front door and out onto the lawn before either of her parents saw them.

"What's wrong?" Betty said, her eyes alert.

"She'll be mad about the nail polish," Sadie said simply. Betty accepted this, as she had always accepted any excuses Sadie made.

They crossed the street to Betty's house, and Betty's sister came out and begged them once more to do the Haunted Woods.

"No one knows what they're doing," she said.

"Maybe we can just help," Betty said.

They would be consultants, Sadie said. They would design and direct, and the older children would construct it all, play the roles of the dead, guide the younger ones through. Sadie said they should make it bigger, have it in the Filleys' pasture this year, instead of Sadie's backyard. They would follow the cow paths. They'd mark out the trail with sticks sprayed with glow-in-the-dark paint. Sadie drew a map and selected the sites: rocking horse boy (under large pine), girl crushed under the rickety bridge (middle of the main path), dead trapeze artist (hanging from sycamore), graveyard with two emerging corpses (on the uneven ground beneath the old apple trees), Gypsy woman with crystal ball (by the barbed wire fence entrance), Victorian man and woman out for a stroll (Roaming: *Isn't this the promenade? Can you tell me how to get to the promenade?*). The Haunted Woods was just a place where ghosts appeared, Sadie said. If one ghost happened to be an ax murderer, well, so much the better. If another was his victim, searching for his lost hand, that worked, too. Betty's sister caught on immediately and began assigning roles.

The first year they put on the Woods, Sadie had agreed to play Laura Loomis. She dressed in clothing similar to the outfit Laura was reported to have worn—the navy shorts, the rainbow shirt, the sneakers. They covered her outfit in fake blood. All of the kids knew it was her but one, a girl who came running out of the woods crying, saying she'd seen Laura Loomis. Sadie had followed her out, protesting and laughing. All of the parents stared at her—some at first shocked into thinking she was the real Laura making her appearance. Mrs. Battinson stifled a scream. (Cynthia Loomis was a close friend.) "This is monstrous," she cried, and the show was called off after only an hour and a half.

That night Sadie's mother had come into her room and sat down on the edge of the bed.

"What could you have been thinking?" her mother said.

Sadie had told her she didn't know. She'd cried, and her mother had hugged her and smoothed her hair. "You're a good girl," she said. "I told them that. You just made a mistake."

Her mother had always been on her side and forgiven her. It felt like now Sadie was supposed to reciprocate, to understand and forgive her mother. Somehow, though, she could not.

The goal with the Haunted Woods was to lure children from the surrounding neighborhoods, and this required the tacking up of cardboard signs on telephone poles all up and down Wadhams Road. Children would come on their bikes, or their parents would bring them in station wagons from neighborhoods farther away. The date was chosen—Friday, July 6.

That afternoon, Francie showed up and asked to be included. She wore a pair of seersucker shorts, her legs emerging wide and white from the cuffed hem. Everyone had moved to sit under the maple tree on Sadie's front lawn. Overhead the leaves fluttered. The grass was dry, the sky inexorably blue. Someone started up a mower on Foothills Road. Francie stood on the fringe of the circle, waiting. Betty said she could have the job of refreshment server. But Francie was adamant about being included in the Woods.

"I want to be the trapeze girl," she said.

Betty's sister, a pert-looking version of Betty, stood up and put her hands on her hips and glared at Francie. "You can't," she said. "That's my job."

Sadie remembered when she had last taken Francie through the woods, two summers ago. The girl hadn't been afraid of anything, even as an eight-year-old. When people came out of nowhere she stood her ground and stared at them, infuriating everyone.

"Well, I want to do something else," Francie said. Her face was pinched.

"You can be the drowned girl," Sadie said, stepping up. "You can be all wet and covered with pond grass."

Francie looked at her suspiciously. "Okay," she said. "I guess that's good."

"Can you moan?" Sadie asked.

Francie assured her she could.

"Let's hear it," Sadie demanded, and Francie made an awful sound, like someone being tortured. Everyone looked at her, agape. Sadie's mother came to the screen door.

"What is going on out here?" she asked.

"It's nothing," Sadie said. "Just tryouts."

Her mother stood behind the screen, a fuzzy outline in a flowered dress. Cigarette smoke billowed around her. "That sounded real," she said. "Did someone get hurt?"

Everyone assured her they were fine. Francie's face was red, and Sadie's mother hesitated. Then she spun around and disappeared back into the house.

"Less tormented," Sadie said to Francie. "She drowned, she wasn't murdered." She told her that the drowned girl wasn't made up, that she'd once existed. "She drowned in that pond out in the pasture in 1775."

Francie made a face. "That's not true."

"It is," Sadie said. "She was one of the Filleys. Ask Beth."

No one wanted to approach Beth Filley, but most of them knew that Sadie had spent time with her, that their mothers were friends.

"Her name was Emely," Sadie said.

"How did she drown?" Francie asked.

"It was terrible," Sadie said. "She was just a teenager, and she was married and had a baby. The baby died, and she drowned herself in the pond."

"Oh, you can hold a baby!" Betty said. She crossed the lawn and hooked arms with Sadie. "Do you have an old baby doll? It will be perfect!"

Betty's sister rolled her eyes. "I'm sure she has one. She probably still plays with it."

A few of the kids laughed, and Francie ignored them.

"I'll be Emely," she said. "That's fine."

"Just be careful you don't run into the *real* Emely," Betty's brother said. He made a moaning sound and walked across the grass, stumbling, awkward, his arms cradling a pretend infant. Sadie bit her lip to keep from laughing.

"That's true," she said. "She haunts the old Filley house. But sometimes she escapes and wanders the woods."

"She'll sound sad," Francie said. "Mournful."

Everyone looked at her again. Francie turned then and headed away across the lawn, away from them.

August 21, 2003

I T ONLY TOOK THAT FIRST ROUND OF HARVEY WALL-
bangers to make ending the day at Kate's a tradition for
the women of the neighborhood. They tromp down and
Kate is waiting, and the children get their Popsicles, or pretzel
sticks, and the women get sloe gin fizzes, or tequila sunrises,
or Singapore slings. Sometimes they sit in the yard on Kate's
rarely used cast-iron furniture, or in their folding chairs, the
aluminum legs still covered with brook sand. Kate serves
them from a tray. She asks about the pond, their day, where
they plan to vacation, an inevitable breach in their routine.
Everyone has someplace to go each summer—to the mountains in New Hampshire, to Nantucket, or to the cottage at
Point O'Woods. They don't all go at once, but the missing
women and children are acknowledged like place cards at a
table. Kate makes it a point to remember where everyone is
going and when.

"Jane's off to Franconia," she announces that week. She
gives the children calamine lotion for their bites. She sprays
on Bactine and blows on their small injured knees. She is a
mother, a friend, a benefactress. She advises them all on what
to wear to their husbands' company functions, to the club for
lunch with their husbands' mothers. With her they wear their
five-year-old bathing suits, the elastic sprung, T-shirts stained
with jelly, spit-up, dirty handprints. She knows the women
they become when they put on their black sheath dresses,

their grandmother's pearls. The drinks, after the long day in the sun, release them all, briefly, from restraint. While Jane is gone they talk about her suspicion that her husband is having an affair.

"I think she's overreacting," Sadie says. They are sipping margaritas, licking the salt from the rims.

"But the receipt," Maura says. "Two diners ordering the exact same meal? That's not two men."

Kate agrees. "It sounds like she ordered, and he said, 'I'll have what she's having.'"

"Or the other way around," Sadie says. And then she holds her drink up, and cocks her head, and pretends to be a woman having an affair, a scenario that is almost true. "I'll have what he's having," she says, her voice pitched up like a question, her eyes wide.

The other women break out in laughter. "You're good at that," Kate says.

Outside the children scramble in the grass, playing freeze tag. Their voices come through the window screen, and the mothers can tell they are playing nicely. Every so often someone volunteers to check. The shyer kids are in the den, still watching television, and Maura's oldest reads a thick, hardback novel, the paper cover removed. Sadie has asked Maura what her daughter is reading, but Maura just shrugs. "She gets them from her grandmother's house," she says. "Old books, you know." Sadie feels urged to lean over the girl's shoulder one day and see, remembering the books she used to read, the dark, adult worlds she often entered. She wants to tell her to put the book away, to find friends her own age and play.

None of the women at Kate's have ever admitted they've fallen in love with someone else, as if this is a phenomenon not possible in their world. Sadie imagines the women discovering the cache of letters she's collected all summer from Ray, perusing them in shock. When the first arrived in her mailbox at the curb she felt a shameful thrill that made her catch her breath, look about the neighborhood to check if someone was watching. Inside her house she took the letter to her bedroom and shut the door, even though it was a week-day and no one was at home. She was suspicious, at first. She remembered, with a sick feeling, the letters to Francie she'd dictated—how easy it had been to pretend to be someone else. And yet Ray's letter sounded just like him, and it told her things she'd longed to hear, things that proved he cared for her, that there was more between them than sex. The next day, another one arrived.

She didn't want to be drawn in, so she put the letters away, hiding them when they came, in a book, or in the bottom drawer of her bureau under her sweatpants. But then the children were in bed, and she'd head out to play practice, the letters tucked in her bag. She'd pull over in the Cumberland Farms parking lot and find herself aching for the man in them. In the first one he told her that he had made up an elaborate story for Beth about a new woman he was seeing, a story that Sadie would be proud of. Sadie imagined him sitting alone in the old house at the scarred kitchen table where his father once poured out shots of Bushmills, where his grandfather sat cleaning his Winchester, writing the letters, licking the white business envelope with no return address.

He talked about missing her, not just her body but the questions she asked him about music, and his childhood, the way her eyes brightened when she smiled, the freckles on her shoulders. He mentioned the clothes he'd seen her wearing, and clothes he imagined she might wear—dresses made of fine, sheer fabric, and hats with wide brims. He pictured her walking the streets of New York City with her children, visiting galleries, attending plays and readings. Sadie tries not to wonder what woman has given him his inspiration. Instead, she imagines herself as he sees her, and slowly a version of who she might become emerges. Each day a new letter chronicles his time without her—providing details of the store, of the fields and what is blooming, of the strawberries and the children arriving with their parents to pick them, and how he feels as if everyone is going on about their lives and he is always going to be there *on the outskirts of town, like an outlaw*. He tells her about the old movies he watches—Cary Grant, Jimmy Stewart, Deborah Kerr, Audrey Hepburn. Sadie has rented the movies he says he's watched, checked out the books he says he's read from the library, and imagined what he saw in them that reminds him of her. Yesterday, she went to Lord & Taylor and bought a floral-patterned skirt, a blouse, clothing that would match the woman Ray's created. This morning, looking at them hanging in her closet, she realized she'd chosen an outfit her mother might have worn, and she could just see her with her silk blouse, her straw purse and Ferragamo flats, slipping behind the wheel of her car to run errands.

In the Currys' kitchen, Kate pulls out the restaurant receipt that Jane has left at her house, and they examine the time and date, the server's number. They analyze it like detectives, their heads leaning in and touching. Maura thinks the restaurant, a little trendy spot by the river where boaters come and dock to eat gourmet sandwiches, sounds just like Howard, Jane's husband. Sadie has to agree. Howard is more a boater than a golfer. She can see him leaving during the workday and driving down to the marina with some girl from the office. Maura thinks her husband has given Howard some tips. They talk, for a while, about last year's Labor Day cookout and the "great disappearance"—when Maura's husband left to get ice and didn't return for two hours.

This discussion of husbands always comes around to Craig, with whom Sadie can never find any complaint. Stalwart and smart, never a harsh word. Gray suits, hair cropped neatly around his ears. She won't tell them about the sex, the way he braces himself over her in bed, his movements quick and efficient like a wound-up toy. And then after, lying on the damp sheets, mystified with her. "You won't tell me what you want," he'd say. "You won't even help me out here." She imagines this has been the only thing keeping Craig with her—this desire to please her that is constantly thwarted. If he knew everything about her he might leave, she thinks, and so she's kept so much of herself hidden she's become her own mystery.

The women want her to confess things so they will be assured she will not reveal their secrets. They know she is keeping something from them. The more she insists that Craig is wonderful the more this signals to them real trouble she is afraid to discuss.

"He can't be perfect," Maura says. "No one's perfect."

She says she's heard from her own children that Craig likes to scare his. Sadie looks at Maura, surprised.

"You mean monster time?"

Sadie explains how Craig sneaks upstairs and hides under one of their beds at bedtime. "Then, when they go to climb in, he grabs an ankle."

Maura gives Sadie a look. "That's terrible."

Sadie laughs, but then she thinks about it more. The drinks throw a new light on everything. "Do you think? The children love it. They love their daddy."

"They don't know that's who it is," Maura says.

"Of course they know," Sadie says. "He does it all the time. They love for him to do it."

Kate wonders aloud how much they love it. There is a long discussion of each woman's own childhood, and her own excitement about being frightened, and Sadie is happy for the diversion. She tells them about the Haunted Woods, and Maura and the others who grew up in town remember it.

"That was you?" she says. "You and your friends put that on?"

"We did it a few summers," she says. "We charged a quarter a person. We served lemonade and popcorn for refreshments while the kids waited to be led through. My friend Betty made the popcorn at her house with their electric popcorn popper."

Kate asks about the Haunted Woods. Some of the women seem to be finishing up their drinks and calling to their children, as if they are getting ready to go, and Sadie has noticed Kate always seems desperate for them to stay.

"We held it at night. The kids paid and then one of us was the guide. One year I wore a sheet I dyed black, draped like a cowl over my face. We led the kids one at a time along paths we made behind my house. We'd have a graveyard where kids would jump out of buried cardboard boxes. We'd have things flying out of the trees—ghosts and witches."

The women all marvel. Maura says she remembers the dark path, and things jumping out, and how terrified she was. "Wasn't that when that little girl disappeared?" she says suddenly.

Sadie sets her drink down carefully. "I don't know," she says.

"I could have sworn that was when it happened," Maura says.

A few of the other women who grew up in town nod their heads, remembering. They are sure it was during one of those Haunted Woods events.

"It wasn't," Sadie says, decisively now, and visibly annoyed. "That must be a rumor. You know how people associated the wrong things with each other."

She shouldn't have brought up the Haunted Woods—anything related to that last summer leads, inevitably, to her mother, a topic she has never discussed with anyone, even her husband. There is a pall then over the room, a silence like those granted for the dead, each of them remembering her own version of the past but sensing Sadie's mood, knowing better than to mention it.

Kate turns away and busies herself at the sink, as if she will be questioned next and wishes to avoid it. No one has asked her why she left her job, or why she doesn't talk about her husband, Walt, or son, Michael. Sadie imagines the two of them together on some sort of vacation—trekking the Alps with backpacks, studying the flora, Michael a future biologist, an entomologist, someone who will one day work in a university, and Walt, the supportive father taking a leave of absence from his job. There are photos of Michael as a child wearing glasses, a sandy-haired boy with bony arms and legs. Others of him posing with Kate and her husband as a teenager—tall and filled out, and looking like a paler version of his father. Michael's absence is something they accept, like that of Kate's husband, their own husbands. Kate's grown son has simply been swallowed up by the same world where the men reside— a childless place, filled with *work, lunch, meetings*.

Women from surrounding neighborhoods with ties to the walking path have also discovered the pond. They are from places beyond Gladwyn Hollow—from Pudding Hill and Whittle Lane, names stolen by developers from early town founders. They stake out their places with bedspreads and towels. They bring floats for the children, a two-man raft with paddles. They plant umbrellas and dole out cups of lemonade from large thermoses. On any given day they appear at Kate's—women she doesn't even know, sitting in their folding chairs on her soft grass, or changing babies, their children running up and down her driveway, drawing on the tarred surface with colored chalk. Kate always keeps diapers and snacks for the little ones. She circulates and makes introductions. She is a hostess, a greeter, and Sadie imagines that her life is suddenly filled by these women who are everything she suspects Kate, with her career, has never been.

On days when thunderheads threaten lightning and rain Sadie and the other women always plan trips to the movies, to the bowling alley or the children's museum. They assume Kate is having a fine day free of them and their children with their demands and quarrels and uncontested needs. They never invite her along. It is as if she is a fixture, like the path and the pond, all things upon which they rely to remain the same, perennially in wait of their return.

The next morning, hot and hazy, Sadie announces to the women at the pond that she is going on a little *expedition* through the woods. In previous weeks they've explored and found the stone remains of a homesite, the rocks toppled into piles along the foundation, sprung from their places by frost and spring thaw, by passing fox and deer and clumsy hunters. Once this area was an open field, long before hickory and oak grew to fill it in. Two hundred and fifty years ago a family plowed and planted hills of rocky soil where their houses now sit. The settlers had their own names for places: Mount Misery, Bare Hill, Hell Hollow. Maura mentioned researching the site but this idea was quickly discarded. Most of the women have grown up nearby and have heard about family grave sites and ghost legends. As teenagers they sought them out on Halloween: the grave of the two-year-old girl who died of diphtheria, whose grief-stricken mother saved the apple she'd eaten that held her little tooth prints; the woods haunted by screams of a Native American woman murdered by British soldiers. Everyone remembers the more recent history, the land combed for missing girls. No one wants to know too much, to dwell on the past. That morning, they all decline a hike through mosquito-infested woods.

Sadie goes anyway. She brings along Sylvia, and Sylvia's best friend, Anne, Maura's youngest daughter. They circle the pond looking for some sign of a path through the woods on the other side, and it is Sylvia who notices the small break in the pine. The trees on this side of the pond are older, the woods darker and cooler, dotted with wood aster, bloodroot, swaths of cinnamon fern. The girls hold hands and shiver in their suits. They wear flip-flops with glued-on bows and jewels. Sylvia imitates a ghost, and Anne does a tiny shriek, like a banshee. Sadie gives them a look. She feels the edge of what must be irritation and is dismayed with herself. Was the look the same one her mother used to give her? "Now," her mother would have said, "don't be a giddy goose."

The path is narrow and rutted with tree roots, but it is a definite path, one that someone has once treaded. Sadie imagines a Colonial woman walking in front of them, her long skirt sweeping the dead leaves, catching the leaves up in her petticoat. The path goes up a short way and then down again, and comes out in a meadow. In the distance, up on a rise, is the old Filley house—its trap rock stones shining, the wooden ell in back deteriorated from this perspective and de-serted looking. Sadie stops. The girls flank her, each looking up, shading their eyes in the sun. Daisies fill the meadow. On one side of the house is an orchard, the trees bright and green. Sadie remembers them in spring bloom, the blossoms blown across the gravel drive. She looks at the upper-story window to the room where Ray took her that day, the first time they had sex. The glass is dark. Ray's green truck is in the drive.

She holds the girls' hands and smells the waving grass. The sun glints off the house's lower windows.

"A castle," Anne says.

"Where the princess lives, trapped by an evil spell," Sylvia says.

Their voices are soft and high. The white door in back is suddenly thrown open, and Ray Filley comes out. He is talk-ing on the phone, his tone sharp, and the girls gasp, sensing they are trespassing. Sylvia yanks on Sadie's hand as if to tug her back into the woods and the shadows. Ray carries a plastic garbage bag. Sadie can tell he is talking to Beth. His angry voice carries over the field of grass and flowers.

"Old Farmer Filley. The lying son of a bitch," he says. "Did you really think he'd quit drinking? He had you all fooled. I can't wait to tell Ludlow this bit of news."

He shuts the door behind him and walks along the side of the house to a row of cans. Sadie watches the way his shoulders move when he hefts the bag and drops it into the can. She hears the sound of glass bottles clinking together. He seems, to Sadie, so vulnerable performing this household task.

"I found ten bottles," he says. "And I wasn't even looking. Wait until I start prying up floorboards." He says something indecipherable that Sadie imagines is *horseshit,* which makes her laugh. Then he turns and looks at them. Sylvia makes a whimpering sound.

"He sees us," she says.

Anne stands immobile. "Oh no, oh no," she whispers.

Sadie doesn't know what to do. They all stand still, looking at each other. Ray shades his eyes, trying to make them out. He sets the phone on the window ledge and waves an arm in greeting. "Hello!" he calls, his anger dissipated.

"Hello!" Sadie calls back.

The girls grip her hands so tightly she can't wave. She tries to take a step but they hold their ground. "We'll ask if we can pick the flowers," she says soothingly. "I'm sure he won't mind."

Their hands loosen a bit. Ray starts across the field toward them, tramping down the grass. Dragonflies flit around his head. He wears a white button-up shirt, untucked, and jeans. His hair is long around his collar. To the girls he seems different from their fathers—men who never leave their dress shirts untucked unless they are in the process of dressing and in a hurry, rushing through the kitchen to grab a glass of juice. Their fathers have their hair cut regularly by the barber in town. Ray reaches them and stops. Sadie says they were on a hike and found the meadow.

"The girls would love to pick some flowers," she says.

He looks at her and then looks at each girl in turn. She knows he wants to ask her which is hers, but he does not. He squats down in front of them and smiles. "Of course you can pick them!" he says. "Make daisy chains. My sister used to make those." And then he focuses his attention on Sylvia, with her straw-colored hair. "I'm sure your mother made them, too."

He glances up at Sadie, his eyes brimming with desire.

She wants to reach out and touch his hair, his face. The girls hold her hands tight.

"Didn't you?" he says.

"Of course I did," Sadie says. Then she squeezes the girls' hands. "Go pick the daisies, the white ones with yellow centers. I'll show you how to do it. We can make necklaces, or crowns."

Both girls say, "Crowns *and* necklaces!" their little voices like small birds. They go out into the field to gather the flowers. Ray sits down in the grass and tugs Sadie down beside him.

She has written him back, tentative letters, ones she reads and rereads before they are mailed, making sure her identity will not be ascertained if a letter is intercepted. His notes are full of passion and a certainty that they are destined to be together, and hers are stilted, sounding like some sort of clever code. *You haven't considered the appendages,* she writes. *There are limbs that I cannot sever.* His replies signify a stubborn refusal to consider her situation. His plans are selfish, self-serving. He tells her she should choose to be happy, that happiness is possible, if only she will grasp it. In his last letter he set a date to meet—Friday before Labor Day, at the old house. She cannot go, she knows she can't. She can tell him now, in person, rather than spending hours composing the letter that will convey this news. Still, the result of her not going is something she fears she will always regret. Will the letters cease? Will he go away? Will he decide that any number of appendage-less women may be more pliable?

The sun on the grass, the smell of the pine woods behind them, makes her light-headed, and she says nothing about the meeting. When the girls' voices recede Ray leans in and kisses her—first one eyelid, then the other. Sadie wants to be in his arms, spread out in the grass, or in the shadow of the pine on the needle floor. She wants him to ravish her. He pulls away and looks at her. Sadie wears her swimsuit, Craig's shirt over it, and he slips his hand inside the shirt, inside the top of her suit. He slides his fingers over her breast. Sadie bites her lip to keep from sighing. "Not now," she whispers. "Please."

He moves his fingers up her thigh and down again. She clenches her fists, digs her nails into her palms.

"We could be inside, upstairs," he says quietly, moving his fingers.

She wants to laugh, to brush his hands away, but she cannot. She closes her eyes and begins to lower herself down into the sweet-smelling tussock grass. And then he is pulling her arm, yanking her up, and Sylvia is there with her flowers in her hands, quiet and watching. Later that night, when Sadie puts her into bed, Sylvia will tell her that the man in the castle was a magician who can cast spells, and that he's put a spell on Sadie, and taken away her real mother, and Sadie will tell her that is impossible and reassure her, even while she recognizes that in many ways this is true. But there in the field they sit cautiously beside each other, and Sadie shows her and Anne how to slice the flower stems with their fingernails and thread the stems through each other to make their necklaces, their crowns. Ray leaves them, but Sadie knows he is up in the room, watching through the window. "Next Friday," he whispered to her before he went. "I'll wait all day."

They head back through the pines to the pond, and this time Sadie knows that it is Emely Filley showing them the way, the path the one she must have taken the day her baby died, when she was filled with despair and purpose. They return to the other mothers and children, the girls showing off their jewelry, Sadie sinking back into her lawn chair, her body sore and aching. She has never felt this way before. She doesn't know what to make of it, how she might shake it or at least keep the feeling at bay. How will she cut the vegetables for the pot roast, change the sheets, drag the laundry up from the basement to fold and put away? How can she arrive at play practice, say her lines, organize the neighborhood Labor Day cookout? How can any of these things exist together with her longing?

June 27, 1979

THE BEST TIMES TO PLACE OR RETRIEVE A LETTER AT the dead end: early morning, the air cool, the grass wet; in the evening when the fireflies dipped and pulsed along the perimeter of the woods; in the afternoon during the lull, when mothers watched *As the World Turns,* the curtains drawn against the glare, the lives of the Hugheses, the Stewarts, the Talbots, the Lowells, and the Turners playing out in real-life Oakdale time. The sound of the soap opera—the low, quarreling voices; the soft endearments; the discussion of what to do over coffee—was a backdrop for Sadie's naptime as a child. She'd be consigned to her bedroom, and the daylight streaming in, the actors' voices, soothed her—even though she never knew the plot threads or understood the characters' complicated attractions, affairs, jealousies, and pregnancies. She'd smell the sulfur of the struck match, the smoke from her mother's cigarette. Her mother would have the laundry basket beside her and the clothes surrounding her in neat piles on the coffee table, on the sofa.

That summer Sadie's new desire to be away from her mother and her moods sent her outdoors, or to Betty's, or to the basement rec room. She would meet up with Betty in front of Betty's house by the curb, where her dog, Heidi, panted in the shade of the hickories. They'd have stolen the cigarettes to smoke. They'd walk on the lawns, along the tar road, the grass dry and brittle beneath their bare feet, the ciga-

rettes damp in their closed hands. In the pasture insects would
flit up around their faces, and they'd walk to the shade, under
the pines, to read Francie's letters.

They came to know her flourishes and games, her mun-
dane details: what color she painted her nails (*Skinny Dip*),
how much money she'd saved from her allowance, and what
she intended to do with it (*buy a ticket to France to meet my pen
pal Chantal*). They learned of her disappointment in never
knowing where the balloon she released in science class ended
up (*Oh, where oh where? Zimbabwe? Tahiti? Scranton?*). She described her weeklong beach vacation (*seaside manse*), her father
in his swimsuit (*hairy thighs, and the conspicuous lump, like something alive stuffed in his skimpy trunks*).

They never knew exactly what to make of her revelations.
She still spoke of events in her life in fairy-tale terms—the
king and queen were always her parents, and almost everything was depicted as fantasy or pretend. Still, Francie's letters were increasingly filled with details that struck Sadie and
Betty as things they should not know, like the questions and
answers in the "Playboy Advisor" column.

> *Dear Hezekiah,*
>   *The king is on a rampage this morning. The queen has*
> *awoken for a day and spent too much money on summer*
> *clothes and groceries and other means of existence. Meanwhile*
> *the king is busy with his hobbies and refuses to seek another*
> *position in the kingdom. Tonight we dine on canned*
> *Beefaroni. The queen puts it on the Royal Doulton. "Don't be*
> *a cunt," the king says, in the foulest of humors.*

Hezekiah, the farmer boy, had a limited domain. Faced
with Francie's letters, growing longer and more intimate, they
had to invent things to fill his life, to flesh out the simple
aspects of his day: *Work to do today,* he'd write. *Build the fence*

down by the road. Caught some nice perch this morning. Francie's new theme was a desire to escape her "castle prison." Sadie told Betty to write that Hezekiah, too, wanted to escape the drudgery of the farm. *But it's not possible for me to leave,* he wrote. *It's as if I am chained to the farm. You would understand the strength of such spells.* Sadie put in lines from Bud's letters to Bea Brownmiller: *My darling, let's pretend we can be together. Let's just talk about our own invented life.* She could only imagine Bea's responses, guessing she must have mentioned her cottage when Bud wrote: *Yes, that little house by the sea will be where we spend our later years. I can imagine all of the children, and the grandchildren coming for visits, and all that you've written is what I want, too, my dearest Bea.*

Sadie imagined Hezekiah loping through the fields, squatting down by the stone at dusk. Hezekiah was always Ray Filley when she pictured him, but in the letters he was the type of boy who read the *Farmer's Almanac,* who wore a white T-shirt and drove a tractor. He harvested the corn that summer. He painted the barn. He wore a brimmed hat down over his eyes. He told Francie about a trip to Woodbury, about apple harvesting, and cider making, and hayrides for children at Halloween.

We always do it up big on All Hallow's Eve, he wrote. *We serve hot cider and give rides up the hill through the woods on the wagon. We have the road lined with jack-o'-lanterns, and people dressed in costumes ready to jump out, to leap onto the wagon and walk among the riders.*

Betty had wanted to write *and scare the shit out of them,* but Sadie objected.

"He's not that crass," she said, a word her mother applied to her father.

Betty had been on a similar Halloween hayride with her cousin in Ellington.

"The jack-o'-lanterns were amazing," she said. "Each face

was different and frightening. Once in a while there'd be one that wasn't scary, but it wasn't happy either. It would be this wide open mouth, like a scream or surprise."

Sadie stared at her. Betty stared back. Sadie was thinking, trying to come up with something. Francie talked about her parents, and Hezekiah was strangely silent about his family.

"We should give him a sister," Sadie said.

"Why not a little brother? Or better, one of each?"

Sadie said that was too much to keep track of. "Why not a sister who is sick?" she said. "A sister with some disease."

"Leukemia," Betty said.

They were in Sadie's basement, sitting on the mattress they used for practicing back handsprings, or when they were younger as a bed in their games of house or an island in their shipwreck game. It was old ticking, with buttons, and covered with stains from years of use. The other things from their games—the cherry drop-leaf table, the old couch with its sewn-on lace doilies, the black cast-iron pot, the stones they'd used as a fireplace—were gone. Sadie missed them, as she missed most of what had passed of her childhood. She was acutely aware of how she had changed recently, and it made her sadder than she thought she should be. A sister with leukemia would work, she thought. Like Beth in *Little Women*. Sadie couldn't help but imagine Ray's sister Beth, her pathetic attachment to Ray, the much-perused map she'd shown her that afternoon when they were little, one charting routes of escape. Hezekiah would be a caring brother, tender and considerate. Francie would be all the more attracted to him.

We are taking my sister for her treatment tomorrow. She is ten and has leukemia. I don't usually tell anyone about this. She is weak but still a happy kid. She likes butterflies.

Betty said it was perfect. The basement door opened and Sadie's mother called down the stairs, "What are you girls doing?"

Sadie hoped she would not come down, but then she did, a little unsteadily, and appeared behind them. The sliding glass doors let in the light through the trees, and the speckled shadows of leaves spangled there on the indoor/outdoor carpet. Her mother was wearing her swimsuit and sunglasses. Sadie had folded the letter up and slipped it under the mattress, and they were sitting there with blank pages and the pen they reserved for Hezekiah's letters—a fountain pen Sadie's grandmother had given her when Sadie said once she wanted to be a writer.

"What are you writing?" her mother said.

"We're trying to come up with a script for the Haunted Woods," Betty said quickly.

Sadie would not have said that. She would have said they were making a list of kids and their roles. She would have said they were adding up how much money they might make. Her mother would have turned and left them alone. Instead she came forward and plopped down on the mattress, smelling of Sea & Ski. She stretched her long, tan legs out in front of her. She propped her sunglasses up on her head. "Let's see," she said.

Betty showed her the blank pages. "We don't have anything yet."

Sadie's mother rolled her eyes. "Well, you have to begin somewhere." She told them that a good plot would keep the kids interested as they walked along the path. "Maybe they see a headless woman, and she is just wandering by. Then they see a man holding a woman's head, crying. It's a beautiful head, with cascading hair, and a gorgeous face, and he holds it up and talks to it, 'Oh, my darling Rosalee,' he says. And the head tells him, 'I won't rest until I find my child. Please find her for me!' Then they come upon a child dragging a bloody hatchet."

Betty stared at Sadie's mother, her mouth open.

"You look like those jack-o'-lanterns at the farm," Sadie said.

Her mother turned to her. "Have you heard a word of what I was saying?"

Sadie shrugged. "I guess," she said. "It sounds okay."

She wouldn't admit how much she liked the story her mother told, how perfect it was.

"Did the child with the hatchet cut off the mother's head?" Betty asked.

Sadie's mother put her arm around her and squeezed. "Maybe, sweetie."

"But we have a drowned girl," Sadie said. "And a wandering Victorian couple."

"And a girl crushed by a bridge," Betty said.

Sadie's mother waved her hand. "Oh, you don't need all of that."

"Then we'll have to cut out a lot of kids," Sadie said to Betty. "They won't be happy."

Sadie's mother stood up and stumbled a bit. "Then you'll have to cut them out. They'll survive. They can work behind the scenes, for God's sake. Do you want a good show or a hodgepodge of a thing?"

She turned and Sadie noticed the pale blue veins on the back of her legs, the way the fat rippled there, all imperfections that gave her a certain satisfaction. Her mother tugged down her suit. "Good luck," she said. She went to the sliding glass door and then out into the backyard.

"Where is your mother going?" Betty asked.

They watched her walk in her bare feet to the woods and then disappear into them. Every now and then they'd see the bright white of her suit moving among the trees, climbing the path.

"No idea," Sadie said. She stood up. "I think we should use that script."

Betty sat on the mattress, biting her fingernails. "You don't think it's a bit, well, much?"

Sadie said it wasn't. It would be fine. They could still have the drowned girl. The theme would be the dead seeking those they loved. Men seeking their lost loves, women seeking their children. "Even in death," she said, "they are searching for them."

"Is the mother whose child killed her still searching for her?"

Sadie gave Betty an exasperated look. "Love doesn't always make sense."

The date was moved back for the Haunted Woods. Parts would be reassigned. That evening Sadie spent the night at Betty's, and they slipped out and hid the note to Francie. Moths fluttered by lampposts. Through the open windows they could hear Mrs. Frobel yelling at her children and smell the meals that had been prepared in each house. Mrs. Sidelman's was dark, and Sadie remembered that she hadn't watered the plants, and after they left the note they went there with Sadie's key. They flipped on all the lights, fearful of the quiet and the dark. Sadie showed Betty the Aquacade playbill with Mrs. Sidelman's name. She kept the letters hidden under the cashmere sweater. They were in the kitchen at the table in front of the sliding glass door to the patio when they saw the bobbing light in the fields. They both watched it move and saw it go out. Sadie wondered if her mother was home, if she was still out in the woods, and she felt a twinge of concern for her.

"What do you think it is?" Betty breathed.

"Hezekiah just left his letter," Sadie said. She laughed, half afraid, half believing that what they'd invented had taken on a life of its own.

PART THREE

POLICE FEAR WINTONBURY
GIRL IS KIDNAPPED

Wintonbury—June 19, 1974

If 9-year-old Laura Loomis is not found today, state police said Monday, they will assume she was either kidnapped or wandered from the search area near her home. The girl was reported missing Thursday, but hundreds of volunteers have combed the dense, wooded terrain more than once, and a pond has been dredged. State police spokesman Dan Fontaine says that since it doesn't seem the girl has left the area on her own the focus will shift to the possibility that foul play may be involved in her disappearance, and the massive search will then end. Fontaine commended the police chief and the hundreds of volunteers who the family hopes will continue the search indefinitely, although some now seem pessimistic about the prospect of locating the girl. "After six days she's probably either dead or kidnapped," volunteer Jim Thompson said. Police are questioning persons who have been charged with morals offenses in the Wintonbury area.

August 29, 2003

WHEN FRIDAY ARRIVES, THE DAY TO MEET RAY, Sadie finds that everything she does, everything she says, is mechanical and stilted. Bringing laundry up from the basement, brewing the coffee, calling the pediatrician to make appointments for the children's physicals, putting dishes in the dishwasher—she does it all in a wind-up-doll kind of way, and she thinks this has been her life and she's never known it. She kisses Craig good-bye, a lingering kiss that he accepts without question. She watches his broad shoulders in his gray suit move through the door and then the grayness of him flashing in front of the picture window, and she wills him back. She is crushed that he does not return, that he continues to back his car out of the driveway, oblivious. The lawn men show up, parking at the road, revving their big mowers.

She looks around at her house. Things have caught up with her; she has left it all untended for too long and the rooms, like the flower beds that flank the front stoop, have gone to weeds. Dust has accumulated under the couches and chairs. It leaves a pale coating on the cherry tables, on the bookshelves. The silver tea set is tarnished. There are cobwebs high in the corners near the plaster ceilings. Sadie has pretended not to notice these things, but she sees them now, and it is as if she is looking at an image of herself stripped naked, and she is surprised to feel embarrassment. She has slowly, cautiously,

135

been pulling away, tucking herself into herself. She cannot decide when it started—after Lily, or after Ray? Both events seem inseparable. She packs up for the day and takes the children to the pond.

Max complains, grouchy about his tube being deflated, unable to comprehend her insistence that she will blow it up when they get there. "When—we—get—there," she says, each word bitten off, containing her irritation. Sylvia is her little helper. She takes her brother's hand and tells him a story about the wood elves. "They live in the trees," she says. "They get in through the roots. There are little hidden doors." She steps off the path and goes up to a beech and knocks. Max stands by, transfixed, the deflated tube forgotten.

"No one's home," Sylvia says brightly. "Maybe they're up at the pond!"

Once there, Sadie settles into her chair. She notices that the sunlight through the trees is different, the pond's water altered to a deeper color. Her lost girl, Lily, would have celebrated her first birthday yesterday, she thinks. She let the day pass without comment to Craig, and she wonders now if he acknowledged it and was too afraid he'd upset her to mention it. She is filled with regret. It is too late now to get balloons, to make a cake. Summer is already fading; the start of school looms. The dragonflies are gone and the field is filled with bluestem, lobelia, purple coneflower. The children know. They putter in the sand. They huddle at their mothers' feet and listen to them talk about school shopping and sales. Sadie is tired, more tired than she's ever been before. She tries to think back through the summer days. When did she begin to leave the housework undone, let the laundry pile up? When did dark mold grow in the cracks of the shower stall? All she's needed is her bathing suit, washed out each night in the sink. It is an addiction, the haze, the dappled leaf shadow, the sound of running water. She hopes for Indian summer.

She doesn't know what to make of any of this, or what she has become—an unfaithful wife, an unreliable mother—or what the use of all her striving to be good was, if only to end up in this place, unable to move one way or another. The way to the old Filley house is clear, through the pines, then down through the meadow. She might ask Maura to watch the children and go there now. She imagines Ray waiting for her, pacing the wide floorboards. Isn't this all it would take— a quick walk through the woods, sex in the upstairs room? Would anyone ever know? But Sadie understands Ray now wants more from her than that, and she thinks there is more she wants as well, though what, yet, she is still unsure. Her limbs feel heavy. The sky is a white blanket. She hears the short, high yelp of a child at play, and she closes her eyes and decides, for now, that she is not going anywhere.

After lunch, Sadie, Maura, and Jane, back from vacation, pack up early. Kate has asked them to come before the other women, told them she is ready to share it with them, a *little hobby*. On the way down the path, Sadie suggests that maybe this is what Kate's been working on all day while they are at the pond, and Maura and Jane agree. While the children play in the den Kate leads the women with their drinks down the basement steps. Her dark hair is loose today, and she seems almost girlish with it brushing her shoulders. Sadie descends into the basement and imagines painted bookshelves or restored antique chairs. She pictures, in the recesses of the basement, a sewing machine and the old-timey patterns she once pieced together in home economics, or yards of brocade upholstery. She almost tells the story of the plays she would put on in her own basement as a child, but she decides against it. She and the others clutch the wooden rail and step carefully. It is dim and cool and smells, much as their basements do, of mildew, damp, and laundry soap. Jane says, "Where's the light?" and stumbles around looking for the string pull for an overhead bulb, but Kate says to wait, her voice pitched high with anticipation, and she flips a switch somewhere ahead of them in the darkness, and the room illuminates, a cavernous space decorated, inexplicably, for Christmas.

She has tacked up swags of fake greens filled with tiny white lights along the ceiling, threaded among the exposed pipes. There are imitation Fraser firs covered with glass balls and ribbons and tinsel, and those motorized dolls dressed in Victorian garb, their mouths opening and closing to music they can't hear. There are fake deer that dip their heads to eat and raise them to listen for predators, a miniature town set up on a large platform covered with fluffy snow batting—churches and stores and houses, a mirror pond with ice skaters, a train doing its mechanical whir around the perimeter. There are ornaments that later Jane surmises must be the result of years of collecting—Nutcrackers, angels with trumpets, glass fruit covered with glitter. They ooooh and aaaah, make the expected noises. But none of them understand. Is it for the children? What is it?

Kate tells them she burns the pine-scented candles when she works, but still Sadie imagines the feeling on first entering the basement is one of dampness and decay. She remembers it herself, the times she'd go down to her basement to play practice or to play Old-Fashioned-Days House. Sadie guesses Kate must use the overhead light while she constructs the little village.

"Michael loved them as a child," Kate says, referring, for the first time, to her own son.

She tells them they would go to the Christmas Barn in Wilton, and he'd lean forward in his stroller, his eyes level with the scene and lit with wonder. Even when he was older—a toddler, a young boy, up until he was ten or so—he loved the villages erected on the snow batting. Kate has made each building light up, and inside each house is a small scene of merriment: dancing, caroling, gift unwrapping, parties, eggnog. Sadie thinks she's constructed this village as if the child he was may one day see it. She leans down and looks at the scene. In a blue Cape that sits on a cul-de-sac are three miniature figures—a mother, father, and young boy. The father wears a tweed suit, the mother a dress that might have come from a Butterick sewing pattern circa 1970. The boy is in jeans and a green sweater. His face is tiny and plastic, and poorly painted. They gather around a table. There is a decorated tree in the window, a fireplace with stockings. Sadie sees Kate has re-created scenes in each house. It reminds her of her old dollhouse—the brilliantly colored metal walls with painted-on wallpaper, rugs, bookshelves, the children's nursery wall covered with scampering squirrels. The furniture was all plastic. Kate uses real wood pieces she tells them she special-orders from catalogs. The houses are vintage dollhouses: Colonials, split-levels, midcentury modern ranches. She's put in small roasts on platters, cups and bowls and silverware on tiny place mats. She has vintage television sets, toasters and blenders, beds and bedding, miniature pillows, pets, even books— tiny leather-bound ones with blank pages. The houses are electrified with wires that illuminate lamps and chandeliers swagged with imitation greens, tiny trees lit up with strands of colored lights.

Jane widens her eyes and is the first to make an excuse to leave. She has the meatloaf still, she explains. She is up the stairs before anyone can stop her. Maura goes on nonstop about Christmas being her favorite holiday, and how growing up there was one house in her neighborhood that really did it up big, and Sadie knows her chattering is done as a kindness to fill the silence. She and Maura make a show of walking about and fingering ornaments, commenting on their uniqueness. In the shadowy place beyond the laundry room, where the black oil tank sits, Sadie sees an odd pile of things: boating magazines, a Burberry overcoat, stacks of file folders, neat piles of folded clothes—not enough things to be a man's total possessions. Sadie imagines they are Kate's husband's but finds it odd that they are piled there where mice might burrow into his starched shirts, nibble at his leather shoes with the cedar inserts, shred the paper in his stack of old reports.

Sadie trips over an extension cord and her drink spills its bright tropical colors onto the pristine village snow. She and Maura watch Kate's face lose its softness, stiffen with apprehension.

"Oh, don't worry about it," she tells them. She laughs and waves her hand, but neither of them is convinced.

They end up standing by the stairs. "This is lovely," they say. "This is so creative."

"It isn't *normal* to have Christmas in your basement," Jane says when they gather afterward in her driveway. She is winding and rewinding her hair, clipping it back up—a nervous habit. Maura does her *Oh well* look, as if nothing can surprise her. They surmise that Kate, still out of work, needs to find a way to channel litigious energy.

"Have you seen her husband's car at all this summer?" Jane asks.

Maura says that maybe he's been out of town. They imagine her waiting for him to return, gluing plastic carolers outside a miniature snow-covered house. But Sadie remembers the pile of things by the furnace and suspects that for whatever reason her husband is gone, and Kate is the keeper of the items he's left behind. Sadie, with her own secret, doesn't share her suspicion with Jane and Maura. She silently excuses Kate's hobby, feels almost traitorous about her reaction when Kate shared it with them. She found herself entranced by the intricate scenes, the miniature re-creations of what she always expected her married life to be—perfect, happy, fixed. The basement Christmas throws everything into strange relief. Nothing is as it once seemed. Sadie sees herself glued into place in her own house, her life filled with the predictable sameness that Kate seems to long for. *I'll wait all day,* Ray said. Sadie feels a small flutter of panic, as if she's known all along what she will do and is now incapable of stopping herself.

June 30, 1979

SADIE WOULD SOMETIMES WONDER WHAT BEGAN THE series of events that came to mark that summer as blighted. Was it the note under the stone? Was it the Haunted Woods? Was it long before any of these things, when Francie was taken for the irritating girl no one wanted to play with, her family ostracized by the neighborhood and held suspect for no explainable reason? Was it the setting—the waving elms and hickories, the way the sun rose over the hills of corn, the cow paths twisting over tree roots and stones, the pale violets that sprang up among mosses, the smell of the air through rusty window screens? Or was it the cicadas, their harsh whirring like something rending the air, like a spacecraft hovering over their neighborhood?

One morning, she woke up before anyone else in her house. She could hear her father's heavy breathing across the hall. She went downstairs and emptied the ashtrays since no one else seemed to. She sat on the couch in the den. Last spring she'd taken a small plastic hinged box—the type that might hold costume earrings tacked to imitation velvet and cardboard—and she'd filled it with things that identified her: a sheet of paper on which she'd written facts about her life and a poem, a small wooden medallion with a metal letter "S," a penny with the date. She'd folded the paper up tightly into a square. She'd covered the box with black electrical tape. And then she'd tossed the box out into her backyard, into the bare, wet branches, into the patches of melting snow and the twigs of thorny bushes dotted with red berries. That girl was a mystery she couldn't solve, residing in a place she couldn't return to.

But she remembered the box now and decided to find it. She went out the back door to the deck. She peered over the railing into the depths of the woods—green and flickering, the birds starting to make noise, the light dappling the porch floor. She didn't know how she could ever locate it under all the ferns and layers of decomposing leaves, but she would try.

In a moment she was down the path and in the woods, near the spot she believed it might have landed. When she glanced back at her house she was surprised to see her mother standing in the basement in front of the sliding glass doors. She held a cup of coffee, a cigarette. She wore her pale-colored summer robe, and Sadie watched as she smoked and stared out the doors. She couldn't see Sadie there in the woods. She moved back and forth in front of the glass, and then she untied the robe and let it slip from her shoulders. She wore only a pair of panties, blue and shimmery. Her breasts were full, outlined by the darkness of her tan. She stared out the doors, and Sadie realized she was looking at her own reflection in the glass, the outside world still dark, the sun just hitting the rim of the hill behind her. Her expression was pensive. Even then Sadie could feel her terrible longing. Her mother reached out and touched the glass, bent down and retrieved the robe, and disappeared into the basement, as if she'd been summoned.

Sadie turned away and continued to look along the floor of the woods, though it seemed to matter less now if she found the small box. She parted the ferns and found a tarnished silver candlestick, left there from one of their old games. It saddened her to see it, this reminder of the girl she once was, who seemed about to slip away from her.

"What are you looking for?" a voice said.

Sadie spun around. There was Ray Filley, leaning against a tree with his cigarette. She realized she was still in her pajamas.

"What are you doing there?" she asked.

"Oh, I'm spying on you," Ray said. He exhaled and laughed. "What do you think I'm doing? Having a cigarette. What do you have there?"

Sadie dropped the candlestick. "Nothing."

She felt childish in the pajamas, the baby-doll kind everyone's mother bought for her in the department store's children's section. "Mortified" is the word she would have used if she'd decided to tell Betty. *And there he was, just standing there in the ferns, watching me. I was in pink baby-dolls and I was mortified.*

"You're up early," Sadie said.

"I guess we're a couple of early risers," Ray said. He put his cigarette out on the tree. Everything he did was cocky. Oh so full of himself, Sadie thought. She hated him, and loved him. She wanted to grab the candlestick and throw it at him. She wanted his hands to slide beneath her pajamas and up her bare back the way the characters' did in Mrs. Sidelman's books. Instead, the two of them just stood there in the woods, staring at each other.

"Do you have an extra cigarette?" she said.

Ray smiled. "An extra one?" He took out a crumpled pack and shook it. "No, sorry. No extras."

He had on a pair of madras shorts, a sloppy T-shirt. He wore tennis shoes. Every so often he shook his long hair away from his eyes. "You should run along back to bed," he said.

Sadie slitted her eyes at him. "What for?" she said. "I'm up now."

"Go have yourself a Pop-Tart or play with your dolls," he said.

Sadie put a hand on her hip. "And what will you do?" she said.

Ray's face seemed to still. His laughing eyes darkened. "None of your business," he said.

Sadie remembered times that Ray Filley would throw the football with the other boys on the street, when he'd helped build the tree fort, dragging heavy sheets of plywood from the new development going up on Butternut Drive. At one time, he'd been a child, and now suddenly he was not. She saw a furtive, darting movement in the woods behind him, and she tilted her head to get a better look. Ray spun around to see where she was looking.

"What?" he said.

Sadie shrugged. "I don't know. I can't see anything now. Maybe it was just Beth, following you." She knew this would anger him, but she didn't care. He moved through the woods and came down the path into Sadie's backyard and stood in front of her. He smelled of sweat and cigarettes. He brushed back his long hair and grinned, the smile false and sarcastic.

"You know you look just like one of Beth's friends—what was her name? Linda? Lisa? No, that's right, it was Laura. Aren't you afraid to be out in the woods by yourself? You wouldn't want to end up like her."

Sadie felt a spark of fear, but she refused to show it. "You're in my yard," she said.

"Once, all of this was *my* yard," Ray said.

Sadie was certain that her pajama top was sheer, that he could see her breasts. She felt her face flush. *Oh, the total humiliation,* she might have told Betty. He bent down beside her and retrieved the candlestick. He hefted it in his hand, the fingers long, the tendons flexing and tightening.

"You should bring this inside," he told her. "Seems like it's worth something."

Then he handed it to her, and turned and headed back up the path into the woods. Sadie watched him until he'd disappeared within the green shade of leafy saplings. She returned to her house, and when she got to the top of the porch steps her mother was there at the screen door.

"What are you doing out there?" she said, her voice sharp. Sadie startled. Her mother still wore her robe. Sadie smelled the coffee, her perfume, the scent of her skin, and the cigarettes. She was breathing as if she'd been running or dancing. They looked at each other, their chests rising and falling.

"I was looking for something," Sadie said.

"What is that? Where did you get it?"

Sadie held the candlestick up. "We used to play with it—I found it in the woods," she said.

Her mother opened the screen door. And when Sadie stepped into the house her mother reached out and slapped her across the face.

"What kind of girl are you walking around outside like that?" she said. "What is wrong with you? What if someone saw you? What will people think of us?"

Sadie felt the sting on her cheek and the anger from the indignity all at once. She tasted blood in her mouth where she'd bitten her tongue. She slipped past her mother into the house, everything dark and cool, the light just coming through cracks in the drapes, the family room foggy with cigarette smoke. Behind her she heard her mother begin to cry. She got to the stair landing and her father emerged from the bedroom.

"What's wrong with your mother?" he said.

And then her mother weeping behind her. "I'm so sorry, Sadie," she said. "So sorry!"

Despite the burning mark on her face Sadie was prompted to accept the apology, to allow herself to be held by her mother, enfolded in her arms, the Chanel No. 5 slightly sour on her skin. Her mother's tears wet Sadie's shoulder, seeped into her pajama top and into her hair. She had to wrap her arms around her mother in the semblance of an embrace, while her father ambled down the stairs, scratching down the back of his shorts. But Sadie was starting to realize that her mother never felt any remorse. All of this was just a manifestation of some other sadness—one that flitted around her wry smiles, that revealed itself when she stared into her drink or exhaled after a drag of her cigarette. Maybe a dreamy, sweet look masked it, but Sadie knew it was there, had always known it.

Her mother finally let her go. Her face was wet. "Don't ever make me do that again," she said. "Good girls don't talk to strange boys in the woods, Sadie."

Sadie felt a little bolt, like a charge, run through her. She had been watching her. They had been watching each other. "It was only—"

Her mother reached out and put her hand on Sadie's slapped cheek. "It doesn't matter who it is," she said quickly. "You don't ever really know someone."

August 29, 2003

AT THREE O'CLOCK SADIE DRESSES IN HER NEW SKIRT and blouse and takes Max and Sylvia back to Kate Curry's. She is jittery, as if she's drunk too much coffee.

"I need saffron," she tells Kate. "I need it for a recipe and it will be so much quicker if I can go alone." *Saffron,* something she knows the woman won't be able to pull from her orderly spice cabinet.

"Oh! What are you making?"

Kate leans on the counter, chin in her hands. If Sadie's grocery-shopping outfit gives her pause, she doesn't let on. Outside the glass doors the humidity has broken. The backyard trees thrash their leaves, signaling a late-afternoon thunderstorm. Sadie has no idea how to answer Kate's question. She cannot remember the last time she made something requiring any spice more complicated than pepper. She is flustered, thinking about Ray waiting for her, the smell of the meadow flowers through his windows, his hands on her hips, his mouth. She staggers toward the woman's door. "Oh God," she says. She waves her hand. "I'll tell you if it turns out."

"Drive carefully," Kate calls. "It looks like it might storm."

Her children are seated in the wood-paneled den in front of the television. They don't respond when she calls goodbye, so she returns to the doorway and says it again. Although she feels an overwhelming desire to go to them and take them in her arms, a simple trip to the grocery store doesn't merit it, so to avoid suspicion she stands in the doorway waiting, her heart thudding.

"I love you," she says. "I'll be back soon."

Sylvia chews on a hank of her hair, absorbed in the television, but she turns, as if sensing something in Sadie's voice. She nudges Max, who says, "Bye, Mommy."

Sylvia waves, her eyes suddenly wary. She takes in the skirt Sadie's wearing, the blouse. "What time?"

Sadie makes a pretense of looking at her watch. "In a little bit."

As she closes the door she hears Kate ask in her bright voice if they want an ice cream cup. How she envies this woman whose beds are made, laundry folded—her efficiency in attending to all of it. She drives away from Kate's, from Gladwyn Hollow, and feels a weight lift; the things behind her dissolve, as if she's never been responsible for any of them—the dishes in her sink, the cobwebs, the clothes the children have outgrown that need to be replaced, the handprint on the front window, Craig's creased brow, his sighing on his side of the bed. She's left her cell phone at home inside her nightstand drawer. Craig is always after her to take it with her, but most times she does not. Leaving the phone behind will not make him suspicious should he discover it, and she feels let loose in the world—unmonitored.

She turns quickly, recklessly, into Ray's gravel drive and leaps from the car, eager to fall into his arms. She knocks, a noise that resounds through the empty rooms, but he doesn't come right away, and she stands there, watching the sky darken, feeling the wind pick up, listening to it drag at the tree limbs overhead, and wonders if she's made a mistake, misread his letter, his whispered reminder. She thinks she's come on the wrong day. But then there's a sound of footsteps and he is there, his white dress shirt damp with sweat, his eyes blank and cold. He apologizes. He tells her he is working on the house, things are a mess.

"I didn't know if you would come," he says.

He takes her chin in his hand, and his expression changes, his eyes slowly warming. He draws her into the house. "I can't believe it," he says. He pulls her into his arms and lowers his head to her shoulder like a child. Sadie holds him and feels his sweat-stained back, his alarming trembling.

"What?" she says. "What is it?"

"I'm just so glad that you're here," he says.

He leads her toward the stairs, and she follows, not sure if she believes him, not sure now about anything, the darkness of the storm outside seeping into the house's rooms, a presence enclosing them. She tells him she has left the children with Kate. "I can't stay long."

"Who?" he says. "Who is Kate?"

He takes her into the same bedroom, to the unmade bed and the scattered clothing, and he pauses there in the doorway.

"I have to make a phone call," he says, to her surprise. "I'll only be a few minutes."

And then he is gone; his footsteps sound on the stairs. She is left in the room filled with shadows, the sky darkening beyond the window. She hears faint, far-off thunder. She sits on the bed to wait, torn between staying and leaving, hating herself for her indecisiveness. She hears Ray downstairs pacing, then his voice—short phrases that sound like an interrogation. *Beth,* she thinks. She can tell from the tone of his voice he is talking to her, and she feels slightly resentful. Then she sees the suitcase. It is still there, behind the chair, and she stands up, unsteady in the darkened room. She squats down by the suitcase, lays it flat, and this time the latches flip easily and the suitcase pops open. She smells the perfume first—that scent she's shunned as an adult, because it is forever her mother's—attached still to the clothing inside. For a moment, she just looks at the contents before putting a hand in and stirring the clothing about—the panties, underwire bras, a dress made of silk in a bold black-and-white pattern, one she saw her mother wear out to the Officer's Club for dinner, to a cocktail party at a neighbor's. She tells herself that surely her mother must have loaned the dress years ago to Patsy Filley, that these are really Patsy's things left here in this old suitcase.

Sadie reaches in and takes the dress in her hands, holds it up, and smells the decay beneath the Chanel No. 5, sees the sad little rings of perspiration under the arms. She puts it back and sorts some more: toiletries in pink-capped bottles, facial cream, tweezers, manicuring scissors, a compact with pale powder, Chanel eye shadow and mascara. She recognizes her mother's linen slacks, a cotton blouse and bright print skirt she wore that last summer. Sadie finds her bathing suit—smelling still of Sea & Ski, of chlorine. The gold sandals. She imagines her mother choosing the items, placing them inside, but she cannot imagine how this has arrived here, in the old Filley house. She takes one of the gold sandals in her hands, traces her mother's toe prints marked on the insoles. She places it back and reaches into one of the satin pockets and discovers an old piece of construction paper, folded like a card, and her own first-grade handwriting, *Happy Mother's Day*—a loopy cursive, written with the heavy pencil handed out to each student. There's a drawing of a blue bird on a branch, a sun, and inside: *You are shinny like the sun / You are sweet like all the flowers / you are the only one / I want to be my mother*. There's more in the pockets, but she hears Ray's voice downstairs—suddenly sharp, raised in anger.

"What's in the hidey spot, Beth?"

Sadie stands up. She hears Ray's footsteps on the stairs, his angry cursing, and she bends again to the suitcase, quickly closes it with her shaking hands, and returns it to its place behind the chair. The smell inside the suitcase seems, as if by some magical force, to fill the room—she sits on the bed, wishing it away, her head spinning. Ray appears in the doorway. Rain strikes the window behind her, and she startles. The shadows of the blown trees mark the bed, the floor.

Sadie stares at him, wide-eyed, numb, and confused by the suitcase and its contents, by his behavior. His gaze darkens with suspicion, and he glances quickly to the suitcase in the corner, then back to her face. Then he goes to the closet, pulls down a duffel bag from a shelf, and begins to stuff clothing into it—items from the floor, items that she notices now he folded on the bed. He grabs a set of keys off the bureau.

"We need to go."

His urgency frightens her, and she lets him take her arm and lead her back along the narrow hallway, down the stairs, and out the front door. He moves so quickly Sadie senses they are escaping something in the house.

"What is happening?" she manages to ask. They are on the stone front walk, and the rain lashes their faces. He tells her to hurry and put her car in the barn, and he points down the drive to a barn near his parked truck. Beyond the barn stretches the field, its grasses blowing. Beyond that—the woods. She stands by her car and shrugs off his arm. "Why?"

"Beth might be coming over," he says.

His face is white, and pinched and altered. The wind brings the rain, harder now, and Sadie feels it through her blouse.

"I told her not to come, but you know Beth," he says. "She'll probably just show up."

"Why do you have your bag?" she asks him.

He looks down at the bag in his hand as if he's forgotten it's there. "I'll tell you later," he says. "We'll go in the truck."

She shakes her head at him and turns toward her car, and he yanks her back by the arm, his hand gripping her tight. "Don't tell me no, Sadie."

Then before she can protest he's dropped the bag on the gravel drive, taken her face in his hands, and pressed his mouth to hers, a kiss that makes her weak-kneed, that she doesn't ever want to end. "You came here today," he tells her, his mouth by her ear. "You must want the same thing I do."

And without examining what she wants or doesn't want, she realizes that Beth may arrive at any minute, and so she does what he asks, pulls the SUV down the drive to the barn. Ray opens the barn door, and after closes her car inside, hidden from Beth's prying eyes.

"Hurry, hurry," he calls.

They return to the truck. Sadie yanks the door open. She is soaked through, her hair, her clothing, and inside the truck is warm and sticky. The lightning brightens the sky beyond the windshield. Ray starts the truck up, turns it around. It bounces down the gravel drive, and the tires spin on the street, where they hurtle away, as if in flight. Sadie half expects Ray to check the rearview mirror. They curve along Duncaster, onto Route 187. His cell phone rings and he works it out of his pants pocket, glances at the screen. He rolls the window down—the sound of the rain rushes through the cab—and Sadie watches in shock as he tosses the ringing phone out the window into the woods. His mood changes afterward, and they leave the town behind.

"Where are we going?" she asks finally.

He makes an exuberant hoot and tells her that they can go anywhere she wants.

"Anywhere in the world, sweetheart." He laughs, one hand on the wheel, the other holding hers, shaking it like loose change. The only problem is that Sadie doesn't know where he expects her to want to go. She is still flummoxed by the suitcase filled with her mother's clothing. Weren't the gold sandals given away years ago to the League of Mercy? The rain and wind rock the old truck on the highway. Sadie looks over at Ray carefully. She feels a little burst of fear, like a bubble rising to the surface and breaking.

July 2, 1979

Dear Hezekiah,

I am so sorry to hear about your sister. And I feel we are now compatriots in sadness. It is a heavy curtain that is drawn around us. Even your sunny fields, your busy days, aren't enough to waylay that sorrow. I wish we could follow through with our plan to run off together. There's been another addition to the already frightful tradition of suspense and upset in the kingdom. The queen put all of the king's woodworkings in trash cans and set them out at the curb for the garbage collector. Thankfully, he found them before they were taken. Next time, she says, she will light a bonfire in the backyard. I am happy to have the summer end, to return to the normalcy of study. Where do you attend? I am looking forward to your All Hallow's Eve hayride. I'd like to bring your sister a gift— it is a small china box painted with dragonflies. [Drawing included.]

Yours in understanding,
Francie

Dear Francie,

My sister has taken a turn for the worse and is now watched over by the nuns in a private hospital. She is peaceful there and likes the sound of their rosaries. She says she has a good view of the rolling hills that reminds her of our farm, and

*a birdhouse where the finches come to feed. Sorry to hear that
your mother doesn't appreciate your father's art. It seems you
are an artist as well. I've shown your drawing to my sister, and
she has pasted it up on the wall of her room. I feel that soon we
may be able to put our plan in place.*

Hezekiah

Dear Hezekiah,

    *I have often considered joining a cloister, but I must be of
a certain age before they will have me. I am not very religious,
but I am used to being persecuted and alone. The queen is
once again comatose on the couch. "Passivity is a form of
rebellion," the king says. I often think about the little girl who
disappeared five years ago, and I picture her living out in the
woods in a little hut made of pine branches, hunting with a
handmade bow, reading books she's stolen off shelves of houses
she slips into at night. Sometimes I wish I was her, rather
than me. I am set to play a character in our neighborhood
Haunted Woods—a grief-stricken ghost named Emely Filley
who drowns herself in a pond over the loss of her infant. You
remember the girls you first met? They are the ones planning
the event. I think they are creative girls, but very stuck-up.
They think they are clever, but they are not. When do you
think the time will be right?*

Yours truly,
Francie

Dear Francie,

    *I do remember those girls—but they don't understand me
like you do. Corn to harvest this week. I feel obligated to stay a
little longer. Wait for word from me—I promise it will be soon.*

Hezekiah

Work on the Haunted Woods became a daily activity. Each morning everyone would meet on Betty's front lawn and then move through the backyard to the pasture. One of the boys stole his father's wire cutters to make an opening through the barbed wire fencing. They used one of the old cow paths, narrow and meandering, as their main route. The path curved under pines; around the old swamp; through an abandoned apple orchard, the tree trunks mottled, the branches like spines; and finally through a small field. From the field they made their own path back, marking it with the fluorescent spray-painted sticks and rocks. In the heat of the day when the cicadas were the noisiest they took breaks under the pines, the needles fragrant and soft, the bases of the trees covered with moss. Sadie had a handwritten script. The props required were elaborate—her mother's long evening dresses, the candles and the candelabra, a maple table and four chairs, stacks of books, wood for the construction of perches in trees, platforms for beds, fishing line, copper wire, nails, an old push lawnmower, galvanized buckets, pots and pans, assorted dolls, bedspreads and sheets, the fake blood and red tempera paint that could only be purchased at Drug City.

Constructed in the pasture and woods was a domestic nightmare—the rooms of a house like any of theirs, set off from the path, filled with scenes of horror: a kitchen with a woman in an apron holding rusted gardening shears, a living room with a headless man watching television, a child's bedroom in disarray, bloody footprints across the floor, a library with books covered in bloody handprints. The children who paid the twenty-five-cent entrance fee would be led along the path and shown the rooms, the story of what happened in each slowly unveiled by visitations from the dead. Each dead visitor had lines to say that told part of the story, and each longed for someone who had died and for whom they were searching, but the nature of their death was part of the mystery.

Francie objected that her character didn't have a place in any of the rooms. They were all sitting in the shade, swatting the bugs. Francie's face was sunburned. She'd been relegated to the open field, where she was to stand, dripping wet, with her baby, and where she'd wait, most afternoons, for her cue. Her glasses slid down her nose.

"Why can't my baby have a nursery?" she asked.

Sadie considered this. She hated for it to be a good idea, to admit this to Francie or to Betty, who'd lately been wondering why they kept up the letter writing.

She claimed she'd gotten bored with Francie's letters, complaining that she was strange, that her family was weird. But Sadie suspected Betty had begun to feel guilty about fooling her, as if Francie had guessed who they were and they might be caught and suffer consequences. The more that Francie confessed (*How I so long for a kindred spirit; I do dream of becoming a famous singer; Even though I lock my bedroom door it is always open in the morning*) or begged Hezekiah to run away with her, the more Betty protested that they should stop. Sadie hadn't told her that she looked forward to the letters, that she'd picked up on a hidden context that intrigued her. For some odd reason she had begun to feel aligned with Francie and her desperate sadness. This was only one of a number of things Sadie kept from her friend that summer, and it bothered her, but not enough to ever confess. She turned to Betty. "Don't you have an old crib?"

Betty looked at her askance. "Yes. But my sister is using it."

Francie said they'd given their crib to the Frobels. Giving away the crib meant that the parents were finished with having children, that their family was complete. Once in a while a family had to get the crib back—like the Gruenbergs, whose children were grown and gone, the crib long ago handed down to some needy relative, when Donnie was suddenly conceived.

"There's one in your basement," Betty said. She bit the inside of her cheek and pretended to be absorbed with the fringe on her jean shorts. Sadie hadn't wanted to bring that up, and Betty knew it. The crib was hidden in the back by the furnace, disassembled and leaning against the cement wall with the mattress. Francie looked at her hopefully. Sadie rolled her eyes.

"I guess," she said. She wasn't sure how to get the crib without anyone seeing. Her mother had been different since her latest hospital visit. Sadie knew it wasn't a change brought on by a new medication. Those altered her mother in other ways. She'd become sleepy and dazed. A new smell would come off her skin. This time she was simply trying to be nicer—baking cookies for Sadie, imploring her to take them with her to share with her friends. Coming into Sadie's room and sitting on the end of her bed at night, reminding her how she used to tell her stories. "Which was your favorite?" she said.

And Sadie, annoyed, mistrustful, told her she didn't remember.

"None of them?" her mother said, as if she should have known her stories would make no lasting impression.

Sadie had just wanted her out of her room, her weight off the end of her bed. She dreaded these confrontations, the way her mother had recently been giving her odd looks, then quickly looking away when Sadie caught her.

"How did you grow up so fast?" her mother had said that morning.

She'd sat at the kitchen table in her matching nightgown and robe, the nylon fabric airy and insubstantial, the sleeves edged with lace. She had a cigarette and a glass of orange juice. Her hair, recently lightened a platinum blond, was held away from her face with a tortoiseshell headband, and without makeup her face was open and childlike, her normally red lips pale and chapped. Sadie noticed her hand holding the cigarette shook, and she looked away, not wanting to feel sorry for her.

"I know you're still mad at me about what happened," her mother said.

Sadie hadn't realized that was the case until just then. Her mother had never attempted to explain her mysterious hospital visits before. Sadie glared at her. "So?" she said. "What do you care?"

"It won't happen again," her mother said. "I've already promised your father."

Sadie didn't think this mattered at all, but as she sat in the pine shade she felt the day had been altered by her mother's promise. The sky outside the screen door had been blue, the air cool and absent of humidity. Bees swarmed the clover in the lawn. "Have fun today," her mother had called, and Sadie, stepping outside onto the porch, let herself imagine she was like any other mother. Taking the crib now seemed wrong.

"I don't know if I can use it," Sadie said.

Betty laughed. "Oh, like your mother is ever going to have any more kids," she said.

"Why don't you ask her?" Francie said.

Sadie glared at them. "I don't know," she said. "Maybe I will."

Francie gave her another pleading look. Betty said she was going home to eat lunch, and she stood and made her way down the path. Usually, Sadie went with her, but today Betty didn't once look back. The other kids had taken off as well. Sadie told Francie she had to go, and Francie got up and followed her out of the pine woods and into Betty's backyard. In two days it would be July 4, the day of the annual lobster bake, and the parents had already begun their own preparations, hauling the long picnic tables to the Donahues' side yard. Some of the kids had gathered around the fathers, who'd been digging the pit. "Stand back," Mr. Donahue said, his shirt wet under the arms. "Back, for God's sake!" The cicadas screamed overhead, their dark bodies and shining wings dotting the leaves, the shrubbery.

"I can help you get the crib if you want," Francie said. "We can sneak it out tonight."

Sadie said she didn't think nighttime would work.

"Early tomorrow then?" Francie said.

Sadie felt drained by her persistence. "We'll see," she said.

It was the same with the letters—Francie insisting that Hezekiah meet her and make good on his promise to flee, and Sadie having trouble coming up with some excuse to avoid it. They parted at the street, and Sadie watched Francie get on her bike and pedal down under the hickories to her house at the bottom of the hill. Betty came to her screen door.

"Is she gone?" she said.

Sadie laughed, and then Betty laughed, and Sadie went inside to make herself a sandwich, the bread and ham and cheese spread all over the counter, and Betty's sisters and brothers stepping up to make a mess with the mustard, dropping crusts of bread on the floor and stepping on them, spilling Hi-C down the sides of their glasses. Sadie and Betty took their food outside to the back deck. Here, under the umbrella, Charlene Donahue sat with her feet up.

"How's your mom doing?" she asked Sadie. Betty's mother wore her red hair in a shag. She wore her usual summer attire: Bermuda shorts, a sleeveless cotton shell, and no makeup—a *regular mother* was how Sadie described her, making Betty roll her eyes. Charlene lowered her dark sunglasses and peered at Sadie over them, and Sadie felt ashamed of all the things Charlene knew about her mother.

"She's fine," Sadie said cautiously.

"I heard the play opened," Betty's mother said. She plopped a bean bag ashtray on the arm of her chair and lit a cigarette.

Sadie knew they were Virginia Slims—Betty stole from her mother, not her father.

Sadie nodded. The play would run for three weeks.

"I can't wait to see it. She's always so good." Betty's mother sighed and smoked the cigarette, staring off at the pasture behind the house. Then she stubbed the cigarette out and pushed herself up. Sadie heard her inside cleaning up the kitchen and wondered what dreams Betty's mother had for herself, if all mothers had them, bottled up beneath their mother exteriors. Betty said that Francie was the most irritating person she'd ever met.

"You know you can't take that crib," she said.

Sadie chewed her food slowly. She nodded. Once, she and Betty had dragged the crib out for one of their games. They'd set it up in the basement themselves, and put their dolls in, and played with it an entire winter afternoon, until Sadie's mother came to the basement stairs to tell Betty her mother had called. Betty had said she'd be right up, but Sadie's mother had come down and noticed the crib. She had walked up to it and put her hands on the railing, standing there a moment staring at the dolls, watching them as if they were alive and wriggling, or rolling over, or doing some other kind of live baby activity—cooing, batting at a rattle. Sadie's mother had even reached her hand in and placed a finger on one of the baby dolls' rubber hands. Sadie had watched her mother's face darken, her smile falter, and then she'd turned toward the stairs where they had retreated, her voice hard with anger.

"I never said you could take this old thing out," she said. "What made you think you could rummage through my things?"

Betty had mumbled something that sounded like an apology and hurried up the stairs. Sadie was left with her mother's rage and accusations, with her insistence that they take the crib apart again, demanding the tool they'd used and stabbing at the screws, until her father came home and found them, took off his suit coat, and under the bare basement bulb took the crib apart himself. Sadie had relayed the story to Betty in school the next day through a rebus letter—half pictures, half letters, their own secret code formed back in fifth grade.

"You don't want your mother to get mad again," Betty said. She glanced at the kitchen window where her own mother stood, washing cups.

Sadie doubted her mother would notice it was missing. "It's because she saw it," she said. "We reminded her." Though of what they reminded her was still unclear, and neither of them mentioned it now.

"I can't believe Francie called us *stuck-up* in that letter," Betty said.

"Who does she think she is?" Sadie said.

And like that, the rift that seemed to be forming between them disappeared.

August 29, 2003

RAY DROVE FOR AN HOUR AND STOPPED AT A MOTEL near the Connecticut shore, a shingled building built low to the ground, surrounded by a salt marsh. The motel was Ray's idea, and Sadie wonders, lying in bed, what other women he has brought here. They have just had sex, yet her body still aches for him. This is the meaning of the word "cleave," she thinks: a bond forged through violence. He props his head up in the semidarkness, his face inches from her mouth.

"Sadie, Sadie," he says. "Your hair is dirty."

"I didn't have time to wash it."

She is sickened by what she has done—betrayed her children, her husband with his happiness and pressed shirts, his careful concern.

Ray drops his head to her breast. He sighs. His hands slide along her body, find a place to settle. He has yet to explain the duffel bag, left in the truck. There was never a plan in place for this, and it didn't even occur to her to pack a bag. They drove mostly in silence—Ray deep in thought, his brow furrowed, and Sadie too afraid to hear the answers to her questions: *What are you running away from? Do I even figure in your plan, or did I stumble in at the wrong time?* She closes her eyes. *If I had come an hour later,* she wants to ask, *would you have even been there?* The motel sheet is starched and cheap. She doesn't know how she will go back, so she refuses to imagine that yet. This, like her

164

escape from her neighborhood earlier, gives her an odd sense of relief. Outside the summer storm has followed them with its heavy skies and thunder.

"I love this," she tells him.

He makes a sound of agreement, a kind of grunt. She isn't sure he understands that she means the weather, that she's leery about admitting she loves the sex. Him.

"I used to run outside in thunderstorms with an umbrella," she says.

"You had those cutoff jean shorts. Skinny legs." His voice is deep and thick, satiated.

"The tar road would have that smell."

She tries not to imagine what is happening without her, but the images surface like those in the View-Master she had as a child—the 3-D scenes falling into place at the click of the button, whole little worlds opening up, ones you could stare into for a long time, so filled with detail you might never see everything. Ray falls asleep. She gets up and puts on her damp skirt and blouse, a decisive action, but now that she stands at the screen door of the motel, she is paralyzed. She watches the rain puddle in the sand and ground shells of the parking lot. If she breathes in deeply she can smell the briny scent of the tidal marsh. It is nearing dinnertime. Other women will have come down the path, and she imagines Max and Sylvia swallowed up in the confusion of their children, all of them vying for an ice cream cup, the women settling into chairs around the kitchen table. They will have just beaten the rain, and maybe a handful will have gotten caught up in it, emerging from the woods to dash across the Currys' wet lawn.

Kate will make them the tequila sunrises she made for Sadie, Maura, and Jane earlier. She wishes, for a moment, that she could be there with the neighborhood women, sipping her drink, listening to the talk. Max would tug her arm and tell her he had to use the bathroom. She feels a small, dull ache. Your sister will help you, she'd say. Go get Sylvia. For every little thing that Sadie does for her children she can easily come up with someone else who might do it for them. She suspects she is entirely replaceable. It is as if, after having given birth and nursed them, her use has ended. When she tries to picture returning to the scene she has left, she cannot. There is no place for her.

Sadie knows Kate will give her a reasonable amount of time to have completed her errand. Maybe they didn't carry saffron at Shaw's, she'll think. Maybe she had to go into the next town to the A & P. She will call Sadie's house, letting the phone ring and ring. Once the storm passes she'll take the children by the hand and walk them over. She'll peer into the front bay window and try the door, which is wide open. Sadie feels her heart sink, imagining Kate stepping inside, seeing the laundry heaped on the couch—sundresses and shorts, T-shirts and pajamas, Craig's boxers, undershirts, and socks. There is the dust on the cherry tables, toys scattered on the floor. Kate will see the house is empty and take the children back to hers.

"Who wants macaroni and cheese?" she'll say.

Max will sit dejected on the den couch. "I want ice cream."

"Maybe ice cream after dinner," Sylvia will say. Sadie realizes that Sylvia will sense something is amiss, that she needs to step in and play her role. She'll sit down beside Max and take his hand in hers. Max will swat her hand away. Sylvia won't be deterred, and she'll take his hand again.

"Who wants to play upside-down house after we eat?" she'll say. She'll raise her hand in the air, and Max will look at her glumly, then raise his hand, too.

Kate will prepare macaroni and cheese, which Sadie knows Max will not eat. He will refuse to take a bite, until Sylvia says, "No game . . . ," in her sweet, high voice, and he will relent. Afterward, the children will ask Kate for a hand mirror, and they will walk around her house side by side looking down into it, pretending they are walking on the ceiling. Sadie doesn't know what Kate will think of her children and the odd game Sadie taught them. She'll continue to call Sadie's until Craig answers, home from work. She'll speak to him in hushed tones on the phone. Then, Sadie thinks, his footsteps will sound on her slate walk, a metallic ring of his shoe soles on the slate. He will yank on the screen door, scrape his feet on the mat. Kate will hand over the children to Craig, who will stand there in the foyer clutching their hands, his eyes lost and dark, as if to say, *What now?*

Sadie can see his baffled expression. She knows Kate Curry will not be able to rush him out the door. His eyes will beseech her.

"Do you have family you can call?" she'll ask him.

The streetlights will come on, buzzing to life with their pale violet beams. Someone will be mowing a lawn; a group of children will play in the twilight, catching fireflies. Max will squirm at the end of his father's hand. Sylvia's eyes will be wide with the knowledge that something is wrong, that her father, commander of the household, keeper of checks and balances, bedtime despot, is at a loss.

Craig will shake his head. "No one locally."

"Sadie's family?"

Craig will do a short shake, almost irritated. "No."

"Grandpa is in Brightview," Sylvia will say. "It's assistant living."

Kate and Craig will both glance at her, surprised.

"Grandma died a long time ago," she'll say quietly, awkward now that their eyes are on her. "She lives with the elves and fairies now."

"Now, don't you worry about anything," Craig will tell her. "We'll go home and get ready for bed and wait for Mommy."

Max will look up at his father. "Is she having another baby? Will this one come home with us?"

Craig's face will darken with an emotion that even as a product of her imagination Sadie cannot decipher. He will tug on the children's hands and turn toward the door without any reply. Sylvia will cast a longing look back at Kate. As Sadie stands by the screen door of the motel, her heart feels tight.

She hopes that Kate will offer to help put them to bed, that maybe she will offer to let them stay with her. She doesn't want Sylvia or Max to cry. She can see Craig refusing out of annoyance or pride, pushing open the screen and moving down the front steps and the walkway, tugging the children along, before he stops and turns, his face white.

"I'd appreciate your help," he'll say stiffly.

At Sadie's house, Kate will try not to notice the evidence of Sadie's despair. She'll take the children up the carpeted stairs. The bathtub she'll run water into will have a ring of grime. Sylvia will bring Max pajamas that look as if she has picked them up off the floor. The children are unused to someone else preparing them for bed, and they will be quiet, compliant.

"I take a shower, not a bath," Sylvia will tell Kate, who will have bundled Max up in a towel and then helped him with his pajamas and brushed his hair with her father's old hairbrush. Sadie will remember that Max's bed is unmade, but Kate will fluff the pillow, reshape and turn down the sheets on one side. She will have agreed to read as many books to him as he'd like. It is a warm night, and he will wear little cotton pajamas comprised of shorts and a T-shirt decorated with pictures of a cartoon character Kate won't recognize. Sadie knows the room is in disarray, and she wishes she had tidied it up for him the way he likes it: deposited the toys in the old wooden box, lined up others just so on the shelves—a model car, an airplane, small plastic army men. Instead, she's been spending her free time sitting alone on the back deck with a drink, talking on the phone, dreaming of a man who is not their father. Sadie is overcome, suddenly, with regret like a flush, a warm dousing. Max will have chosen a stack of books and will be sitting on his bed, waiting. On his face will be an expression of watchfulness.

"Where is Sylvie?" he'll say. His eyes will shine in the light from the bedside lamp. Sadie closes her eyes, opens them. She attempts to compose herself. If she could she would fly back to Max's room, to its neglect, its boy smell, its bedside lamp in the shape of a baseball bat and glove, the books—*Mike Mulligan and His Steam Shovel, Caps for Sale*. Sadie never needs to read the words—these are books she can recite—but even if Kate remembers reading them to her own son, she will have to squint in the dim light to see the print, and she will get some of it wrong, and skip pages in an effort to finish quicker.

Kate will offer to help Sylvia, her face in the dim hallway pale, fringed with her dark hair, but Sylvia will have dreamed up some fairy tale to make sense of the evening's strangeness, casting Kate Curry as a witch. She'll remember some version with the children's victorious escape. Sadie hopes she will block out all the rest—the awful captivity, the fear of the oven, the old woman's transformation into a hobbling creature with warts and vile breath and long arthritic fingers, her bunions pressing against the leather of her outdated shoes. Sylvia will shut the bathroom door and turn the lock.

Sadie imagines the dark hallway, the soft carpet, her husband downstairs calling the authorities. Kate will know by now what she has suspected for hours—that Sadie's need for saffron was a ruse. There isn't a recipe set out on the kitchen counter. Sadie wonders if Kate will tell the police this when they come, if they will ask her only what Sadie said or if they will solicit her opinion. Kate must know Sadie has gone somewhere in secret, a place where she does not wish to be discovered, that she has for some time neglected the life she once lived and has surreptitiously forged an idea of another. She can tell this from the collected dust, the fingerprints on the storm door, the sink filled with plates from breakfast and lunch, the crumbs on the counters.

Ray turns on the bed behind her. Sadie hears him ease himself into a sitting position. She feels the cool rain through the screen.

"Why are you by the door?" Ray says. His voice is thick with sleep, confused.

"I like the rain."

"You look like you're going to leave."

Sadie breathes in the smell of the oil paint on the door frame. The sky is pale, the rain slowing. "I'm hungry," she says.

She hears him move on the bed and then he is standing behind her, his body pressed against hers. He places his face in her hair and sighs, runs his hands down her arms.

"Don't don't don't don't ever leave," he says softly.

He encircles her with his arms and she falls back against him. It is easy to give in, to pretend whatever he wants her to, be whoever he wants.

"Lobster," she says. "Let's get lobster at Cherrystones."

This was her mother's favorite meal, her favorite restaurant at the shore. Ray laughs into her hair and spins her around. There is a moment when their eyes meet—brief, fleeting—and Sadie sees something like disappointment, as if he believed he was holding someone else, someone just like her. But it is there and then gone, so brief that she cannot be entirely sure. She watches him pick up his clothes from the motel room floor and dress. She stays by the door. The rain has stopped, but the awnings drip and the air blows into the room, cool and clean.

That long-ago summer is suddenly here, in sharp relief. It has been worrying the edges of her consciousness for weeks—a fleeting, amorphous presence—and now it has arrived, fully formed. Sadie realizes she has been seduced by Ray, by his let-

ters, by her own desire to find out who she really is. With Ray
she is becoming someone other—a new person, transformed.

He grabs the key and stands by the scarred bureau.

"Ready?" he says.

Sadie pushes open the screen door and steps outside, and
lets it bang shut behind her. She feels his eyes on her as she
walks to the truck. She feels the sway of her hips and brushes
her hair back from her forehead. She knows she's been playing a character, but now she suspects that character is her
mother. As she climbs into the truck, she wants to laugh. This
is a new script.

Ray backs out of the motel lot. The shells grind under the
tires. The seagulls swoop into the puddles. Sadie flips down
the visor mirror.

"I look messy," she says. She tries to brush her hair with
her fingers, then she pulls it all back into a ponytail. No matter what she does the face in the small square mirror is her
mother's—the way her eyebrows are positioned over her eyes;
the eyes themselves, having taken on the foggy, dazed look
of a harried housewife. She wonders when that happened, if
Ray's nearness has prompted this alchemy.

"There you go," Ray says as she secures her hair back. He
glances at her as he drives, maybe worried she is thinking of a
way to get home, coming up with an excuse to explain where
she's been.

"He's going to worry," she says.

They have never discussed Craig, as if Ray assumes he
knows all he needs to know about him.

"The husband returning from work," Ray says now. He
laughs softly. "Pulling his fancy car into the garage and wondering why dinner isn't ready. What's he drive, Cadillac?
Benz?"

Sadie offers a flat smile. Ray imagines him in a pressed suit,
a man unflappable and assured of his wife's love. The man

he pictures is one from their childhood sitcoms—the kind who takes out his cigarettes after a meal, who pours himself highballs from a glass decanter and has a casual method of whistling, as if he was once a boy who walked along split-rail fences or delivered newspapers on his bike with his dog running beside him. Sadie knows Ray doesn't think about her children. To him they are just a girl with wise, knowing eyes, threading daisies. A boy's round head in his car seat. Sadie is grateful she can keep these two lives—the one with Craig and the children, the one with Ray—separate. She didn't imagine herself beyond the bedroom of the old Filley house, but now that they've left she feels the space between who she was and who she is widen with the distance.

He reaches over and puts his hand on her thigh. They have time, she thinks, before anyone comes looking. They will have this night, and then a discussion of where to go next. Time to plan it out. Sadie knows he relishes the secrecy, the hiding. It excites him to imagine having her to himself in the motel room. Sadie thinks he will ask her to say some lines from the play, and she will pose in the room for him, both of them pretending they've left nothing behind. She remembers Ray and her mother running through lines together at the Filleys' pool that summer. Her mother was always a flirt. Sadie would notice her with men at cocktail parties at their house—leaning up close to them, whispering in their ears.

They pass the Italian place and he suggests they eat there.

"No," she says. "It has to be Cherrystones."

He laughs and glances at her. Sadie finds herself giggling too and she cannot stop. The two of them, laughing, their eyes wet, pull into the Cherrystones parking lot. Next door is the driving range, two boys sharing a bucket of balls. The sun has just set over the salt marsh, and the air is cool. They get out of the truck and Sadie feels once again the approach of fall, sees it in the color of the marsh, the way the birds wing overhead.

She sits in the truck, laughing and crying. Ray glances at her, and she wonders, suddenly, if Ray and her mother actually spent time alone together, what her mother was like with him. Ray was just a teenager—but one her mother might have led on, enjoying the attention. The light continues to deepen over the marsh—pale violet now, with streaks of an orange the color of sherbet. She hears her own heartrending laughter and they sit in the truck a moment, until she catches her breath. She wipes her tears out from under her eyes.

"I need a drink," she says into the car's quiet interior.

"Let's get you a drink," Ray says. "Let's get you that lobster." He opens the truck door and Sadie hears its metal scrape. The seat springs groan. He tells Sadie he's gotten used to the sounds of the old truck, that he even imagines his father hearing the same things and staring out of the same splattered windshield and feels close to him because of it.

"You're more generous toward him," Sadie said. "Now that he's gone."

"Since I found the bottles," he says.

Ray steps around the truck to open Sadie's door and tells her he hated his father more for giving up the drinking than the drinking itself. "He was so righteous when he quit," he said. "At least when he drank he could be pitied. We could see he felt guilty for being a bastard, and he was smothering his guilt with drink."

Ray said it was as if when the drinking stopped the guilt disappeared as well. "He was still a bastard then, just sober. Always telling us what to do and how to do it. Faulting us for the slightest mistake."

Finding his father's bottles, hidden in the linen closet, tucked inside a crocheted tissue caddie, was like uncovering the man's weaknesses, bit by bit. Ray tells her he found the first bottle and went on a search of the house, digging through cabinets and bureaus, even under loose floorboards.

"I found fifteen bottles in all," he says, explaining that the old man must have forgotten where he'd hidden one and bought another, evidence of years of covert drinking.

"And that makes you happy?" Sadie says skeptically.

Ray stands beside her, his face bright with vindication. "Yeah," he says. "It was pretty pathetic. I found a bottle in a bag of birdseed."

"Did he put any in the hidey spot?" Sadie asks. She remembers his angry phone conversation with Beth at the old house.

Ray's face clouds and he stares at her with a dark look like the one he gave her in the bedroom. "No," he says, shutting down the conversation, taking her hand. They walk across the parking lot to the restaurant, strangely somber.

As a child Sadie's parents would bring her to Cherrystones for dinner when they vacationed at the shore. They would come in and sit at their regular booth, and her father would have the cook make her mother a special lobster thermidor, and Sadie would have a club sandwich. She'd sit quietly while her parents drank martinis, and her mother would begin to criticize her father for something he'd done or said that day. These arguments would be conducted in soft, conversational tones—unlike those at home—and only Sadie, small and unable to leave, would witness the escalating anger, the biting remarks that could never be taken back.

The restaurant is much as Sadie remembers from her childhood: smoky bar, dark wooden booths, shuttered windows. Everything is varnished, like the deck of a ship. The light fixtures are lanterns hung by coiled ropes. Ray leans in close to her ear. "Shiver me timbers," he whispers. His lips brush her neck. There is no hostess to seat them, and they wander into the dark looking for a table. The bar has a television, the noise of drunken sunburned vacationers. Sadie tugs Ray into the dining room. Here there are tables and booths, mostly empty. A family is at one long table, and they barely glance up at Sadie and Ray. The waitress ambles past, her arms filled with baskets of fried clams.

"Sit anywhere," she says. "It's just me tonight."

Her voice is careful and low, a calm, almost musical sound. She wears jeans, a T-shirt. Her belly is swollen with child. The arm holding the tray is a tattoo sleeve: deep-pink-petaled flowers, a swirl of green stems and leaves. Sadie feels an awful yearning. She and Ray slide into a back booth. It is so dim, and the booth so wide, that they could lie down together on the bench. When she is with Ray, every place is an opportunity to have sex. She turns to him, playfully trying to squelch her sadness, and pushes him back. He laughs and shakes his head. "Oh no you don't," he says.

The waitress appears, tugging down her T-shirt. She wears her jeans below the mound of her stomach, and a strip of skin shows. "I'm Emma," she says in her music-box voice. She looks at them. She has wavy red hair, blue eyes. Her mouth is a half-smile. Sadie remembers only too well the tranquilizing effects of pregnancy, the way her body made the rest of the world seem under a gauzy haze. She envies the girl and her beautiful skin, her baby. She looks at her and smiles, one that feels false and stiff on her face.

"When are you due?" she asks.

Emma puts her hand on her stomach as if for confirmation. "She'll be here October eighth," she says. "Do you need menus?"

Ray is staring at Sadie, and Sadie stares back. "Menu?" she asks him.

He nods and Emma turns to retrieve two large sheets of what looks like parchment, covered in plastic. The edges are burned, like a treasure map Sadie made once in fourth grade. The restaurant is quiet—the family at the long table is busy eating. The restaurant smells of spilled clam broth, of Old Bay seasoning. She realizes she has never brought her children here, and she feels something like terror at what she is doing. She imagines Craig appearing in the doorway. What expression would he wear? Disappointment? Fury? Sorrow? She has no idea, and this is more frightening than the idea of being discovered by him.

"I'd like a Bloody Mary," Sadie says.

Emma nods. She leans against the booth and crosses her arms. *And you?* her look says. Ray orders a beer. She leaves them to get their drinks.

"We don't need the menus," Sadie tells him.

She can't be bothered to look it over. His nearness, their situation, distracts her. They sit side by side. She thinks it odd that she can know his body intimately and yet find everything else about him still a mystery.

"What do you think Beth did when she found you weren't at the house?" Sadie says now. "Would she have waited for you to get back?"

Ray makes a face. "Oh, I'm not going back. And she knows exactly why."

Sadie's skirt and blouse are still damp. The restaurant's air-conditioning is cold. And yet she doesn't think these things cause the chill she feels. She stares at him as if she hasn't heard him correctly, and he turns to her, his expression blank, difficult to construe.

"I mean, what did she think for the last seventeen years?"

"Ray," she says.

"Yes, Sadie."

"Where do you plan to go if you're not going back?"

"You mean where do *we* plan to go?" He leans in and kisses her, slowly, and then pulls away. He keeps his face close to hers and grins, boyish and silly.

Sadie wonders what he is giving up to be with her. Nothing. He is giving up nothing at all. She ignores his suggestion that they are running off together. *They* are not running off together. The only clothes she has are the ones she's wearing. But it is getting later and later, and soon it will be too late to go back. She imagines being ousted from her old life, a reviled imposter. As with most things unseemly she will go unmentioned, disappear like she was never there. They are all tethered to their houses, the rooms and the people inside calling them back with needs to be met. Somehow, Sadie thinks, she has cut her own tether. She thinks of Craig's smiles, his soft, shaved cheeks, his persistence. All those years ago she loved that he loved her without knowing very much about her, assuming he knew all he needed to. Even as she is thinking about leaving him, Sadie is aware that she loves him still.

Emma brings their drinks and they order food, too much for two people to eat. Sadie recalls doing this as a teenager—she and her friends scrambling into booths at the Farm Shop restaurant, ordering specialty cheeseburgers called Golden Abigails, fries and onion rings, sundaes and milkshakes. The food made them happy, like a drug. Now she orders chowder and lobster, the club sandwich the restaurant still offers. Ray orders fried clams and fries. They will share it all, they tell Emma, who smiles her little smile and nods. She doesn't write any of it down. She gives them a slightly suspicious look, as if they are children who will dine and dash and leave her with the tab.

"Don't worry," Sadie tells her. "We're responsible restaurant patrons."

She sucks her drink through a straw and chews on the celery. Ray puts his cold mouth on hers and they kiss. She tries not to see herself as she looks now, giddy, making out in a restaurant, the kind of woman she would normally despise and talk about. It is a relief to be the type of woman she despises, a woman like her mother. She sees that it is so much harder to be the other.

"I feel like I could just burst," she tells him.

Ray grins and kisses her again. He is all intensity and focus. Sadie feels he has closed out the rest of the world for her.

Other patrons enter the dining room. Two couples, the women in sundresses, the men in polo shirts; another older couple and a young girl that Sadie imagines is a granddaughter or a niece; and an older woman who seats herself at a small table near them. She has on a peach-colored sleeveless blouse. Her shoulders are tan and strong for a woman her age. She wears her white hair back in a chignon. Sadie looks at her, and cannot stop looking. She is someone she knows. Sadie cannot place her—not a woman from Gladwyn Hollow, not a Tunxis Player. She feels light-headed with the threat of being recognized. One of the children's teachers? A historical society member? She doesn't want Ray to see. But he is busy cracking the lobster claws and pulling out the meat. The table is littered with the bright remains of the lobster shell. He dips the meat into the butter and holds it up for her and Sadie opens her mouth. The older woman orders a drink from Emma. Sadie can hear her voice, low and authoritative.

"A Manhattan, please," she says.

Sadie thinks if this were the era in which women wore gloves this woman would have now taken the opportunity to remove them, tugging at the fingers of each hand, setting them inside her old-fashioned purse. And in a flash she knows who it is. She remembers the letters: *My darling Bea, you must never forget me.* She remembers a fall day filled with the scent of swirling leaves and car exhaust, and she feels her stomach drop the way it did on the Ferris wheel as a child. Ray leans over to kiss her and she is suddenly wary. What will Mrs. Sidelman think of her? She pulls away, just a bit. Ray freezes.

"What?" he says.

Sadie sees him take in the dining room, lighting on each of the guests, looking for the source of her refusal.

"Nothing," she says. She kisses him lightly on his mouth. His lips taste of butter, the tartar sauce that came with the clams. "It's nothing."

But Ray has seen Mrs. Sidelman. He slinks down into the booth as if he is hiding.

"You've got to be shitting me," he says. "It's that old bitch from the neighborhood."

Sadie shushes him. "Mrs. Sidelman," she says.

Then Ray reaches out and takes Sadie's face in his hands. His eyes are haunted and mournful. She cannot imagine what has come over him.

"It's just Mrs. Sidelman," she says softly, reassuring him. "She's harmless."

But between them is now a widening painful silence, into which pour their respective memories. *Summer 1979.*

"It's nothing to do with us," Sadie says. "Don't think about it."

The food is unappetizing now, the mess of the table an embarrassment. Sadie's head is foggy from the drink. Emma comes by and removes some of the plates and asks them if they'd like another round. Ray says yes. He has his chin in his hand. Every so often he peers around Sadie to look at Mrs. Sidelman. Sadie dreads glancing her way. She won't do it.

"We should go," she whispers.

"Why are you whispering?" Ray asks.

The dining room is fuller now; the voices of the patrons rise and fall, a regular din.

"She can't know who we are, can she?" she says. "It's been too long."

"She must be ancient," Ray says. He is fiddling with his fries, stacking them up in a small pile in the plastic basket. When his beer arrives he gulps it down. Emma pours out water from a pitcher, her arm rising over them, languid and colorful.

"Have you picked out a name?" Sadie asks her.

Despite the waiting customers, the orders she must be tallying in her head, she smiles and leans against the back of the booth. "Cecilia," she says. "From Frances Burney."

Emma places her hand on her stomach. Her T-shirt rides up and Sadie can see a bright blue vein under the pale skin. Beside her Ray sings, *"Cecilia, you're breaking my heart / You're shaking my confidence daily / Oh, Cecilia, I'm down on my knees / I'm begging you please to come home / Come on home."*

Sadie stares at him in surprise. His ability to sing is another thing she's forgotten about him.

"Simon and Garfunkel," he says.

Emma laughs, a sound more melodious than her speaking voice. "You're good."

And then Mrs. Sidelman leans toward them. "Burney was a brilliant satirist," she says. "Cecilia was an heiress who could only keep her money if a man agreed to marry her and take her name."

Emma turns and smiles at Mrs. Sidelman. "That's it exactly," she says.

Sadie feels she should announce herself now. I'm Sadie Watkins, she could say. She might invite Mrs. Sidelman to sit with them. But she says nothing. Emma looks at them, then back at Mrs. Sidelman.

"Check?" Ray says, his voice low, a mumble.

Emma saunters off, slowly, slowly, as if she is walking through a field or easing herself into cold water. Sadie worries that Mrs. Sidelman will continue to speak, but she has turned to her drink and seems to be absorbed in thought. She remembers Mrs. Sidelman's house, the shelves filled with books, the carefully placed vases and crystal on the sideboard, the painting of the woman whose eyes bored into you like an accusation. She was a retired teacher. Her family helped found the public library, and she wrote arts reviews for the newspaper. Sadie remembers her mother standing on the back deck with her drink, watching Mrs. Sidelman in her backyard with slit eyes after the woman had reviewed *The Glass Menagerie.*

"Clare, don't be such a bad sport," Sadie's father said. He was sitting at the patio table with the paper. The grill smoked, and every so often he folded the paper and got up and checked the steaks.

"Everyone else said that my Laura was brilliant. What's wrong with her?"

"She has to say something interesting. Reviewers like to rile things up. What do you care?"

"I hate the way she fiddles with everything over there. Look at her plucking up weeds with those veiny hands. Look at her flat ass and her old-fashioned shorts. She hasn't had sex in years."

"It's just the *Hartford Times.*"

"What are you saying? *Just* the *Hartford Times*?"

"I'm not saying anything." Sadie's father sighed and folded the paper and lifted the grill lid. Smoke billowed up, the smell of burning fat.

"You mean it's not the *New York Times.* You mean it's nothing," her mother said softly, almost petulantly.

Sadie was in her bedroom above the porch, listening through her window. She heard her father shush her mother. She pressed her face to the screen and looked down and saw that her mother had climbed into her father's lap, and he was smoothing her hair.

Emma takes her time coming back with the check. She's busy, they can see that. She brings Mrs. Sidelman a bowl of chowder and then she leans over Sadie and tucks the check under Ray's plate. Ray doesn't even look at it. He has the money in his hand, ready to go. Sadie feels as if their time together has been spoiled by Mrs. Sidelman, even though the woman hasn't acknowledged them.

"God, I hated that woman," Ray says. "Didn't you?"

Sadie isn't sure why Ray feels this way. Mrs. Sidelman would let Sadie play with her old reading textbooks, with the workbooks and the dittos left over from her days as a teacher. Sadie had a pretend school and taught the younger neighborhood children how to read, sitting in rows on Mrs. Sidelman's picnic table benches. Sadie's mother would catch her over there and make her come home, sometimes sending her to her room with no explanation.

"I did hate her," Sadie says quietly, remembering her mother's irrational punishment. She is angry and sad and doesn't understand why.

Ray tells Emma to keep the change, and she smiles her mysterious smile and thanks him with her jingle-jangle voice and moves away. Sadie begins to slide from the booth, but Ray takes her face in his hands and brings his mouth to hers in a slow, luxurious kiss, as if she is some exotic food he craves. And suddenly she could stay there in the booth forever, kissing with Mrs. Sidelman's eyes on her, imagining her mother watching as well. *Look at me,* she wants to say. *Look, look, look at me.*

July 2, 1979

AFTER LUNCH AT BETTY'S THEY COMPOSED THEIR last letter to Francie. They went back out into the pasture to work on the Haunted Woods sets—positioning items in the various rooms, smearing more fake blood. Francie returned, smelling of the Noxzema her mother must have awakened long enough to spread on her sunburn.

"I'm not allowed in the sun," she said. She stood in the shade, stubborn and somewhat forlorn. Sadie tried not to feel sorry for her. Late that afternoon one of Ray's dogs appeared, sniffing around the kitchen and the empty pots and pans.

"Shoo," Francie said. "Shoo!"

Ray himself appeared in the open field, the other dog by his side. He stood there for a moment, watching them. Francie seemed to disappear behind a pine, while the other kids looked at him and then looked to Sadie. Ray came up to the living room set. He scratched his stomach under his shirt and glanced at the headless dummy, positioned in a folding aluminum lounge chair covered with a quilt. They'd made a television out of a square of plywood, and Sadie had painted a scene of invading aliens, their silver saucers marking a night sky.

"What's all of this? Dear old Dad's lost his head?" Ray said. He wore his tennis shoes and a pair of seersucker shorts. His hair had grown long, lightened from the sun. He glanced at Sadie and then pretended not to notice her.

Sadie hated the way he mocked them, and she hated that

183

she was in a position to be mocked. She turned to Betty. "Let's go," she said quietly.

"Games all over for today?" he said. Sadie felt her heart step up, but she said nothing. Ray walked along the path to the next set and picked up the candelabra. This time he looked directly at Sadie, as if he knew this was all her doing.

"You have candles out here?" Ray said. "You know that's a fire hazard."

"We'll be ever so careful," Francie said, stepping out suddenly from behind her tree.

Sadie wished she had never allowed her to be part of this.

"Please, don't ruin the show," Francie said. She had her hands together, pleading.

Ray looked at her, amused. "Who are you?"

Francie seemed surprised at his question. Sadie held her breath, waiting for the revelation. She suspected then that she'd made Hezekiah too much like Ray. Francie bit the inside of her cheek and got a sly look, as if she was going to play along with his pretense of not knowing her.

"I'm Francie," she said. "Francie Bingham."

"Bingham?" Ray said. He smiled. "So, my father says that your father whittled your two little brothers in the basement."

Betty glanced at Sadie and put her hand over her mouth to stifle a laugh. Sadie watched Francie's expression flatten out to become no expression at all. "That's not very nice," she said.

Ray ignored her and began to walk up the path, perusing the rooms.

"Look at all of this," he said, marveling.

He turned to them with what seemed like a new appreciation. But then he narrowed his eyes at them.

"You'll need to get all of this junk off our property when you're done," he said. He shook his head and laughed softly.

He left the woods and went back across the open field.

They could hear him singing, his voice carrying over the trees. *"Your everlasting summer / You can see it fading fast / So you grab a piece of something / That you think is gonna last, / You wouldn't know a diamond / If you held it in your hand, / The things you think are precious / I can't understand."*

"What's he singing?" Betty said.

"How should I know?" Sadie said.

"It's Steely Dan," Francie said. " 'Reelin' in the Years'?"

Betty exchanged a glance with Sadie. "How do *you* know?"

Francie smirked. "I listen to the radio?"

She stepped past them with her Noxzema smell. "I have to go home now." She stopped a little ways up the path and turned. "If you want me to help you with the crib, I will."

"I don't have the crib anymore," Sadie said.

"We looked this afternoon and it's gone," Betty said.

Francie paused, as if she doubted them.

"You'll have to find one somewhere else," Sadie said. They watched her leave the path. They knew where she was going, through the field to the dead end to find the letter they'd left.

Dear Francie,

The time has come for us to escape. I can barely contain my happiness. Can you meet me just before midnight on the 4th? Take the path through your Haunted Woods, across the pasture. Through the woods on the other side is the pond. I feel it is only appropriate we meet at the place where your character, Emely Filley, met her fate. I'm enclosing a token of our bond. I will look for your letter of confirmation.

Hezekiah

They'd enclosed a bracelet they'd made—tiny multi-colored beads strung on elastic. Betty was satisfied that this would be the end of the letter writing, and Sadie had talked her into inviting her to spend the night on the fourth, so that the two of them could sneak out to hide in the woods and watch for Francie.

The next day they returned to the pasture midmorning to discover a battered-looking crib set up in a section of the woods along the path. Francie was there, her eyes swollen from her sunburn. She'd had the boys trample down the spot she'd chosen, and she'd decorated the area with cast-off children's toys that Betty recognized from her own garage. Francie explained that she'd gotten the crib from the Battinsons, that Betty's mother had given her the toys that morning. Jimmy Frobel announced that they were out of fake blood, that someone needed to go to Drug City to replenish it.

Francie came up to them in a huff. She had a bucket in her hand, and she pointed out an empty pack of Parliament cigarettes and three cans of Schaefer beer. "I found these," she said. "Someone was hanging out here last night."

Sadie looked into the bucket. She knew that Francie believed Ray was Hezekiah, and she wanted to separate herself from the Haunted Woods, from childish things. She wanted the upper hand. "Oh," she said. She glanced at Betty. "I thought you said you picked them all up."

Francie's eyes widened.

"Sorry about that," Betty said. "Guess I didn't see them all in the dark."

Sadie tried not to laugh. "You won't tell on us, will you?"

Francie's mouth tightened. Sadie put her hands on her hips and turned to Betty.

"Let's find a ride to the center," she said.

They left Francie in the woods. They planned to check the dead end for her reply letter, but Mrs. Donahue was heading into Shaw's Supermarket and offered to drop them off at Drug City. On the way there, past the roadside grasses, beneath the overhang of old trees, Charlene Donahue chatted about the lobster bake. "Can you believe it's tomorrow?"

She would pick up corn at Filley's stand.

"What games would you girls like to play?" she said. "What about the ring toss? Or the egg relay?"

Betty looked to Sadie in the backseat. Sadie rolled her eyes. Mrs. Donahue must have been looking back at her in the rearview mirror. She grew quiet, and Sadie felt a rush of guilt. Mrs. Donahue had provided for her numerous times—a bed and meals, sometimes even clothes, a lunch for school. From Betty's mother, Sadie learned how mothers were supposed to be.

"What about the sack race?" Betty said cheerfully.

Mrs. Donahue sighed. "I know you girls are older now," she said. "But it would be fun for the others."

Sadie agreed. She tried to sound sincere, but she'd lost her enthusiasm for an event that was so clearly designed for the adults, with lobsters steamed over an open pit, the redwood tables stretched end to end, the table of Beefeater and Smirnoff and Chivas, the ice in the bucket—all reserved for their parents, and only a few games halfheartedly set up for the children, and hamburgers and hot dogs thrown on the grill as an afterthought, charred by a drunken cook, so that even as an adult Sadie would still associate the taste of burned hamburger with the annual summer event. The parents regaled and drank around the fire, and the children were let loose in the neighborhood after dark, pedaling their bicycles up and down the street, wondering when to go to bed.

"The sack race is fun," Sadie said.

Charlene said she thought Mr. Frobel still had the burlap sacks in his shed, and Sadie's father had gone down to the shore today for the lobster. "Girls, it's going to be so much fun this year," she said.

And Sadie chimed in to say what she was expected to say and not what she was thinking, which was easier than hurting anyone's, especially Charlene Donahue's, feelings.

The town center was simply a crossroads that had grown to include—along with the library, the town green, and the Congregational church—a new outdoor mall composed of a maze of sidewalks and shops. That day it was overtaken by young people, who carved their names into the benches by the large fountain and chased each other around with plastic cups of water. Betty's mother dropped them off at the drugstore and said she'd be back after she did the grocery shopping. The kids by the fountain were from their class at school, but Sadie felt instantly leery. She paused in front of Drug City and watched the way the boys grabbed the girls around the waist, the way the girls laughed and slapped at the boys' arms. It seemed as if a glass wall separated her from them. Betty waved, but Sadie said she didn't like gangs of *children,* and Betty agreed she didn't want to get wet, so they steered clear of them. They went into Drug City, down the cool linoleum aisles, looking for the fake blood. Sadie eyed the lip gloss, the dangling earrings on display. After, they paced the sidewalk near the parking lot, waiting for Betty's mother to pick them up. A car idled alongside them and the driver called out.

"You girls need a ride?" he said.

Sadie felt Betty stiffen and grab her arm. The car was an older-model Mustang in need of a paint job. The driver was fair haired and blue eyed, his pointed chin covered with a patch of blond scruff. The car's passenger leaned over him and called out, too.

"You sure look like you need a ride," he said.

The radio played the Guess Who's "No Sugar Tonight." Sadie stopped walking and bent over at the waist to see inside the car. The boy in the passenger seat had long brown hair. He wore tinted aviator glasses.

"We have a ride," she said. "But thank you anyway."

The boys smiled at her, and the car stopped.

"Are you sure?" the driver said. "What's your name, little girl?"

Betty grabbed at the back of Sadie's shirt, but Sadie laughed, confident that no real kidnapper would use this classic kidnapper's line. She stepped off the curb and went up to the driver's window. She leaned on the car door and smelled the Christmas tree air freshener hanging from the radio dial.

"I'm Sadie," she said.

"Sadie Mae," the passenger said in a singsongy voice. "I'm Rob. This is Mack."

Sadie asked them what they were doing, and Mack told her they were driving around. A pack of Winstons sat on the dash. Sadie bummed a cigarette and asked Betty if she wanted one. Betty stood back on the sidewalk.

"Yeah, Betty, you're welcome to a cigarette," Mack called to her. He held the pack out the window and shook it.

"Sadie, my mom will be right back," Betty said.

"We have time," Sadie said. She bent down to the boy's match. She heard the music coming out of the old car radio, the shrieks of the kids near the fountain.

"You aren't playing with your friends?" Rob said, nodding toward the fountain where the kids still chased each other around.

"Those aren't my friends," Sadie said. She realized as she said it that this was true. She sat beside them in class, at the same table in lunch; she traded papers to grade when the teacher demanded it, paired up with them during gym. But they knew nothing about her, and if they'd been curious to learn who she really was, she'd have had nothing she'd have been willing to tell them.

She heard Rob laugh in the car. "I was kidding," he said. And then his voice changed, seemed to deepen with genuine interest.

"Why don't you ride around with us?" he said.

The song ended, and the eight-track tape clicked and whirred. Sadie smoked her cigarette and smiled. "Not today," she said. "Sorry."

"Too bad," Mack said, and he put the car in gear and drove off. Sadie watched the car's taillights, watched the boys turn out of the parking lot, and she wondered where they might go, and she envied the girls they'd find who'd go with them. Betty insisted Sadie chew gum before she got into her mother's car, so they went back into Drug City, where Sadie slipped a tangerine lip gloss into her shorts pocket while Betty paid for the gum at the counter.

August 29, 2003

I N THE CHERRYSTONES PARKING LOT SADIE KNOWS SHE is drunk. She hasn't allowed herself to be drunk in years. There are always children waiting at home with a babysitter, dishes to pick up and wash before bed, an early morning with Max and Sylvia asking for breakfast—their tiny voices crying out, *"Belgian waffles!"*—needing their hair brushed, clothes picked out. Their needs, the elaborate waffle-making preparations, all require a clear head. But mostly, she has never wanted to be like her own mother, a woman who awoke with a hand pressed to her forehead, who vomited and returned to her own sour-smelling sheets to sleep well past midday. "Mommy's head is splitting," she'd say, one of those phrases—like *tear the heart out of you*—that made Sadie fearful as a child. She considers turning to Ray and telling him what her mother was really like, but she does not.

The asphalt, cracked and threaded with small weeds, rises up at odd angles. She is wearing sandals she kicks off, the parking lot easier to navigate without them. Ray has her arm, laughing.

"Oh boy," he is saying. "Oh boy oh boy."

Sadie leans on the truck. "What?"

"You did *not* like my singing."

She stares at him in the fluorescent glare. Nearby on the driving range there is the crack of a golf ball being hit, then another. The air is filled with salt. "What are you talking about?" she says.

191

She is spread out against the side of the truck, a ready victim. She's allowed this to happen and she is giddy at the prospect of her own vulnerability.

"You didn't like my singing in there. You stopped me cold with that look."

"Why is that important?" she says. The word, "important," sounds wrong, slurred, hard to spit out. "I liked it fine."

"You didn't seem to like it. You seemed out of sorts."

"It's that woman," she says. "That woman from the neighborhood."

Ray spins around and glances behind him. "Where?"

Sadie feels exasperation, and then laughter, rise up in her chest. "In there," she says. But she is laughing at his face, his worried eyes. She is doubled over, and dizzy, and then he has her face in his hands, and his mouth on hers. This time, though, she cannot stop laughing, and he has to pull away. "You're drunk," he says, a little taken aback.

She waves him off and tries to open the passenger door. Her hand slips from the handle and she falls back in a heap on the asphalt. Ray stands over her, his hands on his hips like a chastising parent.

"What's this?" he says. "What's going on here?"

"I don't usually drink," she tells him.

"Obviously," he says. He reaches down and yanks her to her feet.

"I think your singing is fine. It's wonderful. The waitress liked it. You impressed her."

"Emma," he says.

She hears something in the way he says her name. She thinks of the waitress's tattooed arms, the swell of her stomach, that bit of skin showing below her shirt. Everything whirls, speeds up and slows down, like the merry-go-round on the school playground, the kind they now say is too dangerous to play on, with the metal bars. Sadie stares at him.

"The waitress?" he says. "Emma?"

"You keep saying that," she says.

The lights on the driving range illuminate the grass, bright and green from the rain, the line of trees—barely visible beyond—a dark curtain. Ray opens the truck door and helps her inside. Sadie bites her lip. She feels her eyes well up. *What is so sad?* she wonders. But something is off, something has shut down. She has never been prepared to start a new life— no new life is beckoning her, really—and for the first time, she hopes there might still be time to return, to slip into her house under cover of darkness, as if she has never left.

"I'm ready to go home," she says weakly, half-afraid of his reaction.

Ray climbs into the cab beside her. "No you're not," he tells her, his voice matter-of-fact. He starts the truck up. "I don't believe you."

They sit in the cab with the truck rumbling. Sadie imagines the rust on the tailpipe leaving bits of debris in the parking lot, the oil leaking in the spot they will soon abandon.

"Why am I crying then?" she says.

"Because you're so happy," he says. "You're happy to be here with me. You can't believe how happy you are, how much I love you, how much you want to run away with me."

Sadie imagines what that might be like—happiness bubbling over, free of all the guilt and trepidation that comes with the burden of memory.

"I am happy with you," she says.

"I'm the man you've been waiting for," he tells her. He reaches over and takes her in his arms. She hears the springs in the truck seat, smells the butter and beer on his mouth. He holds her tight against the front of his shirt, so tight that she must angle her face to breathe, to speak.

"No," she says before she can stop herself. "You're the dream boy of my childhood, *Hezekiah*."

She doesn't think she's said it out loud, but she must have. Ray's arms stiffen. He lets go of her and rights himself behind the wheel. She sees the deliberately impassive side of his face. He puts the truck in gear and they leave the parking lot and drive in silence down Shore Road. Sadie imagines clicking the View-Master to the scene of what is happening without her. By now the children are in their beds. Kate has returned to her house, perhaps slipped down her basement stairs, gritty with dust, to work on her little village, to try not to think about Sadie or where she's gone. It will have occurred to her that when people are missing they aren't necessarily somewhere. They aren't delayed at an airport or staying the night with a friend. Sometimes their bodies are trapped in wreckage or hidden in a wooded area, and the person they once were is gone forever. What if Sadie has had an accident? What if she has been forcibly taken away? These things are disconcerting, but isn't what has really happened worse—that she has run off of her own free will? That she has left everything behind for a reason, and that reason is her own sanity, her own sense of well-being? Sadie believes Kate will understand this better than any of the mothers she has come to know this summer. Kate with her little village, her desperate wish to be surrounded by women, to be made whole. Women, Sadie realizes, who would be appalled at what she's done and vehemently denounce her. She can see them once they hear the news, sitting about Kate's kitchen, nursing their bright drinks.

"I can't imagine leaving my children behind!"

"Poor, poor Craig!"

"How will she live with herself?"

"She will never be happy."

They will pretend that it is unfathomable, but if they are honest they will know, somewhere in the deeply knotted center of who they really are, that they sometimes imagine it.

When they think of Sadie running away they feel a surge of envy so powerful it borders on fury.

Sadie rides along beside Ray, conscious of his body beside her. Yet, she cannot shake the image of Craig and the children alone in their white Colonial. She imagines one light lit downstairs and Craig pacing, on the phone, his arms waving, jerky and angry. Sadie wishes, suddenly, that she'd thought to leave a note behind. *I am fine,* she might have written. *Do not look for me.* One imagined line leads to another, until the note she never left becomes a series of instructions about housework (the coffeepot goes on the top rack of the dishwasher), about Max's Little Bear T-shirt being in the dryer. At the end she would have to say, *I'm sorry.* But these words, after all of the things of which she has made him sole trustee, seem insignificant.

Ray takes a turn and they wind down another narrow road past a gravel drive marked *Private.* He parks by an old split-rail fence and a wide field. The sky is still strangely lit. In the middle of the field is a tree. They are only ten minutes from the restaurant, and yet the sense of isolation is complete.

"Let's go to the beach," he says.

Sadie stares out at the field. "Where?"

"Just beyond the tree," Ray says. He rolls down the window and they can hear the tide coming in, the waves striking the rocky shore. They leave the truck and walk across the wide field. Sadie finds the fresh air, the walking, sobering. This is land owned by a friend of his father's from years back, Ray explains. They reach the shore—the rocks piled up, the wind coming in off the sound. The water is alive in the moonlight. The rocks are damp, covered in snails, the water rushing in between them and sloshing up to wet her feet, her ankles. They are two dark shadows. She can barely make him out as he picks his way across the rocks.

"We'd come here and make bonfires when I was a teenager," Ray says. "Here or the old barn, until it was struck by lightning."

Sadie remembers meeting up with Beth one winter night as a teenager, and driving with Beth and her friends from school down a winding lane, through pine woods, to a barn that used to stand on the Filley property. Her friends had names like Bogie and Digger and Griz, names that she could not remember because she had never heard any like them before. They wore Stetsons and hats with fur flaps, and smoked pot and drank Amstel beer. They sat around the barn in the light of a gas lantern, drinking and smoking and playing cards. Sadie sat in a corner, listening to them talk about ski trips to Stowe, and St. Thomas vacations, and the various boarding schools they attended before landing at Skidmore and Bennington and Dartmouth. She didn't see Ray there, but she wonders now if he was, if she simply didn't recognize him wearing a hat, or a beard, or any of the other costumes the people there seemed to wear.

"I remember the barn," she says.

Ray pauses in his hopping from one rock to the other. His white shirt is billowing in the wind. "You do?"

"Those were the good old days," Sadie said.

"They were?" Ray scrabbles his way over to her. "What are you talking about? You never went to the barn."

"Beth brought me once," she says. "I was there."

He looks at her in the darkness, his features suddenly unfamiliar, and she wonders if hers are equally strange to him, what he sees when he looks.

"No, you were always home studying your French," he says. "You stayed in watching *The Carol Burnett Show* on winter nights."

Sadie shakes her head. "Not me," she says. "You've got the wrong girl."

And then Ray grabs her, forcibly, both of his hands gripping her upper arms, his eyes boring into hers. "I know who I have," he says, protesting so much that she wonders if he is ashamed of being caught imagining her as someone else.

Sadie thinks, for a moment, that she will be pummeled, thrown down onto the rocks, the sea-worn basalt slick with green lichen. She will be raped and killed and left for the tide to drag down the coast to Rocky Neck State Park. But he gives her a little shake and lets her go.

"Stop the playacting, Sadie," he says. "You were always good at that as a kid. Too good."

"Why are we having this conversation?" she says. "Why aren't we back at the motel?"

"Because you said you wanted to go home," he says. He rubs his face with his hands.

She wishes her fear would subside, but it does not. "I shouldn't have said that," she tells Ray to pacify him. "Of course I like being here with you."

He approaches her again. He cups her elbows with his hands. "Maybe it is too much. Maybe we should go about this differently."

Sadie can't see his face fully in the dark. She wishes they were in the motel room with its big bed and its sole purpose. "Is this some kind of reverse psychology? My mother was always big on that. 'Oh, Sadie, don't wash the dishes. I do them so much better than you do.'"

She mimics her mother's voice, something she hasn't done in years. There's a heavy silence after, filled with the sound of the sea. She didn't intend to mention her mother—she's never wanted this to be about her. But something about tonight has made her mother unavoidable. Maybe it's that Sadie is now playing the role of "bad mother." Finally, she hears Ray sigh, a quavering sound that surprises her with its emotion.

"No, this isn't *reverse psychology*," he says finally. And then, "Jesus, Sadie, you sound like you hated her."

"You don't know anything," she says.

The sound draws in and out, the pebbles and shells tumble. Ray stands with his hands on his hips, watching her. "I think you're still drunk."

But it isn't the alcohol that's taking her over now, and she senses that her mother's ghost, hovering over them all this time, has decided to descend and inhabit her body.

"It will all work out," Ray says, but Sadie hears the falseness in his voice.

"You're starting to wish you'd never done this," Sadie says. "Admit it. You're thinking you should have left town and gone back to Florida before you ever saw me."

He takes her hand and leads her away from the waves, back across the salt-parched grass, under the stars. The sound of the water breaking fades. The moon moves beneath the clouds, then emerges to make the field luminous, the lone tree a stark sentry. She clutches his hand. She isn't sure which one of them wants her to be her mother, but the nagging memory of the packed suitcase in the old Filley house means something she doesn't yet want to think about.

Ray says nothing. He watches her suspiciously, as if she might break from his grip and rush headlong into the sound. He keeps hold of her hand, even though she tells him to let go and tries to wriggle free.

"Don't drag me along," she says. "I'm not a child. Let me walk."

"No," he says. "You're staying right here."

"I won't run away," she insists.

"How do I know that?"

"Because I'm telling you. Because I promise."

She says this and expects him to believe her, even though she has left a husband and children, people to whom this promise was implicit. She says this, even though the fragments of that summer are flooding back, adding up to create an entirely new memory. She flashes to the June morning she saw her mother at the basement door in her robe, and she imagines more, perhaps the part she did not see—Ray slipping through the pasture, along the cow path, rapping lightly on the glass door with his knuckles, her mother coming to the door with her finger to her lips, sliding the door on its runner. She wants to ask him if they are alike in *that way*, too, imagines her mother pulling him down onto the old mattress there on the floor, the mattress smelling of mildew.

Did her mother and Ray meet at the old Filley house on a similar afternoon of thunder and lightning? It would have been before his father moved in, when the roof leaked and the plaster walls were damp. The windows in the front would have been broken, and maybe small animals or birds had gotten in. The air outside may have been filled with the smell of wet grass. Cows would have speckled the fields. Sadie wonders if the suitcase was there because they had a real plan: Tickets purchased for the train to New York. Hotel reservations made. Would they have disappeared under assumed names?

The rush of the sound is replaced with the strange quiet of the deserted gravel road, the wide darkness of the sky. Sadie feels as if she's stepped into an empty room and shut the door. She wants to share with him the puzzle pieces she's just now put together about her mother, about the suitcase, the basement sex. She sees that her mother's seduction of a neighborhood boy was criminal, but she doubts her mother recognized this. In her haze of pills and alcohol she was simply acting out a role she'd invented for herself. But Ray *was* a boy, heading back to school soon, and something intervened. Sadie feels a catch in her heart.

Francie.

Sadie wrenches her hand free of his once they reach the split-rail fence. She opens the truck door and climbs in, slam-

ming it with a violence that surprises her. She doesn't know
where her anger comes from, what he's done to prompt it.
She watches him go around to the driver's side and open the
door.

"It was that old bitch from Cherrystones," he says, intimat-
ing that Mrs. Sidelman has caused Sadie's wavering moods.
The two of them sit in the dark truck in silence. From far off
is the sound of the waves on the rocks, a sound that might be
mistaken for passing traffic on a nearby highway, for wind
through trees.

"Yes," Sadie says, her voice hard. "My mother hated her,
too."

She gives Ray a chance to admit an affair with her mother,
but he does not. She turns in her seat to look at Ray. "I never
liked you, you know that? I only liked the version of you I
made up." She doesn't say "in the letters." She doesn't go
that far.

PART FOUR

~

FAMILY STILL HOPES
MISSING GIRL ALIVE

Wintonbury—August 16, 1974

It's been nine weeks since Laura Loomis was last seen by a girlfriend, heading up Hickory Lane to her home. In a phone interview, Mrs. Cynthia Loomis, Laura's mother, claims the fact that nothing has been found gives her hope her daughter is still alive. She wants to thank the state police, who have been working tirelessly to solve the case, and the many volunteers who searched the wooded area near the Loomis home for a week without discovering any evidence of the blond 9-year-old. "It's the uncertainty," Mrs. Loomis says. She's sought medical help and been prescribed tranquilizers, which she takes occasionally. "I've had trouble sleeping," she says. Her husband, Mr. Richard Loomis, an attorney, has recently returned to work. State police told her that they have no solid leads.

July 4, 1979

THE MORNING OF THE LOBSTER BAKE SADIE HEARD her father up early, moving around the kitchen, and her mother's voice, a flurry of admonishments about the size of the lobsters he picked up at the market the day before, the brand of gin. "Bittersweet chocolate?" she said. "I hope you remembered!" Her mother planned to make her famous chocolate cupcakes. Sadie imagined her downstairs, perched at the kitchen table with her juice and her cigarette. She felt an almost peaceful sense of normalcy. Through her window she could hear the sounds of the children already gathering outside in the yard across the street, Charlene Donahue calling hers in for breakfast. "Not until you eat something, missy," she said. Sadie could picture her framed in the doorway, drying her hands on a dish towel.

The fathers steamed the lobsters in a metal trash can over the pit, a bit of chicken wire soldered near the bottom of the can. This had been Sadie's father's invention. The Donahues' yard, with its level topography and minimal tree cover, was the place delegated each year for the bake. The tables, stretching across the entire backyard, bore flapping plastic cloths held down with stones. Gusts of wind filled the trees with a sound like applause. Sadie met Betty in the backyard by the tables. Along the side of the garage, more metal trash cans had been filled by noon with beer and ice, the sides sweating in the sun. The entire neighborhood came to the bake—although conspicuously absent each year were the Binghams. Some years they packed up their station wagon and left for the day, as if they'd been invited elsewhere. But from Francie's letters Sadie and Betty knew that was not the case today, and Sadie imagined them sitting in their hot house, listening to the sounds of the party going on up the street.

The girls, as promised, participated halfheartedly in the egg relay, Betty standing with one line of children, urging them on, helping place the egg on the spoon, and Sadie standing by another, both of them irritated with the children's fumbling movements. Charlene Donahue smiled at them from her lawn chair, her drink balanced on the arm. Sadie's mother, in a teal and bright green Lilly Pulitzer shift, entertained a group by the fire pit, tipping her head back in laughter, leaving her lipstick on her plastic cup.

Sadie sat down at one of the picnic tables.

"Filleys," Betty said, sliding alongside her on the bench.

Sadie glanced up. Patsy and Beth Filley crossed the side-yard grass from the street. Patsy held a bottle of Mateus by the neck. It swung at the end of her long arm like a dumb-bell. Beth kept a few paces behind her, arms folded across her chest, making it clear to everyone that she was there against her will. She had on the same boy's oxford that Sadie had seen her wear before and which she now thought must be Beth's favorite shirt. She had her hair in two braids.

"Pippi Longstocking," Betty whispered.

Sadie smiled and tried not to laugh. The Filleys were invited every year to the bake but were often away on vacation and rarely made an appearance. Patsy spotted Clare Watkins immediately and held up the wine. "We're here!" she called across the lawn. Sadie's mother lit up and rushed to Patsy, and Beth locked eyes with Sadie and approached the picnic table. She slid onto the bench across from Betty and Sadie and stared at them, chewing a piece of gum.

"This is it?" she said in her deadpan voice. "It's got to be a hundred degrees out here."

Sadie thought she saw a bead of sweat slide down Beth's neck. She hoped Betty wouldn't comment on Beth's choice of clothing, but Betty sat silent and immobilized by Beth's presence. Beth's eyes darted around the yard and lit on the line of trash cans, where one of the fathers had just pulled out a can of Black Label. She smiled. "Perhaps the day is not yet lost." She leaned in toward Sadie, ignoring Betty entirely.

"My brother and his friend are up in the woods. Why don't we sneak some of that beer to them?" She widened her brown eyes. "They would be ever so grateful. Our house is dry. Dear old Mom has taken the car keys, so no sneaking out for a trip to the packie."

Sadie could smell Beth's mint gum. She turned and glanced at the trash cans. Their placement on the side of the garage kept them relatively hidden and easily accessible to the path into the pasture. But Sadie wasn't sure she wanted to be around Ray, with his flippant comments and his disregard. "I don't know," she said.

"I can't carry enough of it by myself," Beth said, adopting a whine. "And my brother would love us. We'd be his heroes."

Sadie glanced at Betty, who still seemed to be stuck in her frozen state. "What do you think?" Sadie asked her.

"Oh come on, Betsy! Help us out here," Beth said.

Betty eyed Beth. "My name is Betty," she said.

"Oh, we're both Elizabeth, aren't we?" Beth said. "But we can't really choose our own names, or even our nicknames, when we're born. I have a friend whose parents call her Bunny. Can you imagine that? When I'm an adult I'm changing mine to Serena."

Betty smiled. "Yeah, I'm changing mine to Roselyn."

Sadie said that if they all walked over to the cans and stood in a group, one person could take out the beer, shielded by the others. They all stood up and crossed the backyard to the garage.

"Look at this," Beth said. "Not a single person is paying any attention to us."

And she was right. The adults in their circles were transfixed by each other or occupied with children, setting out paper plates that the wind promptly blew across the yard. They were bent down tending the fire pit or coming in and out of the Donahues' porch door. They refilled their drinks at the drink table. Sadie's small group by the line of beer-filled cans seemed invisible.

Beth lifted off one trash can lid and pulled out a six-pack of beer, the cans held together by the plastic rings. Sadie thought they would move quickly toward the break in the barbed wire, but Beth reached in again and rummaged around until she found another four beers attached together. Betty kept up a high-pitched, fake conversation in the kind of voice she'd have used when they were playing house.

"So, yeah, I always liked your horse. Do you still have it? What's its name? Really? Oh, sure, I like that. When do you go back to school?"

Beth handed the four beers to Sadie. "What is she saying?"

"I'm pretending we're standing here talking," Betty said.

"Let's pretend that we're going for a walk now," Sadie said.

"Yes, here is where we'll begin the Haunted Woods," Betty said, again to the air.

The three of them moved away from the picnic, clutching the wet beer to their chests. Behind them they could hear Sadie's mother's laugh, a loud whoop, and then others joining in, and the shouts of children who had turned on the sprinkler. Once they'd breached the fence and gotten under the cover of the pines, all three of them started to laugh. Beth took one of the beers and opened it, and Sadie did the same. Betty said she'd rather not, and Beth simply shrugged.

"It's not too bad," she said. "It tastes a little like watered-down cigarette ashes."

Betty made a face and looked at Sadie, and Sadie took a sip, pretending it was fine, that the taste wasn't exactly as Beth had described. They walked along the Haunted Woods path and drank the beer, and Beth talked about how clever the sets were. This made Sadie cautious. She wasn't at all sure if Beth meant it. They stopped at the kitchen scene, and Beth set the beer on the table and pulled out one of the chairs.

"Why don't you have a seat?" she said in a voice that Sadie imagined was an imitation of her own mother. "Would you like some coffee? A pastry?"

Betty sat down. "No thank you," she said.

Beth laughed then. "That's how you do it, right? Play house?"

Betty's face turned pink with irritation. It seemed best to not reply to Beth, who in her odd way may have been serious. Sadie wondered if Beth had ever played anything other than backgammon. She watched her sit down at the table and take a long sip of her beer. She shook the empty can and then tossed it over her shoulder. "Next," she said.

"You should save some for your brother and his friend," Betty said.

Beth shook her head. "Early bird catches the worm. First come, first served."

They heard a snapping of twigs and the lowered voices of boys, and the girls turned to where Ray and his friend appeared from the swamp. Their sneakers and the bottoms of their shorts were wet. They had their T-shirts tied over their heads, and Ray's chest was smooth and tan. The other boy was shorter and pale white in the dim woods. He took his shirt from his head when he saw them and put it on, out of politeness, Sadie surmised. He came up and introduced himself, holding out his hand for the girls to take. "Hans," he said. He shook back his long, fine blond hair. Ray kept his shirt tied around his head and leaned over to grab two of the beers.

"I see you were resourceful, as always, Beth," he said.

"What were you two doing?" Beth said.

Hans displayed his good rearing by turning to her and answering. "Why, we were just swamping," he said.

"Looking for some swamp hoydens," Ray said. "Backwater hussies."

The boys snickered. Hans smiled politely toward them. "No offense."

They pulled out their cigarettes. Hans sat down on a stump, and Ray leaned against a tree. The sun came through the pines in shifting patterns on the floor of the woods, on the patches of ferns. Beyond, the meadow filled with a brightness that hurt her eyes. The boys drank the beer quickly, as if a race was on to finish it, and when it was gone they decided to visit the lobster bake trash can coolers again. Sadie's beer had grown warm in her hand. She watched the two boys saunter up the path. She'd said very little while they'd been there. Instead, she'd listened to Beth's chatter and the boys' low chuckles, their comments to each other barely audible.

Now Beth turned to her. "Hans thinks you're cute," she said, as if in some secret way he'd passed her this information.

Sadie didn't quite believe her. She'd noticed that Hans smiled at her pointedly, but she took that to be his good manners.

"I think she's right," Betty said. "He kept looking at your chest."

Beth tipped her head back and hooted. "He likes swamp hoydens."

Sadie didn't know whether she should laugh with them or get angry.

The boys came back up the path. Ray had another six-pack wrapped in his T-shirt. "They replenished," he said.

Sadie couldn't imagine drinking any more beer, but Hans lifted her old one out of her hand and gave her a new cold one. "Drink up," he said, grinning.

They smoked Hans's Parliaments, and listened to the boys talk about the teachers at their boarding school and the antics of their classmates, and Sadie thought how different it seemed from the settings in books she'd read, from her mother's nightmarish stories—where children slept in dormitories and died of consumption, where headmasters had paddles and punishments involved long, laborious writings in cursive.

"My mother went to boarding school in New York City," she said.

Ray turned to look at her, setting his beer on his knee. "Really?"

Sadie didn't know if he was truly interested or making fun of her.

"The nuns beat them. The food was horrible. She ran away when she was sixteen, but they caught her and made her go back."

Betty stared at Sadie. She'd never heard any of this before, and Sadie knew she thought she was making it up. "Really," she said to her.

Her mother had told her once about going to a friend's house for the weekend in Weston, Connecticut—about the neighborhood cookout, the large houses on their wide lawns, and how she'd always dreamed of that for her own children. Sadie remembered she'd said "children," not "child." Sadie thought all schools had both good and bad. At her middle school the walls pushed away to combine classrooms, and they did their math work independently from cards chosen by color from a box set in the front of the room. She was part of a high-achievement class that went on field trips, and learned to write Japanese characters with a brush and ink. But she still had to ride a bus to and from school, breathing in the exhaust, suffering the anxiety of hills covered in ice, the crazed behavior of one boy or another that at times justified his removal by the driver.

Sadie drank her beer, and then Hans was next to her, asking about the path and where it led, for a tour of her Haunted Woods, and then she was walking with him on the rutted cow path, the roots of the trees tripping her up, the sound of the cicadas so lulling she thought she might lie down and sleep on the mossy earth. They passed the living room with the headless father, and when Hans wanted to go off the path, toward the meadow, she relented with the intention of describing Francie's role as the ghost of Emely Filley, clutching her baby. He smelled of soap—years later she will identify the scent as sandalwood—and his hand was soft on her elbow. At one point he slid it down to take her hand and lead her into the grass, into a sitting position, the dry blades sharp on her bare legs. And then she was aware of his hands in other places, softly insistent, and his mouth, a gentle pressure on hers. She heard Betty calling her as if from some far-off place, and she sat up.

Hans applied his gentle force to pull her back down, but Sadie saw he'd shifted her T-shirt up, and she yanked it down and stood up in the grass, light-headed with sun and beer and shame. Even years later, in her memories of this afternoon, Sadie will always imagine that Hans was Ray. She stumbled across the meadow to the woods, to Betty standing there with her hands on her hips, her mouth a terse line.

"Where have you been?" she said. She stared past Sadie at Hans, then took Sadie's arm and dragged her back down the path, through the barbed wire, to the lobster bake. Ray and Beth had disappeared. The activity in the Donahues' backyard made Sadie dizzy. The parents were singing some made-up ditty and laughing at each other's singing voices, collapsing at the waist, the women's hair wildly untidy, the men clutching their stomachs, the backs of their madras shirts wet. There were the bright shards of lobster left on paper plates soaked with butter, the paper towel rolls unfurling in the wind. There were charred burgers still left, so Sadie and Betty put two of them on rolls and took some chips, and went upstairs to Betty's bedroom, closing the door against her sister, who followed them, asking where they'd been. Even after they shut the door she kept up her knocking, and threatening—"It's my room, too," and "I'm going to tell"—until Betty shrieked for her to go away. They didn't talk about what had happened. The room, with its chenille bedspreads and sheer curtains, its soft carpet, felt like a haven, close and quiet.

They ate their food in an awkward silence. Beth kept glancing up at Sadie, and Sadie pretended not to notice.

"Where did Beth and Ray go?" Sadie asked her.

Beth shrugged and made a face. "I don't know."

"They just left Hans there by himself?"

"They said they were going home," Betty said. "Maybe they figured he knew how to get there." And then, finally, "He was cute."

Hans's cuteness had nothing to do with what had gone on in the field. Sadie had been unprepared for what boys wanted, and now she vowed she wouldn't be caught unaware again. She admitted none of this to Betty, even though she felt it was something she should know. Knowing it while Betty didn't made her feel stronger somehow.

Betty said they had never checked to see if Francie left anything under the stone.

"I thought we were done with that," Sadie said.

But she saw that Betty felt the differences beginning to separate them, and that this was something she and Betty still had in common now, and it seemed a little sad and pointless to refuse to play along.

They weren't careful about being followed. The bake was still going on, and the kids were everywhere—riding bikes in the street, playing in wading pools, mostly unsupervised. The day was hot but winding down, the sun sitting just above the line of trees. Sadie could hear the parents' singing, smell the greasy smoke that meant another round of burgers was on the grill as they started up toward the dead end. Betty's sister joined them, stepping in her jaunty way alongside them, her arms swinging.

"Where are you guys going?" she asked.

Betty looked at Sadie, and Sadie shrugged, resigned. It didn't matter. They didn't expect to find anything. By the time they reached the stone a small gang of kids, suspicious from the beginning, had descended on them—some on bikes towing others, some walking. Sadie bent down and lifted the stone and uncovered a small folded square of blue paper, and a pair of girls' underwear.

In her shock at the discovery, Sadie didn't care what happened next, only that she and Betty wouldn't be tied to what lay there in the dirt. She took the letter quickly into her hand and she and Betty backed away. Betty's sister stepped forward in exclamation and sent one of the little kids for a stick, then used it to pick up the underwear. It was a simple pair, pale and slightly grayed from washing, a small flower attached to the elastic waistband. The kids made joined sounds of surprise—some laughed, others shrieked, *Cooties!* Betty's sister, holding the stick, lurched at a boy and he recoiled. Some of the kids began running away, making a game of it.

Sadie and Betty had already walked partway down the street when one of the Schuster boys rode by on his bike, the underwear on the stick held up in the air, like a flag. Sadie imagined her own underwear, tucked in the darkness of her top bureau drawer, exposed against the contrast of sunlight and waving grass, the starkness of the stone, the asphalt, the barbed wire tines, the decaying cedar post. She and Betty exchanged looks. They'd learned from health class about the bright blood that could bloom there at any time, that it could be soon—and it terrified them. Sadie clutched Francie's letter. The group of kids paraded back down the street, the boy at the lead, looking like the benign children depicted in Joan Walsh Anglund prints, with their chunky limbs, large foreheads, heavy bangs, eyes like dark pinpricks.

Sadie and Betty snuck back to the Haunted Woods to read the letter at the old maple table where they'd sat earlier, surrounded by empty cans and cigarette butts and casting tentative looks over their shoulders.

Again, my locked door has been breached. Someone came into my room last night, Francie had written. *His breath smelled of crème de menthe. His hands were furry, like a wild beast's. I am so happy to finally escape this cursed place! Thank you for the lovely bracelet—I will cherish it always. I am leaving you something of mine as well. Until tonight!*

With Francie, it had become difficult to decipher where the fantasy ended. Betty bit her lip. "Is she serious?" she said. "What is she talking about?"

"She's going to meet him, that's the important thing," Sadie said.

Betty looked unsure. "Maybe we shouldn't have set up the meeting."

The light had begun to fade in the woods, and she stood up and began to stuff the cigarette butts into the beer cans, to gather the cans up.

"She'll know it's all a fake when he doesn't show up," Sadie said.

"What about the other things she wrote?" Betty said. "Maybe we should say something."

Sadie considered the note again. She thought, briefly, about Hans in the field, and she imagined him slipping into her bedroom at night. The idea of his body close to hers in the dark made her flush with warmth.

"What would we say?" she said. "That the Beast from 'Beauty and the Beast' went into Francie's bedroom? That we have a note that proves it?"

Betty smiled tentatively.

Sadie shook her head. "It's nothing."

Then she crumpled the note and dug a small hole in the woods, and buried it. Betty stood nearby, still unsure. "We could just give it to her mother," she said. But by then the note was gone and the dirt covered over with leaves. They put the beer cans inside a cardboard box and headed back out of the woods. Neither of them could believe Francie had left a pair of her underwear for Hezekiah.

"What was she thinking?" Betty said.

Sadie took a deep breath. "We can't tell anyone," she said.

That evening, as if enacting a sort of penance, they organized yard games for the neighborhood kids: freeze tag; Red Rover; Mother, May I; What Time Is It? They played until dusk, when they could no longer see each other in the darkness, until the fireflies began their heated blinking, bobbing and elusive along the edge of the woods. The party continued around the pit, the remaining parents circling the fire in their aluminum folding chairs, the lit ends of their cigarettes and their low voices the only indication of their presence. Betty's sister had the idea that they should all take their positions in the Haunted Woods and do a run-through. Betty and Sadie appointed one of the older girls to be the guide, and they pretended to be the kids being led. "Don't show any emotion," they instructed her. "Don't feel sorry for them when they get scared." The fluorescent markings showed up perfectly, the boys made the right noises in the trees, the ghosts moaned and shuffled, the sets were garish and surreal in the flashlight's beam.

Francie's set, the empty crib, remained empty. None of the kids had seen Francie all day, and someone thought the Binghams had gone away for the holiday. Even though Sadie knew better, she used this as an excuse not to send someone to get her. She and Betty kept an eye out for her as it grew later, wondering when she would set out to meet Hezekiah, if she would set out at all. Betty's mother and father got into an argument and decided at the last minute that there would be no sleepovers, and their tentative plan to meet at eleven thirty in Betty's backyard was thwarted by the stragglers who kept a vigil at the pit. Instead, Sadie went to bed with grass-stained feet, her hair smelling like sun and sweat, all the summers of her childhood becoming this one last night.

The next morning Mrs. Schuster, Francie's next-door neighbor, came to Sadie's front door with a birdlike rapping of her bony fist. Sadie was the only one up. She had peered through the living room window first and seen the woman waiting there, her arms wrapped tight around her chest, her hair flattened from sleep on one side.

She hesitated to open the door, but the woman kept up her urgent knocking, and Sadie's father and mother were roused. They appeared at the top of the stairwell, her father in his robe, her mother behind him in her sheer nightgown, both of them nursing headaches, her mother disappearing into the bathroom with a moan. Sadie watched as her father quickly descended the stairs, opened the door, and listened to Mrs. Schuster through the storm door screen. Her voice was high-pitched and panicky. Sadie heard her father tell her *calm down, Lenore,* in a tone that intimated years of neighborhood cookouts and reciprocated dinners with cocktails. The open door let in a clean morning smell, the sound of birds alert and sharp in the maple tree. Mrs. Schuster slipped inside the house, her arms still clasping her chest. She wore a cotton cardigan that smelled of camphor, her hair still in the bouffant style of the sixties. She only had a minute, she said. She had to go to other houses. Sadie's mother appeared in her robe, and her father summoned Sadie, who pretended to appear from the hallway to the den. She was interrogated, first by Mrs. Schuster, and then by her father and mother, each chiming in with further questions:

"Did you see anything unusual this morning?"

"When was the last time you saw Francie?"

"What was she doing?"

"Who was she talking to? Was anyone around that you didn't know?"

"Have you seen anyone around the neighborhood that you don't know lately?"

The questions weren't explained, but they left Sadie's heart thudding.

"What happened to Francie?" Sadie finally asked.

Mrs. Schuster's eyes grew wet. She put her hand over her mouth, and then she bent down to look into Sadie's face. "She's missing, honey."

August 29, 2003

R AY STARTS UP THE TRUCK, AND THE SOUND IS OMI-
nous on the quiet road. The day Francie disappeared
some of the searchers found a loose sheet of paper
blowing about the cornfields. It had been the letter to Hezekiah that Sadie and Betty had lost in the field weeks before.
No one knew who the boy was or where he lived, and all
of the neighborhood boys were questioned, the police going
house to house. It reminded Sadie, in true Francie fashion, of
"Cinderella," when the prince goes through the village trying
to ferret out the young woman whose foot fits the slipper.

Ray turns to her. "Do you know it was old Mrs. Sidelman
who told the police she used to see me in the woods. 'Lurking
in the woods,' she said. Those were her words on the police
report."

Sadie wants to say that Mrs. Sidelman was partly right in
accusing him, that it was a version of him that caused Francie's
disappearance.

But then she would have to tell him everything, how she
remained silent, even when the police drove up the street to
his house and put him in the back of the cruiser to take him
in for questioning. Everyone had seen the cruiser head up the
street. The neighbors had all been gathering every day on the
Binghams' front lawn, and the lawn was littered with cigarette
butts. The fire engines and buses of searchers who moved
like ribbons through the pastures were parked on Wadhams

Road. Sadie remembers Ray's face in the backseat as the car drove by her house, how he looked out the window, directly at her where she stood with her parents on the front lawn. At the time, the weight of her guilt convinced her he was staring straight into her. She wonders now whether that steady look was for her mother.

Ray turns the truck onto Shore Road. They've only gone a short way when the headlights light up a woman walking along the sandy shoulder. Sadie recognizes the waitress at once.

"It's Emma," she says as they pass her.

Ray pulls the truck over.

"Why did you do that?" Sadie asks. "She's going to think you're some stranger. She's going to be scared to death."

Ray opens the truck door and calls out. "Hey, Emma! It's us, from the restaurant." And then he sings a bar of "Cecilia" out into the darkness.

"You just did that to make me mad," Sadie says. "You think I hate your singing, and you did that to bother me."

Emma walks up to the passenger window. "Hey," she says in her soft voice. She brushes her hair back.

"Need a ride?" Ray asks.

"I'm not sure," Emma says. "I was expecting a ride from someone and he's not here. I'm a little worried."

Sadie thinks that the boyfriend has ditched her. Certainly it isn't a husband. But then Emma says it is her husband, and that he is always on time, and she thinks something must have happened to him. Sadie wants to tell her that (an hour away) her husband is saying the same thing about her. Instead, she scoots over and Emma climbs in. Sadie feels the sweat of her body, the heat radiating from her abdomen.

"Sorry it's so hot," Ray says. "No air conditioning in this thing."

The wind whipping into the truck makes it difficult to talk. Emma leans forward and says she likes the fresh air, and that the truck is a *fine relic*. Sadie thinks the wording is a bit dramatic—it's an old truck. There is nothing particularly valuable or meaningful about it. She's run off with a man who drives a junker, and somehow that hasn't mattered to her until now. Her hair blows over her eyes. Emma holds hers back with her hand, her tattooed arm balanced on the door frame. They drive down Shore Road and take a left where Emma points, and then down a narrow lane among cottages with little name plaques on the front—*Eeny, Meeny, Miney,* and *Mo, Winkin, Blinkin,* and *Nod*—past a tennis court and a little general store. They pull up to a small cottage, pale blue, with an outdoor shower, and a clothesline, and the open water right behind it. The cottage is dark, and there isn't a car in front. All down the tar lane the cars are parked haphazardly in front of other cottages with beach towels flapping on lines, different colors with small painted porches, all of them dark. Sadie sees a candle flicker inside one. And then someone approaches them as Emma climbs out. He has a camping lantern, and the light swings back and forth as he walks.

"None of us have any power," the man calls to her. "Someone hit a power line up the road."

Emma puts one hand to her mouth, the other to the mound of her stomach. "Oh."

"Do you have a flashlight?" Ray asks. He climbs out of the truck, walks up to the bottom of the steps. Sadie sees Emma turn to talk to him, but she can't hear what she says over the crashing of the waves on the beach.

Ray comes back to the truck and leans in. "I'm going to help her light some candles," he says. "Now she's all freaked out about the wreck."

"Okay," Sadie says.

Ray looks at her, waiting. "Are you going to come in?"

Sadie wants to wait in the truck. She watches Ray go into the house, sees the candles being lit through the windows—

one placed on a table, another on what looks to be a kitchen counter, the rooms beyond the windows lighting up, and Ray and Emma there inside as if they belong together. Sadie knows this is what has hardened her against Emma from the beginning. She is the kind of girl Ray dated—the type she saw with him the few remaining times he came back to the neighborhood after the Francie incident. He'd be with a girl with long hair wearing a man's T-shirt, a pair of washed jeans so pale they looked white, who wore rings on all her fingers, jangly bracelets, and a paisley scarf in her hair. She would be dreamy eyed, one languid arm draped out the car window.

Sadie, on the other hand, was smart and secretive. She was good at facades. She wore the suburban costumes assigned to her, even as a teenager—corduroys and clogs, turtlenecks and Fair Isle sweaters. She still does. Ray has no reason but one to have chosen her out of the innumerable women he might choose as a single man accustomed to living in Florida, a state where minimal clothing is necessary and women are always tan. Sadie recognizes this now, and sees, suddenly, her mistake in believing he loved her. Only one woman alive looks so much like her mother.

He comes out onto the porch and lets the screen door bang shut. Sadie can hear the sand grinding under his boots. Then he steps down and comes back up to the car.

"Why don't you come in?" he says. "We can sit with her for a little while until her husband gets back."

"What if he doesn't come back?" Sadie says. She gives him a small smile. "What if he's run off with some girl he knew from his old neighborhood?"

Ray stares at her. His face is the same as she pictured it all those years when she didn't see him. Older, with lines around his eyes, but the same. He is still slight and boyish, though his body has filled out to that of a man. He wears the same sloppy clothes.

"Really, Sadie?"

She wonders if she's always been this heartless—then thinks about Francie and knows the answer is yes. But now she tries to consider Emma in her fragile state, alone and pregnant, worried about her husband, and she opens the truck door and gets out. She is tired, as if she's reached the end of an exhausting day with the children and she wants only to sit down for a minute to rest. She has no fresh underwear, no hairbrush. She thought she'd be back for dinner. The porch steps bend under her weight. The cottage is tiny, a playhouse. Inside the candles flame wildly, blown by the wind that comes in through the screens facing the water. Emma is on the phone, an old-fashioned type with a spiraled cord. They hear her describe her husband's car (Subaru, maroon) and her husband (five feet nine inches, one hundred and sixty pounds, brown hair). His name is Pietro Rovella, and he doesn't speak much English. She is worried because of the accident, she says. And then she listens and nods and hangs up.

"They say it was a truck that hit the pole," she says.

She rises from the table. "You don't have to stay."

Sadie says they don't have anywhere they need to be. "But if you'd rather we leave—"

"Of course not—I'm glad for the company."

Ray sits down on the end of the couch and Sadie sits beside him. The candle nearby lights up his eyes, burnishes his hair. Emma sits in a wing chair and folds her legs up. Sadie can tell it is her chair, the place where she always sits. Emma says they are sending someone over to talk to her about her missing husband, to take her statement.

"Was he at work?" Ray asks. "Maybe he got held up."

"Pietro works from home," Emma says. "Sometimes he goes out and explores and gets lost. That might be what happened. Maybe he went to the movies in Niantic and got caught in the traffic. Lots of reasons why he didn't make it to the restaurant."

They finally introduce themselves. They make awkward small talk, unable to really answer any questions truthfully, Sadie taking over and creating, with some of her old resourcefulness, their false history. She wonders if they should leave before the policeman arrives and asks them their names, and then she wonders if the police have gone to talk to Craig. But she is very sleepy, and sitting on the couch beside Ray—his warmth, his smell—she forgets herself and closes her eyes. She opens them once, and hears Ray and Emma talking, but their voices lull her back to sleep, and she doesn't wake until she feels the wind, colder now off the water, and senses that Ray has gotten off the couch. She sees him at the little table with Emma, and a man in a police uniform. The man's badge glows in the sputtering candlelight. He is a short man with a round chest. He writes things down and nods, and Sadie pretends to be asleep when she hears him ask Ray who he is, and who she is, and hears Emma interrupt to tell him they are friends of hers, that they came to give her a ride when her husband didn't show up.

"Any reason your husband would take off?" the officer asks. "Was there an argument? Did you check to see if any clothing or other personal items are missing? A suitcase or bag? Any jitters about the impending event?"

Sadie imagines Craig answering these questions—his emphatic *no,* his objection to this line of questioning. Emma answers calmly, truthfully, and manages to keep the annoyance out of her voice. "He is excited about the baby," she says. "He would never just leave."

"I'm sorry, but I have to ask," the officer says. "And you'd be surprised how many spouses say the very same thing—not to upset you, or imply that your husband has run off, of course. Few expect it, is what I'm saying."

Sadie imagines he will confess to them that just tonight he got another call from a man whose wife was missing. "Just up and left him with two little kids." Her heart races as she waits, and her cheeks burn. But he does not say anything. He is an Old Lyme town cop. He wouldn't know anything about her or Craig. The officer takes a step toward the door. His weight shifts a nail in the pine floor, a sound like a rusty spring.

"My guess is that he'll be here soon," he says. "Probably got held up in the jam."

Sadie hears the man leave, Ray and Emma talking on the porch. She doesn't move from her spot on the couch, feigning sleep. Where is Pietro? she wonders. Has he decided to flee his wife, his unborn daughter? Is he now at a gas station in Rhode Island buying a Coke and a map, trying to figure out how many bills to give the cashier, making a face and bewitching her with his broken English? Has he run off with a girl he met on the beach during the hours when his pregnant wife was working? Will he see that the life he left behind had its own delicate perfection, its moments of happiness? Will he turn the car around? Will he pull into the sandy drive and pretend he never left? And then the refrigerator sputters to life, and the room is suddenly illuminated—thousands of white twinkling lights are strung around its perimeter, draped over the swinging light fixture, looped along the beams of the ceiling, outlining the screens on the porch. Sadie sits up. Ray and Emma step into the room. Emma spins around in astonishment.

"It's my birthday," she says softly in explanation. She moves around the room to each lit candle, blowing it out. Sadie remembers the sad little party she gave Craig, the way he acted surprised for the children as he opened the gifts. In each strand of lights strung about the cottage is the joy she could not offer her own husband.

July 5, 1979

THE PHONE BEGAN RINGING SOON AFTER MRS. Schuster left with her news about Francie's disappearance. Sadie's mother took up her station at the kitchen table, her orange ashtray filling with butts. Sadie's father dressed and met the other fathers outside where they'd gathered in the street, a small, ragtag group of men in Bermuda shorts and Top-Siders, their faces bloated from drink, their appendages, usually white from days under the fluorescent lights of the workplace, burnt red. They talked in hushed tones and looked about with their hands on their waists, waiting for someone to take charge, to direct them where to go. The debris of the lobster bake still blew about the neighborhood. The tables remained with their flapping cloths, the empty chairs still stationed around the pit. The police parked in front of Francie's house. Sadie and Betty stood with everyone at the end of Francie's driveway, waiting for word. Francie's mother was there, roused from her couch, her eyes red rimmed, her hands large and veined and clutching something they learned was the baby blanket Francie still slept with. Her father was there, an older-looking man, hunched over in a sports shirt.

"Geppetto," Sadie whispered. She and Betty laughed, nervous laughter they believed Francie might have forgiven them for.

Francie's bike was found at the dead end. No one had for-

gotten Laura Loomis, the photos of her on flyers—blond hair
and blue eyes, a slightly crooked smile—that still flapped in
store windows five years later. Sadie had begun to grow out
of her resemblance to Laura, but she'd always been plagued
by Laura's eyes staring out from her fourth-grade school por-
trait, haunted by the way life shone in them, alert and potent,
waiting to be lived.

She and Betty stuck together and waited for the letters
they'd written to be discovered. They imagined Francie had
hidden them in some old book—*Grimm's Fairy Tales*—the
pages carved out beneath the mildewed cover. They thought
they knew her then, as well as they knew themselves. Still, they
said nothing, their hearts soft and quick like the robins the
boys would leave near death, that they'd find and cup in their
hands, trying to save them. Search parties were organized—the
neighborhood fathers, volunteer firemen from a town over,
state police organizing searchers to fan out through the swamp
and the surrounding woods, forming a long line of people an
arm's width apart, taking careful steps, separating only to avoid
the wide trunks of trees. Local women made sandwiches from
meat and bread donated by Shaw's. The searchers combed the
woods along the little brook, climbed over barbed wire, and
waded into the maze of cornfields. *Francie! Francie!* The sound
of her name became a refrain. All morning Sadie listened to
the way it passed, back and forth, from all sides surrounding
the neighborhood, echoing off the rows of houses, the shake
shingles and the aluminum siding.

Sadie and Betty slipped away on their own. They knew
where Francie had gone—the place Hezekiah had arranged
to meet her—and their plan was to find her first. They would
become her friend, no longer the stuck-up girls. They'd give
her a sip of their canteen water, and smooth out her hair, and
tell her the shirt she was wearing was cool. They would tell
her they were sorry without ever saying the words, without

explaining what they were sorry for. They wandered along the cow paths, past the marsh with its tall hummocks, and up along the ridge of the cornfield where the blackberries grew in thick tangles. They could hear the other searchers, and occasionally they'd see them in pairs, a flash of their bright summer clothes across a fallow field. It was late afternoon when they reached the pond.

"We should have picked a place that was closer," Betty said. Her bangs were damp on her forehead. Her freckled nose was pink.

They had never before been past the last line of woods, the pond like a mirage seen from a distance. They stood on the edge in the grass and watched the insects flit across the still surface. They were hot, and they took off their shoes and waded in. Years later when Sadie found the pond again she would remember this moment—the cool water, the cicadas' whirring, the heat of the day dissipating, the sound of the brook, the shadows of the trees that rimmed the clearing. She was tired, ready to give up. They could hear the calls of the searchers, and Sadie was becoming less convinced that Francie was just hiding, refusing to come forward. She'd already missed two meals. Mrs. Schuster had said her bed hadn't been slept in. For the first time Sadie considered that something might have actually happened to Francie to prevent her from returning, and she remembered Laura Loomis's mother on the news, her glassy eyes, her strained voice pleading for information about Laura's whereabouts weeks after her daughter never came home.

Sadie scanned the pond's surface. "What's that over there?" she said.

There was something bobbing, a log, or a clump of weeds.

"It's part of a beaver's dam," Betty said. "Isn't it?"

"Looks more like clothes, some sort of material."

She was wading in, deeper now. Her feet sucked at the

sandy bottom. Her shorts were wet, and then she was up to her waist, shading her eyes, looking. Betty stayed by the shore, calling to her. "Don't go any farther," she said. "Please, please don't go any farther."

Sadie stopped when the water reached her chest. She felt it cold on her breasts, and lower, near the bottom, a little rushing of current, the small fish slipping between her legs. She closed her eyes and slid under the surface. From far away she heard Betty's voice crying out. If she swam out she might get closer to the thing in the water, she might see what it was. But then she remembered the story of Emely Filley and felt the tug of the water on her shorts, her shirt, imagined the way it might have pulled on the girl's long skirt. She imagined the water turned to ice, the trees overhead bare save for a few clinging brown leaves. She began to fear what might be in the pond and tried to stand but found she had floated out beyond the place where she could touch. In her panic she flailed, and suddenly Betty was there, tugging on her hand, pulling her up.

"What?" she said. "It isn't her, is it?"

Sadie said she couldn't tell what it was. A pile of pond grass—or hair. A snagged piece of trash, blown miles from the nearest road—or a pink shirt. She felt suddenly sick. Her head ached. It was the sun, she thought. But then Betty said, "What if it's her? What if she threw herself in when Hezekiah didn't show up? What if it's our fault?"

"You mean Hezekiah's?" Sadie said.

Betty glared at her. "Oh my God," she said.

"She wouldn't do it," Sadie said. "That's not sane."

They both stared at the thing in the water, stirred about by the current. In the glare of the setting sun they couldn't be sure about anything, but Sadie felt the first jolt of fear, and astonishment. What if Francie had done it? What if she had shown them all?

"Let's go," Sadie said. They got lost on the cow paths that wound toward home, and the woods grew dim, and they didn't emerge until dinnertime. Their mothers' fury was unmatched. Betty and Sadie were consigned to the front yard like the younger children. Francie still hadn't been found, but the searchers had come upon the site of the Haunted Woods, and the Hanged Girl, a dummy so lifelike that Mr. Frobel had fallen to his knees and cried out, "Oh Lord!" Sadie and Betty learned that Francie's underwear, tossed over the fence into the pasture, trampled into the grass by the farmer's cows, had also been discovered and cataloged as grim evidence. They might have explained the underwear, but not without revealing the entire story—their own complicity. The general fear of the unknown took over, and everyone gathered in hushed groups to speculate what might have happened. Betty was called home earlier than usual, and she and Sadie separated, each worrying what the other might, in a moment of weakness, confess.

The contentment of the day before—the festivity of the lobster bake, Sadie and Betty's reprieve from the letter writing—now seemed distant, forever lost. That night every dead bolt turned. Sadie lay in bed listening to the crickets, the frogs in the brook, the pinging of beetles against the metal window screen, sounds that she can still imagine, that make her think of the child she was, and the woman she is now, and how little she understood of her life, and how little she still understands.

August 30, 2003

IETRO RETURNS NEAR ONE A.M. THEY HEAR HIS CAR in the sandy road, the engine ticking when it's cut off. He enters the house with an expression of solemn regret that he casts around the room to each of them in turn, even Sadie and Ray, strangers to him.

"I got lost," he says. He throws his arms up in the air. "I knock at doors and no one comes to answer me."

He is holding a brown bag of wine purchased at the liquor store in Old Lyme five hours before. From his garbled English Sadie understands that Pietro remembered a book Emma had seen at the antiquarian bookshop, and he tried to make his way there, and got on the highway instead. By the end of his story he is near tears, relaying his frustration, his sorrow in attempting to navigate the road in the dark and missing Emma's birthday. Sadie imagines this slight, handsome man in his somewhat short trousers and fine knit vest, crossing front lawns to knock on the doors of suburban housewives. She notices that Emma is crying now as well, and then they are in each other's arms, and she feels Ray take her hand, pull her toward the door so that they might make their awkward escape. But Emma turns to them and grabs his arm to stop him.

"Oh, no, please don't go."

And Pietro is insisting they stay and share the wine, and Emma is getting glasses, and Pietro is beside her opening the bottle, getting out a cake that looks tall and white like it belongs at a wedding. Sadie can sense that Ray is conflicted, unsure, looking to her to see what she wants. Return to the motel and his tentative plan, or stay here in this lit-up cottage with these happy people.

"No drive so late," Pietro says. "We have room."

Ray looks at her. "They have room. We could stay."

They step out onto the front porch together. The lights inside the house twinkle on the sand. Ray stuffs his hands in his jean pockets. Sadie can tell he wants to light a cigarette.

"We don't even know these people," Sadie says.

Ray glances back into the kitchen through the screen door, as if he is worried Emma and Pietro might hear. "They don't even know us."

Sadie looks at him carefully. She wants to say, *We don't even know us,* but says nothing.

"You're going to leave me in suspense here," he says. He looks down at the toes of his shoes, then glances up at her, his face stony. "It's too late to go back, anyway."

He pulls his hands from his pockets and places them on her shoulders. Sadie can hear Emma's soft laughter. She feels her own brittle resolve, and she shrugs Ray's hands away, as if with his touch she will break into pieces. He nods and they step back into the cottage.

Inside Sadie smiles at Pietro and Emma, and thanks them. She takes a glass of wine and sits down at the wooden table, where the cake is placed in the center and four mismatched china plates are laid out. She is perfectly amenable, has stepped into her cordial mode, a role she is familiar with that makes her feel at ease, that of "perfect guest." The cake is dense and sweet, and Pietro launches into another story, parts of which are translated by Emma, who seems to understand his charadeslike movements and signals more than the words he uses. Sadie feels Ray watching her. Another bottle of wine is opened, and Ray drinks as if he is celebrating his own special occasion. In the kitchen, clearing plates, Emma admits how relieved she is that Pietro made it home safely. She tells her she can see how much Ray loves her.

"He doesn't take his eyes off of you," she says. She almost smirks, so satisfied is she with her interpretation.

Sadie doesn't tell her the truth—that he is afraid if he takes his eyes off of her for a moment she might flee. His love is nothing, she wants to say, in the face of their history. Ray and Pietro are sitting on the porch with glasses of sambuca, and Emma and Sadie join them. The waves are whitecapped; the wind buffets the porch screens.

"We should have a bonfire," Emma says.

"Too much wind," Pietro tells her. He takes her hand and brings it to his mouth, then leans in and kisses the place where their child lies beneath her skin. Emma puts her hand in his hair. Sadie feels a kind of protracted longing. Whether Pietro was truly lost or waylaid at a motel with a woman, if he took a wrong turn or planned an evening tryst—none of these things matter. There is a truth that may never be revealed, and the two of them have chosen one version of it to believe. The waves rush in and out, creating a palpable mist. Emma and Pietro both say they are going to bed. Emma points to a door under the stairs and tells them they must be tired. After they have gone Sadie sighs. She turns to Ray and takes his hand. She is resigned to what can happen in this moment, deter-mined to take full advantage of it.

"Let's go to bed," she says.

Ray smiles, slow and sloppy. Sadie sees that now it is his turn to be drunk. She stares at him. The tiny lights inside the cottage seem, in their dazzling way, to send out heat.

"Of course, of course," he says in a rush to reassure her, to lead her, stumbling a little, into the room under the stairs. The doorknob is old, rusted metal. Inside the room Sadie can make out a double bed covered with a chenille spread. They shut the door. She hears the soft murmuring of Emma and Pietro through the floorboards. She unzips her skirt and steps out of it, unbuttons her blouse and lets it slide down her arms. She turns to Ray and undoes the clasp to his jeans while he yanks at the buttons of his shirt. They slip into the bed, into each other's arms. Ray buries his face against Sadie's breasts. She finds that the murmuring from above urges her on. She moves her mouth to his lips, biting them, tasting the anise from the drink, then down across his chest, over his body, his body in its entirety something she needs to taste. He is aroused, begging her, and still she holds him off until he pries her legs open by force and pushes inside her. He moves slowly, inexorably, and then more rhythmically, and when the bed's springs give out their small twinges, he says, "Clare," into her ear, breathing the name out, soft, panting breaths.

She loosens her grip on him, becomes very still, but Ray doesn't seem to notice as he finishes, rolls off of her with a large exhale. She sees that each time it has been Clare he's summoned. Their differences fade away when he's inside her, and then after, she is just Sadie.

In the dark of the little room he touches her face, smooths her hair, kisses her mouth, her ear, her neck. "Go to sleep," he says. Their bodies press together under the sheet, damp and sticky. She hears his breathing, in and out like the sound of the waves on the beach. High tide, she thinks. Upstairs, Emma and Pietro are still. Ray murmurs that he likes the idea that they have all had sex at the same time. She is quiet, her silence seeming like agreement. She knows he has let himself picture Emma's body, her swollen stomach, her full breasts, the tattoo snaking up her arm.

He is not a very nice man. He is *not to be trusted,* a *bad influ-ence, selfish,* all things she imagines he has been called through-

out the years, all things she has been called as well—by her
father after she drove his car off the road, took his money for
apartments, for clothes, and then refused to keep in touch
with him. Even now, in the nursing home, he asks the aides
to call her, to ask when she will come. She has lied to friends,
to lovers, betraying them in small ways, over and over, always
sorry after. She has tried, with Craig, to be a good wife. She
guesses that soon enough he will join the others in classifying
her. They all decide, eventually, there is something wrong
with her, something missing.

"What *happened* to you?" they say, shaking their heads.

Only Sadie doesn't ask this question of Ray. She accepts
him, as if she's always known who he is, what he is capable of.

She lies beside him now, unable to sleep. She blames this
on the sound of the waves, their tumultuous rushing. On the
gentle creaking of the house, its pine-board floors, its cedar
supports, its beadboard walls all expanding, absorbing the mist
off the water. She hears an old clock ticking in the other room.
She hears Pietro's snores. Ray turns over and faces her. He is
awake, too.

"It's strange," he whispers, his voice slurred. "But it all
seems like it was supposed to happen."

"What?" she asks. She knows what he means—she feels it
too—but will not admit it.

"The old woman in the restaurant," he says. "You."

Sadie lies on her back and stares up at the pine ceiling's
knots and whorls.

"Even that girl, Francie Bingham."

Sadie feels the heavy beating of her heart. "What about
her?" she says.

"Those bumbling detectives," he says. "They tried to
blame me for her disappearance, showing me some letter,
suggesting it was written to me. And then I'm up at the old
house the day after they dragged me down to the police station

like a criminal to question me, and there she is looking in at me through the parlor window."

"Francie? What was she doing there?" Sadie asks. She feels vindicated, suddenly angry. If Ray saw her then, it means that Francie had been avoiding the searchers for three days.

"She must have been hiding out," Ray says, picking up on her tone. "She must have been using the house. She had on these bright pink shorts with purple flowers. She had mosquito bites on her legs."

"Did you talk to her?" Sadie turns in the bed to face him.

Ray laughs. "Oh yeah, we had our little conversation. I told her I was going to call the police and tell them where she was. She was pretty clever, hiding out from everyone. I told her she'd gotten me into trouble, and she said she didn't care."

"She said that?" Sadie asks, although she can easily picture Francie saying such a thing.

"I told her it was going to storm, that she needed to go home, and I would drive her," Ray says. But she refused, and he threatened to drag her back, although even as he said it he worried about how it would look.

"They already suspected me," he says. "You know?"

Sadie sees that he is asking her to understand something, to see his side. But she doesn't know, doesn't understand why he wouldn't bring her back, go to her parents and tell them he'd seen her. She breathes in and out, slowly. "What happened then?"

Ray tells her that Francie ran away, turned and fled into the field. He was almost relieved. He watched her go, knowing he could chase her down and catch her, knowing it now, and wondering if given the chance he would have done anything differently.

"I always figured she kept on running—hitchhiking on

I-95, ending up in some other town, with the hippies at the commune in Voluntown, with the runaways in New Haven or New York City. I used to see them all the time on the streets, and I'd look to see if she was one of them."

Sadie suddenly doubts him. She can't understand why Francie wouldn't have been found. The woods were filled with people searching. If she made it to the road and walked along it out of town, she'd have been seen—a chubby girl in bright pink shorts? The second girl in five years to go missing?

"You really think she ran away? That she's alive somewhere?" Sadie asks.

Ray is suddenly quiet. His tone changes. "What are you suggesting? I *saw* her alive. She swore she wasn't going back. She got all upset."

"What about?" Sadie asks tentatively.

"She told me she put it all in the letter, and I must be dense not to have gotten it. I tried to explain to her that I didn't know anything about any letters. I didn't write them, I didn't receive them."

Now Sadie knows he is being coy, playing with her. He props his head up in the darkness and she can feel his eyes on her. "Did I?"

Sadie can't speak. She doesn't think she can take a breath. But he is looking at her, waiting. "No," she says finally.

He rolls away from her and tells how when he left the old house that afternoon the rain had come on, and the lightning, and an oppressive semidarkness. He said it was bad driving home. He took his mother's car, and the leaves were stripped from the trees and blown across his windshield. "Just like this afternoon," he says triumphantly, assured that the co-incidences have meaning. He pulled up the long drive to the house and his mother opened the door, furious.

"Beth had said she'd cover for me, but she'd taken off. I

wasn't supposed to leave the house," he said. "I think my parents really thought I did something to that girl, that if I was seen around town people would become more suspicious." Ray laughs darkly. "I wanted to tell them I'd just seen her, but I couldn't."

It was only July, but they made arrangements for him to return to school early, to live off-campus with one of the teachers, to work in the boathouse.

"Shipped me off," Ray said. Then, musing, "Sometimes I think I might have imagined her."

Ray is quiet. He shifts in the bed and the springs squeak. Sadie wants to pretend to be asleep, but there is the troubling problem of her mother's suitcase, and she has to ask.

"Why did you go to the old house that day?"

"I was looking for her," Ray says. "I wanted to clear my name."

"For Francie," Sadie says.

"Of course," Ray says. "Who else?" He rolls away from her then, as if he is settling in for sleep.

Sadie wonders if she should tell him that during sex he called her by her mother's name, but she realizes that utterance may be the only confession she will have from him.

"And yet you let her go," Sadie says.

"I know," Ray says. "I know. I shouldn't have."

The room is dark, the darkness calm, like Emma and Pietro, two people who fit together.

"But don't think you aren't responsible, too," he says, and his voice shifts—a different, darker note. "You know more than anyone, don't you?"

"What do I know?" she whispers.

The sound of the water becomes less urgent, the tide withdrawing, more like a long intake of breath.

"What she was running from," he says, his voice heavy with sleep.

Sadie feels her eyes fill with tears that spill over her face to wet the pillow. If he hears her he doesn't say anything.

"I'm sure I don't have to tell a man as experienced and knowledgeable as you, Mr. Shannon, that everything has its shadowy side?" she says.

But Ray is quiet. Maybe he has already fallen asleep.

July 6, 1979

I T HAD BEEN ANOTHER DAY OF HEAT AND HUMIDITY
when the police took Ray in for questioning. Sadie had
wanted to go to Betty's but her mother had forbidden it.
She had her arm looped around Sadie's chest and held her
close.

"You aren't going anywhere alone," her mother said.

The fathers who had all participated in the search now
resignedly took their briefcases and suit coats and headed in
to work, each Eldorado and Continental Mark III joining the
procession from the neighborhood into Hartford, and Sadie's
mother dragged Sadie over to the Filleys'. Patsy opened the
door, her face swollen with tears. Beth was behind her, crying
in her pajamas, her face covered by her hands. Sadie's mother
told Sadie to go to Beth, and she took Patsy's arm and they
went outside onto the patio. Sadie imagined this was what it
was like after someone died. She wondered if Beth was remembering Laura Loomis. She approached her and patted her
shoulder. "It will be okay," she said.

Beth lowered her hands and glared at her. "Not if your
bitch of a mother can help it," she hissed.

Sadie jerked back. She removed her hand.

"My brother had nothing to do with that fat little girl's
disappearance," she said. "Now we're ruined. He's ruined for
life."

Sadie sensed that Beth had obtained this last part from Patsy.

238

But she was confused about her mother being implicated—before this summer Beth had always loved Sadie's mother, and Sadie had always been put out about it. Now that she sensed Beth might be an ally against Clare she became more interesting. "My mother is a bitch," Sadie said. "You've got that part right."

"You don't know the half of it," Beth said.

Sadie gave her a wry smile and stared at her wet face. "Is there anything I can do?" she said. Beth turned away and Sadie heard her thump up the stairs and slam her bedroom door. She stood in the foyer at a loss. She went into the den to watch television until Beth came back down an hour later. Her face was blotched, but she was dressed, and her hair was brushed. She seemed to have made an attempt to pull herself together.

"Do you want some lunch?" she said.

They went into the kitchen. Here the walls were lime green. The floor was checkered black and white. A bowl of oranges sat on the counter. Beth took out a jar of pickles, opened it, and began to eat out of it, one pickle after another. Her eyes glazed over. Then she realized what she was doing and stopped.

"Want one?" she said. She held out the jar. She wore a macramé bracelet, and her arms were tanner than Sadie's.

"Where do you think Francie is?" Beth said. She had gotten down a jar of peanut butter and was unscrewing the lid, her face scrunched up with the effort.

Sadie never considered telling Beth about the pond and the floating object. She shrugged. "No idea," she said.

"What about those letters from some *boy*?" Beth said. "What is that all about? What boy would write to her?"

"Seems kind of weird," Sadie agreed.

Beth made two peanut butter sandwiches. She took out some potato chips. "Do you like chips on it?" she said.

"No, thank you," Sadie said.

Beth dropped a handful of chips on one of the sandwiches, placed the piece of bread on top, and pressed it down. She handed Sadie a paper plate with a sandwich, and chips and pickles on the side. She half-filled two glasses with Hi-C and then topped them off with Smirnoff she took from another cabinet—a large bottle she unscrewed expertly and then returned so quickly that Sadie barely had time to register surprise.

"This whole disaster calls for a drink," she said. She lifted the glass and took a sip. Sadie had no choice but to do the same. She took a bite of the sandwich, the peanut butter thick in her mouth, and swallowed the drink, harsh and awful. Beth looked at her and smiled.

"You'll get used to it," she said. "If you're anything like your mother."

She and Beth had poured another drink after that, and maybe another one, the two of them lying out in the yard under the trees, the pasture land rolling away from them, the gladiolas and peonies in the garden wilting in the sun. Sadie asked why Hans wasn't considered a suspect, and Beth laughed, a harsh little sound.

"Oh, your boyfriend's father picked him up right after your little make-out session. Drove him all the way home to Stamford, so *he* has an alibi."

Sadie felt her face redden, but Beth was still looking up at the sky and didn't notice.

Occasionally they'd hear bits of their mothers' conversation, and then the phone would ring, and Patsy would drag the phone on its long extension outside, and they'd hear her talking to Beth and Ray's father, intermittently crying, and screaming into the receiver. Beth would raise her head up and glance down at her mother, her face lit with fear. Sadie's mother gathered her cigarettes to go and let Sadie stay with Beth to keep her company. "You're my sweet, generous-hearted girl," she whispered before she left, her breath smelling of gin. When she tried to hug Beth, Beth pulled back and made a face over Sadie's mother's shoulder.

Sadie had laughed after she went. She'd made fun of her mother, and Beth had joined in.

"I'm so sorry I don't like her anymore," Beth said. "It makes me sad not to like her."

"I'm not sorry," Sadie said. "She's vile."

"You really have no idea," Beth said. She stared at Sadie, a long, intense look. "I just wish things could go back to the way they used to be."

Sadie still didn't know what had made Beth turn against Clare, and since she liked it better this way, she didn't ask. She didn't want to seem as if she cared. They lay back in the dry grass and felt the thunderstorm return, the leaves overhead whipping up, the gray clouds rolling in.

"It's like Rip Van Winkle," Sadie said. "Maybe Francie is playing nine-pins with the strange little men. Maybe she will sleep for twenty years and suddenly reappear in the neighborhood looking like her mother, with wide hips, graying hair, and the beginnings of a double chin."

Beth told Sadie twenty years was too late. "We need to find her *now*," she said. "Oh where oh where is that piggy little girl? If I knew where she was I'd drag her back and make her tell the truth!"

And right then Sadie, *not drunk, just tipsy,* almost told Beth everything. She felt the urge to confess bubble up, a feeling like knowing the answer in school. She saw herself explaining about the letters and clearing Ray's name entirely. But Beth's eyes were lit with a dangerous intensity, and Sadie felt suddenly afraid of her.

"Maybe the dead end is an alien landing place, and she's been taken off as a specimen," she said instead.

Beth stared at her, her eyes suddenly vacant. "You're the

most imaginative person I've ever met," Beth said. "But you're a drunk now, too."

"No, I'm not," Sadie said, but when she stood up she nearly tumbled over. Beth began to laugh and point at her.

Then Ray's father's car pulled into the long driveway, and Beth jumped up and ran down the hill, falling and stumbling, calling, "Ray! Ray!" and Sadie was left alone to watch Ray emerge from the car, sullen in his wrinkled shirt and madras shorts. Beth threw herself into his arms, and he shrugged her off of him. He looked up the hill at Sadie, and then the two of them went into the house. Sadie was left to walk home, the grass and then the tar road tilting and spinning, the wind from the storm whipping the leaves off of the trees, the rain starting up and soaking her through her clothes. She threw up, once into the sewer grate in front of Mrs. Sidelman's house, and again in the row of pine trees that separated the Donahues' from the Frobels', and hoped that no one noticed. She told her mother she had a stomach flu, and her mother chastised her for walking home alone.

"You aren't allowed to be out by yourself," she said. "We don't know what nutcase is stealing little girls."

"I'm hardly little," Sadie said, irritated.

Her mother sighed. She led Sadie upstairs to her own room and pulled back the satin comforter and told her to get in bed. She brought her ginger ale and set it on the nightstand, and then stretched out beside her, and smoothed her forehead like she used to when Sadie was little. Sadie lay there smelling her mother's scent on the pillow, thinking about the pond, and the still water, and the way the insects landed and stirred it, the way the current moved the mysterious object out near the center, raising it up, spinning it about.

August 30, 2003

S ADIE ISN'T SURE WHAT HAS AWAKENED HER UNTIL she hears the foghorn again, a low, mournful sound that seems to enter her body with her breath. The shade flaps gently against the window. The room appears around her, gray at first, then lighter so she can make out the pale painted walls—the leaves of a tree, the birds in its branches, the white crib in the corner. Emma has put them in the nursery. She sits up and slides out of the bed. Ray is asleep, his arm thrown back over his head, his face averted. She puts on her clothes, furtively, and steps over to the crib, and touches the bumper pads, the little knitted blanket draped over the rail. She touches the painted tree, the leaves, the birds and their feathers so real she imagines she might feel their smoothness, their little beating hearts. Behind the tree, painted in the distance, is the cottage she stands in, and beyond that the sound. These aren't store-bought images stuck to the wall with adhesive like hers. These have been painted by a gifted artist—Pietro or Emma, or the two of them, working together.

In the mornings at her house Max wakes first, padding into her room to tug at the bedsheet, often climbing up into the bed with her after Craig has left for work. Max slips into the curl of her body and falls back to sleep, and then Sadie will go downstairs to make coffee, and Sylvia will come down holding Max's hand.

"Why doesn't he sleep in his own bed?" she'll say. "He needs to learn."

Sylvia is envious of Max, and yet she is still the little mother. She makes sure Max has his favorite bowl for cereal—the blue one with Thomas the Tank Engine on the bottom. She helps him pick out clothes that match. Sadie imagines that this is what is happening now, while she is away. She thinks *away*, rather than *gone*. Children adjust; she knows that. Craig will be there to help, and Sylvia will be happy to have her father make her breakfast. She looks a bit longer at the mural on the wall, at the crib, the changing table, the little stack of diapers, the tiny nightgowns folded on a shelf. She knows the bliss that went into setting everything out, putting the crib together, arranging the furniture. She knows how impossible it feels to *get rid* of all of these things. You do not know how to take it all down again, to give it away. That isn't something you imagine you'll have to do. She remembers the old crib in the basement of the house she grew up in, the little appliquéd bears on the headboard, and she wonders how long her mother, too, dreamed of more children.

They brought the baby to Sadie and Craig in the hospital and let them hold her. She was wrapped in the same sort of hospital-issued flannel blanket that Max and Sylvia had been wrapped in, and Sadie noted her perfect features, her stillness, in disbelief that she couldn't bring her home, change her diaper, hold her to her full breasts. Over a year has passed, but Craig has said nothing about the nursery she's left set up, absorbed back into the world of work, believing, perhaps, that it is already dismantled behind the closed door.

It was Sylvia who finally brought it up a week ago.

"Will that room be another baby's?" she said. Her eyes were bright and hopeful.

Sadie had to tell her that no, there wouldn't be another baby, even though she had not discussed this with Craig yet.

They had the two of them, and wasn't that enough? Sylvia said that sometimes she went into the nursery with her doll and pretended she was the new baby. "I put the clothes on her. I change her diaper. I wind up that thing over the crib and listen to the music."

Sadie knows she should have taken it all down by now, put an ad in the *Yankee Flyer*. Someone would have happily come with a truck and hauled it all off—immaculate things, brand-new, never used. Of the women in the neighborhood, only Maura knows about the nursery. Her daughter, Anne, told her after playing at the house. She came by the other day with the excuse of dropping off a school announcement, tapping on her back porch door.

"You know, that extra room would be a great playroom for the kids," she said. She had brought Sadie a catalog filled with playroom items—shelves and baskets, tiny wooden kitchens, pretend food in real-looking packages, a vanity with a mirror, a table with little blocks and drawers built into it for storage. Sadie agreed, and Maura hugged her and left her with the catalog. But she has still not ordered anything. She often found herself at all times of day in the nursery. She'd sit down on the carpet in the center of it and cry. One day Max had a temper tantrum about his Little Bear shirt being dirty, and Sylvia led him into the room and shut the door.

"Where is your brother?" Sadie asked.

"I put him in the crying room," she said.

Sadie accepted the room's new distinction, and it became the place each of them went to be alone, to stare at the flitting birds, the pale green walls, at the way the light came through the blinds and threw the shadows of the leaves there. Sadie wonders if Sylvia is in the room now, having a quiet cry about her mother being gone. She wonders if Craig knows where the waffle mix is kept, how to blow on Max's food first so it isn't too hot, which shorts are his new favorite pair, how he likes his hair wet to keep the cowlick down. For the first time Sadie allows herself to see the limitless list of things that Craig does not know, the things, vital and important to her children's lives, of which he is oblivious. She lets herself acknowledge what must surely be their confusion, their frustration with their father, whom Max will not allow to tie his shoes because he doesn't know how to make the bunny ears first. She sees the place she fits, the gaping space that she has left behind—cavernous, like the hole left by an excised tooth.

She looks over at Ray, asleep on the bed, his hair over his eyes, his soft mouth. She is as complicit as he in this whole seduction. She slips from the room and closes the door. The house is quiet save for the clock. She can see that the tide is out, the water still and the fog floating over it. She goes out onto the porch and through the screen door to the beach. Emma and Pietro have wooden chairs, old heavy Adirondacks, and she sits down in one and buries her feet in the cold, wet sand. If she doesn't plan anything, if she simply lets Ray take her away, the future is a comforting unknown. Yet, when she tries to actively imagine a life with Ray—an apartment in the city, a career—things shift and distort, as if there is a series of doors sliding open and closed that she must navigate in order to exchange one life for the other, her children always trapped behind the one she doesn't choose.

Out along the fog line Sadie sees movement, a breaking of the water, and a small white bobbing. She watches it come from one end of the beach until it is directly in front of her, and she can make it out—someone swimming in a white bathing cap. Whoever it is has long arms and accomplished strokes, measured but steady, the splash barely perceptible, the small froth kicked up by her feet like the churning of a boat's motor. Sadie watches the figure slide through the water past her, past the next jetty, where she turns and begins her slow pace back again. A sailboat unfurls its sails, the rising sun making them bright on the horizon. The fog begins to burn away, and the swimmer's approach seems to falter. Sadie watches with concern. The strokes have stopped, and the person is paddling in feebly, until she is near Sadie's beach and she can stand in the shallow sandbar. The woman wears a navy blue suit, an old-fashioned style with an anchor sewn onto the skirt, the top portion jutting out, filled with wire. She seems to drag herself through the water, and Sadie stands, worrying, and goes down the beach to the water's edge to see that it is Mrs. Sidelman.

"Are you all right?" Sadie asks. She splashes into the water and takes Mrs. Sidelman's arm and helps her up the beach to the chair. Mrs. Sidelman allows herself to be aided, leaning a bit on Sadie and wetting her clothes in the process. She breathes heavily and lets herself be helped into the chair. She leans her head back and raises a shaky hand to remove the cap.

"I thought I could do it," she says. "I used to be able to. I felt strong enough starting out."

Her voice is thin, filled with exhaustion. Sadie remembers that Mrs. Sidelman was once an Aquafemme, and she smiles at the memory, opens her mouth to share it, but then realizes that she cannot. Mrs. Sidelman looks up at Sadie, and her eyes grow wide.

"You're the woman from last night," she says.

"You're Mrs. Sidelman," Sadie says. "I'm Sadie. Sadie Watkins?"

Mrs. Sidelman shakes her head. "Yes. Yes, the daughter, of course. You look just like your mother."

Sadie knows people think it is a nice thing to say, a compliment, so she smiles and keeps quiet.

Mrs. Sidelman looks behind her at the little blue cottage. "Are you staying here?"

"We're visiting friends," Sadie says.

"You and that Filley boy," Mrs. Sidelman says.

Sadie hears her disapproval, but she nods. "Ray," she says. "Are you cold? Would you like a towel?"

Mrs. Sidelman says that she is fine, her cottage is right down the beach.

"So, you still come every summer," Sadie says.

Mrs. Sidelman looks at her then, cocks her head, her eyes intent. "Yes, I do," she says. "So, you're married to the Filley boy."

"Oh, I'm separated," she says. "From my husband."

Mrs. Sidelman eases herself forward in the chair and stands. "Oh," she says. "Well, I'd better get home."

"Just separated," Sadie says, standing up. "Just lately. Would you like me to walk you back?"

"Like a dog?" Mrs. Sidelman says. "It's mortifying to grow old. Yes, you can walk *with* me." She reaches out and holds on to Sadie for support. Sadie feels the papery skin, the slender bones of the woman's arm. Mrs. Sidelman seems tiny now, not the tall, imposing woman she remembers.

She looks up and Sadie is surprised to see that her eyes are warm, filled with kindness. "I always picked the most responsible girls to take care of my house," she says.

They walk down the beach, past the rows of shingled cottages, some quiet, others with occupants just awakening to sit on the porches, the steam from their coffee spiraling through the screens. Sadie says the coffee smells good, and Mrs. Sidelman invites her to stay for some. Her cottage is the largest on the beach—brown shingles with a copper roof.

"Oh, I should get back," she says. And then she thinks about where "back" is and feels a wave of confusion and guilt, as if Mrs. Sidelman already knows what she's done and is passing judgment. "Back to Ray. He'll be waking up."

"Sit down here on the porch. The coffee is already made. I'll bring you a cup."

Sadie protests, but Mrs. Sidelman ignores her and goes

into the cottage, the screen door banging shut behind her. She comes out with a tray—coffee and buttered triangles of toast. Sadie sits down. The porch is open, the breeze coming off the still water cool. The fog is slipping away in strips. "It's just that they'll wonder where I am," she says.

Mrs. Sidelman stares at her. She pours cream into her coffee and stirs. "Who?" she says pointedly. "Who will wonder?"

Sadie shakes her head. "Well, Ray and our friends." But she knows that isn't the answer.

Mrs. Sidelman's spoon clinks against the side of her cup. She begins to tell her about the neighborhood. "Mrs. Hoskins passed," she says. "You would probably have guessed that. The Battinsons are still there, and the Frobels. The Schusters moved away, and I'm sure you know about the Donahues." She glances up at Sadie, her eyes searching. "Poor Mrs. Bingham died this year—cancer. But young families have moved in, and I have a new girl watering my plants this summer."

Sadie lifts her cup to her lips and finds her hand shakes.

"Do you have any children?" Mrs. Sidelman asks.

"I do. A girl and a boy—Sylvia and Max," Sadie says.

Mrs. Sidelman smiles at her. "I'm sure you're a wonderful mother. You were always so imaginative as a child."

Sadie feels cornered, the way she did at Cherrystones when she first spotted Mrs. Sidelman and there was suddenly someone present who knew the girl she was, the woman she was destined to become. It doesn't matter that Mrs. Sidelman is old and out of touch, that her ideas are from another era when marriage and child rearing weren't options you questioned. Sadie realizes that all of this time she has believed what she has done is forgivable, an offense that might be explained away, and now, sitting across from a woman whose saved love letters prove she, too, had choices, she's afraid she's been wrong.

"Don't be so sure about that," she says. "I may not be as good a mother as you think."

She tries to say it lightly, as if she is joking, but Mrs. Sidelman doesn't respond. She places her spoon on her saucer carefully, letting the quiet expand.

"Some days I think I may be as terrible as my mother," Sadie says.

Mrs. Sidelman looks up at Sadie sharply, her expression fierce. "Your mother made a mistake she couldn't correct."

No one understood that Sadie had, at times, wished for her mother to actually succeed at killing herself. The multiple hospitalizations could only have been other times she'd tried, she'd reasoned long ago—enough times for Sadie's initial terror to transform to resentment, to believe that her mother's attempts were games, that she would always emerge victorious in the hospital, watching her soap opera in her matching nightgown and robe. Truthfully, that last summer her mother had surprised her each morning by being alive, each afternoon by baking brownies and Rice Krispies treats, her hair washed and styled, her clothing clean and pressed, as if she'd just come in from bridge club. So, when Sadie got off the school bus that September afternoon, only two months after Francie's disappearance, and went up the leaf-strewn walk into the house, she expected her mother to greet her. Instead, the house was empty. She called for her and then hesitantly investigated the rooms—trying not to imagine her mother twisted in the bedsheets, or in the bathtub in a puddle of blood, or hanging from a rafter in the basement. When her search uncovered none of these things she was more relieved than suspicious.

Sadie shrugged off her coat. She made herself a peanut butter sandwich. The kitchen was spotless, as usual, but there wasn't a note folded on the table, telling her where her mother had gone. She took her food and her book bag up to her room and sat on her bed. That part bothered her, a little. Her mother always left a note, and since school had begun she rarely went out when Sadie was expected home—as if Sadie might be next in line to be taken, like Francie and Laura Loomis. Outside the window, bright leaves flapped on the tree branches. Sadie pressed her face up against the cold window and peered into the backyard and the woods. There was Mrs. Sidelman, standing with her rake, paused in her work and staring over toward Sadie's house. "What?" Sadie asked out loud, her breath fogging the glass.

Sadie's bedroom was adjacent to the garage, and she heard it then—the sound of a car engine running. She thought her mother was just getting home from the store, from an afternoon play practice, from Westfarms Mall. She went down to the den, and tugged the door to the garage open, and peered in at the Coupe de Ville. The light was dim with the garage door closed, the smell of exhaust strong and noxious. There was her mother behind the wheel. She wore her camel-hair coat. Sadie heard the radio playing under the chugging of the engine. She called to her mother, but she saw that she just sat there, staring out the one window into the woods, into the spaces between the trees where the dried cornstalks lined the fields. Through the window Sadie saw Mrs. Sidelman peering in, clutching a rake. Their eyes met, the horror of the moment equally shared, a parcel shifted back and forth and back. Something in Sadie clicked.

Her mother was dead.

She knew it with a matter-of-factness that surprised her even then. There was no clutch of panic, no rush to open the garage door. She didn't stumble back from the sight. She turned and shut the door. She went to the kitchen phone and called her father at his office. He was out, his secretary said. "Can I take a message?" Sadie said to tell him that her mother was in the garage in the car, and she hung up. Since Francie's disappearance she'd been waiting, apprehensive, for the punishment she deserved—for Betty to confess and implicate her, for Francie's body to be found—and yet she never expected her mother's suicide to be the outcome of her fear. That day, something at her core seized up into a hard, impermeable knot that she now sees has never loosened, that as time passed she must have grown used to.

Mrs. Sidelman came to the back porch door moments later. She was there, knocking, demanding to be let in. "Sadie Watkins," she said, her teacher's voice firm. "Open the door."

But Sadie did not do it. She went up to her bedroom and sat on her bed until she heard voices downstairs, the rush and stumble of strangers' footsteps. And then Betty's mother came up the stairs and entered her room. She sat beside Sadie on the bed, cautiously, as if Sadie were a wild animal that might bolt. Sadie could feel her trying to control her sobs, and she looked over at her, dry eyed, knowing that she, too, should be crying. But she only felt relief. Charlene put her arm around Sadie's shoulders, and then helped her pack a small bag of clothes and walked her across the street to her house just as the ambulance, turning into Sadie's driveway, bumped up the curb.

Sadie remembers the expressions of the people around her, first at the Donahues', and then later at the funeral—their tear-stained faces, the women's smeared mascara, the men's red-rimmed eyes, their awkward embraces. She recalls being held by strangers, inhaling their various complicated smells. For a long time after there were those looks—soft, sad smiles. None like the one Mrs. Sidelman gave her through the garage window, the one she gives her now.

"I went out to rake leaves," she says. "I heard the car running, but it was like background noise, and I didn't give it much notice until I realized what it was. I wish to this day that I had gotten there first, that I might have spared you that."

Sadie remembers the leaves blowing about the driveway, the swirls of them, their beautiful flattened shapes on the walkway. Mrs. Sidelman reaches out and takes Sadie's hand in her own.

"Your mother loved you very much," she says. "I remember one Easter she had you in the most adorable matching dress and spring coat. You had a straw hat and a little purse and white gloves. She brought you over so you could show me before you left for church. She always told me how proud she was of you."

Mrs. Sidelman went on to describe her mother's praise—stories of Sadie's good grades, the poems Sadie wrote her for her birthday, her confidence that Sadie would one day find a greatness all her own.

"Oh, she had such high expectations of you," she says.

Sadie feels she is hearing about some other child, some other life. Then she remembers the card in the suitcase, and realizes that at one time she had high expectations for her mother, too—and her mother wanted to remember that. Mrs. Sidelman pours more coffee. Her spoon hits the side of the china cup. A seagull squawks from the jetty. Her smile is calm, her silence a space waiting to be filled. Sadie wishes she could take it all back. She thinks about Ray asleep in the cottage nursery, about his plan for them to run away together that doesn't seem like a plan at all anymore, just a series of beds and sex. She feels the first cold edges of shock at what she's done, and her urge is to shock Mrs. Sidelman in turn, to startle her so she's not so alone.

"I've been sleeping with Ray," Sadie says. She doesn't say "having an affair" or name Ray as her "lover," words that sound adult and old-fashioned, that might be ascribed to her mother. "We met, secretly, twice. And then we planned to meet last night, and somehow—I don't know—we drove off together."

She wants the woman to stop smiling. She is furious with herself, with Ray and his foolhardy life, with her mother, who left her with an emptiness she has no idea how to fill, much less name. Why she wants to lash out at Bea Sidelman is as inexplicable as anything she has done in the last twenty-four hours, the last twenty-four years.

"I've left them," she says then. "My children, my husband."

Saying the words makes them real, the finality leaden.

Mrs. Sidelman watches Sadie, her eyes fixed, and Sadie keeps talking, telling her more. She talks about Lily, the little girl she lost, how she went into labor, how it was only three weeks early and they were safely checked into the hospital.

"I could see," she says, "if it had been back in the days when women had babies in houses without heat and running water, without modern medicine, with just herbs and roots to treat complications." She remembers the graves in the old cemetery, the markers for the infants with the inscription *Born and died,* followed by a single date. As a child, Sadie hadn't understood how this might be possible, much less imagined a time it might happen to her.

She tells her how the labor was normal. "She looked perfectly fine," Sadie says. "I couldn't quite believe it. Sometimes I still don't. Sometimes I think she is somewhere else, living a life with other parents. Stolen from me."

Like Francie, Sadie thinks. She won't confess about the letters. Despite Ray's accusation that she is complicit, she isn't sure how much the letters contributed to Francie's ultimate disappearance. In the light of what she's learned—about Ray, about her mother—the letters are only a part. Sadie has eaten one of the triangles of toast, and then another, and now discovers she has eaten them all. She sits back. Mrs. Sidelman has remained silent all of this time. The sun heats up the sand. The tide has shifted and the water laps at the jetty, fills the pockets between the stones with a hollow slap.

"I don't know what to do now," Sadie says.

On her fingers are the buttered crumbs, and the taste of

the toasted bread still fills her mouth. She feels desperate, depleted. Mrs. Sidelman's eyes watch her with the kind of sorrow that cannot be ignored.

"Can I be honest with you?" Mrs. Sidelman says. "I feel I owe you that much."

Sadie nods, curious. Mrs. Sidelman tells her that when her mother first moved to the neighborhood they became friends.

"We would have coffee," Mrs. Sidelman says. "Like you and I are doing now."

Over coffee, Clare revealed her dreams of an acting career, and also personal things about her husband—how he insisted on having sex on Friday nights, and no other night would do. How he made strange faces when he climaxed. She told her about her feelings for other men. It would be one she met at a party or someone she saw at Drug City, who held the door for her and whose cologne she could not forget. Mrs. Sidelman, Bea, encouraged Clare to join the community theater, tried to discourage her from obsessing about the men.

"I told her to buy the cologne for her husband," Bea says. "I said, 'Close your eyes when you make love.' Well, she didn't want my advice."

Bea tells Sadie that her mother came to her one afternoon, brimming with news.

"She was pregnant," she says. "I worried, of course, about who the father of the baby was, but I didn't let on. She was happy, and that was all that mattered."

Sadie can't imagine her mother pregnant, but this is another woman Bea's describing, someone Sadie didn't know. "She lost the baby," Sadie says, finally understanding.

Bea nods solemnly. "And the one after that. And then another."

Sadie remembers the wary happiness, the crushing sadness of her own lost pregnancies.

Bea says she called Sadie's mother and her father would tell her she couldn't come to the phone. Bea baked a lemon pound cake and left it at the house, and she found it later in the day on her own front porch. Sadie's mother made it clear she wanted nothing to do with her, for whatever reason. "This was long before I wrote the reviews," Bea said. "At the time, I didn't know why, but maybe she felt she'd shared too much." She finally accepted this and stopped trying to contact her. "I heard later that she'd taken an overdose of pills."

Bea sips her coffee. She looks up at Sadie over the rim of her cup, her eyes softened.

"But I couldn't sit by and allow what was happening with that Filley boy," Bea says. "I saw him that summer before I left for the shore—slipping into your basement. At first, God forgive me, I thought you were letting him in. But one morning your mother came out with him—and they embraced. I was standing on my porch, and your mother saw me watching."

Bea looks to Sadie, waiting, her mouth tight.

"Blame me for her suicide, if you want. But don't think you're destined to become her."

Sadie wonders how many people claim responsibility for her mother's death. Hasn't she thought back through it all herself—over and over again? How her mother had pressed a new shirt for Sadie and made her a lunch to take to school. How she was dressed and standing by the door as Sadie left to catch the bus—the white silk blouse, the herringbone skirt. She tried to kiss Sadie good-bye, but Sadie felt awkward in her arms and pulled away. Her mother called to her as the bus chugged up the hill, but the other kids were there, and Sadie only glanced back and didn't hear what her mother said. Was it an important message? Some instruction that Sadie neglected to follow? She imagines her mother putting on her coat, mixing the drink they found with her in the car, cutting the lime they found on the counter, gathering her cigarettes. What journey did her mother take, watching the woods waving beyond the garage window?

Mrs. Sidelman gives her a long look. "It's not about judgment. It's about how you choose."

Sadie realizes that she's been involved in a long pursuit and sees now that having recognized it, she cannot go on any longer. Her mother is still gone, and she is still floundering, unsure. She remembers the Mary Vial Holyoke diary, the entries that chart the death of Mary's daughter, Polly, the women all coming to sit and *watch*—the word conjuring up figures by a bedside, their presence a balm, bearing witness. Sadie shunned the women trying to *watch* her, hid herself away with her sorrow rather than share it and move on. She never considered that her mother did the same. Pretending it had never happened, seeking her own method of escape.

"I should leave," she says. She stands up, suddenly, and knocks her china cup onto the stone patio, where it shatters, a sound that is both delicate and deafening. Sadie looks down at it in despair.

"I'm so sorry," she says, and stoops to pick up the shards. Mrs. Sidelman waves her hand at Sadie's apology. "It's an old cup," she says. "Don't worry about it." But Sadie bends down and gathers the little floral-patterned pieces, her eyes stinging with tears. When she stands Mrs. Sidelman is standing as well, and they look at each other—Sadie with the china pieces gathered in her hand, Bea Sidelman with her hands clenched like a warrior.

"You're going home," Bea says in that way she has of making an order out of a question.

Sadie is afraid to imagine it, to allow herself to entertain the idea. "I could go wake up Ray and ask him to take me back," she suggests.

"I'll drive you," Bea says. She takes the china pieces from

Sadie's hand and disappears inside the cottage. She emerges in a caftanlike cover-up, jingling a set of car keys.

"I don't want to bother you," Sadie says.

"Nonsense," Bea says.

They climb into her long Grand Marquis, the sand from their feet falling onto the floor mats. Sadie settles back into the leather upholstery, already hot from the sun, but she cannot relax. They pass Pietro and Emma's, Ray's truck still there in the sandy lot in front.

"What if it's too late?" Sadie says. She doesn't say anything about Craig refusing to take her back, the children with questions she cannot answer.

Bea reaches over and pats her hand. "Never too late," she says. "You'll tell him you ran into an old friend of your mother's, and I invited you to my house. We had too much sherry, and you fell asleep."

"The children will hate me," she says. "They won't ever trust me again."

"They'll forget," Bea says. "It won't matter in light of everything else."

Sadie understands what she means, the way that memories come like postcards pinned to a board, standing in for years of a life. And even though she isn't entirely convinced she can return, that Craig will accept Bea Sidelman's outlandish story, she lets herself imagine the smell of her children—Max like sweat and earth, Sylvia cleaner and sweeter, like her Bonne Bell perfume, like her Johnson's Baby Shampoo. She imagines the swell of Craig's chest beneath his work shirt, his brusque, familiar way of saying good-bye in the mornings. She thinks about the casserole recipe that Maura gave her two days before—Indian inspired, with raisins and almonds—and imagines what it will taste like. Ray's truck disappears in the rearview mirror. They turn onto Shore Road and head toward the highway, and Bea turns on the radio to a station playing old forties and fifties hits and she begins to sing along, softly, to "Baubles, Bangles, and Beads." Sadie knows she cannot ask Bea about her hidden love letters, but she remembers the longing in them, Bud's desire to make a life with her, the lost opportunity. Bea made her choice, and yet she kept the letters all those years. Sadie doesn't think she could keep Ray's letters, not when she sees them as devices to lure her into having sex, letters written to a dead woman, a character she tried to play. "Clare," he said, his voice low and tremulous, a fleeting sound that might, as time passes, be yet another thing she tells herself she only imagined.

Bea signals and changes lanes. The radio is lost beneath the rush of morning traffic composed of commuters heading into Hartford, vacationers anticipating the holiday weekend. The cars merge and speed past them, and she worries about letting Bea, an eighty-year-old woman, drive on the interstate highway, about a tractor-trailer nudging them off into the metal guardrail. The traffic slows and jams and then inches along, the heat rising off the car bumpers. Sadie tries to remain calm, but she is filled with a sudden urgency. Now that she's decided to return she is faced with the exasperating possibility of being prevented from doing so.

July 7, 1979

THE SEARCH FOR FRANCIE MOVED INTO ITS THIRD day, and still there was no mention of finding a body in the pond. It was a Saturday, and the fathers gathered at the end of the street to meet with state police and firefighters, with people on horseback, with the National Guard. They were placed into search parties and sent out into the same woods, the same swampy ground they'd searched for the last three days, that they'd searched five years ago for another girl. Already, a few had expressed frustration. "Maybe there's a black hole in the woods," one said. "Maybe there's a Bermuda Triangle thing going on here." Sadie heard her own father downstairs that morning.

"It's just getting depressing," he'd said before he left.

The mothers gathered around kiddie pools with the younger children, their voices lowering and then ceasing altogether when Sadie and Betty approached. Each car that drove by was noted and its make, model, and tag recorded: maroon Oldsmobile Toronado, blue wood-paneled Chrysler Town and Country wagon, black Cadillac Calais. The list was supplied to the detective, the cars checked out, the occupants verified: Mrs. Holmes going to visit her daughter, Jill Mandell bringing doughnuts to her sister's family, a priest going to visit the Mansfield kids' grandfather and administer last rites.

Betty and Sadie sat up in Sadie's bedroom in the sweltering heat, eating root beer Popsicles. It was late afternoon.

Before Betty came over, Sadie had passed by her mother's bedroom door and seen her packing her suitcase. She'd stood and watched her through the crack in the door placing items in, the suitcase open on her bed. Then her mother had closed the suitcase and stood before the mirror, fixing her hair, and Sadie had slipped away from the door and into the hall bathroom, where she'd watched her mother with her suitcase head downstairs, the hem of her sundress brushing the carpeted steps. Sadie heard the garage door, and when she went downstairs the garage was empty and her mother's car was gone. Sadie wondered where she'd go, whether she was coming back. Her father came into the garage, his T-shirt damp, his face and arms sunburned and scratched in the search.

"Where's your mother gone?" he asked.

"To the store," Sadie said. "For some ice cream."

Two hours had passed since her mother had left, and the prospect of her never returning filled Sadie with a buzzing sense of apprehension. Betty sat across from her on the bed, and relayed how she'd heard her mother on the phone with her grandmother and that she was thinking of taking them all to her grandmother's house in Farmington. " 'Another girl is *missing*,' " Betty said, imitating her mother's harsh whisper. " 'They already took a neighbor boy in for questioning. What about all the other neighbors they haven't questioned? What about the people who drive through that we don't see? I can't sit at my window all day thinking everyone is a kidnapper, or worse!' "

Betty's grandmother must have suggested that Francie ran away. "This girl isn't like that," her mother said. Betty imitated her mother taking a long drag of her cigarette. "She's a little, dumpy thing."

Betty said her grandmother must have asked whether Francie was a *Mongoloid*.

"It's called Down syndrome, Mother, and no, she isn't,

she's a smart girl, smarter than my kids. They found sheaves of notebook paper in her bedroom, practically a book she'd written, some fairy tale with kings and queens and magic spells."

Sadie eyed Betty. They'd gotten some of that in the letters. But not a book, not a whole story. "I wonder if we can find that," Sadie mused, preoccupied. She still half-believed that Francie was running away—escaping whatever it was that came into her room at night.

Betty dripped her Popsicle onto her leg and then dipped her mouth down to lick it off. Outside the wind picked up in the trees, and they could smell the air, cooler, filled with the approaching afternoon thunderstorm. The sun flitted in and out of clouds. The curtains billowed out. They talked about poor Ray Filley and wondered what would happen to him next.

"It's all our fault," Betty said.

"No," Sadie said, jaded by her experience with Beth at her house. "It's not."

"What if she was really taken?" Betty said.

Sadie shifted back onto her pillow. "Who would take *her*?"

Betty gave her a halfhearted smile. "I guess."

"After five minutes anyone would kick her out of the car." Sadie sat up and made a Francie face and assumed her Francie voice. "Excuse me, but I'd like a general idea of the direction we're heading. I do have a vocal lesson this afternoon, and I told my boyfriend, Hezekiah, that I would meet him at two o'clock precisely. I'm a stickler about being on time, and I really appreciate that in others as well. A ride in a car with the windows down is a nice change from my routine, but getting back *on time* is a priority."

Betty fiddled with her Popsicle stick, and Sadie kept on, believing she could make Betty laugh. "I like this part of town, it's really new to me, and it's been a pleasure taking this sight-seeing tour of New England's quiet country roads, but I hate to worry my family unduly."

"Stop," Betty said.

Sadie widened her eyes and puffed her cheeks up. "I'm quite certain that it is past my lunchtime, and a regularly scheduled mealtime is essential for children's health and well-being. I haven't noticed any restaurants on our drive through these scenic woods, so perhaps you have a picnic lunch packed? I enjoy peanut butter and jelly, but bologna is okay if it's been kept cool."

There was a soft knock on Sadie's door, and Betty jumped. Then the door opened just a bit, and Sadie's mother spoke through the crack.

"I just want you to know that I hear you," she said, her voice hoarse and quavering. "I'm so very disappointed with the way you're behaving." And then the door closed, and Sadie and Betty heard Sadie's mother's soft footfalls moving down the hall. Her bedroom door opened and then closed. Nothing remained of her mother but her words, and the almost imperceptible smell of stale Chanel No. 5. Sadie felt a joyous relief, sure her mother had left them, had a change of heart, and returned. Betty said nothing. She bit her lip.

"Oh my God," she whispered.

Then Sadie's father came upstairs. They heard the creak of the stair treads, heard him open the bedroom door and accost Sadie's mother in his booming voice.

"Well, where's the ice cream?"

Sadie's mother said she didn't know what he was talking about, her voice muffled by the pillow.

"Why aren't you out searching?" she said.

"They sent us home," her father said, his voice lowered. "They don't want us to be the ones to find her body."

Betty's eyes widened, and Sadie put a finger to her lips, signaling her to be quiet. Once they heard her father retreat down the stairs they emerged from Sadie's room. They stepped quietly by Sadie's mother's bedroom door, and Betty moved past it to the stairs, but Sadie paused, listening, and heard only her mother's sobbing, stifled by the pillow. She felt all of her gladness depart. In its place was a hollow worthlessness—weren't she and her father enough to make her happy? And now there was her mother's concern for Francie.

Betty started down the stairs, but Sadie made her Francie face.

"Yes, I'm thrilled to spend the night! No one asks me. This is exciting, almost like a campout. I'll just snuggle up here in the backseat."

"What kind of girl are you?" her mother cried out from inside the room, her voice close to a wail. "I can't believe you are my daughter."

Sadie told her mother she was going to Betty's, and she followed Betty down the stairs. They went to the screen door and watched the wind whip up the poor maple tree, the green leaves flapping violently, the sky a roiling gray. Upstairs they heard the bedroom door open.

"We'd better run," Sadie said, and they took off across the front lawn, the wind yanking their hair, bending the trees. They reached Betty's house, and inside her mother clanked the pans around in the kitchen, and Sadie felt the strangeness she always felt, no matter how many times she'd been there, of being a guest in another house—allowed the opportunity to be served first at the large kitchen table, having to bow her head for the blessing, mouth the words she did not know, having to observe the petty arguments of a large family, from the size of the servings ("He took more!") to the proximity of chairs ("Move *over*! You're touching me!"), and endure the questioning of Betty's mother playing amateur sleuth.

"You girls sure you didn't notice anything unusual that day?"

Charlene kept her cigarettes and her ashtray on the window ledge near her chair. Her mouth was narrow and tense, and between small bites of food she squinted at Betty, then at Sadie.

"Nothing at all?" she said. "No cars on the street? What about the Filley boy? Did you see him? Was he anywhere around?"

Betty whined and sighed, imposed upon and humiliated. Sadie offered as much information as she could invent without giving herself away. She wanted to divulge the location of the pond, and she decided Betty's mother was the conduit.

"The other day when Betty and I went looking for Francie and got lost, we did find this pond, a big one, on the edge of the woods." She took a bite of pork chop and chewed.

Betty's mother perked up. "Really? A pond?"

Betty's father sighed and shifted in his wooden chair. "Charlene," he said.

"But a pond? I don't know if that's been checked out. That's a hazard, you know? The kids should be warned away from that."

"The kids are smart enough not to go into a pond if they don't know how to swim."

"I swam in a pond once and they have mucky bottoms. Lots of weeds," Sadie said.

Betty's father took up two spaces at the table. His face, perennially red, made him seem as if he was always holding his breath. He gave Sadie a paternal look, his eyes kind.

"That's true," he said.

Betty's mother set her fork down on her plate. "We should mention the pond to the police," she said.

"The entire area has been searched. I'm certain the pond was—well, searched, too."

"A girl did drown there once," Sadie said.

"What, sweetie?" Betty's mother said.

"In the pond," Sadie said. "Back in the seventeen hundreds."

Betty's mother and father exchanged a glance. Betty's siblings, their faces all a version of Betty's—younger, shorter, thinner, with only slightly varying shades of hair color—all looked up at Sadie, then at their parents in turn.

"Who wants dessert?" Betty's mother said, her voice high and sweet.

"I'm pretty sure it was that pond," Sadie said. "A Filley girl."

Betty elbowed Sadie. Her siblings were already stacking the plates, clearing the table, distracted by the mention of chocolate pudding. The rain came slashing against the window, pooled in the sill, and Betty's mother quickly shut it. The second-to-youngest Donahue child, Joey, was afraid of thunder and lightning, and Betty and Sadie were required to take him with them to the subterranean level of the split ranch to distract him with a rerun of *Wild Wild West*. Sadie sat on Betty's modern couch, the cushions stiff squares, the fabric a nubby tweed that left its imprints on her legs. While Betty's brother sat immersed in the television she leaned toward Betty.

"What if she's out there?" Sadie said. A wet leaf, ripped from a tree, pressed up against the high window. The temperature dropped with the storm, and the rain would wet Francie's clothes, her hair. Her glasses would be smeared, rendered useless. Maybe she would huddle at the base of a tree, but Sadie remembered the warning about trees and lightning. There might be an old abandoned fort, a cave. Sadie imagined Francie in the trunk of a stranger's car. The thunder sent Joey Donahue up onto the couch between them, and at the moment that James West in his tight pants thwarted Dr. Miguelito Loveless, the evil dwarf, the television clicked off, and the room, once lit by its rays, was thrown into darkness. Betty, Sadie, and Joey all shrieked, and from upstairs came Mr. Donahue's lumbering footsteps.

"The lights are out," he said. "I'm coming down."

He appeared behind a wavering beam of light and showed them the way upstairs, where Betty's mother was moving about the kitchen, lighting candles, telling the children who seemed to be glued to her clothes, "Don't touch! Don't touch!"

Betty and Sadie took a candle back down to the rec room and sat on the couch and watched the wax melt around the base of the candlestick holder. "Remember Old-Fashioned-Days House?" Betty said.

Sadie had been thinking more about James West's blue eyes, his tight clothes, the vest he wore over his nice white shirt, than about wandering the woods in a long dress. The strangeness of these thoughts, their allure, made her feel oddly empty, as if the girl she once was had gone forever, and in her place was someone she was afraid to know. She stayed at Betty's another half hour, watching out the window for a light to come on in her house, but it remained dark, and she dreaded going home. When Betty's mother started calling the younger kids for baths, Sadie told Betty she should probably go, hoping she'd say no, but Betty didn't invite her to spend the night, and Betty's father gave her his golf umbrella and stood at the door watching her as she crossed the street.

The rain had slowed to a soft pattering. Sadie only pretended to enter her dark house, waiting for Betty's father to leave his post at his front door, then walked down the street in the rain. The streetlights were out, but the clouds had moved on, and the street seemed as she'd once imagined it—magical and moonlit. In this strange light, Sadie saw a figure approaching—smallish and wet, covered in mud—and she stared in amazement, sure it was Francie finally relinquishing her hiding place, newly thankful for her warm house, her comfortable bed, still oblivious of what Sadie had done. Sadie stepped up her pace and almost called out. But as she got closer she saw the figure was Beth. She wore the oxford shirt she'd had on the afternoon of the lobster bake, now streaked with dirt, and a pair of shorts. Her shoes were caked with mud, her hair soaked to her head, as if she, and not Francie, had been outside these past two hours in the storm. Sadie held the umbrella for her, and Beth stepped beneath it, and Sadie felt Beth's body shaking, the kind of uncontrollable tremors Sadie would get after swimming too long in very cold water.

"Where have you been?" Sadie said, shocked at Beth's appearance.

"Where have you been?" Beth said, her voice quaking.

"At Betty's," Sadie said.

"At Betty's," Beth said, the strange hiccuping not masking her snide tone.

"Why are you mimicking me?" Sadie said. Betty's younger brothers and sisters often mimicked each other. It became a game to see how long one child could keep it up until the other resorted to violence. Beth didn't answer. Instead she continued her shaking and allowed Sadie to walk her up the street to her house, then up her driveway, through the iron gate, to the back door by the pool. As they stood there the power suddenly returned, and the pool was illuminated, the shrubbery surrounding it lit by carefully positioned lamps. The light by the back door had come on, too, and Sadie saw the true state of Beth's clothing: the mud on her back, on the sleeves of her shirt, and on the front another smear—a rusty color, like blood.

"Were you up in the woods?" Sadie asked. "Are you hurt?" She wondered what Beth had been doing, if she'd been following Ray, like she always threatened to, or if she'd been frightened by something instead—kidnapped by the same person who took Laura Loomis and Francie, and made a narrow escape.

"What were you doing up there?" Sadie asked, desperate

now to know. "Did you see something? Did you see some-one?"

Beth stared at her, her hair wet along the sides of her face, her eyes dark and wide, and said nothing. Then she flung her back door open, and Sadie set the umbrella on the patio and followed her inside into a dim tiled hallway. She watched as Beth slopped mud across the white tiles into the laundry room. Here she kicked off her shoes, took off her shorts and her shirt, the whole thing performed quickly despite her un-controllable shaking. She left the clothing in a sodden pile, glanced up, and seemed surprised to see Sadie still standing there, staring.

"Don't look at me!" she shrieked, and slammed the laun-dry room door. For the second time that day Sadie stood out-side a door, listening to sobbing.

PART FIVE

MOTHER TRIES TO GET ON WITH LIFE

Wintonbury—December 13, 1974

Six months ago, Laura Loomis's mother took her and a girl-friend for an afternoon of swimming at the Wampanoag club pool. After, she dropped Laura at the friend's house down the road with the instruction to be home by dinnertime. "I walked her to the door," the girlfriend said. "I watched her go down the front walk to the road." Though there were no signs of a struggle, Mrs. Cynthia Loomis, Laura's mother, knows that Laura wouldn't get into the car of just anyone. "Sometimes, I still can't believe this has happened," she said quietly, sitting at her kitchen table, looking out a window into a snow-covered backyard woods. Laura's drawings are taped up on the wall. "Laura was a smart girl in school. She was very artistic—she loved to draw." Mrs. Loomis hopes the FBI, which has been called in to the case, will provide some answers. Life at home will never be the same. "We can't ever get over it," she said. "You just find yourself waiting."

August 30, 2003

BEA SIDELMAN PULLS THE GRAND MARQUIS ALL THE way down the old Filley house's gravel drive. The rain the day before has left the grass damp and green, and there are still puddles. Sadie has the window down and breathes in the thick air. "It'll be a hot one," Bea says. They pass a white Audi convertible parked in front of the house. Bea glances at Sadie and tells her that the car belongs to the sister, Beth.

"She's always tooling up and down the street in it," Bea says.

She pulls up to the barn and stops. She keeps her hands at ten and two on the wheel. "Take care now," she says, back to her schoolteacher manner. "You were always a smart girl, Sadie Watkins."

Sadie leans over in the car and puts her arms around Bea. She feels her narrow shoulders tense and then relax, and the woman's arms come up and Sadie feels a soft patting on her back.

"Go on home," Bea says, her voice breaking.

She watches while Sadie gets out and opens the barn door to reveal her car, and then she waits, the car's big engine idling, while Sadie gets inside and starts the SUV up and pulls out. The smell of the barn—the hay, the oiled tools, the bags of lime—has seeped into her car's upholstery. She watches Bea Sidelman disappear down the drive, and when she hears her accelerate out onto the road she pulls up alongside Beth's convertible, climbs from the car to stand in the old house's shadow, thrown now onto the grass. She feels a vague unease. She moves up the slate walkway, around the overgrown rho-dodendron, to the front door and knocks, the wait interminable. She knocks again but, impatient, tries the door and finds it open. She steps into the hallway, onto the old wide chestnut floorboards, and then moves farther into the house, hesitantly stepping into the open room with the fireplace—*the parlor,* Ray called it. Today the room is bright with sunlight. There is a couch pushed against one wall, an old television on a stand. A crystal chandelier throws prisms of light onto the plaster walls. The windows are open, and on the chestnut floors are swaths of wetness, as if they were left open during the storm and the rain was allowed to come in. Sadie imagines Francie peering in the window, her eyes eager behind her glasses, her hair hanging lank and dirty to her shoulders, looking like a ghost waiting for Ray, much as she stood at the fence in the kindergarten playground, expecting Sadie and Betty to bring her the candies they'd promised. Sadie could see her, defiant, her hands on her hips, her dirty face, her wide eyes and pale skin dotted with insect bites. *Maybe she did keep running,* Sadie thinks. *Maybe she's finally made a life for herself somewhere and is happy.*

She turns from the window toward the fireplace and sees that a panel is swung open on invisible hinges to reveal a wood-framed space beside it. The *hidey spot.* Inside, in the shadowy interior, is a dull-colored pile of something she cannot discern and a bit of still-bright fabric. Pink and purple. Before she can step closer she hears footsteps, a sharp-heeled clicking down a staircase somewhere.

"What are you doing?" Beth says. She emerges from a doorway, her hands on her hips. "You just walk right in?"

Sadie notices Beth's clothes—a flowered dress cinched

with a belt, a stone necklace, and sandals with sensible heels. Beth looks the part of a schoolteacher, but Sadie remembers her as the sad, somewhat pathetic girl of her childhood. Her bobbed hair swishes along her shoulders the same, but Sadie notices once again that Beth seems much older—the grooves around her mouth deep, her eyes ringed with smudgy makeup, the skin crepelike. She is aged, beyond her years.

Sadie is aware of how she looks in her own wrinkled skirt and blouse. "I apologize for just walking in, Beth," she says. "It's me, Sadie Watkins?"

Beth clenches her jaw. Her eyes flit around the house, as if something has caught her attention—a fly or a bee caught in the room.

"I know who you are," Beth says.

"I came to pick up something of mine," Sadie tells her. "I left it here."

"Here? I don't know, I don't think so," she says. She stares wide-eyed at Sadie, a look that makes her old face seem child-like, guileless.

"It's upstairs in Ray's room," Sadie says.

Beth smiles then, a false smile of the type with which Sadie has long been familiar and that in any other circumstance, from another woman, would have put her at ease.

"Oh, I haven't seen anything of yours," she says, her voice higher pitched, moving into the register of propriety. "And I was just heading out."

Beth means to corral Sadie out the door, but Sadie brushes past her, down the front hall and up the stairs. Behind her she can hear Beth's protests, the angry tapping of her heels. In the bedroom Sadie doesn't look at the bed, its rumpled sheets, the imprint of Ray's head on the pillow. She finds the suitcase, just where she last saw it, and she grabs it by the handle. Beth has followed her up and blocks the doorway. She stares at Sadie and laughs.

"*That* old thing?" she says. Sadie glares at her, and Beth's expression falters. "You might be able to use those things since your mother couldn't."

But Beth's voice has lost its conviction. The suitcase is like a charm or a portal to the past.

"At least we know now why you hated her," Sadie says.

Beth shrugs, but her eyes fill with something like regret. "She made me hate her." Beth is still the girl she was all of those years ago—she has never moved beyond that time. Sadie wonders if any of them have, and then decides she cannot let that happen to her.

"Their little love escapade never happened," Beth said. "My brother had tucked that away in the closet. Not a very good hiding spot—" Beth stops. She looks as if she's bitten into something hard and hurt her tooth.

Sadie pushes past her out of the room, and Beth follows Sadie downstairs, close on her heels. They stand in the doorway to the parlor. "Speaking of my brother, where is he?" Beth asks her.

Sadie suspects Ray is just waking up at Emma and Pietro's, discovering her gone, and making up an excuse for her. "Oh, she has friends in the area," he might say. And now he is driving up and down the narrow sandy roads in his truck, past the colorful towels on lines, the beach toys stacked under cottages, the smell of eggs and bacon, expecting to come upon her. He'll run through everything he said, making sure he didn't slip, making sure he didn't say something that might have given his love for Clare away, although the night will be a blurry-edged thing he cannot bring into focus. He will drive back to the motel, hoping she will miraculously be there. He said he wasn't coming back here, and Sadie now wonders if he meant that, if she will be forced to endure sightings of him in town, or if he truly has decided he's shared this house with ghosts long enough.

The heat suffuses her, cottony air filled with the scent of the wet floorboards and plaster. Sadie hefts the suitcase from one hand to the other. She remembers the odd bundle in the hidey spot, remembers, suddenly, Ray's phone conversation with Beth before they left yesterday—the way his voice rose in fury—and she looks toward the place again, trying to make it out. Beth turns to see where she is looking, her face suddenly bright with alarm.

"Get out!" Beth shouts. "Just get out!"

Sadie is taken aback. She stares at Beth, a grown woman who has transformed into a frightened girl, and feels an uneasy sense that this has all happened before. She whirls on her heels and steps out the door onto the front stone steps. Beth is right behind her, her hand on the door. In the sunlight Sadie sees Beth's dress is soiled. On the heels of her shoes are what seem to be divots of grass, as if she's been hiking through the meadow in them.

"Where's my brother?" Beth asks again.

Sadie ignores her and puts the suitcase in the back of the SUV, her chest tight. She remembers Ray describing Francie, the shorts with the purple flowers. Sadie feels suddenly weak, dizzy in the climbing heat. From across the field of waving grass comes a calling voice. Sadie pauses. She imagines it's Craig, calling her name.

"What have you done with him?" Beth says. Her face is pale, shining with perspiration.

Sadie looks at her. She needs to get home, she knows that.

But first, she repeats the question she overheard Ray asking the night before. "What's in the hidey spot, Beth?"

Beth's hands ball tightly into fists. She wears a beautiful ring, a platinum watch. But beneath her fingernails are slivers of dirt, and on her face is the expression from the night Sadie saw her stripped of her clothes in her laundry room.

"He was letting her *go*," she says, her voice soft, frightened.

And then there are two voices that rise out of the woods. A man and a woman, calling someone. Sadie realizes she is the one who is missing, and they are seeking her in the woods.

Beth hears it, too. Her eyes become glassy with tears.

"I didn't mean to do it," she says, her voice a near whisper.

And then she takes a step back into the house and slams the front door. The morning sun brightens the glass in the upper-story windows. The mica glistens in the trap-rock stones. Sadie feels an implausible sense of dread take hold of her. From the woods behind her she hears the voices calling, calling.

She drives through the center of town, home to her family, quickly, quickly, taking the three hills at whatever speed she can manage safely, and turns into Gladwyn Hollow, her tires sliding on the sandy shoulder, her heart racing with a strange apprehension. The bit of colorful fabric, so like a girl's item of clothing; Beth's odd admission—these things have made her anxious, physically sick. Her street is quiet like an empty movie set, and she calms, tells herself she has only imagined the calling voices, much as she's imagined everything that has happened without her here. She pulls into her driveway and enters through the front door. It is a Saturday, and she expects to find Craig making breakfast, to smell the waffle batter and the syrup, to discover Max and Sylvia in front of the television. But the inside of her house mirrors the street. She walks from the hallway through the living room to the kitchen and breathes in the smells of her family, climbs the carpeted stairs, calling each of their names.

She pauses in each doorway, notices the space of the rooms, as if the people have only just left and she is a visitor to a preserved place, like a museum. In Sylvia's room there is a cup filled with water by the bed, her pink purse slung over the doorknob, her bathing suit tossed on top of the bureau. Max's room reveals the same sense of silence and disorder—clothing hung on the bedpost, his little train cars pushed into a corner. In Sadie's and Craig's room the bed is still made from the day before, the spread rumpled as if someone slept on top of it, and abandoned on the rug Sadie sees a pair of women's leather flats, beautiful shoes that are familiar but not hers.

Kate's, she thinks. She leaves her house and walks up the tarred road. She rings Kate's doorbell and knocks, calling Kate's name, until two police cars appear, gliding like strange fish, and pull up in front of her own house down the street. Someone calls her name and Sadie turns to find Jane rushing through Kate's side yard toward her, eyes lit with fear. Sadie understands that something more has happened, even before Jane grabs her hand.

"It's Sylvia," she says. "Craig woke up this morning and she was gone."

Sadie stares at Jane, the realization settling, her body going cold. Still, she can't believe it. "What are you saying?" she says, expecting that when Jane repeats the words she'll discover they mean something else. But Jane's face tells her all she needs to know. The voices weren't calling her, they were calling Sylvia. "This is my fault," Sadie says.

Jane doesn't ask her to explain, she just takes her in her arms. "It will be okay. Kate and Craig are looking around the pond. Max is with Maura."

Sadie looks down the street toward the police cars, and Jane waves her hand. "Let Maura talk to them."

They head up the path through the woods, the way trampled and cleared by the women's and children's passage throughout the summer. Pale light filters down through the trees, although the path keeps its shadows. Jane tells her she was waiting for her. "Kate called me last night. We racked our brains trying to figure out where you'd gone. We called the hospitals, the police. Craig found your cell. They told him he had to wait until this morning, and now this."

Sadie is mute with fear, but Jane doesn't really expect her to answer.

"I told Craig you'd just gone off for a bit, to get away. Maybe an old friend, I said. I told him not to worry. Kate was with him at the house."

At this, Jane glances at Sadie, to see how much she is taking in.

"I can't believe she'd come this way at night," Jane adds. They are moving quickly, and she is talking too much and out of breath. "But Max told Craig this is where she was headed."

Sadie says Sylvia has never been afraid of the woods, that she tells Max stories about fairies and elves that live there, and Jane glances back at her again, and then takes her hand, and they continue on this way, like two girls.

They reach the clearing, and the pond is soft and still, the late-summer insects hovering over the surface. They walk the perimeter and see nothing. Sadie listens, but the calling voices have stopped. She remembers the day she and Betty sought Francie and came upon the pond. She thinks that finally it has come, that this is the payment she will make for Francie's disappearance—not her mother's death after all, but this: one child. It is possible that Sylvia is somewhere below, tangled up in a tree branch, captured beneath the surface, but Jane tells her she isn't there, her face as fierce as Bea Sidelman's. Sadie hesitates by the pond, watching its calm surface, thinking about how deceptive it is. She looks at Jane, her face a question.

"She's too smart," Jane insists.

Sadie doesn't say anything about Francie Bingham or about how smart she was. They forge on through the pine woods, taking the path Sadie knows, the one she and Sylvia and Anne took the day of the daisy crowns.

Laura Loomis's mother, Francie's mother—both waited

back at the house while the neighbors searched, tranquilized to calm their frayed nerves, their terror building as hours, then days passed and their children remained unaccounted for. Sadie couldn't have imagined it then, but she experiences it now, her chest heavy with panic. She calls out Craig's name. Sadie knows her daughter, quiet and imaginative, and tries to think like her now, a child who once created a bed for a plastic dinosaur out of an old Sucrets tin, a house for a small dime-store doll out of an apple crate. Her drawings, pages of fairy-tale characters, all depict events in a long-running story. Sylvia would walk through these woods having imagined conversations with nymphs and sprites and elves. She and Jane haven't walked far when she sees something glittering on the path, and she bends down and picks up a sequined star. She scans the path and sees another, then another, and as her eyes adjust to seeing them she realizes there are hundreds of stars scattered among the pine needles like constellations. She stops and smiles.

"Like Hansel and Gretel," she says. She points, and Jane sees them too, and she lets out a laugh, her loud hoot she uses when one of the children surprises her.

"It's from her arts and crafts kit," Sadie says.

She yells Craig's name again, and this time there is an answering call: "We've got her! She's here! She's fine!"

Her knees tremble with relief. Jane exhales and finally releases Sadie's hand. They see Craig farther along the path, his dress shirt bright like a signal flag. He approaches with Sylvia in his arms. She sees Sadie and struggles to be let down. Kate is with him. Sadie sees they are all wearing the same clothing they wore the day before, and she is filled with guilt and regret. She has no idea what went on while she was gone. Sylvia runs into Sadie's waiting arms. Her body is all bony limbs. Her little fingers are cold, her eyes dark. She seems to be fine, shivering a bit in her T-shirt and shorts, her hair knotted, her

arms scratched, but otherwise unharmed. Craig approaches
Sadie and nods once, his face stiff with restrained emotion.
When she whispers his name he makes a noise that is either a
sigh or a groan, she can't tell which. He wraps his arms around
Sadie and Sylvia both.

She apologizes, over and over. She tells him she's been
with old Mrs. Sidelman.

"She knew my mother," Sadie says. She glances at Kate
over his shoulder—this story is for her, too, but Kate is looking away, not wanting to witness their reunion. Bea has
planned to call later in the afternoon to apologize for keeping
her overnight. But none of this is necessary now.

"Oh, Sadie," Craig says. "It doesn't matter."

Behind the exhaustion in his voice, she hears the place
where she fits, her old life waiting and comfortable like a
leather glove. His breath smells of bourbon. His face is drawn
and lined, his eyes wet. Sylvia tells her in her little high-pitched
voice that she was looking for her at the castle house, and Sadie
reassures her that she will make the waffles for breakfast, and
that she will wash Max's pillowcase that smells like his tears.
They emerge from the woods at the pond to see that women
and children from other neighborhoods have just arrived with
their folding chairs, their blankets and towels, their striped
umbrellas. They rub sunscreen on their children's shoulders.
Behind them three police officers appear from the path. It
is the children who spot them first. The women all glance
up, their faces marked with astonishment. They sit in a circle
and stare at the officers, whose shoes flatten the drying grass,
whose buckles and badges flicker in the sunlight. Heads pivot
and pivot back, their faces poised for what might happen next.
They suspect heart attack, stroke, car accident. All of it a loss
they steel themselves against, none of it seeming to fit here at
the pond, with the brook's gurgling and the wind in the leaves.

Craig approaches the officers and reaches out a hand to

each. Sadie hears him explain that all is well, and they form a small circle.

"I'm just glad we have a happy outcome," an officer says. He's older, gray haired. He wipes his brow. "We've searched up here before, all of this Filley land. Days of looking, you know?"

The younger officer beside him nods. "I was a kid then, but I remember the last one. She was in my class at school—funny little thing. So sad for the family."

"Still live in town. The mother died recently."

"Saw that in the paper. Brave lady."

"The other family moved away right after—the Loomises."

Sadie holds Sylvia and listens to the police officers talking, the occasional static buzz coming from their radios. Jane is beside her, an arm flung protectively over her shoulders, as if she hasn't forgotten that Sadie, too, was lost.

Craig steps up to the pond and looks down into it. His reflection wavers on the surface.

"*This* is where you've been bringing the children?"

Sadie suddenly sees the trampled-down grass, the pond's dull reflection, the scattered toys and paper cups. The women instinctively cover their stretched-out suits, their bug-bitten legs, smooth down their unruly hair with its neglected roots.

"You know there might be fertilizer runoff here," he says to no one in particular. "Contaminants." He suggests they collect a sample and send it to the EPA for analysis.

The officers nod in agreement. "There's a perfectly good pool in town," one of them says, his voice bouncing off the ring of pines. The women stare back at him as if they've been reprimanded. They glance to Kate, who moves among them, smiling, offering her calm expression. They've never seen her at the pond before, and as is often the case when seeing people you know in unexpected places, they don't all recognize her.

"Was that Kate?" someone asks Sadie.

Their unusual entourage makes its way to the path and down into Kate's backyard. Kate remains quiet. She gives Sadie a look that Sadie cannot decipher and slips her hand around her wrist, a soft, firm grip.

"Everything has worked out," she says, as if she can hardly believe it.

The heat is rising in waves from the asphalt. Entire families, alerted by the police officers' cars, have gathered with Maura and Max on Sadie's front lawn. A pack of children on bikes pedal past from another neighborhood, emissaries sent to see what's happening here. Craig and Sadie and Sylvia approach, and Maura rushes toward them to scoop Sylvia up in her arms. Max buries his face in Sadie's lap. Sadie thinks the group of them there, poised on the green grass, must look like a tableau. She glances up the street and sees Kate at the end of her walkway turn to head into her house. She has forgotten to mention her shoes.

Sadie imagines Kate descending into her Christmas basement. She'll throw the switch and all the houses will flame into life, the people inside them placed just so lit up on display, each scene so carefully manipulated: the wife carrying the turkey to the table; the father heading up the caroling party; the little girl on the rug by the fire, coloring; the boy on the couch wearing a cowboy hat, watching television, his legs jutting out, just reaching the end of the cushion. But Sadie imagines that when Kate goes down today, she will discover that the mothers and fathers and children in her village will have shifted position, moved into other rooms, other houses, stepped out into their snowy yards to stand together without her intervention.

August 15, 1979

THE PARENTS DECIDED THE HAUNTED WOODS WAS no longer appropriate, and the event was canceled. No one wanted to go into the woods anyway, fearful of Laura's and Francie's ghosts. Larry Schuster claimed he'd seen their spectral presences on the swings in his backyard. Others had their own Francie sightings—sometimes alone, eating a sundae at the local Farm Shop restaurant, or with Laura Loomis, riding the Tilt-A-Whirl at the Sacred Heart Church's Strawberry Carnival. Reports had come in from as far away as Ohio and Florida of girls matching Francie's description. It had been over a month and the local search—conducted by the police, fathers and grandfathers, volunteer firemen packing thermoses of coffee and ham-on-rye sandwiches—had nearly halted, the group that met each morning dwindling to a few bitter loners who trampled the yellowing fields arguing about the fallout of the Three Mile Island accident. The focus had shifted to the children who were not missing, who needed new school clothes and shoes. Sadie's mother dropped Sadie and Betty off at the town center the Saturday before Labor Day, and Sadie was allowed to pick out new outfits at the Youth Centre, the Weathervane, to place them on hold so that her mother could return to pay. They didn't need to be reminded not to talk to strangers, to stay together. Her mother threatened them both with a pointed finger before taking off in the Cadillac, and Sadie had made fun of her after she'd gone, not knowing, then, how little time she had left with her.

The stores were located in the outdoor mall. Sadie and Betty had worn their jean shorts and midriff tops. They picked out their school clothes and went into Drug City, where Francie's picture was taped to the door now, alongside Laura's, her expression wistful, apologetic. *I'm so sorry I've caused all this trouble,* her face said. Sadie pretended not to see it, but Betty stared at it, and then when she saw Sadie watching her, she looked away. It had become something they didn't discuss—a firm block of coldness between them. They left Drug City and Sadie saw the same Mustang trolling the parking lot.

"Look, it's Mack," she said. And before Betty could reply she'd raised her hand and called to him. The car made a wide arc and slid alongside them.

"Well, well," Mack said. He had on a work shirt with his name stitched on the pocket. Rob sat beside him, fiddling with the radio dial. They each had a can of beer cradled between their legs. Rob glanced up.

"Look, it's Sadie Mae and Betty."

Sadie was slightly flattered that he remembered their names.

"Can we ride around and do nothing with you?" she said.

Betty's eyes widened. "We're getting picked up in twenty minutes. Your mom is coming."

But Sadie suspected that she would not, that she would be passed out in her bed, taking her afternoon nap, that they would be stuck at the outdoor mall with the kids from their school, the ones giggling and gathering once again by the fountain, the ones who would head over to the movie theater to see *Meatballs,* the boys holding the girls' hands in the air-conditioned dark. She was tired of being on the outside of things. She wanted her own place to fit.

Sadie knew Betty wouldn't let her go alone, that she would

be forced to slide into the backseat with her, and she was right—Betty climbed in beside her. The car was old but clean. There was a cooler on the floor, and Sadie asked if they could have a beer, and she and Betty shared one. Betty grimaced, her eyes watering, and Sadie did her best to keep her face passive, her eyes dry. They bummed cigarettes, and Mack drove around town, up and down the streets that they'd known since childhood—the road the bus took to school, the one that led out to the reservoir, the one that took them past the historic homes of early town founders, past the Filley produce stand, the stalls filled with summer squash, tomatoes, the fields waving late-summer flowers. They kept the windows down, and the breeze blowing in and the smell of the pasture grass made Sadie sleepy and dazed. Every so often Rob would turn around and ask them something—how old they were, where they went to school, questions adults asked children to make small talk. Sadie told them they went to private school, that they were sixteen.

"Don't you want to know my favorite color?" she said.

Rob turned in his seat and smirked. "What's your astrological sign?"

Rob and Mack had graduated from high school the year before. One of them worked at the local gas station, the other at a company that put up aluminum siding. They lived at home with their parents. In ten years they didn't know what they'd be doing.

"No hopes and dreams?" Sadie said.

Betty leaned over and whispered, "Losers," in Sadie's ear.

"I heard that," Mack said, looking up into the rearview mirror.

They pulled into Penwood Park and took the narrow road that wound up through the woods, around the lake. Betty leaned over to Sadie and whispered in her ear.

"Is this the park where the girl was raped?"

"Don't worry," Rob said, swiveling to look back at them. "We'll protect you from the rapist."

Betty grabbed Sadie's hand and sank her nails in.

Mack drove up to a clearing where they parked alongside a group of other cars—Chevelles and GTOs and Road Runners, cars that looked poised at a starting line, their paint jobs shimmering in the sun. Mack and Rob got out, their bodies unfolding from the car to reveal their height and bulk—broad shoulders, low-slung jeans, men more than boys, Sadie noted. Rob opened the door to the back and stared in at them.

"You two just going to stay in there?"

Sadie and Betty slid out and leaned against the car, their arms folded over the skin exposed by their midriff tops. In three years Sadie will meet up with Mack again and discover that Rob died in a car wreck in Hamden, and she'll ride on the back of his new motorcycle to a motel on the Berlin Turnpike. But that day she and Betty just moved to a picnic table in the shade. Rob and Mack leaned on the car hood drinking and joking with the other boys, who cast occasional looks over at Sadie and Betty, but for the most part ignored them. Sadie listened to the discussions of who would run in the demolition derby at Riverside, who would race who that night on Dudley Town Road. She heard one boy ask Rob if they'd stolen Sadie and Betty from the middle school playground. There was nervous laughter, and the boy, who was met with stony silence, became absorbed in his beer. Sadie decided that Mack and Rob, as older boys who had achieved some fame in their world—through car racing and drinking, through fistfights and a general disdain for the accepted paths mapped out for them by their parents—were not to be questioned. She felt a keen sense of having been chosen, as if these boys sensed the same potential in her.

Betty kept up a low mantra. "I cannot believe we are doing this, I cannot believe we are doing this." They were the only girls there. When they left Rob climbed into the backseat, and Betty was asked to sit up front, and rather than argue, or maybe because she felt chosen herself, Betty complied. Riding this way back down the twilit roads of town, Sadie leaned boldly into Rob and Rob put his arm around her. His shirt smelled faintly of sweat, and Sadie tried not to compare him to Hans and his expensive-soap smell. Up front, Mack slid his hand over the gearshift to Betty's bare leg, and Sadie watched her knock it away. She gave directions to Mack, and they drove to Hamlet Hill and deposited them at the end of the street. Rob tugged Sadie in and kissed her, long and hard, his aviator glasses pressing into her cheek, his tongue searching the inside of her mouth. He slid his hand between her legs, wedging it there like a brick, lifted Sadie's own hand and pressed it against the V of his jeans and the swelling there. Sadie felt aroused and sick at the same time. Betty was already outside of the car, waiting by the asphalt curb, when Sadie got out. The car with the boys drove away, the tires leaving a thick, black mark on the road. Sadie and Betty walked in quiet, stunned silence up the hill to their houses.

"What if they hadn't brought us back?" Betty said, her voice choked.

Sadie looked over and saw Betty was crying, her round cheeks wet with tears. Sadie felt her own chest zinging with the nicotine and the beer, the excitement of having been released into the wild, and the relief of returning. She felt a little ashamed when she thought about Rob's tongue in her mouth, the groping, and so she didn't think about it. She thought of Francie, wondering if she'd been lured into the car of a stranger, the ways this was accomplished not readily known to children at the time. It seemed inconceivable that someone would choose Francie, in the way Sadie herself had just been chosen, and so instead she preferred to think of her as a runaway. Hadn't Sadie planned this often enough herself, imagining what she'd bring, how she could live in the woods, how she'd survive on dandelion and wild berries, the hard little apples that grew in the old orchard? She'd drink brook water, build small fires for warmth. In the fall she could eat the hickory nuts that fell in multitudes onto the lawns. She could slip into houses at night and steal Swanson TV dinners.

In a week Sadie would go to the junior high school, a place foreign to her, its building old and its linoleum marred, an in-between place fraught with unknowns. It seemed that, unless she was found, Francie, like Laura Loomis before her, would have the luxury of avoiding the return to school, the dreaded early-morning alarm, the wait for the school bus in all kinds of weather, the cold vinyl seats and toxic exhaust, the frightening sense of being trapped all day at a desk, unable to use the restroom when needed, to get a drink of water.

"But they did," Sadie said. "They did bring us back."

Betty wouldn't look at her. "Is this a venial sin?" she said.

Sadie stopped walking. "What?" she said. "What are you talking about?"

Betty stopped too. She stamped her foot, and her long ponytail swished. "All of this," she said. "Everything we've done."

She didn't wait for Sadie to respond. She turned and picked up her pace and left Sadie behind. The Frobels' sprinkler wet the side of the road. From inside the houses Sadie could hear the clink of cutlery, smell pork chops and Hamburger Helper. She watched Betty let herself in her house, watched it all happen from a distance. In two days she turned thirteen. She felt the widening rift between herself and that world of mown grass and tree canopies, the race of years, their rush to overwhelm her.

August 31, 2003

I T IS THE SUNDAY BEFORE LABOR DAY. CRAIG TELLS
Sadie to forget the cookout, but a few of the women have
already called to ask about the plans, and Sadie insists the
tradition will continue. She will head out to Shaw's to pick
up what's needed. She is heady with exhaustion, with relief,
eager to restart her old life. Craig offers to go to the store
himself—he raises his eyebrows at her. "What if you run into
another friend?" he says. Sadie smiles, then laughs, and Craig
sighs, pulls her into his chest, lays the palm of his hand gently
on her head, like a benediction. "Take your phone," he says,
and hands it to her, and Sadie accepts it, glances down to see
the missed calls, the messages—an archive of Craig's and her
friends' growing fears in her absence.

Max is taking a nap. Sylvia has been asleep, too, on the
couch, but awakens as Sadie prepares to leave and asks to go
with her. Sadie has given her a bath, and washed her hair,
and combed out the snarls. She has dressed her in her little
seersucker sundress, her white sandals with the flowers. Sylvia
climbs into the car and notices the suitcase in the back.

"What's that?" she says.

Sadie tells her it's her grandmother's. She circles the town
so that she passes the old Filley house. The driveway is empty,
and her heart stretches tight with longing. Sylvia leans forward in her seat and watches the house recede.

"That's the castle house," Sylvia says excitedly.

Sadie sighs. "It is."

She drives past Vincent Elementary School, where *The Night of the Iguana* is scheduled to open the following weekend, and she tells Sylvia about attending her mother's plays, how she would sit in the front row with her father, waiting for her mother to appear onstage. She felt a little afraid, she tells Sylvia, in expectation of her mother. It was always some other woman who stepped out into the lights in a costume, one who lived with different family members and had different problems, who wore outdated clothing, and sometimes a wig, her face altered with heavy makeup. Sadie recognized, as a child, her mother's long arms, the ring on her finger, a certain timbre of her voice, but all of that only served to confuse her further. She would watch the perspiration build on her mother's face, listen to her voice lower or raise in entreaty or paralyzing fear. Afterward, she and her father slipped into the makeshift dressing room—usually the art room, where a mirror was propped—and they presented her mother with flowers, roses and orchids, clouds of baby's breath. Sadie's mother would gather her in her arms and press her cheek up against hers, the powder, cold and damp, transferred to Sadie's skin.

"Oh, I love love love my little girl," she'd say.

Everything was abundant and swelling with happiness. Her mother clung to Sadie's and her father's hands.

"When can I go to your plays?" Sylvia asks.

"When you're older," Sadie says.

"When is that?" Sylvia says.

"A long time," Sadie says.

At some point her mother must have grown weary of pretending, she thinks. She herself has worked hard to be a different kind of mother, to keep her life simple and straightforward and free of secrets, and yet she has found that she could not. Still, she knows she need not follow her mother's trajectory. She has already learned things her mother failed to.

She and Craig have decided not to punish Sylvia for sneaking out of the house and wandering off. They're convinced she now knows to stay out of the woods.

"I went on an adventure," Sylvia says from the backseat. She begins to describe the darkness in the woods, how the moon was out.

Sadie tells her she saw the sequin stars Sylvia dropped. "Weren't you afraid of animals?" Sadie asks.

"No," Sylvia says. "I knew you weren't at the pond. I went through the field of flowers to the castle."

She tells Sadie she wanted to bring Max, but he whined when she told him where they'd be going, and she couldn't risk alerting her father or Mrs. Curry, who were downstairs.

"What were they doing?" Sadie asks.

"Talking very quietly," Sylvia says. "Drinking."

At the edge of the pines, Sylvia says, she paused. She could see the castle house and all the lights lit. She expected to find the man, but she saw someone else moving around inside, passing back and forth in front of the windows.

"I thought it was you," Sylvia says.

The woman was throwing her hands in the air. Sylvia wondered if she was dancing, or laughing, and then she thought of the Twelve Dancing Princesses and how they slipped out at night to dance with men in a secret place, wearing out their slippers, vexing their father. Sadie remembers the fairy tale: the princesses dancing all night, exhausting their lovers, then giving them up—like Ray, she thinks. Sylvia says she moved through the field and crept up to the house. The woman was not her mother; that much she could tell. The woman had short dark hair, like her friend Anne's mother.

"Maura?" Sadie asks.

"Yes," Sadie says. "I thought, what if all the mothers from the pond snuck out at night to dance, just like the princesses?"

Sadie laughs. "Imagine if they all met up there wearing the clothes they put on to go out on Saturday nights, their earrings and necklaces, their pretty sandals."

"Yeah," she chirps. "That's what I thought!"

Sylvia says that when she stepped up closer to the window she could only see a big room with a fireplace, the light coming from a crystal chandelier. No other women were visible, and she knew the woman there was not Maura when she came back into the room, her heels clicking. Sylvia says she threw her arms up in the air again, the way her mother does when Max spills his juice.

"How can you do this?" the woman said. "What are you thinking?"

Sylvia imitates the woman from the backseat, and Sadie watches her in the rearview mirror do a near-perfect imitation of Beth Filley. Sylvia says she couldn't see who the woman was talking to. She thought she must be talking to someone in the hall, or in another room. But when no one answered, she wondered if the woman was just talking to herself.

"You go and ruin everything I've done to help you."

Sylvia imitates the woman shouting, and then, to Sadie's surprise, crying.

Sylvia doesn't remember everything the woman said. She shouted some things and then whispered others, then she lay back on the floor and cried. "You were supposed to leave with me," she said. "It was our plan." When she was quiet Sylvia wondered if she'd gone to sleep, so she stepped up closer to check. She still wanted to find her mother, and she wondered if the woman might know where she was. She peered into the open window.

"The floor smelled old," she says. "I could smell the lady's perfume."

Then the woman sat up and looked at her.

Sadie is stopped at a stop sign, and she turns to look at

Sylvia, who is now imitating the look on the woman's face. "Then she screamed," Sylvia says. "She kept screaming, and I ran away through the grass and then into the woods.

"I thought she was a witch," Sylvia says. "I thought she had changed you and the magician into birds or mice. Maybe she put you in a cage."

So Sylvia ran, plunging through the woods, forgetting the path and the little sequin stars, until she reached an open place and a big tree with boughs that dipped toward the ground. She was a good climber—Sadie knew this to be true—and the bark was smooth, the little leaves dark and thick, the branches wide enough for her to walk across. She found a place where the thick branches formed a hollow, where she fit inside, and she huddled there and hid.

Sadie has told Sylvia stories of tree forts, of the old wagon she and her friends found at the edge of a pasture, its metal wheels sunk into the earth. They climbed up on it and pretended they were traveling west. They built a fort out of the graying wood from a fallen-down shed, stole a bale of hay left over in the field, rolling it over and over to the fort and spreading it out on the ground so that in the winter they might return and find it dry and warm.

"I thought maybe the tree was one of your old forts," Sylvia says.

Sadie tells her maybe it was. She drives down Tunxis Road and stops at the intersection. Sylvia says the witch eventually stopped screaming but that there was rustling in the woods, something thrashing through the ferns, breaking small twigs. She slipped down as low as she could in the tree and heard the thing pass by her, heard it mutter and curse and move farther away, and she imagined the witch limping along, changed now into her real form.

"I was going to keep running," she says. "But I thought she might be waiting, and then I fell asleep."

Sadie listens to Sylvia's story, remembers the dirt on Beth's heels. She doesn't let herself imagine how close her daughter was to real danger. She thinks she must be traumatized by her experience. "Were you afraid?"

"No," Sylvia said. "I like pretending for real."

Sadie smiles at her in the mirror. "Yes," she says. "I know what you mean."

Sylvia tells her she awoke when the birds had gathered around her in the branches and something scurried near her head. It was dawn. She felt sore from sleeping in her sitting position. She could see where the woods thinned out and the sun just lighting up the meadow grass. She was there when Mrs. Curry crossed the meadow, and she watched her carefully, wondering if she was the one in the woods last night. She rose slightly to see better through the leaves, and something shifted under her feet. She stepped out of the hollow, onto the wide branch, and peered down. Inside the place where she'd been sitting was a small knapsack with a tarnished clasp, a camping dish, a spoon.

"What kind of knapsack?" Sadie asks, now incredulous.

Sylvia says it is like the one she used to take to the pool—lined with plastic so her wet bathing suit could be carried home. "It had hearts on it, but it was really old and falling apart." When Sadie asked she described what she found inside—a bracelet made of tiny colored beads strung on elastic; a few changes of clothes, shorts and T-shirts, each item filled with holes, as if bugs had crawled inside and eaten through.

"And letters," Sylvia says.

A sudden breeze shifts through the open car windows carrying the smell of the field they have just driven past, of wildflowers and manure.

"What do you mean letters?" Sadie asks.

At the bottom of the knapsack, Sylvia says in her chatty voice, was a packet tied with a thick piece of yarn. Some of the writing she couldn't read because the paper was torn, and the handwriting was messy.

Sadie looks back at Sylvia in the rearview mirror, and their eyes meet—Sadie's dark and startled, Sylvia's earnest and wide with excitement.

She had gone through all the letters when she heard her father calling her name, and she put everything but the bracelet back and climbed down from the tree and went to wait for him on the path. Her father had come, and Mrs. Curry.

"And then you," Sylvia says. "Mommy."

She is going to draw the story of the boy who wrote the letters, of the castle house where he must have once lived, of the girl who was, like her, unafraid of the woods. Sadie tells her that would be nice.

"Maybe we can go back there," Sylvia says. "And I'll show you."

Sadie imagines going at night, following the little sequined stars. She tells Sylvia, "Maybe." She isn't sure how much of Sylvia's story could possibly be true, is half-afraid to find out.

The parking lot at Shaw's is hot, overbright, and the stunted trees planted in the medians blow in the wind that is kicking up and promising rain. Sadie opens the car door and opens Sylvia's door to let her out. She takes Sylvia's hand in hers and they stand there together beside the car. Sylvia pulls a small beaded bracelet out of her dress pocket and slips it on her wrist.

"Is it okay if I keep it?" she says.

Sadie, remembering the day she made the bracelet with Betty, finds she cannot speak and must simply nod her head.

Inside she pushes her cart across the waxed linoleum. The air-conditioning is cool, the store filled with music, with the squeak of the cart wheels. She and Sylvia move through the aisles and find hamburger and hot dog buns, pounds of ground beef, packages of hot dogs, three watermelons. She buys dozens of eggs for the children's egg toss, cucumbers for her cucumber salad.

She reaches out to touch her daughter's blond head and thinks how much she was like Sylvia when she was little—how her games, her pretending, are all replicated in her child. She sees, too, how closely she has patterned her own life after her mother's—joining the Tunxis Players, the affair with Ray. How alike they are in other ways beyond her control—the miscarriages, the grief. She admits to herself that once she discovered the suitcase it was as if her mother's ghost had thrown up one more dare. Clare made plans to leave Sadie and her father, to run off with a schoolboy. As incredible as it seems, sorting through the packed clothing Sadie had admired her mother's nerve, saw her leaving as an attempt at happiness, as an act of bravery against the world that told her how she must always behave. At the time, Sadie thought she was seeking the same thing. But she wonders now why her mother would flee the people who loved her, as if their love wasn't enough, why she made her last flight one from which she could never return. Sadie sees how narrowly she has missed falling from the same precipice. She feels her longing for her mother like a crushing burden, left for her to lug about alone for all these years. She is relieved to have saved her daughter from that weight. She can parse out memories to her—create a version of Clare that is both made-up and true.

She tells Sylvia that they will bake her grandmother's chocolate cupcakes.

"These are the best cupcakes you'll ever taste," Sadie says. She finds that she is near tears, imploring her daughter to believe this. The little beaded bracelet is bright on Sylvia's narrow wrist.

The men will pitch in and line up grills in Sadie's side yard. They will circle their chairs, the legs gritty with pond sand, while the children play manhunt in the darkness, drawing out the last of the summer, every bit of it coursing through their limbs, the bottoms of their feet stained with tar and grass.

November 20, 2003

I N MID-NOVEMBER AUTHORITIES RESPOND TO AN EARLY-morning fire at the old Filley house and discover the skeletal remains of a young girl. Sadie reads the details in the *Hartford Courant.* There are photos of the house—blackened windows and ravaged stonework, the fields around it flattened by frost. The body is reported to be that of Francie Bingham. Investigators claim that the skull shows blunt trauma but suspect no foul play, speculating that twenty-four years ago she may have simply bumped her head and taken refuge in the then-abandoned house. Somehow, she got trapped in a hidden room and died. Sadie thinks that this version of events may spare Beth from any suspicion, but the cause of the fire is still under investigation. "The house was vacant at the time of the incident," the article states. "The owner could not be reached for comment."

Craig is upstairs dressing for work. Sadie hears his shoes hit the wood floor of the closet as he sorts them, looking for his brown pair. It is their anniversary, and Sadie has hired a sitter and planned a special dinner out that Craig knows nothing about. She feels the pleasure, the anticipation of Craig's surprise. The children sit at the table with their cereal, spooning the brightly colored pieces into their mouths. They know about the plans and every so often glance toward the doorway, waiting for Craig to appear so they can feign ignorance. Behind them frost etches the kitchen windows.

Sadie remembers the day Francie went missing, how she watched Mrs. Bingham swoon onto the dewy grass, the way the officer bent and caught her like a ballroom dancer. Francie's father stood apart, shaking his head, his hands on his hips, and she and Betty had joked about wood shavings caught in his gray curls. Neither of them discussed the word he called Francie's mother or the other things Francie had written about in her letters. They were too young to really understand, Sadie thinks. Instead, she lay in bed that night and imagined herself in the arms of a boy she'd invented, a shock of sun-lightened hair over his eyes. A boy she'd always intended to be Ray Filley. She sees Francie's face again, rounded with joy, the way it looked retrieving the letter from under the stone.

In September she drove back to Hamlet Hill to pick up Bea Sidelman for lunch, past the Schusters', the Frobels', the Donahues' old house where the new owners have painted the door a bright periwinkle, past the house she grew up in with its tree grown too large, encroaching on the roof, with its sagging gutter and weed-filled beds. After lunch, she dropped Bea back off and drove up to the dead end and parked her car. She remembered the story Francie wrote to the boy she thought was Ray Filley. *Someone came into my room,* she wrote. Sadie has searched for her letters in boxes of her things from childhood, hoping she saved them. But she didn't need to see the letters again to read beneath the fairy tale, to understand what was really happening at night in Francie's bedroom. The stone was still there, heavy and pocked with mica, and she lifted it one last time, sifted through the dirt, and imagined she saw the decaying pieces of what may have been Francie's last installment.

She left the dead end and drove to the Binghams'. The house, a split-level, had shed chips of paint into the hedges. Behind the house the trees were tall, the leaves turning fiery. At the door she was met by a man who said he lived there now. "And the Binghams?" Sadie asked.

"I'm the son," he said. They spoke through the storm door screen. He was tall and stooped; his eyes took her in and then grew angry. "Look, we get a lot of you people nosing around—psychics, writers, curiosity seekers. It's been twenty-four years, for God's sake."

Sadie shook her head. "No, please. I'm Sadie Watkins. I used to live up the street?"

The man stared at her—she watched his eyes warm with recognition. Then he shook his head. "Well, aren't we both survivors of tragic circumstances. We should form a club."

He opened the screen door. "Might as well come in," he said. "I'm Stephen."

Sadie hadn't ever been in the Binghams' house. The carpet was threadbare gold shag. She went up a short set of stairs to the living room, still decorated in a 1970s style, with long low couches and heavy drapes. "Pretty mod, huh?" Stephen said. He stood in the center of the room and invited her to sit down. "I'm just staying with my father," he said, absolving himself of the condition of the decor.

All around the room were the wooden carvings Sadie remembered from Francie's letters. The late-afternoon sun came in through the picture window and lit up the polished curves and edges of the wood. *Shoe tree,* she'd written. It stood in the corner, as tall as a coatrack, the trunk like a young maple, the branches spiraling out, laden with carved shoes of all varieties—ladies' pumps, work boots, dress flats, elegant wing-tips. Sadie went up to the tree and ran a finger down one of the carved tongues, the laces. Behind her Stephen gave a dry laugh.

"Yeah, he was talented," he said.

"Francie told us about these," she said.

Stephen's mouth flattened. "I never really met anyone who knew her," he said. "Other than family."

Sadie sat down on one of the couches in a patch of sunlight. Stephen sat down on the other across from her. Between them stood a coffee table on top of which sat a large wooden gun that seemed formed out of whorls and waves, dips and eddies comprising the barrel, a seagull perched on a floating log riding a current. "Water gun," she said, smiling.

Somewhere in the house was the father, with his paws and crème de menthe breath, stretched out for a nap in a bedroom down the hall, or taking a shower, or sitting out back in the last bit of sun on the porch. Sadie didn't ask where he was.

Instead, she said, "About Francie?" and Stephen nodded, eyes eager.

So Sadie told him all she could remember about his sister. Stephen listened, leaning toward her, his long face in his hand. Sadie made Francie into the girl she might have been. There wasn't anyone to challenge her version. She attributed aspects of her own creations—the plays, the Haunted Woods—to Francie. She told Stephen about their childhood games, the way the neighborhood used to be. She said that he might even find the ruins of the last Haunted Woods in the pasture behind the old Donahue house—the crib, the maple table and chairs, all of it abandoned there, left to molder. Stephen took her then down the dark hallway to Francie's room and showed her how it, too, hadn't changed—the pink bedspread, the stuffed animals, the porcelain figurines lining her bedroom shelves staring down with their frozen, wise looks. Sadie hadn't come to the house for this. She wasn't sure why she'd come, except to see the father, confront him, and maybe tell him she knew why Francie had run off, why she'd chosen to believe a mysterious boy might save her. She wanted to divide the burden of guilt, hand him his part. But when there finally was a shuffling in the hall and the father appeared in the shadow of the doorway in his wool sweater, Sadie was leaving and had already decided to say nothing. Stephen held the door for her, and the autumn wind buckled the screen and brought the smell of burning leaves into the house. He smiled, grateful. They shook hands as if making a pact to adhere to the story she had told.

Back at home, Sadie shakes out the newspaper, takes a sip of her coffee. Sylvia tells Max that she will trace his hand and help him draw a perfect turkey when they get home from school. Sadie tells them it is almost time to go, to finish eating and brush their teeth. There may be snow before Thanksgiving, and then it will be Christmas, and they will go to Filley's for their tree.

She's seen Beth's white car, occasionally, so Sadie assumes she is still in town, but as far as she knows Ray Filley never returned to the old house. In October, when she took the children to pick out pumpkins, and Indian corn to hang on the front door, she casually asked the woman behind the register about the family. She seemed hesitant to gossip until Sadie told her she was an old friend. Then the woman smiled and lowered her voice to share, a little too happily, Sadie thought, that Beth had spent some time in Silver Hill—the psychiatric hospital in New Canaan.

"The son," she said. "I heard he ran off this summer—with a married woman."

Sadie didn't need to feign surprise. "Really? Who?"

The woman shrugged and placed Sadie's purchases in a bag. "It's a mystery."

Sadie decided she deserved the annoyance she felt at the rumor, since she'd been the one to prompt the woman to talk. She took the bag from her and thanked her, called to Max and Sylvia to carry their pumpkins to the car. She drove back home, accepting that Ray was gone from her life forever, that her assumption that he'd only been using her as a stand-in for her mother was correct.

And then two weeks ago she retrieved the mail and spotted the plain white envelope, the familiar handwriting. She was afraid to open it—afraid to feel anything for him. She took it down to the basement in the laundry basket, the subterfuge ridiculous and unnecessary. In the glare of the overhead bulb she slipped the letter from the envelope and read it.

I feel I owe you an explanation, he wrote, *for this summer—for that other summer. I know you have the suitcase, so you must suspect what happened between me and your mother, what had been happening all summer long. It was easy to meet until Francie went missing, and I was taken in and questioned in connection with her disappearance. Then Clare got nervous, afraid we'd be caught. We would talk about running off together, but it was all talk—until the afternoon she agreed to meet me at the old house like usual, and she showed up with her suitcase. She'd known about my parents' plan to send me away before I did. If Francie hadn't appeared we might have actually done it. I didn't tell you the whole story about that day. Francie saw us both—your mother and me. She was there, staring in the window. We went to the back door and tried to reason with her, but it seemed to only make things worse. Clare and I agreed we had to keep silent when Francie ran off—for my sake as well as hers. She left the suitcase at the old house, and I spent the rest of the summer at school in New Hampshire living with one of the teachers, waiting for my chance to sneak away—but of course, classes began, and then it was too late. I never saw your mother again.*

Ray might have been young—just a teenager—but Sadie didn't doubt that he loved her mother. She leaned back against the washing machine and heard Sylvia and Max cross the kitchen floor above her head. She heard the refrigerator open. "What do you want?" Sylvia asked her brother, and Max rattled off all the things he couldn't have: "Ice cream! Orange soda! Beer!" Sadie heard Sylvia laugh. "No, no, and no!" This was a game they played. "Apple!" Max cried. She heard the refrigerator door close, heard them cross the kitchen again and enter the den, the sound muffled by the carpet.

Sadie returned to Ray's letter, which shifted to that past

summer. He told how all those years ago he'd hidden the suitcase below the floorboards in the bedroom closet, how when he'd moved back into the old house the first thing he did was recover it.

I didn't look inside right away, he wrote. *The lock was jammed, and I admit I was afraid to open it—afraid of what I'd find.*

Sadie thought of the letter in her hand—how she'd felt the same way about opening it—and she smiled sadly.

But that day you were supposed to meet me seemed like the right time. I can't describe how I felt, looking at your mother's old things. Everything was jumbled. I remembered her wearing the dress once to my parents' house—but the clothes are all out of date now. I saw that she'd packed for a little weekend away, maybe lying to her husband about where she was going, sneaking off with me to a motel. The grandness of our plan, my great love, her tragic death—none of it had been real. She hadn't died over any of that.

Sadie understood that he, too, had blamed himself for her mother's death. He had come to see her differently and forgotten she was a mother, with a home and a child of her own, and a husband who may or may not have been attentive enough, and a percolator on the stove like his mother's, and recipes cut out of the newspaper and women's magazines, and a bottle of Chanel No. 5 on her bureau, and that at night she tucked her daughter into bed, and maybe read her a story, "The Elves and the Shoemaker," or "The Ugly Duckling," stories that held some moral message about beauty coming when you least expected it and the duty of selfless service. He'd forgotten about Mrs. Watkins and had become involved with someone named "Clare," whose thighs and breasts and mouth no longer signified *mother,* just *woman,* and whose body, opened to him, became an object he could covet.

I didn't want you to find out, Ray wrote. *I'd been stupid, leaving the suitcase in the room, so I decided to put it back under the floorboard in the closet. The sky was building with clouds that day—it stormed later, remember? And the sun slipped out from behind a cloud and lit up the space below the planks where the suitcase once sat. I could see the light coming in below, too, between the cracks of the panels—the hidey spot—and something else, a bunch of old clothes. I thought maybe something had fallen out of the suitcase.*

Sadie remembered the look in his eyes when he'd answered the door, imagined him prying open the sealed-up space, finding what was in there.

I had to call Beth, but she became hysterical when I asked her what was in the hidey spot. Still, I managed to piece together what had happened—that she'd followed me to the old house the afternoon I met Clare. That she'd hidden in the barn and watched Clare arrive with her suitcase. Beth saw Francie too. She couldn't believe we let her run off into the woods. After Clare and I left, Beth chased Francie down with the intention of bringing her back—to clear my name, to absolve me of any crime. Francie stumbled and hit her head. This is possible. By then it would have been raining and wet. The woods are filled with stones. Beth said Francie wasn't moving—she thought she was dead.

Sadie found her heart beating fast in her chest. She'd never believed Ray had any more to do with Francie's death than she did—though she accepted that each of their omissions played a role. In any event, neither of them had saved her from Beth—whose story Ray seemed to feel a need to defend. Sadie could imagine Beth, fueled by her obsessive love for her brother, her fury at his being implicated in Francie's disappearance, at his plans to run off with Clare, taking up a rock as a weapon to prevent Francie from running off. But Ray chose to believe Beth's story.

She'd tried to protect me, he wrote, and had made things worse. She said she dragged the girl all the way across the meadow, back to the old house. That day I opened up the secret room and called her she was desperate to explain herself—said she was coming over to talk to me, to make me understand. But I understood enough—I didn't want to hear any more. You see, she had to have put her there. No one else knew about it, Ray wrote. *Just the two of us. And now you.*

And then farther down he'd written an apology of sorts—one darkened with threat: *I'd made a mistake, and then another mistake, and I saw that everything I'd done had been wrong. But you weren't innocent in all of this either, were you? Someone agreed to meet that girl in the woods.*

Sadie felt the accusation binding her to him.

I meant what I said on the beach, he wrote. *I knew who I had. I knew who you were.*

He signed it, *Hezekiah.*

After she'd read the letter she felt strangely calm. She stood in the basement under the bulb, listening to the washer move through its cycles, until she heard Craig, home from work, his footfalls on the floor above, the children's shouts of greeting, his "Where's your mother?" She folded the letter neatly and placed it in the bottom of the laundry basket. Later, once the children were in bed and Craig was dozing in front of the television, she took her mother's old suitcase off the top shelf of her closet and put the letter with the others hidden in the suitcase's silk pocket.

Sitting at her kitchen table, Sadie scans the article about the fire again. She thinks if not for the efficiency of the local fire department the old house might have burned to the ground, erasing any outward evidence of the past, depriving the Binghams of resolution, of an end to the waiting that Laura Loomis's family still endures—if any of the family even remain. Sadie doesn't try to imagine Francie's last days in the narrow room, if, as the investigators suspect, she became conscious and discovered herself a prisoner there. But she realizes that Beth does imagine them, has for years—that she knows exactly what it would have been like, and even the destruction of the house would not allow her an escape from the memory of being trapped there herself.

She feels an overwhelming need to call someone from her old neighborhood, but other than Bea Sidelman, there is no one. Betty has made it her life's practice to avoid Sadie, but Sadie imagines her now with the newspaper open to the same page, thinking the same thing about calling her and deciding against it. They are all alone with the stories they have never told, and even now, given Francie's death, there is no real forgiveness. Sadie will not interfere with Stephen's and his brother's grief. She may tell one of the neighborhood women with whom she has made it a point to keep close—not all of the story, of course, just the part about the letters she wrote as a girl, which they may, in their way, forgive her for, perhaps confessing their own small childhood sins in the process.

Just after Sadie received the letter from Ray a Realtor's sign went up in front of the Currys' house, and they all watched as the rooms emptied out, saw the dismantling of the basement through their own windows—the evergreen swags, shards of colored glass, metallic bows, white false snow from the basement all set out in a trash can by the curb. There was an ad in the *Yankee Flyer* for the little houses, the electrical wiring, the miniature sets of furniture. When Kate and Walt Curry's divorce was final Sadie learned that Kate's son had not been in Europe after all, examining insects for an academic thesis, but that he'd died the winter before of an "undisclosed illness." Maura called her and told her, and then said that they couldn't have known. Sadie agreed but still felt the flutter of doubt, the dark brushing of its wings. Kate cared for all of their children and they'd never once asked her about her son. Didn't they all wonder and say nothing? Isn't this just as much a betrayal? She called Kate and left a convoluted message, expressing her condolences, but Kate never called her back. Her beautiful shoes still sit in the dark recesses of Sadie's closet. Someone has seen her at Shaw's Supermarket, her hair dyed a new color. Someone else says she has gotten an offer with a firm in New York City, or was it Boston? She will be spending part of the winter at a friend's villa in Tortola.

Craig comes downstairs and, late for work, drinks his juice at the counter. He leans in to give each child a kiss. "I'll see you two tonight," he says, and they each suppress a giggle, knowing they will be in bed asleep when he gets home, that there is a secret planned for him and they are now part of it. She rises from the table and Craig takes her in his arms, and she presses her mouth to his lime-scented neck. There is time for this, she thinks. Today she and Bea Sidelman will see an exhibit at the Wadsworth Atheneum. She will study her lines for *Our Town*. She will clean out the hall closet. Tonight she will put on a black cocktail dress like one her mother used to wear, low-cut crepe de chine; slip into black heels, her pearls—not as a child playing dress-up, but as the woman she is now able to become. She will celebrate her marriage with her husband at the restaurant where they had their first date.

The early settlers of this land buried their children in family plots, on a rise of land visible from Sadie's second-story window. Here a mother would have paused, her arms heavy with laundry or firewood, with another child on her hip, and then moved on to the baking of bread, to the planting of her garden, to the demands of a house that bring forgetfulness. Sadie still goes alone up the secret path through the woods. The cicada nymphs burrow beneath the leaf litter, down into the soil to feed on tree root sap, keeping their seventeen-year vigil. She sees the trees fan out like a blaze, the pond coated with ice. She watches the fog settle among the bare, black branches and the snowfall, its obscuring blanket. She longs for the sun in her hair and pauses, listening, as if she can still hear the high and happy voices of children—those who have come and gone, those who have never been. Each passing day, filled with the work of her life, is its own solace.

For a long time she would dream she'd returned to her

old neighborhood, where everything remained the same—the houses lining the street, the farm and the farmer's fields in the distance. It would be summer, and the corn would do its fine green swaying dance. A thunderstorm would roll in, the lightning arcing and cleaving and the air sharpened with the smell of rain. She'd enter her house to discover her mother's cigarette burning in the bright orange ashtray on the kitchen table, the phone cord stretched across the tile. She'd follow the cord and find the receiver sitting on the floor of the pantry, the dial tone discordant, her mother nowhere in the house, though she'd search from room to room, pulling open closet doors, expecting to find her. What did she want to tell her? she'd wonder. Now she knows, and finds she has stopped looking.

Author's Note

On July 26, 1973, seven-year-old Janice Pockett of Tolland, Connecticut, left her home on her bicycle to retrieve a butterfly she'd hidden under a rock. She never returned. Janice's case was given attention in the *Hartford Courant,* in often poignant reporting by J. Herbert Smith, Jon Lender, and George Gombassy. These newspaper articles detailed the extensive search, the fear of kidnapping, the effect on the family, and the ultimate struggle to move on.

As a child growing up in a Connecticut suburb, Janice's disappearance was a tragedy that unfolded a few towns removed from mine—one I knew nothing about until I discovered the newspaper articles years later as a curious writer. When I set out to create a fictional world around a missing girl, I wanted to reinvent the feeling of loss captured in the articles, and to provide some sense of closure that remains, as of this writing, sadly absent in Janice's story.

In seeking a setting for my novel I returned to the Connecticut town of my childhood. For information about Latimer Cemetery and a feeling of the town's layout and history, I consulted the Wintonbury Historical Society and its wonderful book *From Wintonbury to Bloomfield: Bloomfield Sketches,* published in 1983. Bloomfield residents will recognize some of the names and places in my novel but will discover that in my fictional version the places have been relocated to suit my needs, the names given to invented people. In an attempt to relay the Colonial history I felt so strongly in my own childhood, my town is a combination of several towns, and the folklore and legends are appropriated from across the New England region.

Finally, I wanted this book to be one about mothers, and mothering, about the nature of that role and its responsibilities, joys, and sorrows, and for this reason I was drawn to Colonial women's diaries. That of Mary Vial Holyoke, a doctor's wife from Salem, Massachusetts, which I found in *The Holyoke Diaries 1709–1856,* seemed to resonate the most for me. Its daily recording of visitors, travel, and chores includes the births of children, and almost as frequently, the deaths. Of the twelve children she bore only four survived infancy. In her spare accounting we glimpse a community of women taking turns at the bedside of her sick three-year-old, the child's death a brief notation that we might miss if we were skimming the pages. I wanted to pause at that moment after the words were written, and then reveal its indelible mark on everything that comes after.

Karen Brown

Acknowledgments

Thank you to Laura Mathews of *Good Housekeeping,* and Michael Koch, of *Epoch,* in whose publications portions of this book first appeared.

I am deeply grateful to Samantha Shea and Valerie Borchardt, for the insightful suggestions that helped shape this work, and for their perseverance in finding it a home.

Thank you to my wonderful editor, Sarah Cantin, whose attention to these pages was subtle, graceful, and wise, and to all of the Atria Books team who shared her enthusiasm.

For the whimsical rendering of my fictional town, thank you to my talented niece, Jess Brown.

For friendship and support, thank you to Susan Wolf Johnson and Tom Ross, and a special note of thanks to Jonadean Gonzalez, Delma Rodriguez, Lorelei Perez, Violet Pullara, Grace Landeta, Sandy Alberdi, and Jane Toombs—the Literary Dames. Your stories, generosity, and wine continually enrich my ideas about books and the people who read them.

And finally, thank you to my family, and to my sister Beth—my first reader.

THE LONGINGS
of
WAYWARD GIRLS

KAREN BROWN

A Readers Club Guide

QUESTIONS AND TOPICS FOR DISCUSSION

1. Read the epigraph of the novel aloud. How does it serve to frame the narrative that follows it?

2. Consider the mother-daughter dynamics that are depicted within the novel. How do you think Sadie's experience of being mothered by Clare impacts how she mothers Sylvia?

3. What do you make of Sadie and Craig's relationship? Why do you think Sadie is drawn to Ray to begin with, and why does she ultimately return to Craig? Do you believe Ray when he writes to Sadie, "*I knew who I had. I knew who you were*" (p. 308)?

4. The weight of history—and the sense that it can repeat itself—is felt throughout the novel. As a group, can you brainstorm moments within the novel in which it appears (as Faulkner once famously said) that "the past isn't dead—it isn't even past"?

5. Consider the theme of female companionship in the novel. In what ways is it shown to be sustaining—and in what ways can it turn sinister?

6. Both Sadie and Clare are involved with the local theater troupe. What is the difference between this kind of formalized acting and other forms of role-playing that are depicted throughout the novel? Using examples of each, compare and contrast.

7. Turn to the scene on p. 137 in which Kate shows the neighborhood women the Christmas village she has cre-

ated in her basement. Why do you think Kate has chosen this hobby? What do you make of Sadie imagining Kate returning the next day to her basement, only to discover that "the mothers and fathers and children in her village will have shifted position, moved into other rooms, other houses, stepped out into their snowy yards to stand together without her intervention" (p. 284)?

8. Think about how fate and free will are juxtaposed in the novel. How could the suitcase that Sadie discovers in the old Filley homestead be seen as emblematic of both—or, put differently, as the perfect melding of destiny and agency?

9. What do you make of Beth as a girl—and later, as a grown woman? In what ways can she and Francie be seen as reflections of each other?

10. Consider the domestic spaces that feature prominently in this novel (basements, perhaps) and those that are rarely shown (for example, kitchens). What kinds of activities are the characters engaged in, in each setting? In terms of tone or atmosphere, how are the scenes that take place indoors different than those that transpire outdoors?

11. As a group, reread the scene in which Clare and Patsy run lines from the Tennessee Williams play *The Night of the Iguana*. Given what lies ahead for these characters, how do you interpret these lines?

12. While many of the novel's characters are guilty of various wrongdoings, do you feel that true malice is at the root of any of their crimes? Are there moments when certain individuals could have acted differently to prevent others

from getting hurt? Discuss using specific examples from the text.

13. *The Longings of Wayward Girls* ends with Sadie describing a recurring dream she has about entering her childhood home and wandering the rooms, looking for her mother: "What did she want to tell her? she'd wonder. Now she knows, and finds she has stopped looking" (p. 311). What answers has Sadie come to by the novel's conclusion? To what extent do you believe she has made peace with her mother's memory?

14. Though not a ghost story in the classic sense, *The Longings of Wayward Girls* is filled with ghosts. Who are they, and how does their presence shape the narrative's development?

ENHANCE YOUR BOOK CLUB

1. The summer of 1979 is a transitional summer for Sadie, and though her thirteenth birthday is still a few months off, in her personality and demeanor she arguably "becomes" a teenager during July and August. Did you have a summer that was similarly monumental to your personal development?

2. As a group, watch the 1964 film version of *The Night of the Iguana*. Imagine Clare (and later, Sadie) playing the role of Hannah Jelkes, here depicted by Deborah Kerr. Does the movie make you think differently about any aspects of *The Longings of Wayward Girls*?

3. Speaking of movies, pretend that you are casting the film version of *The Longings of Wayward Girls*. Brainstorm whom you might cast as Sadie, Ray, and Beth. What about Clare, Bea Sidelman, or Kate?

4. As twelve-year-olds, Sadie and Betty play a seemingly harmless prank on another girl—one that sets off a chain of events with disastrous consequences. Looking back on your childhood, did any of your own transgressions initially seem innocuous but ultimately lead to harmful or damaging outcomes?

roof tiles that cost a fraction of the cost of the machine it would replace. "You have to get up very early in the morning to suggest anything of any real relevance to these people," Raintree told me. "Occasionally, you can. What was nice about working with Ann was she understood the villages and the rural industry situation so well that she could prime me, so that I could find a lot of things that really seemed to make sense. Ann had it all figured out long before I got there."

Using her dissertation field notes as a guide, Ann took Raintree on an orientation tour, giving him the deepest and most insightful anthropological perspective on rural industry he told me he had ever encountered. With Semarang as their base, they would drive up to four hours out of the city to villages all over Central Java. They paid countless courtesy calls on provincial officials, district heads, and village headmen—formal meetings in which Ann would introduce Raintree and their project. The government official would preside from a chair on a dais, looking down on his visitors, seated below. Raintree, who had done fieldwork in the Philippines and was used to villages of tribal people with their own traditions, was unaccustomed to the rigid, hierarchical nature of Java. To do anything at any level, one needed permission from all the levels of government and administration above. It helped that Ann knew what she was talking about and spoke the language. "But she couldn't have gotten anywhere with that if she didn't also know how to be politically correct and formal, and at the same time charming," Raintree told me. "These were all kingdoms before they became bureaucracies within a national state. She knew how to be courtly."

Ann worried about corruption among government officials, who, Raintree said, sometimes seemed to her not to care much about ordinary people. She also noticed that the class background of government planners and administrators, who were mostly men, tended to work against poor women sharing in the benefits of development projects. The Indonesian men she worked with, mainly from the planning office and the Department of Industry, "simply did not believe that the lives of poor village women were significantly different from the lives of women of their own class," Ann would write to a colleague in July 1981. "In other words, they believed that poor village women spent most of their time at home, caring for children and doing housework, fully supported by their husbands except for a little 'pin money' they might earn doing handicrafts or selling something in the market from time to time. Given these preconceptions about the importance (or unimportance) of women's work, it is not surprising that women were seldom selected as participants in projects which could increase their income-generating abilities."

But Ann was pragmatic. She was good at recognizing a felicitous convergence of interests. She believed that improvements could be made even if they were not the top priority of the people she had to convince. The game was to enable her Indonesian counterparts to see why it was in their own enlightened self-interest to help the poor. She was an organizer, always with goals of her own. If a colleague had his own view about how things ought to be organized, Raintree said, he had to devote some energy to seeing that they were not done her way instead. In fact, he told me, "I could understand why a young man would need to go off to school in Hawaii."

On one occasion, Raintree recalled, he challenged a policy of Ann's—and went so far as to discuss the matter with the team leader. "She gave me a stern lecture about how friends don't do that," he remembered. She did not mince words. He saw her angry, too, when she believed others had been treated unfairly. For example, she had a driver in Semarang who doubled as a field assistant. As Raintree put it, "Her driver was much more than a driver." Occasionally, people unfamiliar with the arrangement had a tendency to treat the man as they might a mere driver. Ann would stand up for him, Raintree recalled, with fire in her eyes and steel in her voice. If the cultural context was such that she could express her views, she did. "Sometimes it would involve a sharp anger but not something lingering or smoldering," he said. "She spoke her mind, and that was it."

For village people, one of the biggest barriers to expanding a business, and moving out of poverty, was the lack of affordable credit—the problem Ann had stumbled on while doing the research for her dissertation. The most common source of credit was moneylenders—that is, loan sharks, as Carl Dutto described them. A trader might borrow money at four a.m., walk to the central market, buy whatever she intended to sell, take a *becak* to the suburbs, sell her product by the side of the road, pay back the moneylender at some exorbitant rate of interest, and keep whatever was left. The lenders made a killing, and their customers barely scraped by. Nearly everyone in the villages seemed to be in debt to moneylenders. Foreign development groups and Indonesian organizations such as the one for which Clare Blenkinsop worked were exploring other ways of offering small amounts of credit. By the time Blenkinsop arrived in Semarang in 1979, there were already eight to ten thousand savers in the program run by her organization, which enabled women to become eligible for a loan by demonstrating that they could save.

The Indonesian government, too, was interested in rural credit. To help diversify the economy, redistribute wealth, and promote rural development, the government had mobilized the banking system. In 1970, the governor of Central Java had used a provincial government loan to launch a system of rural and locally run financial institutions to make small, short-term loans to rural families. The system, known as the Badan Kredit Kecamatan, or the sub-district credit agency, grew rapidly in Central Java. But when the units were pressed to repay their government loans and support themselves, many suffered high losses. There was also corruption and mismanagement. By the late 1970s, one-third of the 486 units in Central Java were languishing or had closed.

To help tackle the problem of credit, the U.S. Agency for International Development enlisted the help of Richard Patten, a brainy, irascible development veteran from Norman, Oklahoma, who had worked in East Pakistan, now Bangladesh, and in Ghana in the 1960s before moving on to Indonesia. In East Pakistan, Patten told me, he had worked with Akhtar Hameed Khan, an Indian-born, Cambridge-educated social scientist and development activist now recognized as a pioneer in what is now known as microcredit—the making of very small, or micro, loans to impoverished entrepreneurs. Khan, who had founded the Pakistan Academy for Rural Development, had been working on ways of lending money for small enterprises, including small shops. "We followed what he had pioneered when we did a public-works program in East Pakistan," Patten said. "He was doing group credit through the cooperatives but then using a local bank to support it." The Agency for International Development was interested in trying similar things in Central Java. At first, Dutto said, the agency did not know what might work. They tried lending chicks, ducklings, and goats—to be paid back in other chicks, ducklings, and goats. They also began working with the floundering rural-banking system.

Ann, the credit adviser hired by Development Alternatives Inc., worked with Patten, the credit adviser to the Agency for International Development. From her dissertation fieldwork, Ann had found that rural industries were frequently held back by shortages of raw materials—which they often lacked because they did not have the working capital to keep them in stock. Women had an especially hard time getting even government-sponsored loans. In 1979, Ann evaluated a small credit project being carried out in ten villages in industries such as production of roof tiles, cassava chips, and rattan. In most of the villages, women as well as men worked in those industries—but not one of the one hundred twenty-nine loans had gone to a woman. The provincial development project, for which Ann was working, began providing not only capital but training in management and bookkeeping to sixty-five Badan Kredit Kecamatan banking units in Central Java. Those offices became a proving ground for new initiatives. The best of those initiatives eventually spread beyond Central Java. The system became a permanent government-run program in 1981, and the Indonesian Ministry of Finance made a large loan to the provincial government to strengthen and expand it. Looking back on the provincial development project as a whole, Silverman said it resulted in the setting up of planning bodies throughout Indonesia, which took on an important role in the allocation of government resources at the provincial level. But, he said, "the one major success we had was the small-scale credit and institutionalizing it. It was the one thing that got institutionalized in ways that are close to what was intended."

Ann's days were long and full. She worked on her dissertation before dawn, managed her household staff, saw to the schooling of her daughter. Every day, she wrote at least a couple of paragraphs to Barry, Kadi Warner remembered: "It was part of her ritual." Ann attended meetings, went into the field, spent time in the office, escorted visitors. At night, she presided over lively dinners at home. She liked running her own household, being immersed in her work, being accountable largely to herself. In her element, she was developing a big and unmistakable presence. "She was the grand lady when she was in the village, or in her house, or talking with the *bupati*," Raintree said, using the Indonesian word for a district head. "She was enormously bright; she was fluent in Indonesian; she always had a sort of twinkle in her eye. I always thought she had just swallowed a canary." Even in a difficult negotiation, she seemed to be enjoying herself. Decades later, Raintree remembered a certain look on Ann's face, a trace of which he had begun to notice in her son during the presidential campaign. After making a point, Ann would look down the bridge of her nose, her chin slightly elevated at its usual angle. In Obama, some people had interpreted that look as aloofness, Raintree said, "but when she did it, she had this puckish smile." In her work, she set goals, met deadlines, was a team player, did not bend rules, Silverman said. "This notion that she was this hippie wanderer floating through foreign things and having an adventure is not the Ann I know," he said. "In a sense, she was as type A as anybody on the team."

Ann kept much of her private life private, even with close friends. Glen Williams, who dined with her a number of times during the year they overlapped in Semarang, said he did not know at the time whether or not Ann was married. He knew that Maya's father "was the Indonesian guy," as he put it, but the subject of Lolo never came up in conversation. Ann told Silverman that she and

Lolo had separated. Their marriage reminded Nancy Peluso of some other Indonesian marriages she knew of, in which husband and wife seemed to go in their own directions. "It wasn't like a real marriage," she told me. "It was just kind of a marriage in name."

Sometime in 1979, Ann and Lolo agreed to divorce. According to Maya, Ann received a phone call in Semarang from Lolo, and by the end of the call, it had been decided. I heard several different accounts of the reason the marriage ended, some or all of which could conceivably be true. According to one explanation, offered by Peluso, Ann no longer believed that she and Lolo had anything in common. She was tired of trying to arrange for them to spend time together. According to Alice Dewey, Ann knew from Lolo's doctors in Los Angeles that he had few years left to live. She knew from Lolo that he wanted more children, which she did not. So, according to Dewey, she did the practical and humane thing: She let him go. A third explanation came from Rens Heringa, who became a close friend of Ann's around the time of her divorce and who later divorced her own Indonesian husband. Heringa told me bluntly, "She left him—on the pretext that she had to work, which was an acceptable pretext. The real reason was that it was hopeless. He couldn't accept the way she was, and she couldn't accept the kinds of things he expected."

The divorce became final in August 1980, according to a passport application of Ann's. Lolo married the woman Maya remembered encountering in her father's home the day she and Ann had returned to Jakarta. He went on to father two more children, a son and a daughter, before dying of liver disease in 1987 at the age of fifty-two.

Ann's relationship with Maya, who turned ten in 1980, was close and affectionate. Delightful and dimply, Maya was on her way to becoming extraordinarily beautiful. In many ways, Ann treated her like an adult. She took her everywhere, in a way that some people told me was common in Indonesia. "Many hours of my childhood were spent in the homes of blacksmiths or by their furnaces," Maya has written. "When we visited the blacksmith known as Pak Marto, I would look for the reliably present feral dogs chasing chickens outside his home. . . . Mom took me to see potters, weavers, and tile makers, too." In the house in Semarang, Ann had converted a room into a schoolroom, with desks for Maya and several other children from expatriate families. Lesson manuals, textbooks, workbooks, and school supplies arrived in boxes from the home instruction department of the Calvert Day School in Baltimore. A rotating roster of parents served as teachers, meeting in various households. Kadi Warner, whom Ann enlisted to teach world and United States history, told me that the Calvert system was the oldest formal homeschooling curriculum and was highly respected. "It was the standard internationally then," she said. "If you went through that, you were prepared." But Ann was not satisfied with the arrangement for Maya, Richard Holloway recalled. "That was a source of sadness and disappointment to her," he said. "That she was failing as a mother by not giving her a better education than that."

The dilemma was not uncommon. Some expatriate families were reluctant to enroll their children in international schools for fear that they would know only expatriate children. They wanted their children to appreciate the country in which they were living and to have local friends. So they sent them to local schools. But at a certain age, a child in a local school would not receive the preparation necessary to get into a university of the sort their parents attended. "So there is a real problem," said Clare Blenkinsop, who faced the same issue later with her son. "I think that was the problem for Ann with Maya. She didn't want Maya to be cut off in some sort of international school. On the other hand, the level of education gained in anything going in Semarang was probably well below the level that was needed."

The quandary was especially difficult because Maya was half Indonesian.

In the spring of 1980, officials at the Ford Foundation in New York and Jakarta had begun talking about creating a new position in the Jakarta office. The job would entail encouraging research, at the village level, on rural employment and the role of women. Women, it seemed, were playing a critical role in keeping poor households afloat. But Indonesian government policies and programs would not reflect that reality until there were more data to prove it. Officials at Ford wanted to encourage more village-level studies. Research, they hoped, would not only help explain the causes of rural poverty, it might also suggest how to enable poor households to take advantage of opportunities the government or other agencies offered. In March, Sidney Jones, a Ford program officer in Jakarta, wrote an interoffice memo listing six people who should be sent the description of the job in case they might want to apply. Jones knew Ann through Nancy Peluso. All three of them, along with other scholars, had begun to collaborate on a possible book of articles on women's economic activities in Java, which Ann intended to edit. The six names on Jones's list had come from Peter Goethals, an American anthropologist who was a Harvard classmate of Alice Dewey's and a former denizen of the house in Mānoa. Goethals had been working on the same Agency for International

Development project as Ann, but in another part of Indonesia. All six candidates were anthropologists, fluent in Indonesian, who had done fieldwork in the country. But Ann was described at the greatest length. After listing Ann's scholarly credentials, Jones concluded, "She's a specialist in small scale industries/non-farm employment and would be superb."

Eight

The Foundation

Four Americans lingered at the entrance to a teeming street market in an out-of-the-way neighborhood in Yogyakarta. It was the fall of 1981, and their little landing party must have made an unusual sight—a stout white woman, a six-foot-four-inch-tall black man, and two white male colleagues, all towering above the eddying crowd. The place was a used-book market, Tom Kessinger, the head of the Jakarta office of the Ford Foundation at the time, remembered years later. But a Westerner might have mistaken it for a paper-recycling operation. Sellers trudged in, humping inventory in fabric bundles on their backs. The market was chaotic, densely packed, and dominated by men. One year into her job at Ford, Ann was increasingly immersed in the world of street vendors, scavengers, and others who eked out a living in the informal economy, where as many as nine out of every ten Indonesians made at least part of their living. On that day, the used-book market was being forced to close, under pressure from merchants or the police. Ann was accompanied by Kessinger, who had lived for years in India, and Franklin Thomas, who had overseen the restoration of the Bedford-Stuyvesant neighborhood in Brooklyn before becoming the president and chief executive officer of Ford. "We waded into the market in a way that nobody outside the country would have," Kessinger remembered. "If you weren't someone as big as Frank is, you might even feel physically threatened. It was so dense and out of control." Ann strode into the chaos, leading the way. Thirty years later, Kessinger would remember the ease with which she unlocked the obscure logic of the place, the relationships and patterns of organization. He said, "I could see, and she communicated it nonverbally, just how comfortable and easy it was going to be."

When he had hired Ann, Kessinger had been looking for someone capable of working "close to the ground," as he put it later. The Ford Foundation, one of the leading philanthropic organizations in the United States, defined its mission as strengthening democratic values, reducing poverty and injustice, promoting international cooperation, and advancing human achievement. After going from a local to an international foundation in 1950, it had operated initially by hiring expatriates with specialized knowledge, and making them available to emerging countries trying to build democratic forms of government. By the early 1980s, countries such as Indonesia had experts and institutions of their own, so Ford was becoming a source of funding more than a supplier of outside expertise. Thomas, after ten years in community-based development in New York, believed in local talent. The Bedford Stuyvesant Restoration Corporation, which he had headed, had enlisted neighborhood people in the work of urban redevelopment. At Ford, he wanted local people engaged in every aspect of the foundation's international work. "There was an evolving sense that you probably had more knowledge in the experience of people in almost any setting than you could bring in from the outside, no matter how diligently the outsiders worked or studied," Thomas told me. Tom Kessinger, arriving in Jakarta in August 1979 to head the Ford office, had set about making contact with Indonesia's small but growing universe of civil-society organizations, in which an emerging generation of leaders was working for social and economic change. He wanted to know how those organizations could be nurtured. It was easy to find the bigger ones; they tended to be based in Jakarta and had English-speaking staffs who knew how to write reports. Harder to reach were the smaller, more numerous, less sophisticated, so-called nongovernmental organizations scattered all over the archipelago. "What Ann represented to me was getting out into the NGO circuit beyond what I could do because of my obligations and my poor Indonesian," Kessinger told me. She arrived at Ford, Thomas said, "at a time when the institutional focus had shifted from the elite to the grassroots. She personified someone all of whose ties were at a non-elite level."

Kessinger also wanted someone interested in women. There was a new focus at Ford on gender equality and the status of women. In Indonesia, the position of women had been relatively high compared with what it was in some other Muslim and even non-Muslim countries. But population pressure and technological change were pushing rural women into menial work. The extent of the problem was difficult to gauge, because there had been few studies of village women. Members of the Ford staff in Jakarta had suggested hiring someone to spend half their time as a program officer based in Jakarta, developing and managing projects addressing the need for paying work for village women. The rest of the time, he or she would work as a so-called project specialist at the Bogor Agricultural Institute, helping Indonesian researchers analyze village-level data on women, and teaching younger scholars how to do field research. Sidney Jones, the only female program officer in the Jakarta office of Ford at the time, invited Ann and Tom Kessinger to dinner at her house. Not long after that, Kessinger hired Ann.

"At first impression, you would say she was easygoing," Kessinger told me. "Once you got to know her, she was really quite intense and, in a certain sense, driven." She was serious and focused, and willing to engage with people. "But there was also a little bit of reserve as well, which I never totally figured out," Kessinger said. "I could see that some people might see that as a kind of snobbishness—though I don't mean snobbishness. When someone is distancing, sometimes it's personality or they're protecting themselves. Sometimes it's read as not very open or warm. Ann had that quality. I felt it the first evening we had dinner at Sidney Jones's house. I was doing the interview kind of thing—not the formal interview. I just had a sense that there were areas where I was going to get a certain distance, not further. There seemed to be a time when the conversation had to go in a different direction."

By January 1981, Ann was back in Jakarta with Maya and working for Ford.

"Life in the bubble" is the phrase one longtime Ford employee used to describe life as a Ford program officer in Jakarta. The economy was growing, the oil industry was booming, and Jakarta was becoming a modern city, but Ford families lived in a style that resembled an earlier, colonial-era, expatriate existence. They were housed in Kebayoran Baru, a quiet neighborhood of wide, shaded streets planned by the Dutch, where Ford owned or leased a number of high-ceilinged bungalows with ceiling fans, verandas, and gardens dense with flowering trees. The foundation furnished the houses in teak and rattan or to the tastes of the Ford families. It dispatched its own maintenance crew to fix toilets that ceased to flush. Ann's house was comfortable, not lavish. ("My oven has collapsed!" she wrote to a Ford support-staff member in April 1981. "I have to wire the door shut and it sprinkles flakes of rust on the food while the food is cooking." Some months later, she reported a termite infestation: "The wood is riddled with holes already and in the evening hours literally thousands of termites pour out of these holes and fly about, making the room and the back sitting area unusable.") Ford had a fleet of cars with drivers—though Ann employed her own, a man who had driven her Agency for International Development jeep in Semarang. The foundation ferried expatriate staff members in a carpool back and forth along the twenty-minute drive between Kebayoran Baru and the office. There was annual home leave for the entire family, with travel arrangements made by the foundation. There were provisions for spouse travel and "educational travel for dependent children," annual physicals and vaccinations. Children of the program staff rode a school bus together to the Jakarta International School, where—along with the offspring of diplomats, oil company executives, and missionaries—they performed in Gilbert and Sullivan operettas and recited the poetry of Rabindranath Tagore in the original Bengali. Ford arranged for enrollment and paid the tuition. "Everything seems set at the school for Maya," Kessinger, who served on the school's board, wrote to Ann in December 1980. He had, he said, "personally spoken to the Superintendent and [had] been assured that a place will be saved for her."

Ann worked three days a week in the Ford offices in a

whitewashed colonial-style building with a steeply sloping tile roof on Taman Kebon Sirih (Betel Tree Garden) in Central Jakarta. Formerly a private home, the building sat squarely on a low-lying lot next to a canal. In the rainy season, brown water seeped up through the tile floors, swamping the metal file cabinets, saturating paperwork, and staining the walls. The staff fell roughly into two groups: The program staff was transient, white, and mostly male; and the administrative, clerical, and support staff tended to be permanent, Indonesian, and female. A photograph taken during Ann's tenure shows a dozen Indonesian women, all smiling and many of them dressed in batik, arrayed in front of a half-dozen mostly Caucasian men in neckties and short-sleeved plain white shirts. Floating half hidden in between is the only Western woman, Ann. Kessinger, whose title as the head of the office was country representative, had been a member of the first group of Peace Corps volunteers sent to India in the early sixties. He had worked in community development in the Punjab before returning to the United States to study history and anthropology, writing his dissertation for his Ph.D. from the University of Chicago on the social and economic history of an Indian village. He was a tenured professor of history at the University of Pennsylvania, married to an Indian, when Ford hired him in 1977 and sent him first to New Delhi. In the Jakarta office, Kessinger was a jovial presence, inclined toward the informal management style of academia, not the top-down style of the corporate world. The program officers, with Ph.D.'s in fields like comparative world history, specialized in areas such as natural resources, epidemiology, education, and traditional Indonesian culture. "There was a sense of idealism, but there was also a certain smugness of the 'best and the brightest' culture," said Sidney Jones, who went to work for Ford in Jakarta in 1977, initially in a job she said was known as "the ingenue role," because it was not expected to lead anywhere better. "You never referred to 'Ford.' It was always 'The Foundation.'"

The job of program officer required a mix of skills and talents. As Kessinger described it to me, a program officer had to talk to a lot of people, then think about the issues, then consider the context—within the Ford Foundation, in the Indonesian government, among other donors. As Jones put it, one had to think strategically about how to plant money in different places in order to bring about a desired transformation or change. "If you want to increase access to justice, for example, you think, 'Okay, we've got the legal-aid group that works with one set of people,'" she said. "'It would probably be a good idea to get a couple of really bright people trained in some kind of legal approach so that you can have those people in law faculties in a number of places. It would be good to get some judges or others to have exposure to what's done in places where there is really good access.' You put all the pieces together and you get a program."

As for herself, she said, "I just tended to take really interesting projects and fund them—without thinking very far ahead about what the end result was."

Within a week or two of starting at Ford, Ann flew to India on a trip that would end up shaping her approach to her job from then on. A young program officer in New York, Adrienne Germain, who had been working with the international program staff to increase Ford's involvement in the advancement of women, had invited Ann to join her on a trip she was taking. Unlike Indonesia, India already had a movement to improve the condition of poor working women. Ford was in contact with groups organizing street vendors and other self-employed women. Germain, who several months later would become the foundation's first female country representative and be sent to Bangladesh, had extended the invitation, she told me, "as a way of collaborating with Ann—to say, 'Look, these are the kind of women-specific programs that are going on that are really quite impressive and that you won't yet see in Indonesia.'"

They met with leaders of the Self Employed Women's Association, a then nine-year-old trade union based in Ahmedabad with roots in the country's labor, cooperative, and women's movements, which has since gone on to create a network of cooperatives and India's first women's bank. They visited the Working Women's Forum, started by a former Congress Party activist named Jaya Arunachalam, which within a decade would become not just a union of poor women but a network of cooperatives encouraging entrepreneurship by making low-interest loans. They met washerwomen, known as *dhobis*, in the slums of Madras. Germain had first worked abroad while still an undergraduate at Wellesley College, tagging along for six months on a household survey in Peru that took her to the slums of Lima; she had strong feelings about how one should behave when working in other people's countries. Ann impressed her, Germain remembered many years later. She listened well—not to get information to do her job but because she wanted to learn. She was not, Germain said, "thinking at the top, which is where a lot of Ford was: 'Let's build our universities and let's get our intellectual capital going.'" Ann seemed to believe that you could not help people unless you learned from them first. "It was the most interactive way of being and of taking time," Germain recalled. "A lot of times, in all kinds of jobs, people didn't feel like they had that kind of time; they were there to make grants and move money. Often they didn't think much about: Could the project really be implemented the way it was? What would be the consequences? They weren't going to be around to learn the consequences. Ann was never like that. Ann was very aware that money doesn't necessarily solve problems."

What Ann saw in India left a deep impression. For years afterward, she would point to the organizations she had seen on that trip as examples of what might be possible elsewhere. Occasionally, she would use Ford grant money to send Indonesian activists to India to see for themselves. The size of the women's organizations in India astonished her. "She thought to herself, 'Why can't we do more than these itsy-bitsy NGOs? Why can't we take this to scale?'" said Richard Holloway, her friend from Semarang. Back in Jakarta, Ann wrote to Viji Srinivasan, a Ford colleague in New Delhi who had traveled with her and Germain: "The India trip certainly set my mind moving in some new directions. Could Indonesian women in the informal sector be organized a la the Working Women's Forum? (But where will we ever find a new Jaya Arunachalam?) Could a SEWA-like cooperative bank for women be organized in the Indonesian context?"

Anyone interested in the condition of poor women in Indonesia faced a shortage of data. Only a handful of Indonesian researchers were interested in women's issues, William Carmichael, Ford's vice president in charge of its developing-country programs, would write several years later in a Ford report; and most of those scholars had studied urban middle-class women. The exception was Pujiwati Sajogyo, a sociologist at the Center for Rural Sociological Studies at the Bogor Agricultural Institute. Married to one of the country's top experts on rural development and poverty alleviation, she had studied rural women in West Java in the late 1970s. The Sajogyos were "two of the more original and interesting researchers working on issues that the government thought were sensitive,"

Kessinger told me. Pujiwati Sajogyo's research, funded by Ford, was among the first to shed light on work patterns by gender in rural households and villages. In 1980, Ford gave the agricultural institute another $200,000 to develop detailed data on rural women outside Java and to increase the country's capacity to carry out that sort of research. Under the grant, young researchers from the provinces were to be trained and sent out to study the lives of village women. A project specialist from Ford would help analyze data from village studies and run workshops in field research for graduate students and junior faculty. The aim was to build a national network of researchers on issues involving women, increase the supply of data, and make it available to program designers and policy makers. During her first two years at Ford, Ann was the project specialist assisting Sajogyo.

Twice a week, Ann would be driven south from Jakarta to Bogor, the hill town where generations of colonials, including Thomas Stamford Raffles, the British lieutenant governor of Java during the brief British occupation of parts of the Dutch East Indies, had repaired in the early nineteenth century to escape the swelter of summer. The university lay alongside a wide boulevard, facing the Bogor Botanical Gardens, conceived a century and a half earlier by a Dutch botanist with the help of assistants from the Royal Botanic Gardens at Kew. With fifteen thousand species of trees and plants, the Bogor gardens surrounded the Indonesian president's summer palace. "I might mention that I'm in Bogor every Tuesday and Thursday at Pujiwati's office," Ann wrote in 1981 to Carol Colfer, an American anthropologist working in Indonesia, who had sent a letter proposing that she and Ann meet. "I see from your itinerary you will also be in Bogor on Tuesday, March 17. We could have a picnic in the garden."

That summer, Ann flew with Sajogyo to Sumatra, where they spent a week visiting universities, giving presentations on women and development, explaining field research methodologies, and interviewing candidates for the training workshop they planned to hold in Bogor a month later. Finding the right researchers was not simple. At the University of North Sumatra in Medan, all eleven candidates were unsuitable: Either they were from unrelated fields, such as art, or they had no experience in villages and had never done research on rural women. In Padang, the capital of West Sumatra, the university rector preferred hiring men as instructors because, he said, women went off on pregnancy leave or balked at leaving their husbands. Traveling alone in South Sumatra, Ann found that the cultural complexity of the region presented additional research challenges. There were four distinct ecological zones and fourteen indigenous ethnic groups, each with its own dialect or, in some cases, language. There were also migrants from elsewhere in Indonesia, some relocated by the government from densely populated parts of the country. The experiences of women varied widely from one ethnic group to the next; one, for example, kept teenage girls in purdah. "With all this complexity, the difficulty of selecting truly representative sample villages is enormous," Ann wrote in a report on the progress of the project.

By late September, Ann and Sajogyo had enlisted eighteen researchers from eight universities in seven provinces to meet in Bogor for the workshop in preparation for heading out into the field. Twelve were women. Ann and the Sajogyos taught seminars on a dozen topics, from theories of social structure to the role of women in small industries and petty trade. Well-known Indonesian social scientists gave guest lectures. The government's junior minister for women's affairs spoke on the connection between policy-making and research. The young researchers were to collect data on three subjects: time and labor allocation, income and expenditures, and decision-making. Each also chose a special area of interest. They would be working in Sumatra, Sulawesi, East Java, and Nusa Tenggara Timur, a group of islands in eastern Indonesia. They would be studying a half-dozen ethnic groups—from Bataks to transmigrant Javanese—in villages that made handicrafts, farmed fish, harvested forest products, and grew such things as rice, coconuts, coffee, rubber, and cloves.

Ann went into the field, too. Bill Collier, whom she had known since the early 1960s at the University of Hawai'i and who had known both of her husbands, was working on a separate study in tidal-swamp areas of South Sumatra. His team was studying agricultural systems and the condition of several ethnic groups, including indigenous Malays, Buginese migrants, and Javanese transmigrants. Ann joined the group, moving from village to village on a grid of rivers and canals, traveling by night in wooden boats in crocodile-infested waters. The group slept on the floors of village leaders' houses, built on stilts. Because the Buginese distrusted the Javanese, Collier told me, the Javanese members of the research team would insist that he and Ann step out of the boats first in every Buginese village. In one area where Ann was hoping to conduct interviews, the local leader was said to have a long arrest record for robbery and a murder, committed ostensibly with the help of his wife. He had returned from prison, and everyone in the villages deferred to him: "If you wanted to go anywhere, you had to tell him first," Collier said. The man assigned his wife and alleged co-conspirator as Ann's escort—to convince the Buginese to talk. Through flooded rice fields and swarms of mosquitoes, Ann and her escort crossed from one canal to the next on foot. "Ann ended up up to her chest in water and mud," Collier remembered. "She loved it. She could create a rapport with these people very easily, because she was sympathetic and she liked them. They realized that she was there trying to find out things to help."

Indonesia was "a country of 'smiling' or gentle oppression" when it came to women, Ann would write in a Ford memo the following spring. Extreme forms of anti-female behavior, such as infanticide or nutritional discrimination, were nonexistent or rare, but there was a "social reward system" that led middle- and upper-class women to marry early, forgo further education, and pass up careers. Educated women often stayed out of the workforce to avoid giving the impression that their husbands could not support them. Most Indonesian women worked for little money: In village industries and farming, they made about half the income of men. Yet their income was crucial to the survival of poor households—especially the one in five households on Java that were headed by women because of divorce, desertion, and the departure of men looking for work. Government programs, however, addressed women as homemakers, not breadwinners. Women were required to attend family-planning and nutrition programs, but they were rarely chosen for projects that might help them make money. As a result, young women were leaving the countryside for the cities—where they were ending up as servants, factory workers, or prostitutes. All three of those jobs involved economic and sexual exploitation, Ann said. Ford was working with grassroots organizations that focused on women, she said, but the government viewed organizing as subversive. "While Indonesia has many women's organizations, it cannot be said to have a real women's 'movement,'" Ann wrote. "In comparison with a country like India, for example, the capacity of Indonesian women to articulate their problems, organize themselves and use political or other channels to improve their condition is still minimal."

As Ann had noticed several years earlier in her dissertation field-work, development was not necessarily benefiting poor women. In 1982, she helped persuade Ford to award a $33,000 grant to a legal-aid organization, the Institute of Consultation and Legal Aid for Women and Families, to hold a seminar and workshop on the effects of industrialization on female labor. In preparation, a team formed by three other organizations studied women workers in fifteen factories on Java, looking at the division of labor by gender, differences in treatment, legal literacy of women workers, and en-forcement of labor laws regarding women. The team leaders and their assistants were young, well-trained female social scientists, one of whom later started her own organization focused on women workers. Their report quickly became "our best reference on the condition of women workers in the formal sector in Indonesia," Ann wrote afterward.

Ann was a feminist, by all accounts, but not inclined toward fiery pronouncements. As Sidney Jones described her, she could more legitimately be called a feminist than could anyone previously assigned to the Jakarta office. She had strong convictions on the rights of women. "But she wasn't at all in your face or belligerently ideological," Jones said. Two of Ann's close friends in Jakarta in the early 1980s were more immediately identified as feminists: Georgia McCauley, whose husband worked for Ford, was a former presi-dent of the Honolulu chapter of the National Organization for Women, and Julia Suryakusuma, the flamboyant daughter of an Indonesian diplomat and wife of a film director, who would later quote a friend's description of her as a "feminist and femme fatale." According to James Fox, an anthropologist based in Australia and working in Indonesia, who was friendly with both of them, "Ann was never out there in the same way that Julia was, but they were close." As Fox saw it, some feminists were earnest and literal, and could constantly be teased. You could not do that with Ann, he said, because she would just play along. Her feminism was tempered, he said, by the fact that her overriding commitment was to the poor, regardless of gender. Occasionally, Ann would make jokes about feminists, said Pete Vayda, a close friend of Ann's who was working as a consultant for Ford. Which is not to say she would necessarily overlook a remark she considered demeaning.

"Have a good weekend, honey," said one Australian consultant.

"Don't call me honey," Ann growled in response.

"Okay, sport," the consultant countered cheerily.

On another occasion, Ann challenged a table full of Indonesian activists, all men, with whom she was dining, because she felt they were being rude to the waitress.

"Excuse me," a younger Indonesian friend recalled Ann saying. "You guys make me feel uncomfortable. I'm sitting here and you're doing nothing to me and yet I feel badly. How do you think she felt?"

What drove her?

In the eyes of her children, there was something soft and a bit naive about their mother. In *Dreams from My Father*, she comes off as a romantic, a dreamer, an innocent abroad. Amid the secrets, the unacknowledged violence, the corruption of Jakarta, Ann is "a lonely witness for secular humanism, a soldier for New Deal, Peace Corps, position-paper liberalism." Twenty years after the end of her first marriage, her chin trembles when she speaks to her college-age son about his father. Her wistful expression at a screening of *Black Orpheus* seems, to her son, a window into "the unreflective heart of her youth." In later life, she travels the world, working in villages in Asia and Africa, "helping women buy a sewing machine or a milk cow or an education that might give them a foothold in the world's economy," as Obama describes her work. She stares at the moon and forages through markets of Delhi or Marrakech "for some trifle, a scarf or stone carving that would make her laugh or please the eye." At times, she seems almost childlike.

Maya, too, described her mother to me as what she called "a softie"—a person of acute sensitivity and empathy who would be overwhelmed with feeling at the sight or even the prospect of other people's suffering. In the company of her family, she might weep at a newscast, Maya said, and she could barely watch movies in which children were hurt. "She could be naive when speaking about this country and what people were ready for . . ." Maya said. "There was that sense—like, 'Why can't we all get along?' And, you know, there was a touch of the flower child in her." Perhaps Ann was simply an optimist; perhaps she refused to be cynical. But, Maya said, "it seemed perhaps a little naive at times—this failure to comprehend that not everyone would necessarily have good motives or benevolent intentions."

When I asked President Obama if he saw his mother as naively idealistic, as his book seemed to suggest, he paused a while before answering, then said, "Yes, I do and did see her that way, in part—but not in a pejorative sense. I mean, my mother was very sophisticated and smart. In her field of study and her work, she was deadly serious about what she was doing, willing to take on a lot of sacred cows, and really committed. So as a professional, she knew her stuff. There was a sweetness about her and a willingness to give people the benefit of the doubt, and sort of a generosity of spirit that at times was naive. . . . Now, I like that about her. That's not a criticism; there's a wonderful quality about that. But there's no doubt that there were times when she was taken advantage of in certain situations. And she didn't mind being taken advantage of. Part of the idealism was, 'You know what? If somebody makes me pay five times what the going rate is at the market for this little knickknack that I think is neat, that's fine.' There's an idealism and naiveté embedded in that. But I don't see that as a criticism. I see that as part of what made her special—and also part of what made her resilient. Because I think she could bounce back from disappointments in a lot of ways."

Friends and colleagues described her differently. Many remembered Ann as tough, sharp, and worldly. Most said they had never seen her cry. She was more open than many people, both intellectually and emotionally. She was unusually curious: She wanted to understand the reasons for things. At one point, for example, she became interested in the relationship between Indonesians and the relatives some of them exploited as servants, Pete Vayda remembered. "It was the kind of thing she was very interested in—some kind of injustice based on something structural or cultural," he said. "It was not a matter of saying these were evil people, but something systematic about exploiting poor relatives from the countryside." Her convictions, he said, arose less out of emotional responses than out of empirical data. Her sense of injustice was sharp but informed—not a sentimental reaction. He could not recall having heard Ann "give any passionate speeches about the injustices of the world." She would just comment, rather matter-of-factly, "I'm looking into this." She was fully aware of corruption, the government restrictions, the cynicism of elites. She knew all about people exploiting one another, and she did not romanticize

With friends or colleagues, apparently in Yogyakarta,
about 1977 or 1978

any of those things. At the same time, she believed it was not impossible to make life in Indonesia better. "She saw the good and the bad everywhere," Vayda said. "She was smart about it. She realized these were things she had to accept if she wanted to make a difference." He said he had no evidence that correcting injustices was what drove her—but if something could be corrected, that was a bonus.

"Other people talk about her warmth and compassion and generosity," Vayda said, with some impatience, reflecting on characterizations of Ann in the media during the presidential campaign. "All that's true. But I haven't seen that much about how funny she was—and how hardheaded."

What was striking, James Fox said, was not her passion but her authority.

"Ann had lived how many years with poor people?" he said. "She didn't have to parade it, it was just there. When she talked, she talked as if she knew the villages of Java. You knew she knew. It was a kind of mission, but she didn't put up a flag to parade it." At the same time, he said, "she just couldn't stand some of the bullshit that comes from an expatriate who's been in the country a week and knows the answer to everything. Ann could be very tough. She didn't suffer fools who pretended to know what they didn't know."

To some in the Ford Foundation office, she came off as more of an advocate.

"She was a very tough person, and I mean that in a good sense," said Terance Bigalke, a Ford program officer in Jakarta. At Ford, she did not go out of her way to "nuance" her positions, he said. "In an office setting, you often say things where you're making your point but very carefully choosing your words," he said. "That wasn't her style." She seemed to believe people should be able to take the full force of her opinions; she was ready to do the same in return. Most people seemed to respect her for it, Bigalke said, even if they might not have taken such an undiplomatic stand. They may even have found it endearing. "They could feel how passionately she felt about the issues she was working with," he said. "It wasn't an academic exercise for her, it was something she was really committed to."

Or as Tom Kessinger put it, "It wasn't just a professional job. It was something a little more personal."

One of the Indonesians with whom Ann worked most closely was Adi Sasono, the son of Muslim social activists from Pekalongan on the north coast of Central Java, who had been a student leader at the time of the overthrow of Sukarno. Trained as an engineer and educated in Holland, Sasono had worked in the corporate sector until the mid-1970s, when he had quit and, with a group of young intellectuals who saw themselves as Islamic reformers, formed an organization to explore alternative approaches to development in Indonesia. By the time Ann met him, Sasono was the director of the Institute for Development Studies, an independent organization with a full-time staff of thirty. He was organizing squatters and scavengers in the cities and encouraging the growth of rural cooperatives. Sasono, who would go on to become a minister in the Indonesian government after the fall of Suharto in the late 1990s, wanted to find ways of allowing "development without displacement"; he wanted to integrate the sprawling informal economy into city planning. His ideas were so attractive, Richard Holloway of Oxfam told me, that many of the international-development people wanted to work with him. "Of all the Indonesians I worked with, he was the strongest in terms of a conceptual framework for what he was doing," said David Korten, who was working for the

U.S. Agency for International Development in Indonesia at the time and has since become a critic of economic and corporate globalization. Korten recalled "how far he was ahead of most of us in understanding the dysfunctions of the 'modern' development sector and why it so inexorably increases the marginalization of the majority of the population. He saw the bigger picture that most of us were missing."

It was assumed, Sasono suggested, that rapid industrialization and the exploitation of natural resources were the best route to economic development and high employment. But industrialization was failing to absorb the growing labor force in the cities. Poverty was increasing, and the gap between rich and poor was widening. The benefits of growth were not trickling down. In Jakarta, people were squatting in cemeteries, encamped beside garbage dumps, crowded in shanties alongside railroad tracks. The government was demolishing makeshift settlements to make way for high-rise buildings and the widening of roads, and the police were confiscating pedicabs to clear streets for cars. There was talk of shipping vagrants to a nearby island. Shantytowns, demolished one day, were being reborn the next. "They were doing constant battle with authorities," Bigalke remembered. "Police were needing to be bribed to allow people to continue setting up their stands on the street." Sasono made the case for a broad-based, decentralized approach to growth—"for the people, by the people, and with the people." Even without government help, he believed, the poor would prosper on the strength of their energy and wits. Sasono was a figure not unlike Saul Alinsky, the author of *Rules for Radicals: A Pragmatic Primer for Realistic Radicals* and the father of community organizing in the United States, Richard Holloway told me. Alinsky wrote that book, he said, for those "who want to change the world from what it is to what they believe it should be." Community organizing, of course, was the line of work that Barack Obama would take up in Chicago just a couple of years after Ann began working with Sasono in Jakarta. Alinsky's phrase, about wanting to change the world, echoes what Craig Miner, the historian, had told me about Kansans—that they were people who said, "You're not okay, I'm not okay, and I know how to fix it."

Through Sasono, Ann widened her circle of acquaintances to include a diverse group of labor activists, reformers, people in cultural organizations, and organizers from the slums. Her fieldwork in the handicraft villages and on the provincial development project in Central Java had convinced her, like Sasono, of the vitality of the informal sector, and the value of development from the bottom up. "She was very interested in demonstrating what a significant contribution to the overall economy the informal sector was making," Bigalke told me. That way, the informal sector might be encouraged by the authorities rather than stifled. Ann and Sasono, along with others, traveled together to Malang in East Java to visit the largest grassroots women's cooperative in Indonesia, the Setia Budi Women's Cooperative, which had been set up exclusively to meet the financial needs of women. They attended seminars and workshops in Jakarta, Semarang, and Bali. "They got along well together," said her close friend Rens Heringa. "With him, she could really talk—politics and social and economic problems, that kind of thing." Holloway said, "She was friendly with Adi professionally and possibly personally. Of course, you don't express emotion in Java. So whatever emotion they had was always concealed. They hung around a lot together. It would have been talked about a bit. But no big deal." Through Sasono, Ann told Holloway, "I'm able to find really impressive people that I respect greatly, who are

Indonesians and not privileged foreigners like myself, but who are working with down-and-out and poor people."

Ann had a strong sense of right and wrong about people abusing other people, Holloway had noticed. She knew wealthy women in Jakarta, some educated abroad, who "talked up a great talk about democracy," Holloway said, then went home and gave their own servants no wages, poor food, and abysmal accommodations. He had been struck by what he described as Ann's "vituperation about high-class Javanese women treating servants badly." That sort of thing was a fact of life in Indonesia, he said. "But she was not prepared to just slough that off and say, 'That's how Indonesia is.' She would get angry about it." To encounter Indonesians who felt passionately about challenging such injustices was emboldening. Holloway said, "She would, I think, feel justified in this because, 'I'm not just a foreigner getting angry, there are people like Adi getting angry. This is an Indonesian response, not a foreign response.'"

It was an important point, Holloway added.

"There was always a danger that you would become overidentified with the problems of the people you were working with," he said. "When that happens, you exaggerate the nature of their problems in a way that's meaningful to you but not to them. They have accommodated such problems in their view of life; for you to go on about it seems naive or foolish."

Ann played an unusual role during that period: At a time when fledgling independent-sector organizations offered just about the only opportunity for the exercise of democratic values, Sasono told me, Ann served as a catalyst and a bridge. The Suharto government tolerated a limited amount of activity. But the organizations had a tendency, Bigalke said, "to kind of carve out their own little territory and not be all that interested in interacting with others."

Rarely did one group try to bring others together. "In a way, Ann was doing that through the various grants that she had, and then bringing people together at her home for dinners in the evening, having the kinds of social interaction that we had with the institutes that we were giving grants to," Bigalke said. Sasono, who had been impressed as a young man by the stories of American democratic institutions as told in booklets distributed by the United States Information Service to libraries all over Indonesia, said he learned about pluralism from Ann's example.

"Bridging is not an easy job, because she has to understand the ideas of many people with different ideas," he said. Being an anthropologist, she talked to people as partners, not "as target beneficiaries." Her involvement was emotional, not simply intellectual. Those discussions, Sasono said, gave people ideas and courage. Many became activists in the reform movement that eventually brought the government down. A few, such as Sasono, went on to work in the governments that followed. "Development, like democracy, is a learning process," Sasono said. "People have to learn to have freedom, on one side, and also responsibility, the rule of law, social discipline. It must be done through a social learning process. That's what we learned from both Ann Dunham as well as David Korten, because both come from a society that has learned from democracy in more than two hundred years."

More important than projects, he said, was the selling of ideas.

In mid-1982, Ann made several field trips to tea plantations in the mountains of Java. An Indonesian organization, the All-Indonesia Labor Federation, had proposed to the Ford Foundation a project aimed at improving the welfare of female tea plantation workers. It was also intended to increase the participation of women in labor organizations. Traveling with women, some of whom she had met through Sasono, Ann talked with plantation owners, managers, and pickers. She kept detailed notes, full of observations about the meddling of managers, the hardships faced by the pickers, the comfortable lives of the owners. "She is a Sundanese and she also lives on the plantation in a large comfortable home with diesel-powered electricity, stereo and cassette collection, etc.," Ann wrote of the owner of a plantation between Jakarta and Bandung, where heavy ash from an erupting volcano was falling. "She provided us with a lavish lunch, but attempted in various ways to obstruct our free discussions with her workers." Managers tried to orchestrate the interviews—handpicking the workers and sitting in on the conversations. "We overcame this by rearranging chairs, splitting up and moving in amidst the workers for private conversations," Ann wrote. The area was Islamic, and the women said they were "diligent in praying," Ann wrote. None had ever been to Jakarta or Bandung. None had completed more than third grade. Only two out of seventy-five they met with could read or write. Most could not understand Bahasa Indonesia, the national language. "Claimed school costs prohibitive," Ann wrote. "Includes contributions of rice to the teacher."

Accompanying Ann on one of those trips was Saraswati Sunindyo, a young organizer newly graduated from the University of Indonesia in Jakarta with a degree in sociology. "My line about Ann is, 'She found me in a slum when I was organizing,'" Sunindyo told me when I interviewed her in Seattle, where she was living. Sunindyo was organizing the residents of a squatter settlement in Jakarta for an organization run by Sasono. Later, she moved to Bandung, where, she said, she lived in a shack in a community of scavengers she was organizing into a cooperative. She and Ann met at a meeting of independent and grassroots organizations. "She was this big American woman," Sunindyo remembered, referring to Ann's presence more than her size. "She is a big woman with very little ego. She's not playing the role of an expatriate—not 'I'm an American, I read lots of books, therefore I know.' She worked for the Ford Foundation, but she didn't act like someone who was going to dictate what Ford wanted." Instead, Sunindyo said, Ann "would listen and listen and listen. She was interested in how people are doing things. Rather than, 'Okay, this is a story from another place that I read about. . . .' We all read lots of books, but we don't have to show it. That's Ann. She saw potential in people. And when they needed a push, she really pushed."

In September 1982, Sunindyo traveled with Ann and several younger women to a plantation in the mountains southeast of Bandung. They were housed for the night in a Dutch-period guesthouse with an antique wood-burning stove and a veranda overlooking the adjacent valley and what Ann described as the "tea-covered hills beyond." The bathroom Ann shared with one other woman, she wrote in her field notes, was the size of the bathroom used by many of the workers, as well as their children. To speak with workers, Ann and the others were taken to where women were picking tea. Sunindyo, wanting not simply to gather information but to help out, fell in beside one picker and began picking with her, dropping tea leaves into her basket. The skin on the faces of the pickers was cracked from the weather and the cold.

"And politely, very politely, Ann asked one of the women, 'May I see what's in your lunch box?'" Sunindyo remembered.

There was only rice and *sambal,* a paste made from ground red chili peppers.

"So, we asked, 'What else are you going to eat?'" Sunindyo recalled.

"The leaves," the woman said.

The trip to the tea plantation with Ann was important to Sunindyo. "For us, young women at that time, it was really empowering—in the sense that we were learning from her," she said. "We just watched, said, 'Okay, that's it, that's how.'" To have Ann recognize their commitment and treat them as friends emboldened them to return to their work in their organizations "knowing that we are in this together," Sunindyo said.

"There is Ann, who works for the Ford Foundation," she said. "We see Ann as one of us."

Ann's circle of friends in Jakarta kept expanding. There were anthropologists, artists, activists, academics, curators, writers, development consultants, and filmmakers, among others. Yang Suwan, a Chinese-Indonesian anthropologist educated in Germany and newly returned to Jakarta, had done studies on women in development in West Sumatra and East Kalimantan. She and Ann shared a fascination with Indonesian crafts and textiles. Rens Heringa was studying a group of isolated villages on the northeast coast of Java where women made batik from hand-spun locally grown cotton. In October 1981, in the hot period before the rains broke, she and Ann took a three-day car trip along the northeast coast of Java to visit those villages. They stopped along the way to explore a series of saline ponds where the owners, many of them of Arab descent, trapped shrimp and harvested salt. Wahyono Martowikrido, the archaeologist whom Ann had known in the early and mid-1970s, was back at the National Museum in Jakarta. Ann Hawkins, who had known Ann in Semarang, had moved to Jakarta to work for UNICEF, around the corner from the Ford Foundation offices. By crossing an old Dutch canal on jerry-rigged boards, she and Ann would meet from time to time for lunch. Pete

Vayda, living in a Ford bungalow near Ann's, dropped in regularly for breakfast and rode to work in Ann's car. Her long dining room table was a gathering place, often arrayed with packages of home-made Indonesian snacks. "Please, take these," Yang Suwan remembered Ann saying. "You'll help the poor women if you eat the snacks." Often, Ann had guests. After Vayda introduced her to a graduate student of his who was doing fieldwork in East Kaliman-tan, the student, Timothy Jessup, became a regular guest when he was in town. Was there a place in Jakarta to play squash? Vayda asked Ann. Soon she had arranged, through Lolo, for Vayda to become a member of the Petroleum Club.

Ann could be found at parties at the East Jakarta home of Ong Hok Ham, a Chinese-Indonesian, Yale-educated historian and public intellectual. Newspaper editors, academics, artists, for-eign reporters, foundation program officers, and diplomats with duty-free privileges were regularly invited. The parties served as a kind of salon and a source of inside information and political gossip. "He collected people he found interesting," said John McGlynn, an American translator of Indonesian literature who first encountered Ann in the early 1980s. "He wanted intellect, he wanted argument. I was told you can count on Ann for some of that." Ann was a member of a group McGlynn referred to as "the white women in tablecloths"—expatriates with a taste for wrap-around batik skirts. Ann's laugh was full-throated and spontane-ous, "a cross between a chuckle and a neigh." But her speaking voice was soft—as Heringa put it, "almost Javanese. It was as if she was telling fairy tales. In that way, she had adapted fully." On sev-eral occasions, she gave lectures on topics such as textiles and In-donesian ironworking traditions as part of a series organized by the Ganesha Society, a group of mostly expatriate volunteers at the

National Museum. At other times, she could be found at exhibitions and plays at the Taman Ismail Marzuki Arts Center, where some of the performances were known to be, as James Fox put it, "pushing the edge of things."

"If you knew Indonesian culture, if you knew what was being said, you could recognize the game," Fox said. "But you had to know the language well enough, you had to know the way things were being communicated. Of course, Ann did. Her Indonesian was excellent; it was almost like a native's. She could pick those things up. So either at events like that or parties we'd have with Indonesians, you could participate. In the expatriate community, you would almost have to spell it out and they'd never get it. You'd tell them the simplest thing, and it would be a revelation. Ann was one of those rare birds who knew how things were. She had an edge to her. She was feisty. She had a huge sense of humor, I thought. It was honed to be subtle. She could make a joke without appearing to. It was innuendo."

It was, perhaps, almost Javanese.

"Are you aware that our friends are all people living in more than one culture?" Ann marveled to Yang Suwan on one occasion, being driven home one evening in Jakarta. "We are so lucky to know both cultures. This problem about ethnicity, about race—it is not a problem for us."

Ann's closest female friend was Julia Suryakusuma, the "feminist and femme fatale." On the surface, the two women made an unlikely pair. A diplomat's daughter born in India and educated at the American high school in Rome, Suryakusuma was tall and beautiful, and twelve years younger than Ann. Colorful and outspoken, she prided herself on being, as she put it, "naughty and rebellious." She had married Ami Priyono, an Indonesian film director who was fifteen years older, when she was barely twenty. James Fox considered her "some of the best company in Jakarta," and Rens Heringa described her to me as "a person one gets into trouble with." Ann was calm and measured. Julia was volatile. "The ideas were squirting out of her imagination," Timothy Jessup said. "It was interesting to see them talk, because Julia would be waving her hands around. Ann would be calm, and Julia would be getting very excited. She liked to make an impression and shock people. Ann liked to make an impression in a different way." Yet they were both bright and unconventional, and not terribly interested in conforming. "Ann used to say that I was from another planet," Suryakusuma told me. "Well, it takes one to know one." They shared a scholarly and personal interest in the condition of Indonesian women. They occasionally fought over handicrafts. They went to parties together, hung out, critiqued each other's relationships with men. ("You know, Julia, you're overqualified for him," Ann once told her.) "We shared our innermost secrets, our fears and desires," Suryakusuma told me. The friendship was intimate and turbulent. "She put up with a lot of shit from me," Suryakusuma said. There were periods when they did not speak.

During one of those periods some years later, Ann sent Suryakusuma a letter that, at least at this distance, seems remarkable in its blend of frankness, respect, and bruised affection.

Friends often ask me about you, Julia. . . . Frankly, I don't know what to say to them. The situation is made more mysterious because I am not even sure what you were angry about. I <u>THINK</u> you were angry because I suggested you patch up your quarrels with Garrett and Rens, but I am not even sure about that. If that is the case, I can only say that, as an old friend, I felt I had the right to give you an honest opinion.

It has been more than 7 months since we last talked, Julia. I haven't called you because I felt I should respect your wish to break things off. Also, I don't like you in your arrogant bitch mode, and I did not want to run the risk of encountering you in that mode again. (Who in the hell did you think you were talking to, anyway, Julia?).

That said, I do of course miss you, and I miss the whole family as well. After all, we were best friends for almost 10 years. I hope things are going well for all of you. Will you be moving into your new house soon? . . .

Have a good holiday. Regards to Ami. Love, Ann.

Yet on another occasion, Ann wrote, "Wanted to write and let you know how much I enjoyed our time together in London. . . . I realized when we were there how much you actually mean to me. In a world where most people are such bloody hypocrites, your spirit shines like a beautiful star! I never have to go through a lot of crap with you, so to speak. Sounds corny, but I mean it. I love you a lot, kiddo."

With many of her friends, Ann kept the details of her private life private. Even with some who knew her well, she revealed little about her childhood, her parents, even her marriages. On the subject of her sex life, she was discreet even with close friends—or so they led me to believe. But opportunities for romance did not end with her second divorce. Carol Colfer, who was also a single American woman in her thirties working in Indonesia, said she and Ann used to talk about people hitting on them. "It was very common," she said. "A lot of Indonesians like white skin. And, of course, she had quite white skin. We would joke about people bothering us and thinking we were going to be these wildly sexually active folks. We weren't very wild." If Ann confided on a regular basis in anyone, it appears to have been Suryakusuma. "We were both very sexual," Suryakusuma told me. "We talked a lot about sex and our

With Ong Hok Ham, Julia Suryakusuma, Ami Priyono, and
Aditya Priyawardhana, the son of Julia Suryakusuma and
Ami Priyono, July 1989

sex lives." Ann was sensual, Suryakusuma said. She took pleasure in, among other things, food and sex. Rens Heringa said she and Ann shared an astrological sign, Sagittarius, thought to signify an adventurous spirit. "I never was interested in Dutch guys, ever," Heringa said. "She never was really interested in white guys." According to Suryakusuma, "She used to say she liked brown bums and I liked white bums."

Ann's secretary at the Ford Foundation, Paschetta Sarmidi, noticed that Ann's eyes "glittered" at the mention of a certain Indonesian man who worked for a bank near the Ford offices.

"You like Indonesians," Sarmidi observed tentatively. "The first time, you married an African. The second time, you married Lolo. Now you like the man from the bank."

"She smiled," recalled Sarmidi, who pressed no further.

Ann loved men, but she did not claim to understand them, Georgia McCauley, who became a close friend of Ann's in Jakarta in the early 1980s, told me. McCauley, who was fifteen years younger than Ann and a mother of two small children, remembered once asking Ann for advice about men. "She said, 'I'm so sorry, I have no idea. I just have nothing to offer you. I haven't learned anything yet,'" McCauley told me. "She was befuddled by them. They were interesting to her; she had this intense curiosity. Her relationships had not worked out. Like many women, she didn't understand men. She was a cultural anthropologist, it was a kind of *topic*: 'Interesting, but don't know!'"

Life in the bubble had its downside for an unmarried American woman with a half-Indonesian daughter at home and a half-African son in college thousands of miles away. In a community made up largely of married men with wives and children at home, Ann was an anomaly. "You're more subject to gossip," said Mary Zurbuchen, who had become a single parent by the time she returned to Jakarta in 1992 as the Ford Foundation's country representative. "People might have wondered who she was and who she was hanging out with. They might have noticed things." After attending a meeting of high-ranking Ford people from all over the world, Nancy Peluso remembered, Ann remarked that nearly all the participants were male, and those who were not male were mostly unmarried or childless. "She was really the odd person out," Peluso said. Ann's home life "imposed different kinds of constraints on her life that Ford was simply not cut out to understand."

Suzanne Siskel, who joined the Ford Foundation as a program officer in Jakarta in 1990, ran into Ann at a party in 1990 shortly after accepting the job. "She looked at me," Siskel told me. "She said, 'Hmm. You're going to work for Ford? Get ready for the eighteen-hour workday.'"

The logistics of managing Ann's household could be complex: "Barry will stay in Indonesia +/- one month and then return to New York via Honolulu, taking Maya with him and dropping her off at her grandparents for the rest of the summer," Ann wrote to her boss, Tom Kessinger, in April 1983, laying out the family's travel plans for the summer after Barry's college graduation. "This will count as her home leave. I will either go to Hawaii at the end of the summer to pick her up, staying two weeks as my home leave, or I will have her grandparents put her on a plane to Singapore and I will pick her up there. We will do our physicals in Singapore at that time." For work, Ann traveled often: New Delhi, Bombay, Bangkok, Cairo, Nairobi, Dhaka, Kuala Lumpur, and throughout much of Indonesia. On at least one occasion, she appealed to Ford to rewrite its spouse travel policy to cover dependent children. "This is particularly relevant for single parents who do not have another responsible adult in the household to handle child care during periods of extensive travel," she wrote in a memo to New York in December 1983. On the other hand, the cost of living in Jakarta, combined with a Ford salary and benefits, made it possible to be a single mother in a high-powered, travel-intensive job in a way that might have been more difficult in the United States.

"You managed," Zurbuchen said. Even if barely.

The Jakarta International School, where Ann enrolled Maya, was both extraordinary, in its community and curriculum, and extraordinarily exclusive. Founded by international organizations, such as the Ford Foundation, that put up money in return for shares, it served the families of those institutions. The grounds of the new campus in South Jakarta were landscaped with tropical flowers. There was a swimming pool, air-conditioning, a theater with plush upholstered seats, where students performed plays by the likes of George Bernard Shaw. The faculty was international. The student body comprised fifty-nine nationalities, with the United States and Australia contributing the most. Parents were accomplished and ambitious for their children, and there was an abundance of nonworking mothers available to, say, sew kimonos for a production of *The Mikado*. The school played a powerful and positive role in shaping the worldview of its students. "They came to easily transcend the notion that national identity is the normal referent for looking at people," Tom Kessinger said of his two sons. "And they found early on that friendships take many different forms, particularly over time." One group was glaringly absent, however. Under Indonesian law, Indonesian children could not attend. When Kessinger wrote to Ann, telling her that Maya's enrollment had been approved, he added that the only hitch was that the school would need copies of the first page of Maya's passport and of Ann's work permit: "They need them to satisfy Government of Indonesia regulations for all students, and are somewhat concerned because she obviously carries an Indonesian surname." In that way, among others, the school stood apart. "It was like a satellite on its own," said Halimah Brugger, an American who taught music there for twenty-five years. Frances Korten, who joined the Ford Foundation office as a program officer in 1983 and had a daughter in

Maya's class, recalled, "That kind of insularity of the foreign community was something that Ann, I think, frankly, more than the rest of us, felt was really not good. . . . To have her child going to a school that Indonesians couldn't attend, I think, was an affront."

It was not easy. Ann wanted Maya to have an English-language education, and Maya would have been ill equipped to leap into an Indonesian school for the first time at age ten or eleven. In preparation for entering the Jakarta International School, Ann had made sure that Maya's homeschooling included English. But Maya felt, as she put it, some "discomfort being the only Indonesian in the Jakarta International School." It was a discomfort of which Ann was surely aware. "I think batik-making was the only Indonesian thing that I did," Maya remembered. "I remember taking choir and singing 'Tie a Yellow Ribbon Round the Old Oak Tree.' We did *Pygmalion* and British history." Hoping to gain acceptance, she brought in photographs of American relatives she did not even know. "There were a couple of mixed kids like me," she said. "No full-blooded Indonesians, except folks who worked there. Some. I certainly felt like I was in two different worlds: the world of Indonesia that I knew, populated by Indonesians, and then the world of JIS, which was basically an expatriate school." Ann worried that the nature of her work would affect Maya's shot at social acceptance. "Ann said Maya's friends thought Ann's job was rather odd—going into the field, talking with poor people," Yang Suwan told me. When Maya had friends coming over for the night, Yang recalled, Ann seemed uncharacteristically anxious. The Indonesian snacks would disappear from the dining room table. "Suddenly, there are steaks and soft drinks," remembered Yang. She would say, teasingly, "Ann, this is not locally made!" Ann also worried about Maya's exposure to the excesses of some of her more privileged, jaded classmates. Richard Holloway remembered Ann observing, in some distress, "I'm afraid that this comes with going to an international school, because most of the kids there have too much money."

Ann wanted Maya, like Barry, to be a serious student. "She hates me to brag, but I am forced to mention that she made high honors this term," she wrote to Alice Dewey in February 1984. She made her expectations clear. "Ann was pretty strict with her," Rens Heringa remembered. "I think she needed to be. Maya was too pretty for her own good. Ann talked to her, took her to task— to do her homework, to be a serious student, to not do the things that many of her classmates did." She worked hard to pass on her values. On one occasion, she arranged for Maya to accompany a friend of Ann's who was doing research in a slum area of Jakarta, then was upset when the colleague's methods fell short of Ann's exacting standards. Ann herself took Maya into the field and traveled extensively with her outside the country. In April 1984, Ann used her annual home-leave allowance instead for what she called a "grand tour" with Maya to Thailand, Bangladesh, India, and Nepal. "I had to spend five days en route at an employment conference in Dhaka, but the rest was vacation and great fun, despite beastly dry season weather and dust storms in North India," she wrote to Dewey late that month. "Saw lots of Moghul palaces and forts, rode elephants, rode camels, bought heaps of silk and clunky silver jewelry and useless gew-gaws very cheap—altogether a most satisfying trip."

Ten months earlier, Ann and Maya and a group of Ann's friends had traveled to Bandungan, a hill resort near Semarang in Indonesia, to watch a total solar eclipse over Central Java. The government had campaigned for weeks to convince Indonesians to stay inside with their windows covered in order to avoid being blinded by the sight of the eclipse. The countryside was eerily empty, many Javanese having taken to their beds in fear. The group drove past mosques packed with men, all turned toward the interior, praying. From Bandungan, they made their way to a place where nine small eighth- and ninth-century Hindu temples sit one thousand meters up in the foothills of Gunung Ungaran. Reached by a trail through a ravine and past hot sulfur springs, the place offered one of the most dazzling views in Java, to the volcanoes in the distance. "We sat on the edge of the escarpment and watched the shadow of the eclipse rushing across the plain beneath us and engulfing us," recalled Richard Holloway, who had gone along on that trip. The horizon turned red, according to a later description, "and in the half-light distant volcanoes usually obscured by the glare of the sun became visible. For the four minutes of total eclipse, the sun, almost directly overhead, looked like a black ball surrounded by a brilliant white light."

Ann remained in regular contact with Maya's father, Lolo. They spoke often by phone and met for lunch, according to Paschetta Sarmidi, the secretary who worked with Ann. "They tried to take care of Maya together," Sarmidi said. But Lolo's second marriage had changed Maya's relationship with his family. His new wife was young and "not secure enough to bring me into the family—and certainly not Mom," Maya said. "We stopped going to all family functions. There was a complete loss of contact." Maya continued to see her father on his own, but he never took her to see his family or play with her cousins. Ann complained to at least one friend that Lolo, like a stereotype of a divorced parent, was lavishing Maya with luxuries, toys, and sweets. "That particular thing really irritated her," her old friend Kay Ikranagara remembered. "She felt that he had grown up without material things, and now he put so much importance on material things. He was conveying this to Maya."

One evening, shortly before dinnertime at the house in Kebayoran Baru, a group of young activists was gathered around Ann's dining room table, working on a project, Yang Suwan recalled. There was a knock at the door. Yang went to open it and found a man she had never seen before with his arms full of jackfruits and packages. He was there to see Maya, he announced. When Maya ran in and hugged him, Yang was startled. She glanced back into the dining room. Ann's expression had grown uncharacteristically dark. "I had never seen Ann's face so changed, so not friendly," Yang said. When Lolo left after ten minutes, the young people chided Ann, saying she should have invited him to dinner. After all, he was Maya's father. "She looked so annoyed," Yang remembered. "She didn't want to talk."

Ann's visits with Barry were inevitably infrequent. When she went to work for Ford in early 1981, he was in his sophomore year at Occidental College in Los Angeles. That fall, he transferred to Columbia University in New York City. At least twice during her nearly four years at Ford, Ann arranged for him to fly to Indonesia to visit. "I would like to use my educational travel for dependent children this summer to have my son, Barry, come out to visit us," she wrote to Kessinger in May 1981. Barry spent July in Jakarta, then went on to Pakistan to visit a friend from Occidental on his way back to the United States. A week before leaving Jakarta, he sent a telegram to Nancy Peluso, Ann's friend, who had offered him her apartment on West 109th Street in Manhattan: "DO WANT THE APARTMENT WILL ARRIVE AT LATEST AUGUST 24 IN CASE COMPLICATIONS WIRE MOM." The following summer, Ann and Maya visited him in New York City.

And in May 1983, after graduating from Columbia, he flew again to Indonesia for a month, stopping in Los Angeles and Singapore to visit friends. "After Barry arrives I would like to take a week or ten days off," Ann wrote to Kessinger in April. "If I can get reservations (this is right after the eclipse and right after JIS gets out), we would like to go to Bali."

Richard Holloway, Ann's friend from Semarang, recalled arriving to stay at Ann's house and being startled to encounter Barry for the first time.

"There was this young black lad pumping iron in her garden," Holloway remembered. "Very good-looking, great body, polite, personable."

"'This is my son, Barry,'" he recalled Ann saying.

"'Nice to meet you.'"

Women, however, told me that Ann spoke often to them about Barry.

"Never did we get together where we didn't hear, right up front, the first thing, what Barry was doing," said Georgia McCauley. If Ann had received a letter from him, Yang Suwan said, she would be in a good mood all day. Saraswati Sunindyo, who had described Ann as "a big person with little ego," said that little bit of ego pertained to her son. She would show his photograph "and say how handsome he is," Paschetta Sarmidi, Ann's secretary, said. "She spoke of Barack Obama a lot of times a day."

"You married an African?" Sarmidi recalled asking.

"Yes."

"Is he very black?"

"Yes!"

"How is Barry? Does he have his father's skin?"

"Yes."

"Is it like my skin?"

"No," Ann answered. "Your skin is like a Hispanic. But Barack Senior, he is very black. Barry is very handsome. And he is very smart, Paschetta. My boy is brilliant."

By February 1984, during his first year out of college, Barry was working for Business International Corporation, a small newsletter-publishing and research firm that helped countries with foreign operations understand overseas markets. Ann reported on his progress to Dewey.

> Barry is working in New York this year, saving his pennies so he can travel next year. My understanding from a rather mumbled telephone conversation is that he works for a consulting organization that writes reports on request about social, political and economic conditions in Third World countries. He calls it "working for the enemy" because some of the reports are written for commercial firms that want to invest in those countries. He seems to be learning a lot about the realities of international finance and politics, however, and I think that information will stand him in good stead in the future.

In November 1982, after receiving a call from an aunt in Kenya telling him that his father had been killed in a car accident in Nairobi, Barry telephoned Ann in Jakarta with the news. She had been divorced from Obama for eighteen years and had not seen him since that Christmas in Honolulu eleven years earlier. But when the younger Obama delivered the news of his father's death, he wrote in his memoir, he heard his mother cry out. Ann telephoned Bill Collier, perhaps the only person she knew in Indonesia who had also known the elder Obama. Collier, a classmate and friend of

Obama's at the University of Hawai'i, told me that Ann's sadness was unmistakable. It was clear, he said, that she still felt strongly about Obama. Julia Suryakusuma found Ann in her office on the verge of tears. "I just heard the news that Barack's father died," Suryakusuma remembered Ann saying. Then she broke down and wept.

"I always got the impression that she was critical of her husbands," Suryakusuma said, "but I had the feeling she still loved them in a certain way."

By early 1984, Ann was at a crossroads. She had spent six years fulfilling her graduate course requirements and doing the fieldwork necessary to graduate with a Ph.D. But she had yet to take her comprehensive exams, complete a dissertation, and sit for its defense. The nine-month leave of absence she had requested from the University of Hawai'i in 1979 had stretched into five years. "The major reason for the delay in my return to Hawaii is the need to work to put my son through college," she wrote to Alan Howard, the chairman of the anthropology department, in March 1984. "I am happy to say that he graduated from Columbia in June, so that I am now free to complete my own studies." Her contract with Ford was set to expire in late September. "I will either not extend it, or extend it but request an educational leave of absence for nine months (one school year)," Ann told Dewey in a letter that February. "If I do not need to be physically present in Hawaii during the whole time, it might be better for me to stay in Indonesia through the end of the year. The deciding factor will probably be finances." If she could land a part-time fellowship with the East-West Center, she and Maya would return to Honolulu for the 1984–1985 academic year. If not, she might accept an offer from Pete Vayda, who was returning to the United States, to take over the lease on his house in Bogor. "This would be an ideal, quiet place to work and finish up my thesis draft and the house is available very cheaply," she told Dewey. She hedged her bets. She asked Ford for a ten-month leave of absence, applied to schools in Hawaii for Maya, and approached the East-West Center about a fellowship. At the same time, she began looking into applying for a one- or two-year appointment as a visiting professor in the rural-sociology department at Cornell University, specializing in women in development. It was a long shot: A Ph.D. was a prerequisite for the job. She let Alice Dewey know she had listed her as a reference on applications for fellowships from several foundations and funding agencies. "If anyone asks, you can tell them that I am good with dogs," Ann said.

Meanwhile, she went to some lengths to make it clear to Dewey, still the chairman of her dissertation committee, that she was swamped with work.

Maybe you remember that I am handling projects for Ford in the areas of women, employment and industry (small and large). Jakarta was made the Regional Southeast Asia office last year, so that we are also working in Thailand and the Philippines. This year I have major projects for women on plantations in West Java and North Sumatra; for women in kretek factories in Central and East Java; for street food sellers and scavengers in the cities of Jakarta, Jogja and Bandung; for women in credit cooperatives in East Java; for women in electronics factories, mainly in the Jakarta-Bogor area; for women in cottage industry cooperatives in the district of Klaten; for hand-loom weavers in West Timor; for shop girls along Jl.

Malioboro and market-sellers in Beringharjo (still tentative);
for slum dwellers in Jakarta and Bandung; for street food sellers in Thailand. . . .

During Ann's tenure in the Jakarta office, Ford had backed
the first women's studies center in the country, a fledgling research center at the University of Indonesia. Ann had successfully
made the case for an early affirmative-action program for Indonesian women—a scholarship program aimed at getting more women
trained in the social sciences and working in the upper levels of
university faculties and the civil service. Smaller grants had gone
to translating into Indonesian, for use in universities, a key text by
Ester Boserup, a Dutch economist, on the role of women in development; paying for fellowships for female graduate students doing
dissertations on women in home industries; supporting a conference to familiarize the leaders of grassroots organizations with
women's issues; and sending top staff members from the women's
cooperative in Malang to India to learn from the women's cooperatives and trade unions there. The Bogor project, which continued for some years afterward, had laid the groundwork for a
network of Indonesian researchers experienced in the study of village women. It had generated what Ann called, in a 1983 report, "a
great deal of useful and surprising data, which forces us to change
some of our basic perceptions about Indonesian women." Java was
atypical, as it turned out. Rural women on Java worked long hours,
often in multiple occupations, though their hourly earnings were
low. Elsewhere, women worked few hours, and needed money but
had few opportunities to make it because they lived in places with
few roads, means of transportation, or markets. Under such circumstances, development planning needed to be decentralized—

tailored to each province, even each village. Pujiwati Sajogyo, who went on to serve for a time as a consultant to the Indonesian government's Ministry for the Role of Women, helped shift the government's focus away from simply the health and domestic roles of women to include women's need for income and paying work.

In the end, Ford did not renew Ann's contract. She had been in the Jakarta office for nearly four years, which, several Ford people told me, was becoming the standard tenure after which program officers moved to another country or moved on. Kessinger was interested in trying someone new in Ann's job. Ford was increasingly a grant-making organization, not an operating foundation. No longer were several hundred Ford staff members scattered all over, say, India, teaching in management schools, serving in government ministries, working in agricultural research. Program officers sat behind desks, conceived areas of activity, designed grants, wrote memos justifying what they wanted to do. To Kessinger, Ann seemed less comfortable in the office than she was in the field. Some people were good at one thing, some at the other, he believed. Few were good at both. "I felt that from an institutional point of view, she'd probably given us what she could give us," he said.

Kessinger also believed that Ann should complete the work needed to get her Ph.D. Not infrequently, graduate students drifted away from writing their dissertations because they needed money and found paying work, he knew from his years as a professor. When he had started graduate school, the average time from enrollment to a Ph.D. in history was nine years—in large part because students married and needed to support their families. Ann was lucky in that she had found work that not only paid well but that she loved. But that kind of good fortune made it even harder for people to go back and finish. Those who never did, Kessinger was

convinced, went on to regret it. Your Ph.D. was your union card.
"Get a union ticket," Ben Finney, the University of Hawai'i anthropologist, advised his students. "Become a qualified anthropologist.
Then you can get your own grants or jobs." If Ann ever wanted to
work in a university, she would need a doctorate. Furthermore, as
Kessinger saw it, there was something selfish about carrying out
fieldwork and doing nothing with it. In the village in India where
he had done his fieldwork, the first questions were always: Why
are you here? Why is anybody interested in that? The people you
studied expected you to finish. Kessinger told Ann as much. Looking back later, he did not know how she took his tough love. She
said, at least, that she saw his point.

"She felt she had to do it," her friend Rens Heringa recalled.
"And she did it."

She would go back for a year, she seems to have imagined. She
would return to Honolulu in time to register at the University of
Hawai'i in late August and would stay through the spring semester.
She would audit whatever basic theory courses were offered, take
her comprehensives, and defend her dissertation before the end of
the spring term. To support herself and Maya, she hoped to find a
research or teaching position. "Something in the areas of peasant
studies, women's studies or applied anthropology would probably
be most suitable," she wrote to her department chairman, Alan
Howard. She asked Dewey to look out for a two-bedroom apartment or house-sharing arrangement on a good bus route or within
two miles of campus. Then she set about packing up her life in
Jakarta—finishing up evaluations on several grants, clearing out
her office, moving out of her house, finding homes for her animals.
She would stop in Singapore with Maya for two days for insurance
physicals. She would make one last visit to Yogyakarta and her

villages, on which Dewey would join her. She suggested Dewey pass up the opportunity to make the return trip to Hawaii with her and Maya. "After nearly nine years in Indonesia, I will probably need to hire a camel caravan and an elephant or two to load all our baggage on the plane, and I'm sure you don't want to see all those airline agents weeping and rending their garments," she wrote. Her sea freight shipping allowance of three thousand three hundred pounds, she said, "should about cover my batik collection."

At a farewell party at Yang Suwan's house in Kebayoran Baru, Yang told Ann to choose anything in the house as a farewell gift. In the years they had known each other, Yang had made a point of bringing Ann handicrafts from remote reaches of Indonesia that Ann had not visited. She admired Ann's knowledge and never dared give her anything second-rate. Yang had built up her own collection, too. One of the most beautiful pieces in it was a sarong by Masina, a batik artist from Cirebon on the north coast of Java, where the mixing of Javanese, Sundanese, and Chinese influences had produced a rich culture and a distinctive style of batik. The pattern on the sarong was *mega mendung,* or rain clouds in reds and blues, dyed naturally in just the right weather. The sarong hung on a wall in her house. On the day of the party, the house was filled with Ann's friends—Julia Suryakusuma, Wahyono Martowikrido, Pete Vayda, and many others. When Yang made the offer of any object in the house, Ann spun on her heel without a moment's hesitation and pointed to the sarong, displayed on the wall directly behind her.

"This!" she said.

Perhaps Ann had had her eye on that batik for a long time, Yang thought later. After all, Ann knew everything you had in your house. Ann knew her friends, too, Yang thought, fondly.

"She knew I could never say no."

In early July, a shipping company packed up Ann's possessions: batiks, ikats, *wayang* puppets, wood carvings, wall decorations, paddy-field hats, ten boxes of books, three wooden chests, one trunk of clothes, a rattan sofa, five rattan tables, two rattan cabinets, a rattan bed, kitchen utensils, one mirror, and so on. The total weight fell well short of the 3,300-pound limit.

Then she and Maya headed for Honolulu, leaving Indonesia behind.

"It wouldn't have surprised me if she had stayed forever," Sidney Jones, Ann's colleague, told me one afternoon in Jakarta, where she was still working a quarter of a century later. "I got the sense that she was permanently enamored of the place. It's probably the same thing that I feel: This is where a particular formative period of your life took place, it's where your friends are, it's the place that you've made a second home. And it eventually becomes your first home."

Nine

"Surviving and Thriving Against All Odds"

Honolulu was a comedown. Ann went back to the University of Hawai'i, where she had first enrolled as an undergraduate twenty-four years earlier. She rented a modest two-bedroom apartment in a cinder-block building not all that different from the one she had left behind in 1975. Maya was accepted by Punahou, the school to which Barry had returned from Jakarta alone in 1971. Madelyn Dunham helped make up the difference between Maya's partial scholarship and her tuition. Once again, Ann was living a couple of blocks from her parents. At the university, she sat in on Alice Dewey's course on economic anthropology, reviewing material she had surely already learned. Having never learned to drive, she commuted by public bus or on foot. Without savings, she was in no position to buy a house that might have served as a base for future operations, a repository for her collections, a gathering place for her children and for her friends—that is, a home on the scale of the roomy, bustling households to which she had grown accustomed. The anonymity of urban America, even Honolulu, felt alien after the warmth and intimacy of Ann's life in Jakarta. In her tiny household of two, she was without servants for the first time in years. Fearless abroad, Ann seemed vulnerable at home. She wanted Maya, who had roamed Jakarta at night, to be at home in Honolulu by dark. Eager to go out with friends, Maya would hesitate, worrying about her mother. "She seemed lonely, perhaps?" Maya told me. Ann would have loved a companion, Maya said, but she had too much dignity to go to great lengths to find one. Instead, she worked on her dissertation and planned her escape.

"I sympathize with your desire to get back out there in the real world, writing something with an impact on more people," Ann wrote to her friend Julia Suryakusuma, who was doing graduate work in the Netherlands. "I've made the decision to stay based in Hawaii so Maya can graduate there, but it has not been the most thrilling two and a half years of my life, let me tell you."

On January 1, 1985, Ann opened a spiral notebook she had begun keeping toward the end of her time in Jakarta. It was already filled with methodically numbered lists of all sorts under headings that included "Work + Employment," "Health and App," and "Personal and Travel." There were lists of vegetarian dishes, topics for future articles, calories burned per hour of various activities. One list of debts, titled "Owed to Folks," comprised fifteen entries, including "Punahou $1784" and "$2000 deposited in account by Mom." There was a handwritten schedule of daily activities ranging from what appears to be meditation at five a.m. and straightening up the apartment at seven-thirty a.m. to "read w/ Maya" at nine p.m. and "read and slp" a half-hour later. "People List" contained 216 numbered names, the first five of which were, in order, Maya, Adi, Bar, Mom, Dad. The notebook suggested a woman trying hard to be organized, struggling to be responsible about money, looking for a job, thinking about her children, worrying about her weight, reflecting on her past, sorting out her future. On New Year's Day, she turned in the notebook to page 103 and wrote a list of challenges to herself, without elaboration, under the heading, "Long Range Goals."

1. Finish Ph.D.
2. 60K
3. in shape
4. remarry
5. another culture
6. house + land
7. pay off debts (taxes)
8. memoirs of Indon.
9. spir. develop (ilmu batin)
10. raise Maya well
11. continuing constructive dialogue w/ Barry
12. relations w/ friends + family (corresp.)

If Ann had imagined she could wrap up her dissertation in nine months, as she had told the university, she was mistaken. Eighteen months after returning from Jakarta, she passed her comprehensive exams, having submitted a list of two dozen theoretical issues in anthropology and archaeology that she was prepared to discuss. But her dissertation, on five peasant industries, had ballooned to nearly seven hundred pages. It was already twice as long as many Ph.D. theses, and it was far from finished. "But I'll definitely be through and out of here when Maya graduates in June," Ann wrote to Suryakusuma. A year later, she was wishing she had chosen a smaller topic. Her enthusiasm was waning. "I don't find I care very much about it," she wrote again to her friend. "The creative part was over long ago, and it's just a matter of finishing the damn thing." It was not an uncommon problem. Financial support for graduate students in anthropology was hard to come by. Jobs in international development would turn up, promising good pay plus expenses. Graduate students, burdened with credit card bills, would accept, figuring they could finish the dissertation on weekends. Repeatedly, Ann appealed to the university for patience. "I regret the delay, but hope you can once again hold the fort for me till I get back," she would write several years later to Dewey. Ben Finney, a member of Ann's dissertation committee, recalled drafts "of this and that" coming in and Dewey "pulling out her hair. 'It's too long!'" Dewey received in the mail from Ann a postcard of a painting by Picasso, *Interior with a Girl Drawing.* In the painting, a brown-haired woman wearing a garland of flowers draws blithely on lemon-colored paper. Another woman slumps over a table nearby, burying her face. "Rather a nice Picasso I picked up at the Museum of Modern Art en route," Ann wrote in the letter attached. "I call it, 'Ann writing her dissertation on yellow tablets while Alice waits patiently (I hope) in the background.'"

Ann's parents had little understanding of Ann's professional passions. Stanley, nearing seventy, had never found work that he loved. Retired from selling insurance, he now devoted himself to crossword puzzles and television game shows such as *The Price Is Right.* He started projects—photo projects, albums, a family tree— that as often as not went unfinished. He had an immense repertoire of jokes, at which his granddaughter cringed while dutifully laughing. Madelyn, by contrast, loved her work and did it well. By the time Ann returned to Hawaii in 1984, Madelyn had risen to become one of the first female vice presidents at the Bank of Hawaii. Her marriage to Stanley did not seem, at least from the outside, to have improved with age. They bickered and sniped and took refuge in separate bedrooms. Madelyn drank. Occasionally, Ann told a friend, Madelyn would rent a hotel room in Honolulu where she would spend a solitary vacation. "Well, you know how Mother and Father are," Ann would say to her uncle Ralph Dunham after her father's death, some years later. "They fought all the time, but they really loved each other." Ralph Dunham agreed: As far as he could tell, they couldn't live with each other, or without. Ann sometimes wondered if Madelyn was reminded of Stanley when she gazed on her restless, voluble, dark-haired daughter. "I don't think either one of her parents read her dissertation or really even knew what it was about," Maya told me. "So there was a whole side of her adult life that remained a mystery to them. There was a difference in interests and in manner and in temperament that was difficult to bridge."

At the same time, Madelyn made it possible for Ann to live the life she chose.

"Our mom was the one who gave us the imagination and the language, the storytelling, all of those things," Maya told me. "And those things are really important. . . . But I think that if my grandmother had not been there, in the wings, making sure that we had savings accounts and school tuition taken care of and that sort of thing, maybe I would have felt more torn about the way that I was raised. As it was, I could feel free to love my childhood unabashedly and to love growing up in all those different places with all these

different languages and flavors. And so on some level, I would say
that our grandmother gave our mother the freedom to be the kind
of mother that she was."

As Ann's list of long-term goals suggested, she was not especially interested in staying put. In May 1986, less than two years
after returning from Jakarta, she moved to Pakistan on a six-month
contract to work as a development consultant on a rural-credit
program in the Punjab. The following summer, she was in Illinois,
presenting a scholarly paper at an academic meeting and visiting
Barry in Chicago. Next, she was in New York visiting friends with
Maya, who was looking at colleges. From there, Ann flew to London for three days en route to Pakistan. ("Any chance you could fly
over and spend some time with me in London?" she had asked
Suryakusuma in a letter. ". . . It would be great if we could do London together. . . . If you are still planning to go to India in September, could we meet in Delhi? I'd rather see you in Delhi than
Bombay just because I like the city better, but Bombay might also
be possible. . . . You could also come over to Pakistan. . . .") Back in
Pakistan, she spent three months completing the consulting contract she had begun a year earlier, then returned to Honolulu, stopping off in Jakarta. The dissertation would be worth the wait,
Dewey believed. "Ann would run out of money and go take a job,"
she recalled. "Not washing dishes. She was building up more data.
So she would come and go constantly. We knew she was the kind
of student who was going to end up knowing three times more
than we did—in our specialties. So we just let her go."

Ann took Maya with her when she could. In 1986, they traveled
together to India en route to Pakistan, stopping in Delhi, Agra, and
Jaipur. In Pakistan, Maya stayed with Ann for three months, stud-

ied Mughal dancing, and accompanied her into the field. They took a six-day driving trip from Islamabad to the border of China along the Karakoram Highway, the highest paved international road in the world, following the Indus River gorge, passing through the tribal areas of the Pathans, Gilgitis, and Hunzas to the place where the Hindu Kush, the Himalayas, and the Karakoram Range converge. Pakistan was fraught with difficulties, said Michael Dove, an American anthropologist and friend of Ann's from Java, who worked in Pakistan from 1985 to 1989 and saw her there during that period. Bombs fell in marketplaces and around the house in Islamabad where Dove and his wife were living. Dove said he and his wife were kidnapped by armed Pathans in the upper Indus River gorge. "It was the opposite of Indonesia," he recalled. "It was a difficult culture, much more violent. Everyone had a gun." In border areas, people kidnapped foreigners to raise cash. It was difficult to be a Western woman in Pakistan without a husband. Simply walking alone in public was problematic.

Ann wrote to Suryakusuma:

Pakistan is an interesting experience but I do not love it the way I love Indonesia. For one thing, the level of sexism is almost beyond belief. Even the most innocent acts, like getting on an elevator with a man, riding with a male driver, or talking with a male colleague in your office are subject to suspicion. Since almost all marriages are arranged, and all Pakistani men are sexist, many educated Pakistani women choose to remain single (in Pakistan that means virgins for life!) The people are also quite puritanical in general, although the intellectuals somewhat less so. I did make some good friends when

I was there, however. One of them was my field assistant, a young woman who was active in a feminist organization in Lahore.

Ann had been hired to work on the design and initiation of the pilot phase of the first credit project for women and artisan-caste members carried out by the Agricultural Development Bank of Pakistan, the country's largest development institution. In the Punjab, where she was working, Ann observed that village people fell into three classes. Feudal, landowning families lived lavishly in hilltop villas and sent their children abroad to the best universities. Small landholders lived in walled mud compounds and farmed tiny plots. Artisan-caste members, including blacksmiths and weavers and other craftspeople, made products for the landowning families, to whom they were indentured, in return for raw materials and a small share of grain. Some artisan-caste members, however, had cut their ties with the landlords. They were buying raw materials and selling their products in the markets. Ann interviewed carpet weavers, pottery makers, blacksmiths, leather workers, tailors, and others during her first six-month stay. She talked with branch managers of banks. She surveyed buyers, suppliers, and intermediaries in Lahore. When she returned a year later, she conducted training courses for sixty-five extension workers, including the first women, who would work with the artisans. She also made recommendations for increasing lending to poor rural women. Over a two-year period, she told Dewey in a letter, the program made loans to nearly fifteen hundred artisan families and landless or near-landless agricultural families. "So there are some satisfactions in a job pretty well done under difficult field circumstances," she said.

Details of the pleasures of Pakistan she saved for Suryakusuma, her flamboyant friend from Jakarta. In one letter, dated August 28, 1987, she wrote:

I am now ensconced in the Canadian Resthouse on the canal bank in beautiful Lahore. . . . They don't have any guests at the moment, so I'll be able to stay here at least till October 10 and maybe longer. Meanwhile, I have the whole upper floor to myself, with an enormous verandah that looks out over flowering tree tops, a cricket lawn and the canal beyond. It's a perfect place to drag a blanket out to about 6:00 AM and sit and meditate with nothing between me and God but the sky. (My, I am waxing romantic today.) It's also a good place for a cup of coffee in the evening with friends once the weather cools down a bit. Summers in Delhi and Lahore are ferocious, and everyone with money leaves and goes to London or at least to a hill station, but the weather should be perfect by the end of September when you come. . . . Three or four days a week I drive by jeep from Lahore to my project area about one and a half hours from here. I spend all day in our regional office or in the project villages, getting back to Lahore, hot and dusty, about 7:00. Usually, I stop at the Hilton on my way home and throw myself in their rooftop pool to wash the dust away. After 2 or 3 fresh lime sodas I begin to feel human again. Two of my Pakistani women friends are also brave enough to swim there in the evenings (braving the glares of all the male guests who feel they should be in purdah), so I often don't get home till 9:00. In the village, on the other hand, I have made good friends with a family of blacksmiths (6 big boys, and 4 girls, all very "healthy" and strong, like you would expect peasant blacksmiths to be), and I usually stop for a meal or tea (with lots of sugar and buffalo milk) with them a couple of times a week. So my life is full of contrasts as usual.

Ann's approach to matters of the spirit was eclectic. She would meditate in Buddhist monasteries and make small offerings in the Hindu communities that she visited. When she had a kris made for herself in Java, Maya said, she went through the ritual of sleeping with it under her pillow—a process through which a kris is thought to communicate with its owner through dreams—and having her dreams interpreted. "It was important to just sort of acknowledge that everyone had something beautiful to contribute spiritually," Maya told me. "She always counseled us to be very open-minded, to have deep respect for everyone's religions, to recognize that every religion had something good to offer." According to others, she was skeptical of organized religion and ceremonial excess. Don Johnston, a Southern Baptist from Little Rock, Arkansas, and a colleague of Ann's in the early 1990s, said she seemed at that time to be leaning toward deism or Unitarianism—the religion of the church in Bellevue, Washington, she attended as an adolescent. God, she thought, could be found at the intersection of many belief systems. "As anthropologists, we tend to talk about religion more as ritual practice and part of human society," said Nina Nayar, who became a close friend of Ann's several years later. "Rarely do we converse about belief in God. I would not say Ann was a Christian or a Hindu or a Buddhist. I would not put a label on her. But she had a general interest. And I think she probably had more spiritual stuff in her than most people who profess to be religious and faithful. She never once used words in my presence about being atheist or agnostic. She was not a woman of labels. The only label she would not shun was the label of anthropologist."

In *The Audacity of Hope,* Obama describes his mother, despite her professed secularism, as "in many ways the most spiritually awakened person that I've ever known." Without religious texts or outside authorities, he says, she worked to instill in him the values that many Americans learn in Sunday school. She possessed, too, "an abiding sense of wonder, a reverence for life and its precious, transitory nature that could properly be described as devotional." She would occasionally wake him in the middle of the night, as a child, he writes, to look at the moon or have him close his eyes as they "walked together at twilight to listen to the rustle of leaves. . . . She saw mysteries everywhere and took joy in the sheer strangeness of life."

In the late summer of 1986, Ann arranged for Maya to fly to Jakarta, on her way back to Hawaii from Pakistan, to visit her father. Lolo Soetoro had been hospitalized in Jakarta with the liver disease that had been diagnosed a decade earlier when Maya was a small child. Though Ann had been led to believe by his doctors, during his hospitalization in Los Angeles, that the disease would cut short his life, Lolo had lived another seven years. Now he was gravely ill. Maya, having just turned sixteen, flew by herself to Jakarta, where relatives met her at the airport and took her to the home of her uncle Trisulo. Lolo, released from the hospital, spent a week with her in Trisulo's house. He was more talkative than Maya had remembered. He asked about her school, her favorite subjects, and her friends. He brought photographs of himself that he wanted her to keep. There were moments of affection and tenderness. But their time together felt awkward to Maya. "I felt a

teenage resentment that he hadn't been present in a more meaningful way and that he had left the rearing of me to Mom," she remembered later. "I was sort of feeling like I wanted him to be sorry
about that." Later, she would come to regret not having stayed
longer. But she had been away from Hawaii for three months, and
she was impatient to go home. It never occurred to her that her
father might be dying—and that he might know it. Afterward,
she wrote him a long letter from Hawaii and tried to send it in
time to reach him before his birthday on January 2. She wanted
them to have a meaningful relationship, she told him in the letter;
she wanted to know him better. But the letter was waylaid in the
Christmas rush, she told me, and did not arrive as planned. In
the meantime, a family member telephoned from Indonesia to say
that Lolo had fallen into a coma. In early 1987, he died.

The house in Menteng Dalam, to which Maya and Ann had
returned from Hawaii in 1975, went to Maya (and was sold some
years later, with the proceeds going to help pay for her graduate-
school education). To protect Maya's rights, Ann stopped in Jakarta
on her way home from Pakistan the following November. The
house was being rented by Dick Patten, whom she had gotten to
know while she was working on the provincial planning project in
Central Java in 1979 and 1980. Patten, who had extensive experience in credit systems in Indonesia, had gone on to work as a consultant to one of the largest banks in Indonesia on a program not
unrelated to the work he and Ann had done earlier. The aim of the
new program, run by a state-owned bank called Bank Rakyat Indonesia, or the People's Bank of Indonesia, was to make small loans
on a broad scale to low-income rural households throughout the
country. At a time when the term *microfinance* was not the household word that it has since become, the Bank Rakyat Indonesia

project, launched in early 1984, had gotten off to a remarkable start. By late 1985, the bank had made nearly one million small loans, ranging in value from a few dollars to a few hundred dollars. It would soon be initiating new loans at a rate of 120,000 a month. The program held the potential to benefit small enterprises of the sort Ann had studied as an anthropologist, worked with as a development consultant, and tried to help in her years at Ford. So in the summer of 1988, after Maya graduated from Punahou with plans to enroll at Barnard College in the fall, Ann moved back to Jakarta to work with Patten on what was quickly becoming the most successful commercial microfinance program of its kind in the world.

Once again, her dissertation would have to wait.

"Anyway, they are paying me well and I need to fill up my bank account again. (How's that for revolutionary fervor?)," she wrote to Suryakusuma in August 1988.

The credit program had arisen out of the ruins of an earlier effort at rural lending. During the 1970s, Bank Rakyat Indonesia had set up a network of 3,600 small banking units for the purpose of channeling government-subsidized credit to rice farmers under the country's push for rice self-sufficiency. Lending under that program had peaked in the mid-1970s, after which operational losses had ballooned. So it had been phased out, leaving the bank with an extensive network of fully staffed loan offices with little to do. With the encouragement of the Ministry of Finance and advice from the Harvard Institute for International Development, with which Dick Patten was affiliated, the bank had tried something new.

From the beginning, anthropologists had shaped the new credit program. Marguerite Robinson, an American anthropologist who had done fieldwork in India and spent twenty years teaching, had joined the Harvard institute and been sent to Indonesia to work with the Ministry of Finance. James Fox, the anthropologist from Australia whom Ann had known in Jakarta in the early 1980s, had worked with Robinson and Patten advising the bank. From anthropological fieldwork, including Ann's, they knew that rice farming was just one of many economic activities in Indonesian villages that needed credit in order to grow. They also knew, from village studies, that government-subsidized credit, under the old system, had reached only a small fraction of villagers. It needed to be more widely accessible. So, working with the finance minister, the consultants began exploring a program of unsubsidized commercial microfinance. The bank would lend money for any reasonable economic activity, not just rice farming. The program would soon operate without an ongoing subsidy; instead, it would charge interest at the market rate. The market rate was nearly twice the old rate. But most villagers, if they borrowed money, did so through loan groups or moneylenders, who charged in excess of one hundred percent interest on an annual basis. Even with an interest rate of thirty-two percent, it was argued, the new program would be an improvement.

The project took off. Within two years, with the help of a microsavings program, the new general credit program was self-sustaining. By 1989, the bank had 2.7 million rural savings accounts; it had made as many as 6.4 million loans to 1.6 million borrowers. The microfinance program would become the biggest and most lucrative part of the bank's operations. In 1999, Fox called the program "probably the single largest and most successful credit program of its kind in the developing world."

Ann joined the team in 1988 and worked on and off over the next four years as a research coordinator and consultant under three separate contracts funded by the World Bank and the U.S.

Agency for International Development. Ann had what Patten lacked—an intimate knowledge of Indonesian villages. Working with teams of staff researchers from the bank, she designed and carried out what might be described as customer surveys and market research, the results of which were used to fine-tune and measure the success of the microfinance program. She spent weeks at a time traveling with her teams on field trips through Java, North Sumatra, South Sulawesi, and Bali, meeting with bank branch managers and interviewing customers for hours on end. The teams examined how customers were using the money they had borrowed. They gauged its impact on households and rates of employment. They studied repayment rates by gender, estimated the scope of unmet demand, and tracked the rates at which customers were either keeping up with or falling behind on their payments. The consultants used the studies—original research at a time when there was little like it—to refine the microfinance program and to convince the bank not simply to continue the experiment but to expand it, increasing the size of the loans. For every million rupiahs that the bank loaned, Ann told Kamardy Arief, the bank's chief executive officer, her research showed that one additional job was created.

"Ann provided a justification from the field for the approach of commercial microfinance," said Don Johnston, who joined the Harvard group in early 1990 and worked closely with her and Patten. "She was showing that this was something that was benefiting the customers—not something the banks were doing out of desperation. That left Dick and me free to worry about the operational side. We had our ammunition to deal with outsiders, and we had the information that gave us confidence that the basic product approach and expansion direction we were taking was right. So then we could worry about fighting the internal battles . . . to keep the institution on track."

The microfinance program was an extraordinary success. In June 1990, it was making 115,000 loans a month with a value of $50 million and an average loan size of $437. It was soon a major source of the bank's growth. During the East Asian monetary crisis of the late 1990s, when the repayment rate on the microloans remained higher than that of the small, medium, and corporate customers of the bank, the program helped the bank weather the crisis. As of 2009, the bank operated more than four thousand microbanking outlets in Indonesia. It had 4.9 million microloan customers and 19.5 million microsavings customers.

"If you work in the development racket, you're lucky at the end of ten years or twenty or thirty to be able to look back and say, 'I think I did more good than harm,'" Richard Hook, who was hired as an adviser on the Bank Rakyat Indonesia project the same year as Ann, told me. "The non-successes are all too numerous. Often you inflict collateral damage, albeit unwittingly and unwillingly. This project met Indonesian needs. It was based in a massive Indonesian institution—a state-owned commercial bank. It was run by Indonesians. We were external advisers. The concept was making small loans to low-income rural people. The conventional wisdom was you won't get repaid and these people don't know how to handle a loan, they were too innocent of sophisticated procedures and financial know-how to know how to handle credit. We didn't believe that. A number of Indonesians didn't, either. We worked together and made this project work. That was just such a delight."

Patten was brilliant, creative, and not necessarily easy to get along with. Akhtar Hameed Khan, the microcredit pioneer whom he had known in East Pakistan in the 1960s, once described him as

"the finest development worker I have ever met." The son of a successful midwestern banker, he had grown up on a daily regimen of
meat and potatoes so rigid, his daughter told me, that it drove him
to swear off potatoes for life. He had spent most of his adult life in
East Pakistan, Ghana, and Indonesia—a long way from Norman,
Oklahoma. A divorced father of three, he inhabited the persona of
an inveterate bachelor. He liked people who did not need to talk
all the time, and he hated the sort of questions that began with
"Don't you think . . ." He was hardworking and occasionally napped
on the office floor. For a time, he lived in a house with a two-story
cage that served as home for a black Sumatran gibbon—until the
gibbon terrorized various neighbors and found its way into the
electrical wires above the street, necessitating a neighborhood-
wide power shutoff. Patten was opinionated and blunt but not
without compassion. After three months as office manager, Flora
Sugondo went to him in tears, saying she wanted to quit because,
working for Patten, she had become convinced she could do nothing right. Patten apologized, persuaded her to stay, and vowed never
to treat her that way again. When Johnston, a graduate student in
economics at Harvard, arrived in Jakarta for a temporary stint as a
research assistant in Patten's office, Patten gave him a paper to edit,
and Johnston "marked the hell out of it in red ink," as he put it.
Patten was thrilled. Johnston was suddenly the permanent project
assistant. "When I got there, everybody was so happy," Johnston
told me. "I was one of the few people who could work productively
with Dick."

Ann was another. Patten valued Ann's ability to recognize what
kind of research would be useful in building the microfinance program. They shared a certain midwestern straightforwardness and a
fascination with Indonesian culture and Indonesian people. Patten

operated the house in Menteng Dalam as a kind of guesthouse for expatriate consultants. During periods when Ann was between contracts or not renting a house of her own, she stayed there. She treated Patten like a favorite uncle, said Johnston, who lived in the house. Sometimes she called him her surrogate father. There might be as many as ten or twelve people at the table for dinner—pot roast or meat loaf, and vanilla ice cream for dessert. Patten kept the lights dim and the radio tuned to the BBC. He liked Bach—"up and down music," as Ann dismissively called it. Patten found her good company and entertaining. Once, he told me, Maya telephoned Ann from Yogyakarta, where she was taking time off from college and working for a travel company, leading cultural tours in Java and Bali. An older, unmarried American tourist, who happened to be a teacher, had arranged to have a blind masseur come to her hotel. The woman had become hysterical, accused the masseur of molesting her, and had him arrested. Maya wanted her mother's advice. "First, give the teacher a good, hard slap," Patten remembered Ann saying. "Then go to the police station and make sure nothing happened to the masseur."

Recalling the story, Patten laughed.

"It's so entertaining and so indicative of the way she thought: *Just worry about the masseur.*"

Ann's methodology in the field was meticulous. She designed novella-length questionnaires to be used as a guide for interviewing potential customers about matters ranging from working-capital turnover periods to the number of relatives employed without pay. For inexperienced research assistants, she appended handy tips. "Has the Respondent ever been inside a bank before?" one question asked. If not, why not? If the respondent answered that he or she was afraid of banks, the interviewer was to find out why. "This is an important question, so take whatever time is necessary to discuss it with the Respondent," Ann wrote. Another question required that the interviewer fill out a chart with ten vertical columns under headings such as "type of account," "maximum amount of savings," and "use of withdrawals." The interviewer was to list every savings account the respondent had had in the previous seven years, as well as other deposits through savings-and-loan societies, credit unions, and other organizations. "If the Respondent has any savings in kind, for example in a rice bank, list this also, but give a rupiah value underneath," Ann's instructions said.

She had an unusual ability to adapt. With bankers, she came across as professional, methodical, and not the least bit eccentric. With older Indonesians, her accent and diction took on a precision that Don Johnston thought sounded faintly Dutch. Arriving in a village for the first time, she transformed herself into the beloved visiting dignitary—her bearing regal, her silver jewelry flashing, her retinue in tow. "She was clearly the queen bee of the entourage," recalled Johnston. "Then she gets there and they realize, 'Oh, this is not just a foreigner but this is a foreigner who can speak Bahasa Indonesia, and who knows a lot about what we're doing and who wants to talk to us about this stuff. And she has some connection to this big bank, BRI, but she's not a banker, so I don't need to be scared of her.'" She was even deft in her dispensing with inevitable Indonesian comments about her physical dimensions. When a boatman professed trepidation about whether the personage boarding his boat was going to sink it, Ann switched, humorously, to the role of the grand lady: How dare you! There was showmanship involved, but she was never inauthentic. "Ann was a genuinely complex person who had a really varied background," Johnston said. "So she could legitimately tap those different experi-

Interviewing bank customers, with colleagues, about 1989

ences to build empathy with different people." It made them want
to line up and tell her their life stories.

On a field visit to village banks in the district of Sleman in 1988,
Ann proposed a short detour to the village of Jitar, the home of a
respected kris smith whom she knew. According to Ann's account,
she was traveling with three carloads of bank colleagues and local
government officials. At the smith's house, he invited the group
inside for tea. Members of the group, laughing loudly and making
raucous jokes minutes before, fell silent, sat formally, and then addressed the smith, Pak Djeno, with deep respect and deference.
When Ann said she wanted to buy a small kris, the smith brought
out four blades. "A deadly hush came over the room, and even
whispering ceased," Ann wrote later. For days afterward, her colleagues discussed the encounter. "The very fact that I had known
a keris smith and had purchased a keris also caused a change in
their behavior toward me. They began to show me some of the
deference they had shown to Pak Djeno, speaking with greater

respect and formality. Somehow, a little of his magical power had managed to rub off on me."

Ann combined the discipline of a workaholic with a personal warmth that her Indonesian colleagues and subordinates described to me as maternal. She was not a practitioner of "rubber time": If she had an appointment, she was never late. In the field, she might start work at nine a.m. and not wrap up until thirteen hours later. She would stay with an interview long after colleagues were ready to move on. She traveled with a Thermos and took her coffee black, no sugar. "Coffee is my blood," she said; if she ever got sick, she said, she wanted intravenous coffee. She rarely seemed to get enough sleep. She tested survey questions on herself first, to feel what a respondent might feel. She would never risk insulting her host by declining food. When the manager of a bank branch in South Sulawesi threw her a surprise birthday party, including karaoke, she launched gamely into "You Are My Sunshine." In the town of Garut, she turned her attention to a girl of no more than seventeen who was serving dinner to members of the team at their hotel. Ann asked her about her family, her marriage, her education. How much was she paid? Was it enough? Then, when dinner was over, she slipped the girl money.

On occasion, a misunderstanding across some cultural divide left Ann rattled. On a visit to a village in Sulawesi in 1988, an irate local official pursued Ann and her group, shouting furiously in a local language that none of them understood. He appeared to believe the group had failed to obtain his permission to enter the area. The confrontation subsided after some local residents intervened in the group's defense. But late that night, Ann remained upset and was unable to sleep. She asked a bank colleague, Tomy Sugianto, to accompany her on a walk around the outside of the hotel where they were staying. The hour was about one a.m., Sugianto told me. Ann, visibly exhausted, was on the verge of tears. She seemed haunted by the memory of the local official's fury and whatever misunderstanding had provoked it. She felt wrongly accused. "She only wanted to know why the man was so angry," Sugianto remembered, "and what we did wrong."

To her younger colleagues, she was Bu Ann—Bu being an affectionate abbreviation of the honorific *Ibu,* a term of respect for mothers, older women, and women of higher status. She treated them, they felt, as family. If she went out to lunch in Jakarta, she would order an extra meal for her driver, Sabaruddin, and his family. She helped pay for his five-year-old daughter's surgery and for repairs to the roof and the doors on his house. In the town of Tasik Malaya, she pointed out to her team that the village chief, a successful businessman, had started out as a peddler—evidence that anything was possible. To her young research assistants, she emphasized accuracy, rigor, patience, fairness, and not judging by appearances. "Don't conclude before you understand," Retno Wijayanti recalled Ann saying. "After you understand, don't judge."

She even tried her hand at matchmaking. In the fall of 1989, the bank hired a willowy twenty-four-year-old woman named Widayanti from Malang in East Java, who was soon assigned to help Ann and Don Johnston with a survey of potential microfinance customers. Ann quickly discovered that Widayanti was a Pentecostal Christian. Johnston, the son of a church musician in Little Rock, was a Southern Baptist. Widayanti began to notice that whenever she asked Ann a question about the survey, Ann would say, "Oh, just ask Don." Did Widayanti know that Don had once been a Sunday school teacher? Ann asked her. To Johnston, Ann talked up Widayanti's intelligence, her command of English, her honesty

With Tomy Sugianto (left) and Slamet Riyadi (right),
from Bank Rakyat Indonesia, in Tana Toraja,
South Sulawesi, 1989

and strong principles. To Flora Sugondo, the office manager, Ann confided that she wanted to match up Johnston and Widayanti.

In October 1993, Ann was a guest in Malang at their wedding.

That *Ibu* quality was useful, Julia Suryakusuma told me. "Ann was a very intellectual person, but she didn't come across as being that," she said. "That whole *Ibu* quality took away the threat of being a pioneer, a professional, efficient. It took away the edge." Occasionally, however, Ann found the role of surrogate mother tiring. "I get so tired of having to mother people myself—for example, all my research assistants at BRI—that I actually enjoy being on the receiving end of a little mothering once in a while," she confessed to Suryakusuma in a letter.

Not long after Ann returned to Indonesia in 1988, Suryakusuma's husband, Ami Priyono, asked a young Indonesian journalist, whom he knew, to see if he might help out a friend of Priyono's. A few days later, a secretary in the Bank Rakyat Indonesia office called the journalist, I. Made Suarjana, a reporter in Yogyakarta for *Tempo,* an independent newsweekly, and set up an appointment for him to meet Ann at the Airlangga Guest House in Yogyakarta, where she would be staying on a trip for the bank. Arriving at the hotel, Suarjana was startled to find that the person he was meeting was Caucasian and a woman. From the name, Sutoro, he had expected an Indonesian man. They got along immediately. Soon, he was driving Ann to Kajar, to update her dissertation research in her spare time. Occasionally, she would ask him to visit other villages for her in her absence. They dined together on her visits to Yogyakarta, eating tempeh and *sayur lodeh,* an eggplant stew that she loved. They went to batik exhibitions and visited the ninth-century Hindu temples at Prambanan, northeast of Yogyakarta. For Ann's birthday, she asked Suarjana to go with her to Candi Sukuh, a fifteenth-century temple on the steep, pine-blanketed slopes of Gunung Lawu, three thousand feet above sea level on the border of Central and East Java. The temple, which Ann had known of for years but had never visited, was known for, among other things, its humorous, *wayang*-style carvings, stone penises, and other indications that it may have been the site of a fertility cult. The temple reliefs also included a scene of a smithy with the same double-piston bellows still used in Kajar. To drive to the temple, Ann arranged to rent a car. When it arrived, she and Suarjana were amused to discover that it was a white Mercedes—the car of choice for government officials and newlyweds.

Suarjana was twenty-eight the year he met Ann—one year older than Barry. Ann was turning forty-six. For an Indonesian man, he was tall, nearly six feet, with a taut, high-cheekboned face that reminded Ann of Mike Tyson, the heavyweight boxing champion. He was the fifth of seven children of a Balinese poet, journalist, and politician, Made Sanggra, who had been a nationalist fighter against the Dutch. (The name is pronounced *mah*-day.) Suarjana had grown up in Sukowati, a crafts center in Bali, where his mother had a business buying and selling Balinese clothing. The family was Hindu. As a child, Suarjana had learned Balinese dancing, music, and woodcarving. He had studied Indonesian language and literature at university, married in his early twenties, and become a father three years before he met Ann. His relationship with Ann, he told me, was "a romantic-intellectual relationship," the exact nature of which, he said, would remain between them. The connection was deep, he said, and rooted in shared interests. There was no limit to what they could talk about, no difference that could not be bridged. She volunteered little about her past and, on a visit to Honolulu, even stopped her father from showing Suarjana photographs of her when she was young. She never directly told Suarjana her age. When the question arose by chance in a conversation, she refused to answer—then handed him her passport. Intellectually, the relationship changed him. Perhaps Ann was changed less by him than he was by her, he said. But he was sure he'd left a mark.

They talked about Indonesian art and culture, gender roles in Bali, the reasons for declining production in Kajar. Were government programs flawed in concept or in implementation? Was there a relationship between the salaries of government ministers and corruption? Ann was the scholar in their conversations; Suarjana was the cynic. She spoke from the head; he spoke from the gut. "Oh, Made, *please*," she would complain, in exasperation. She was also the optimist, her mind always bending toward practical solutions. She would assert nothing, it seemed to him, without evidence to support it. She had the spirit of a teacher, a *jiwa guru*. Whatever Ann knew that Suarjana did not know, she would offer to teach him. She gave him a four-volume set of books on English grammar and usage. "How far did you study?" she would invariably ask. Then she would administer a pop quiz on the spot. She corrected his essays in red ink in his spiral notebook. She insisted each of them speak the other's language. If he spoke to her in Bahasa Indonesia, she might refuse to answer at all. She recommended him for a workshop for journalists at the East-West Center and paid his tuition at an English language institute at the University of Hawai'i. From her example, Suarjana said, he learned how to be open-minded and to recognize shades of gray. He learned to look at batik differently, too: In his mind, its importance was no longer strictly cultural and economic. Woven unmistakably into textiles were the lives of the people who made them.

"You're an eccentric," Ann told him. He was not sure what the word meant. But it was a compliment, he was sure of that.

If Ann had a weakness, he thought, it was that she too easily trusted strangers. Her generosity and her compassion got the better of financial good sense. On one occasion, a man came to her, professing to represent a nongovernmental organization and asking for money, Suarjana told me. She gave him two million rupiahs, or roughly twelve hundred dollars, of her own money—and never heard from him again. She was not especially concerned about money. Once, Suarjana suggested that the price of a batik she was considering buying at an exhibition was too high. "It's only paper," she said blithely, before allowing him to talk her out of the purchase on the grounds that most of her money would go to the dealer, not the craftsman. She was not ambitious or acquisitive, at least in the usual sense. She would have liked to have learned to drive so she could have driven Suarjana around Hawaii without having to rely on her father. She would have liked to have found a way to afford a house in Bali where friends and her children could stay. As the latest deadline for her dissertation closed in, Suarjana threatened to end their friendship if she did not finish. When she finally did finish it in 1992, and he congratulated her for it, she told him, "I did it because I wanted us to remain friends."

To those who knew her well, Ann seemed happy with Suarjana. Rens Heringa met her and Suarjana for dinner in Yogyakarta. "It had just started," Heringa remembered. "She was all rosy and happy, and it was quite funny and nice." Ann ordered spaghetti, which Suarjana loathed, and joked that it was his favorite food. She called over a street singer to sing "Bésame Mucho."

Bésame, bésame mucho,
As if tonight were the last time.

In a letter to Suryakusuma, who was skeptical of Suarjana's motives, Ann downplayed her feelings. "I never said I was a woman in love . . ." she protested. "I like him a lot. He has a place in my heart." Suryakusuma believed Ann could be too open, too trusting. In a letter that Suryakusuma read aloud to me, but did not give me, she told Ann: You have a big capacity to love, but you often love uncritically. ("I know I benefit," Suryakusuma wrote.) She told Ann that one of the nicest things about being her friend was that Ann was not judgmental: "You take people as they are, with all their faults." But, Suryakusuma said, often one's strong point is also a source of vulnerability. Your capacity to love, she told Ann, leaves you open to being used by others.

The attention of a much younger man was flattering, Heringa

In the early 1990s

told me, but it cannot have been simple. Indonesians made jokes
about older women who went around with younger men. Hotels
expected couples to be married. "Ann didn't give a damn," Heringa
told me. "She was much less concerned about what people thought
than I was. She just could not have cared less." In the spring of
1990, Ann and Suarjana spent several months together at the
University of Hawai'i, where Suarjana took part in the English-
language institute in which Ann had helped him enroll. They lived
in a dorm at the East-West Center, where, according to Suarjana,
they had separate rooms. He cooked Indonesian *soto*—a souplike
dish with bean sprouts, scallions, cellophane noodles, lemon slices,
hot chili, egg slices, and so on—for Ann's parents. They took a
short vacation to the Big Island. Ann reported to Suryakusuma that
she had enjoyed their domestic arrangement. They had had only
one fight—over his tendency to turn off her fan without asking
first. They enjoyed collaborating on the chores and the shopping—

the novelty of which, Ann confessed, was wearing off for her. "After all, God surely intended me to be a *Nyonya Besar*," she wrote to Suryakusuma with mocking self-knowledge, using a term for "mistress of the house."

Ann's work at Bank Rakyat Indonesia had delayed, once again, the completion of her dissertation. In early November 1989, she asked Dewey to run interference for her with the university. "Have just returned from a long, hard trip to North Sumatra with my field team," she explained. There had been delays getting into the field, she said, "and it has been necessary for me to do more hand-holding than anticipated. My field workers are sharp, but most are economics or business majors who have never worked with village people before." In mid-December, she returned to Hawaii for Christmas. Maya, having finished her job as a tour guide, was back in Honolulu, staying with a University of Hawaiʻi professor, with a temporary job lined up waiting tables in a Japanese restaurant. "Barry is also coming at Christmas with a new girlfriend in tow," Ann wrote to Dewey. "He is still enjoying law school and writing pro-choice opinions on the abortion issue for the Law Review." Ann's dissertation committee, headed by Dewey, and the chairman of the anthropology department agreed to submit an extension request to the graduate division. "So now I must make some hard decisions about finishing my degree vs taking a new job," she wrote to Suryakusuma in January. Bank Rakyat Indonesia had agreed in principle to giving her a two-year contract, but she did not know whether the bank would wait several months while she finished. "My family and friends all say to finish my degree, but there are also practical considerations if I take several months off from work," she wrote. Among them were the usual financial pressures.

To Dewey, Ann wrote, "Am sending a money order for the $1000 I borrowed from you some time back. You can take out interest in batiks or other goodies when I get back."

In early 1991, Dewey persuaded Ann to narrow the focus of the dissertation to metalworking, with particular attention to black-smithing, the forging of iron and steel to make tools. That meant dropping four other peasant industries—basketry and matting, clay products, textiles, and leather—about which Ann had gathered data over the course of a decade and a half. Soon, she was firing off chapters to Honolulu. "Since narrowing the topic to blacksmithing and metal industries, everything is going much better," she wrote to Dewey. Ann's office rented a house for her in her old neighbor-hood, Kebayoran Baru. "I thought if I went to Jogja I would end up eating lesian with Made on *Jalan Malioboro* every night and never get anything done," she told Dewey. (*Lesian* appears to be a misspelling of *lesehan*, a Javanese word meaning to sit on the ground or on a mat, usually with one's legs folded back. *Makan lesehan* is to eat in that position, often at a low table.) In her spare time, she could not resist rounding up even more data, driving with Suarjana to Klaten, where, she exulted to Dewey, "there are iron and brass casting industries which date from the Dutch period (they used to make spare parts for the sugar factories and railway locomotives). Absolutely fascinating!" The following fall, she was back in Hawaii for two months, finishing her dissertation. On November 10, with her draft due at the end of the month, she hand-wrote a short note in Indonesian to her former research assistant, Djaka Waluja. She had heard from the village headman in Kajar, through Suarjana, that Waluja had been in the village. If he had any new information, Ann asked, could he send it along?

Ann's opus weighed in, at the end, at one thousand forty-three pages. She had completed the dissertation, "Peasant Blacksmithing in Indonesia: Surviving and Thriving Against All Odds," almost twenty years after entering graduate school. She had paid for the typing of at least one draft in barter, Dewey would remember: rattan furniture from the house in Kebayoran Baru.

Drawing on data from the fields of archaeology, history, metallurgy, and cultural anthropology, Ann described the occupation as it was seen by the smiths themselves. She recounted the early history of metalworking industries in Indonesia, with its "unbroken line" tying the culture of the Early Metal Age to the present-day smiths. She discussed metalworking technologies, types of bellows, the layout of the smithy. She examined the class position and social status of smiths. She devoted one hundred pages to Kajar, and another seventy to smithing villages in the Minangkabau highlands in West Sumatra, Tana Toraja in Sulawesi, Central Java, Bali, and South Sulawesi. She looked at the future of metalworking industries against the backdrop of economic trends, critiqued government programs, and looked at the implications of her findings for future development. Although economists and bureaucrats had been predicting the demise of village industries since the late nineteenth century, she wrote, she had found that employment in those industries had increased. Social scientists who saw that increase as a sign of a crisis in the agricultural sector were assuming, incorrectly, that agriculture was more profitable than other occupations. In fact, metalworking was more profitable than agriculture in a number of villages she had studied. For that reason, villagers considered metalworking their primary occupation, agriculture only secondary.

I asked James Fox, a respected anthropologist who had worked in Indonesia over a twenty-year period, what he made of Ann's dissertation. Fox, who had degrees from Harvard and Oxford and had taught at Duke, Cornell, and Harvard, was a professor at the Research School of Pacific and Asian Studies at the Australian National University when we spoke. He said he held the view that anthropology, as a discipline, was too fashion-driven: Anthropological theory had a half-life of five years, and graduate students tended to gravitate to the latest theory. Ann, he said, did something unfashionable. She produced an ethnography of the sort Fox believed would be a reference point for many years. "Ann's book will be a monument into the next century," he said. "You can get into it, and you can get a glimpse of life in a certain period. You can't do that with a lot of anthropological theory. It's momentary. It might be stimulating, but it doesn't last long."

When a redacted version of the dissertation was published by Duke University Press in 2009, Michael Dove, the Yale anthropologist and Ann's longtime friend, wrote in a review that her study of Kajar "is one of the richest ethnographic studies to come out of Java in the past generation. This sort of long-term, in-depth, ground-level study, once the norm in anthropology, is increasingly rare." Ann had concluded that development in the villages she studied was held back not by a lack of entrepreneurial spirit but by a lack of capital—the product of politics, not culture. "Indonesia exemplifies the truth that often the disadvantaged do need not assistance but fair play, not resources but the political control over resources," Dove wrote.

Ann signed the dissertation S. Ann Dunham. On the dedication page, she wrote:

dedicated to Madelyn and Alice,
who each gave me support in her own way,

and to Barack and Maya,

who seldom complained when their mother was in the field

On February 8, 1992, less than two weeks before Ann was to defend her dissertation, Stanley Dunham died. He had been diagnosed with prostate cancer more than a year earlier. His condition had deteriorated, his brother said, to a point where he was unable to walk. He was buried at the National Memorial Cemetery of the Pacific, or Punchbowl National Cemetery, a rolling green landscape of finely tended lawns flecked with gravestones overlooking the Pacific. His death hit Ann hard. The tensions between them, which had marked earlier years, had subsided. She had talked about him, at least to some, as the family's emotional glue. "When she talked about her mother, it was with admiration," Don Johnston, her colleague, said. "But clearly her stronger emotional bond was with her father."

Two years earlier, Obama, at age twenty-eight, was elected president of the *Harvard Law Review*—"its first black president in more than 100 years of publication," as the Associated Press reported on February 5, 1990, the day after the election. That initial article, in which Obama was said not to have ruled out a future in politics, made no mention of his parents. An article in *The New York Times* the following day mentioned them briefly—a former Kenyan government official and "an American anthropologist now doing field work in Indonesia." A longer article a week later in *The Boston Globe* went into greater detail. "What seems to motivate Barack Obama is a strong identification with what he calls 'the typical black experience,' paired with a mission to help the black community and promote social justice," the *Globe* reported. It described "his unusual path, from childhood in Indonesia, where he grew up, he says, 'as a street kid,' to adolescence in Hawaii, where he was raised by his grandparents." The article dwelt at some length on the influence of Obama's father, who, it said, was born in Kenya, "studied at Harvard and Oxford and became a senior economist for the Kenyan government." In high school, the article said, Obama began a regular correspondence with his father, "whose heritage was to be a major influence on his life, ideals and priorities." One of Obama's most valued possessions, the article said, was the passbook that his grandfather, a cook for the British before Kenyan independence, was required to carry. "He said that even though his heritage is one-half white, and although he has had a mixture of influences in his life, 'my identification with the—quote—typical black experience in America was very strong and very natural and wasn't something forced and difficult,'" the article said. Of Ann, it said little more than "His mother, who is white, is a Kansas-born anthropologist who now works as a developmental consultant in Indonesia."

In an even longer article in the *Los Angeles Times* a month later, Ann was described simply as "an American anthropologist" and "a white American from Wichita, Kan."

The marginal role to which Ann was consigned in those accounts did not go unnoticed. She had raised Obama, with the help of her parents, after his father had left for Harvard when Obama was ten months old. She had been his primary parent for the first ten years of his life. She had returned to Hawaii to live with him when he was in middle school. She had moved back to Hawaii from Indonesia for several months during his senior year. Yet in those accounts, Obama had been "a street kid" in Indonesia, then sent back to Hawaii to be "raised by his grandparents." Yang

Suwan, Ann's Indonesian anthropologist friend, recalled Ann returning to Jakarta around the time of the *Harvard Law Review* election. As always, she was extraordinarily proud of her son. But on another level, she seemed crushed.

"'His mother is an anthropologist,'" Ann told Yang, quoting an article she had seen. "I was mentioned in one sentence."

The new girlfriend Obama had brought with him to Hawaii the previous Christmas was different from Ann. A young lawyer from Chicago whom Obama had met while working as a summer associate at the law firm of Sidley Austin, Michelle Robinson had grown up on the South Side of Chicago and had returned there after graduating from law school. Her father, Fraser Robinson III, a descendant of slaves, had been employed as a maintenance worker and later a foreman in a city water-filtration plant; her mother, Marian, had stayed at home with Michelle and her brother when they were young. The family was hardworking, churchgoing, and close-knit. As an undergraduate at Princeton and as a law student at Harvard, Michelle Robinson had been active in black student organizations. She moved systematically through her life, making sensible, carefully considered decisions, each building to the next. "I would say Michelle is much more like our grandmother," Maya told me. "And I would say that my mother and my grandmother really were also opposites." After the Christmas visit, Ann reported back to Suryakusuma. "She is intelligent, very tall (6'1"), not beautiful but quite attractive," Ann wrote of Robinson. "She did her BA at Princeton and her law degree at Harvard. But she has spent most of her life in Chicago." Ann, who prided herself on raising her children to have a global perspective, described Robinson as "a little provincial and not as international as Barry." But Ann liked her. "She is nice, though," she said. If Robinson and Obama were to marry after he graduated from law school, Ann told Suryaku-suma, she would not be unhappy.

Graduation rolled around.

"I would have liked to go for the graduation, but both Barry and his girlfriend recommended that the family skip it," Ann wrote to Dewey from Jakarta. "Apparently hotels are a problem and the law school graduates with everyone else so that you can hardly find your kid."

When Ann told Made Suarjana that Obama was graduating from Harvard Law School, he said, "So he's going to be a billion-aire." Ann corrected him: No, she said, he wants to return to Chicago and do pro bono work. Because Suarjana knew that Obama was interested in politics, and because he felt he knew something about American public life, he said, knowingly, "Okay, so he wants to be president."

To his surprise, Ann began to weep.

It was the only time, he told me, that he saw her cry. He was uncertain what it was about the idea of her son one day running for president that brought her to tears. He thought maybe it was fear: What would it mean to be a man with an African father run-ning for president in a country riddled with the racism Ann must have encountered when she had married the elder Obama? Maybe it was protectiveness: Every facet of a candidate's life, professional and personal, would be unearthed and subjected to scrutiny. Maybe it was the anticipation of loss—a mother's loss compounded by whatever regret she might have had about the years they had spent apart and the distance that almost inevitably was widening be-tween them.

"No, not this time," she answered, according to Suarjana. "He's going to be a senator first."

Had they already talked about it? Suarjana wondered later. If Obama was to be "a senator first," perhaps Obama and Ann had discussed what would follow. Obama must have thought about running for president, Suarjana said, or Ann must have thought about his running. What role had she played in cultivating that ambition? Suarjana had been struck by the respect with which Ann treated Obama. It reminded him of the way a mother treated the eldest son in a Javanese family, preparing the boy from an early age to one day inherit the role of father and backbone of the family. Ann's relationship with Obama seemed different from the relationships between mothers and sons that Suarjana had seen in American movies. Conversations between her and Obama, occasionally recounted to Suarjana, had a certain gravity. When Ann recounted stories about her daughter, she sounded less formal and more relaxed. That made sense, Suarjana thought, because Ann and Maya had lived closely together for many years. Nevertheless, he could not help but notice the depth of Ann's admiration for her son.

His life decisions, it seems, carried more than the usual freight.

"She felt a little bit wistful or sad that Barack had essentially moved to Chicago and chosen to take on a really strongly identified black identity," recalled Don Johnston, Ann's colleague at Bank Rakyat Indonesia. That identity, she felt, "had not really been part of who he was when he was growing up." Ann felt he was making what Johnston called "a professional choice" to strongly identify himself as black. "It would be too strong to say that she felt rejection," he said. But she felt, in that way, "that he was distancing himself from her."

At the same time, Ann's example could be discerned in some of Obama's choices. Barry had left Hawaii far behind him when he had planted himself first in New York City and then in Chicago—just as Ann had done when she had made Indonesia the center of gravity in her life. His community organizing work paralleled some of her development consulting work abroad. Then, after all of Ann's efforts to secure for him the best education and impress on him the importance of living up to his potential, he had flourished at Harvard.

"So that experiment I was talking about earlier?" President Obama said when we talked, referring to his account of his confrontation with his mother during his senior year in high school. "Turns out she was actually onto something."

Ten

Manhattan Chill

✦

Ann, at fifty, straddled hemispheres. She was an American citizen who had lived in Indonesia for more than half of her adult life. She had a doctorate from the University of Hawai'i based on work done over two decades in Java. She had a career in Asia but a family in the United States. Her mother, Madelyn, turning seventy, was a widow living alone in Honolulu. Barack, at thirty-one, was a lawyer in Illinois, writing his first book and engaged to a woman rooted in Chicago. Maya, twenty-two, was an undergraduate majoring in English at the University of Hawai'i. Ann longed to live closer to her children and had begun dreaming of grandchildren. But she could live more comfortably in Indonesia, on a development consultant's salary and benefits, than she could ever afford to live in Hawaii, and her work had a degree of impact in Indonesia that she could not begin to match in the United States. As long as she had a job, she could keep renewing her visa and continue to live in Indonesia. She even toyed with the idea of

making it a more permanent base. She thought about one day having a house in Bali, if she could come up with the money; it would
be a place where she and her children and their friends could alight.
But as a foreigner, she could not own property, she could only lease
it. As an expatriate, one heard unsettling stories of sudden lease
cancellations, mysterious property claims, precipitous departures.
If she could park everything that was important to her in another
country, the risks might be fewer. But Ann did not have the luxury
of maintaining homes in two places. She never wanted to fall out
of love with Indonesia because of some catastrophe she could ill
afford, she told Garrett Solyom. An American consular official in
Bali had once told the Solyoms ominously, "If you're at an age
where you don't have the money or connections to be able to get
out of here at a moment's notice when you need to, you shouldn't
be here."

   In mid-1992, Ann made the decision to move back to the United
States. Barack was to marry Michelle Robinson at the Trinity
United Church of Christ in Chicago in early October—an event to
which Ann looked forward with great pleasure. On a visit to Chicago in advance of the wedding, she got in touch with Mary Houghton, the president of ShoreBank, a bank holding company that
Houghton and others had founded in the early 1970s in an effort
to show that banks could play a constructive role in low-income
black neighborhoods. Houghton, who had also advised microfinance organizations, had met Ann at a party in Jakarta in the late
1980s and remembered her warmly as "forthright, sharp-tongued,
opinionated, happy." When Ann contacted her, they agreed to
meet for what Houghton remembered years later as an agenda-free
brunch in downtown Chicago. Ann's contract in Jakarta was to
wind up the following January. She was moving back to the United

States and would need a job. Houghton offered to put her in touch with a nonprofit based in New York City whose interests seemed aligned with Ann's. Conceived during the first United Nations World Conference on Women in 1975, the organization, called Women's World Banking, had set out to promote full economic participation for low-income women by helping them develop viable businesses. Toward that end, it offered support, training, and advice to several dozen microfinance organizations in Asia, Africa, Latin America, and elsewhere, which in turn offered credit and other financial services to women producers and entrepreneurs. The original board had included Ela Bhatt, the founder of the Self Employed Women's Association, whom Ann had first encountered during her eye-opening trip to India in her first weeks at Ford. Women's World Banking was governed by women and run by women and existed first and foremost for the benefit of women.

In mid-September, Ann received a letter from Women's World Banking, alerting her to a job opening. Embarking on a monthlong trip to Hawaii and the mainland, Ann sent off her résumé and a letter asking to be considered. In New York, she met with the president of Women's World Banking, Nancy Barry, in a French restaurant near the organization's offices in Midtown Manhattan. Barry, a Harvard Business School graduate in her early forties, had worked at the World Bank for fifteen years before becoming president of Women's World Banking. Smart, charismatic, and driven, she was a product, she liked to say, of both the decentralized culture of Women's World Banking and the command-and-control ethos of "the World Bank of Men." At Women's World Banking, she wanted to influence the policies of banks around the world to better serve the poor. Ann had more experience with poor women than anyone in the Women's World Banking office, Barry could

see. She had also influenced the design of the services offered by
Bank Rakyat Indonesia, which ran the largest self-sustaining microfinance program in the world. At their first meeting, Barry
found Ann's size jarring, she told me. The staff of "Wild Women's
Banking," as it had occasionally been called, was so young and attractive that it had been suggested Barry had a "looks problem."
But she was impressed by Ann's intelligence, experience, and independence of mind. She could see that Ann had a sense of humor,
the ability to laugh at herself, and the charm to win people over. So
Barry offered her a job that had not previously existed: coordinator
for policy and research. In many countries, government and bank
policies favored big over small businesses, the formal over the informal sector. They favored male clients, who owned property,
over women, who did not. Governments also placed restrictions
on the activities of independent-sector organizations in ways that
held back microlending, limiting loan sizes, rates of interest, and
the outside funding those organizations could receive. Ann's job
would be to help Women's World Banking and its affiliates persuade policy-makers to change all that. "This was not like we had
a position for a policy coordinator," Barry told me. "But in my
mind we had a whole agenda waiting to happen if we had the right
person."

Moving to New York City for the first time was not easy at age
fifty. Ann arrived in Manhattan in late January 1993 during a cold
snap so bitter that her lungs ached when she breathed. Three weeks
into her stay, a truck bomb detonated in the underground garage
beneath the World Trade Center, injuring a thousand people and
killing six. Ann, with a starting salary of $65,000 a year, had ex-
pected to be able to find a two-bedroom apartment for about $1,500
a month within walking distance of the offices on West Fortieth

Street. But because two-bedroom apartments were renting for more than $2,000, she was forced to settle for an antiseptic one-bedroom in a forty-story tower near the United Nations for $1,550. She parked most of her books and belongings in storage in Hawaii, for which she paid another $250 a month. (A "wardrobe inventory" she put together around that time listed a remarkable forty-eight skirts, half of them marked "sm" and apparently not in use.) Women's World Banking paid for two weeks in a hotel near the office while Ann looked for an apartment, but she got stuck there for ten extra days, at her expense, waiting for the credit clearance needed to sign a lease. She spent $8,000 on housewares and furniture from Pier 1 Imports, and another $1,500 on winter clothes. She had never worn panty hose in her life, she told friends. The small amount of savings she had accumulated dwindled, and her credit card debt rose. Afraid of the subway system, she spent money on cabs. *"Aduh! Aduh! Aduh!"* she would say, falling back on an Indonesian expression of pain in the face of the rushing crowds. Ann missed Indonesia. The best Indonesian restaurant in New York seemed no better than the lowliest *warung.* From her room on the twenty-sixth floor of the hotel, she gazed at the sky, remembering the full moon in Bali and wondering why she had traveled so far from Made Suarjana. She told herself she would stay in New York for two or three years, then move to Bali. Suarjana could start a civil-society organization or a publishing house, and she would look for work as a consultant.

Life at Women's World Banking was consuming. The two dozen employees were mostly young, female, unmarried, and childless. Driven by devotion to "the mission" and an esprit de corps cultivated from the top, they toiled long hours in an office culture that more than one of them remembered years later as having the intimacy and intensity of a dysfunctional family. Barry pegged the pay and benefits to those of other not-for-profits; she scrimped, she told me, only on vacations. The staff was international and impressively credentialed. Kellee Tsai, the daughter of immigrants from Taiwan, had come straight from a financial analyst's job at Morgan Stanley, putting away her pearls and lipstick and fully expecting a cohort of hirsute women in vintage clothing. Instead, she found hyperarticulate women in saris and handcrafted jewelry, and Christmas parties catered by a high-end Upper West Side boîte. The financial products and services coordinator was a young Australian woman with an MBA from Harvard who had run the Australian government's food aid program in Ethiopia. The regional coordinator for Africa was a Kenyan-born, British-trained accountant who had been the first in her peasant family to go to university. The communications coordinator, a British-born lawyer, had grown up in Pakistan and Iraq, where she could remember having watched her mother water-skiing on the Tigris in a bikini. Other staff members were Indian, Ecuadorean, Colombian, Canadian, American, Honduran, Haitian, Ghanaian. The calendar was crowded with conferences in foreign capitals such as Tokyo, Accra, and Mexico City. "In many ways, it was one of the most dysfunctional organizations I've ever worked in," said Nina Nayar, who worked at Women's World Banking as Ann's assistant. "But I have never felt such warmth, such passion, such excitement. It was like a soap opera: You're crying, you're laughing, you're celebrating, you miss people, you love people, you hate people, and you know that this is all psychodrama, but you're so hooked on it that you have to be there every day at three o'clock to see this thing."

Office space was tight. Despite her seniority, Ann doubled up in a small, dark room in the back of the building with Kellee Tsai,

who was a few years older than Maya. Accessible only through a
windowless word-processing zone nicknamed "the bunker," the
room had back-to-back desks and a view into the wall of the next
building, a few feet away. Women's World Banking had not lav-
ished attention on developing well-oiled office systems; if a person
needed something done, she might be best off doing it herself. Ann,
for the first time in a long time, was without secretarial assistance.
"She couldn't type to save her life," one colleague remembered. And
on matters technological, she was the opposite of self-sufficient.
An aspiring Irish-born playwright named Donald Creedon, who
had worked as a Manhattan doorman before learning word processing, served as "computer coordinator." He devoted his time
to helping staff members get their computers to do what they
wanted. Ann, wedded to an outdated version of word-processing
software, needed constant assistance. Creedon, ensconced in the
bunker, would hear her cry out in frustration. "Then she would call
my name—without moving," he said. "The expectation was probably, 'You can come and help me type this thing. Because I need
help.'"

Ann's office became a magnet for younger colleagues. When
she was stuck on a piece of writing, she might be found holed up
back there—like the village elder, Creedon thought—telling stories. They were not about her but about people she had met, worlds
she had known, absurdities she had witnessed. Stories sprang from
her head fully formed, many of them endowed with the clarifying
wisdom of myths. Younger women would find excuses to wander
down to word processing for a chat. With her glasses on a chain
around her neck or perched on the tip of her nose if she was reading, Ann seemed perpetually on the verge of smiling. She was mischievous and witty. She worked her dark, shapely eyebrows for

emphasis, her toothy grin for punctuation—sometimes the tip-off that she had made a joke at the expense of someone present, who might catch on a minute or two late. "Maybe because she was an observer, she saw how ridiculous things could be," recalled Brinley Bruton, a young program assistant in the office. "I remember her literally sitting back and wiping tears away from her eyes because she was laughing so hard. She had that kind of laugh—a belly laugh."

One of Ann's stories—at least as one colleague remembered it years later—concerned a group of village women from Africa and Indonesia. On some earlier occasion, Ann had invited them to get together to talk about their lives. During a discussion of similarities and differences, the Indonesian women mentioned an unusual practice: After childbirth, a woman would put a salt pack in her vagina, ostensibly to restore its firmness. The practice was painful, the women conceded. But it was thought to help women remain "young" for their husbands. The African women were incredulous: Why would a woman willingly inflict pain on herself? "The Indonesian women—or so Ann told the story—asked, 'What do you do, then, to be able to continue to please your husbands?'" recalled the colleague who was present. "The African women all rolled about laughing and said, 'We find a bigger man!'"

Sometimes, Ann was the anthropologist in the field, with Women's World Banking as her village. She could capture the essence of a personality in an anecdote, even in a subordinate clause. "She would not be the type who would do well in a conventional organization, because she was very straightforward in her views on everything and often did it with humor—humor that had a bite," Nancy Barry told me. Ann toyed with the idea of writing a murder mystery set at one of Women's World Banking's global meetings, during which sleep-deprived staffers pulling all-nighters in the service of the mission occasionally almost came to blows. It was said that a delegate had returned to her home country after one global meeting and promptly expired. A recurring topic of conversation in the office concerned who would be the murder victim in Ann's book, some of her colleagues told me. Others, however, said the victim was to be Barry; only the identity of the murderer remained up for grabs. "Of course, it could have been anyone," Ann confided conspiratorially to Creedon. "Because, God knows, there were enough people who had a motive."

Several younger women in the office told me that in those days, they wanted to be Ann. Her assistant, Nina Nayar, an Indian woman then in her mid-twenties, had an undergraduate degree in anthropology, a master's in South Asian regional studies, and experience working in Ahmedabad with the Self-Employed Women's Association. The child of supportive but protective parents, Nayar told me that Ann, by example, taught her how to live. To Nayar, Ann seemed unconcerned about society's opinions about working women, single women, women who married outside their culture or tradition—women who, as Nayar put it, dreamed big and pursued their dreams and were fearless in the pursuit of adventure and knowledge. Ann did not seem, at least to Nayar, to feel that marriage as an institution was essential or even particularly important. What mattered was to have loved passionately and deeply, to have had lasting relationships, to have lived honestly and without pretense. She never spoke of her marriages as mistakes or failures; they had simply worked out differently than expected. Nor was she haunted by decisions she had made. "The past was her past," said Wanjiku Kibui, Ann's Kenyan colleague, whom Ann affectionately referred to as her in-law. "But it was not a prison." When

Nayar told Ann that she intended never to marry, Ann suggested Nayar was simply trading one orthodoxy for another. Ann advised Nayar to remain open. Niki Armacost, who became the communications coordinator, said of Ann, "She was the opposite of uptight. It was like, 'Oh, interesting! So *that's* how those people live.' I think she was a very principled person, but she was not a judgmental person. She had a set of principles, and tolerance was one of the principles. But she didn't lecture people about those things."

Business trips became field trips. When Ann and Nayar traveled together, it was Nayar's job to make sure Ann could get coffee at five a.m., as soon as she got up. In Jakarta, Ann took Nayar into the *kampung*s and in pursuit of the best street food: "Oh my God, my taste buds have finally come alive!" Nayar remembered her saying. In other cities, there were outings to anthropological museums and art museums and shops specializing in silver jewelry: "I will have to starve for the rest of the month, but I had to get this silver and turquoise thing," Ann would say, according to Nayar. "Isn't it magnificent?" Several younger colleagues suggested to Ann that they should all live together in Bali. "We talked about Alice Dewey's house, so we said, 'Ann, why don't you set up a house for us in Bali and we'll come there and do our dissertations together?'" Nayar recalled. "'You can be one of our readers. We'll take care of you and you can take care of our dissertations.' She thought it was a brilliant idea." Ann was a mentor to several younger women, but she had her limits. On the elevator one day, Brinley Bruton, who had been trying her hand at fiction, asked Ann if she would read one of her stories. "Which was, in fact, 'I want you to read this story and tell me it's wonderful,'" Bruton remembered. Unapologetically, Ann declined. "I came out of it feeling a little hurt," Bruton told me. "But in retrospect, I have respect for her. She wasn't going to pretend."

Ann arrived at Women's World Banking during the long lead-up to the United Nations Fourth World Conference on Women, which was to be held in Beijing in September 1995. To organizations like Women's World Banking, the conference offered an opportunity to promote their agenda. Discussions of the status of women had tended to focus on matters like health, education, and reproductive rights. But women made up the majority of the economically active poor in the world. Over the previous two decades, institutions had begun offering financial services for low-income women producers and entrepreneurs. As a result, their enterprises had flourished and the role of women in the economy had grown. Yet even the leading microfinance institutions were reaching only a tiny fraction of the women who could benefit. Women's World Banking saw the conference, and a parallel forum for nongovernmental organizations, as a chance to change the policies of governments, banks, and donors so that financial services to the poor could grow. Ann made the case to Barry that Women's World Banking ought to play a role in organizing many of the disparate microfinance institutions into a movement. If a coalition of organizations could agree on an agenda and demonstrate the contributions of low-income women to economic development, it could catapult the issue of microfinance into a prominent place in the "platform of action" that would eventually be endorsed by the nearly two hundred countries expected to be represented in Beijing.

Barry was skeptical about Ann's suggestion of a coalition. She saw the other organizations as competitors vying for the favor of a finite number of donors. Women's World Banking had worked hard in its early years to differentiate itself from the others, defin-

ing itself in part by what it was not. That is, it was not like Grameen Bank in Bangladesh, one of the largest and most successful
financial intermediaries focused on the rural poor; it was not like
ACCION International, another microfinance organization with
a network of lending partners. Barry, who had been on the board
of Women's World Banking during those early years, had been
influenced by what she later called "that kind of insular, go-it-
alone, we-are-the-best, we-are-different mentality." She doubted
that some groups would be willing to collaborate. She worried that
time would be wasted trying to bring together organizations with
divergent interests. Instead, she favored what she described as a
more unilateral approach—that is, one in which Women's World
Banking was in charge. "It kind of made me nervous," she told me.
"Even though I'm a big believer in building coalitions—coalitions
that *we* lead, if you know what I mean."

Barry was "a pretty tough character to deal with," she told me,
looking back on those years with a degree of self-knowledge and
candor that was striking. She had grown up in a Catholic family
in Orange County, California. One uncle was a priest who had
marched with the labor leader César Chávez. A great-aunt was a
nun. A graduate of Stanford and Harvard Business School, Barry
had worked in Tanzania for McKinsey & Company, the management consulting firm, before going to work for the World Bank
for fifteen years. At Women's World Banking, she was bent on
results. She took dissent personally. Small things—say, the wrong
word in a business plan—could set her off. She felt she had to manage everyone—the funders, the board, the affiliates. "It wasn't like
Women's World Banking was the leader of the network," she told
me. "*I* was the leader of the network. So I was like the big brain,
and everybody else was feeding into the big brain." Younger women

on the staff, swept up in the mission, tended not to challenge Barry. "If you're a young twenty-five-year-old and you're working with somebody that is working on something supercompelling, with unbelievably interesting people and with a mission to die for, you're a net learner, so you're kind of into it for at least ten years," Barry said. "By the time you get ten years into it, hopefully you actually know that I'm a good-hearted person and you've learned how to manage me. But for Ann, who was also very strong-headed and strong-willed, I think it was not fun."

Ann was not afraid to take on Barry. She had little patience with the shorthand that is useful and necessary in corporate life for selling an idea, and she was unwilling to make any claim—about, say, loan repayment rates and women—without the data to back it up. She preferred to acknowledge what was not known, then go find the answer. "She would sell an idea by saying, 'Well, we don't know the answer. That's why it's important that you fund us,'" Nayar remembered. "There was no halfway. In the business of development, academics have a very limited role. You can't indulge in spending weeks and months on research. Oftentimes, deadlines are what we're led by. Ann didn't live by those rules. She would say, 'If I have to get this thing ready, I am going to research it, I'm not just going to give you sound-bite stuff. If it's got my name on it, it has to be right.' It used to drive us crazy. We had to push Ann to do something. There would be much 'Oh, c'mon, Ann. Get it over with.' But I understand. She would never produce anything that she was not proud of."

The confrontations between Ann and Barry became, to Nayar, the clash of the Titans. "I had the luxury of being in on all their meetings," she said. "It was horrible. I can understand Nancy, because I'm very much a can-do, will-do, do-it-now person. But

I also related to Mother Ann." Barry needed justification for the policy statements the organization was making. "For instance, 'Women are good clients.' Okay, what are the ways that we can prove that?" Nayar said. "Ann would want to write a dissertation. And Nancy just wants, like, 'For example, boom, boom, boom.'" According to Nayar, "Ann would say, 'I can't whip things together into nonsensical bullet points. I need to have justifications for all my bullet points. So that's a paragraph!' And Nancy says, 'Cut it down, cut it down.'" Colleagues joked that Ann had been in Asia too long. She had a different sense of time, and instead of arguing, she preferred to debate or discuss. Over time, it seemed to Nayar, the conflict forced Ann to become more confrontational and assertive. "Both are demonic once they get on their high horse," Nayar said. "God can't turn them around. It was just two very strong women."

At other times, Ann seemed to fret about not meeting Barry's expectations. "Nancy would be harping on her: 'Are you done with that yet? You're still working on that?'" Kellee Tsai, Ann's office mate, remembered. "Nancy had her in tears so many times, it was horrible."

As Barry herself put it, "Because of my pigheadedness, you actually had to be pigheaded to get your way." Each person in the office had her own approach. Wanjiku Kibui, the regional coordinator for Africa, would call Barry out, in a way that Barry appreciated, when she was, as Barry put it later, "misbehaving." Niki Armacost, the communications coordinator, would find a better time. "Ann would just stay," Barry remembered. "She would stay and fight." On the question of the coalition of microfinance organizations, she would not back down. In a series of long, uncomfortable meetings with Barry, Ann insisted that Women's World

Banking use its influence for a greater good. To do otherwise would be small-minded and selfish. "We have to be grown-ups now," Barry remembered Ann saying, in effect. "She would have used language like that." Intentionally or not, Ann made Barry feel guilty: "I don't think she was ever mean-spirited or nasty, but she could not have been more direct about what was at stake and why it was the right thing."

Eventually, Barry relented. In October 1993, Women's World Banking joined two dozen other microfinance organizations to form the International Coalition on Women and Credit. Its aim was to influence the opinions of policy-makers at a series of regional conferences leading up to Beijing. Coalition members would hold workshops, publicize the successes of microfinance and microenterprise, make policy recommendations, and lobby delegates. Finally, they would all converge on Beijing. At Barry's insistence, Women's World Banking became the secretariat for the coalition. It fell to Ann, as the policy and research coordinator, to marshal the data needed to back the claims that the coalition would be making and to take the lead in dealing with the other organizations.

That was not simple. The organizations were not merely competitive, they also differed as to how best to deliver financial services and the type of clients it was most important to reach. Now they were expected to put aside their differences and support a common objective. "It became like an infiltration," Barry recalled. "If you picture all these regional and global meetings put on by the UN for the year or two in preparation for Beijing—complete chaos, all of these NGO leaders, strident, doing their thing, not at all respectful. If I'm in health, I don't want microfinance to get primacy. Ann got all these coalition members showing up to these regional meetings around the world and getting the health and education people saying one thing: 'The poor woman has to have an income. Then she can pay for education.' So that whole bottom-up approach, getting disparate players to act to common cause? She pulled it off."

Ann believed in it, said Lawrence Yanovitch, director of policy and research at FINCA, also known as the Foundation for International Community Assistance, a leader in village banking in Latin America, who served on the executive committee with Ann. That was simply her nature: She had little ego, he said, and she cared about the issues first. Barry told me, "She could be kind of a fat lady with big hair and a bohemian, but she was trying to do the right thing for the right reasons. And she did it with great intelligence and very strong rigor in terms of preparation and methodology and thinking through strategy."

At the same time, the secretary general for the Beijing conference asked Women's World Banking to chair an "expert group" on women and finance, to be made up of forty representatives of microfinance networks, development banks, government leaders, and others. In addition to Barry and Ann, the group included Dick Patten, Ann's friend and longtime colleague; Ela Bhatt from the Self Employed Women's Association; Muhammad Yunus, the founder and managing director of Grameen Bank, who would win the Nobel Peace Prize in 2006; and Ellen Johnson-Sirleaf, who would go on to become president of Liberia. In September 1993, Women's World Banking sent every member of the group an unusually detailed questionnaire on women and microfinance. The questionnaire bore the unmistakable marks of Ann's research methodology—a total of ninety-two questions, few of them amenable to short answers. ("I think we even had a conflict over the questionnaire," Barry told me. "Something I really know how to do super-well is moderate meetings and create a process where you get consensus in a very robust and detailed way out of a messy process. So I'm very results-oriented. My recollection is Ann would have loved to have gotten more stuff from everybody.") Two hundred pages of responses poured in to the Women's World Banking office. Ann and Nina Nayar, working with Barry, distilled them into an interim report. That report went out to every member of the expert group, along with profiles of leading microenterprise institutions and an analysis of government budgets and the flow of donor aid. Finally, the expert group met over five days in January 1994 to hash out and endorse a final report and recommendations— a framework for how to build financial systems that work for the poor.

"That was considered a huge achievement in the world of microfinance," recalled Niki Armacost. "No one had talked about common standards before. No one had talked about the kinds of criteria that you need to evaluate microfinance organizations, or the policy constraints, or the challenges they would have to deal with, or why it was important to be lending money to women. None of that had been put together before. So it was a seminal document."

Outside the office, Ann was increasingly worried about money and her health. When she had moved to New York, she had understood that she would not be able to live as well as she had in Jakarta. But she had hoped to get by, she wrote in a memo to Barry eight months after accepting the job, "modestly but decently, in a manner suitable for a grownup, meet my basic family obligations, and still save a small amount toward Christmas, emergencies or the future." That had not happened. After less than a year, she was spending more than she was making. She was sinking ever more deeply into debt. After taxes, she expected to take home just $41,000 of her starting salary—a figure she expected to shrink the following year, when she would be eligible to claim fewer exemptions and deductions. The monthly payments on her ballooning credit-card debt had doubled to $600 a month. In her memo to Barry, she had asked for a raise. "To make a long story short, in the seven months I have been at Women's World Banking, I have been forced to exhaust my savings and I am now going further into credit card debt at the rate of about $500 a month in order to just get by," she wrote. "There is no possibility of saving even a penny. Clearly I cannot continue this way, no matter how devoted I am to Women's World Banking or the mission."

Money was not Ann's only worry. She was more overweight than ever, her skin was pale, and her abdomen and lower legs were swollen. When she walked any distance, she would pant and become short of breath. By the summer of 1994, it had become painful to walk. When Maya and others urged her to see a doctor, she seemed to procrastinate and make excuses. She attributed her symptoms to menopause. "You, my in-law, will see when you reach my age," she said to Wanjiku Kibui, her Kenyan colleague, laughing it off. Though Ann appeared to fear little in life, she was uncomfortable with doctors, especially gynecologists. Once, she had told a friend that she had rejected a physician's suggestion that she consider a hysterectomy to address a problem of heavy bleeding. "The indignity of it!" the friend remembered her saying. The prospect of the procedure seemed to violate her sense of privacy and self-respect. She was also morbidly afraid of cancer. On at least a dozen occasions, Nayar recalled, Ann brought up the subject. "If you're going to get it, you're going to get it," she would remark at the slightest reminder of cancer—passing a cancer-awareness ribbon or discussing a new health insurance policy requiring Pap smears. "If it gets you, it gets you."

"The only thing I'm really afraid of in life is to die of cancer," she told Nayar.

"Why do you say that?"

"Well, my father died of cancer."

"A lot of people's parents die of cancer," Nayar would reassure her. "So you're in a high-risk category. You have to take precautions."

It was as if she did not want to know, Nayar thought, or maybe she thought she knew and did not want to see it in writing. Around the time of a review of the benefits package at Women's World Banking, Ann became especially agitated. She had no savings, and she was worried about her health. "I think she realized that if she was going to get sick—even if she was going to get old—this was not the job that was going to help her," Nayar said. "And she would have to think about that rather than depend on her children."

In late June 1994, Ann wrote Barry a letter giving notice that she would be resigning. For months, she had been considering leaving. She had a sense, she told Don Johnston, her former colleague in Jakarta, that Women's World Banking was spinning its wheels— "rushing off to a lot of different places, doing a lot of different things, but not making a really strong impact on women's access to finance anywhere," as Johnston put it. Having finally completed her dissertation, she wanted to get it published. She had prepared an application for a postdoctoral grant to cover the cost of three months in Indonesia updating the research and nine months at the East-West Center revising the dissertation for publication. But she had also been contacted by Development Alternatives Inc., the firm in Bethesda, Maryland, that had hired her for her first big job as a development consultant fifteen years earlier. Development Alternatives wanted to bid on a project aimed at strengthening the Indonesian State Ministry for the Role of Women. To have a shot at winning the contract, the firm would need a certain kind of team leader—ideally a woman, fluent in Indonesian, with the combination of authority and sensitivity that it would take to be accepted by the minister and her staff. "It had to be someone who was basically Indonesian—but an American," said Bruce Harker, who was working for the Bethesda firm, developing technical assistance contracts in Indonesia. He had known Ann in Java. She seemed to him the only person who could do the job. He knew she was torn about whether to be living, at that period in her life, in Indonesia or the United States. But when the firm contacted her, she seemed excited by the job opportunity and eager to return to Indonesia. The base pay was $82,500, well above the $69,550 she was making, before taxes, after her first year at Women's World Banking. In addition to health insurance, the benefits included a housing allowance and a car. "After much agonizing, and lengthy discussions with family and friends in the US and Indonesia, I have decided to accept the position," Ann wrote to Nancy Barry. "I have enjoyed my time in New York, and I have added a lot to my store of professional knowledge, particularly in the areas of policy work and institution building for NGOs. I will leave WWB with great affection for the organization, and all the people working here. I hope there will be opportunities for us to meet and cooperate in the future. (Who knows? Perhaps we will all meet at Beijing.)"

Ann seemed to have a feeling that she was running out of time, Nayar told me. Ann told her, "I just need to go home."

Before she left, Ann made one last trip for Women's World

Banking. In July, she flew to Mexico City for the global meeting of the Women's World Banking network. She seemed worn out by the travel, but she rallied when she arrived. Nayar was struck by Ann's ability to connect with people across regional and cultural differences. "It was not just the Asians," Nayar said. "It was the Africans, because they saw her in her muumuus and her trinkets, and she fit right in to the Mama circle—the West Africans with their scarves and all that." Nayar was also reminded of Ann's effect on men. The Mexican organizers had hired "these stunning, drop-dead-gorgeous male models," as Nayar remembered them, to serve as hosts to the several hundred women. Ann had always been flirtatious, Nayar said. A glimmer in her eye expressed eloquently her interest and delight in men. "These boys were eating out of her hand," Nayar remembered. "They weren't looking at us, they were all around Ann. I think she was probably one of the most sensual women I have met in my life. Size didn't matter, it was what was inside. She just exuded woman."

The young male host assigned to Ann's group turned out to be an anthropology major, fluent in English, who did modeling on the side. Soon, he, Ann, and Nayar were in a taxi, heading to an archaeological dig. Ann took Nayar to the Frida Kahlo Museum at Casa Azul, the house in Coyoacán where Kahlo had grown up and later lived with Diego Rivera. At the National Museum of Anthropology, Niki Armacost recalled, Ann stopped in front of an exhibit illustrating human evolution. "There was an Africa grouping, an Asia grouping," Armacost told me. "She was talking about the Africa grouping. The image they had up on the wall was this incredibly curvaceous African woman who had this huge, curvy bum. And we're all so—kind of unshapely. And she said, 'You know, it's very interesting, because when the white explorers found these African women and took them back to Europe, that's when the bustle started!'"

On an outing to Teotihuacán, the vast archaeological site northeast of Mexico City that was the largest city in the pre-Columbian Americas until it was suddenly and mysteriously abandoned, Ann wanted to climb the Pyramid of the Sun, one of the biggest pyramids in the world. Worried about her stamina, Nayar suggested instead the Pyramid of the Moon because it was smaller but offered dazzling views of the bigger pyramid and the majestic expanse of the Avenue of the Dead. Against the backdrop of a sacred mountain to the north, the two women, a generation apart, ascended together. "It was so hard for her to climb this thing," Nayar remembered years later. "I really thought she was going to pass out or fall. There was no way I was letting her go up on her own. She was also a little afraid of heights. But she was going to do it. And she did it."

Two months earlier, Ann had gone to see a physician with a private practice in obstetrics, gynecology, and infertility on the Upper East Side of Manhattan. She had been given the doctor's name by another physician, who had retired, and had made an appointment for a gynecological checkup. She told the doctor, Barbara Shortle, that she had a five-year history of heavy and irregular periods, for which previous doctors had put her on hormone-replacement therapy. Twice, she said, she had received a dilation and curettage, a procedure commonly done to diagnose the causes of abnormal bleeding. Each time, she said, the test had turned up nothing. Shortle, who had a particular affection for Hawaii, took a liking to Ann, but she also suspected Ann was seriously ill. From the extent of the bleeding, Shortle thought she might have uterine cancer, a rarity in Shortle's practice, which could in many cases be treated successfully with surgery and radiation, depending on the grade of the tumor. Shortle jotted her hypothesis in her notes. She recommended a physical exam, a Pap smear, a pelvic ultrasound, a mammogram, and, most important for a diagnosis, another dilation and curettage, which could be used to rule out uterine cancer. The D&C would have to be done in a hospital, and would for that reason take up the better part of a day at a critical time when the staff at Women's World Banking was especially busy. Ann went ahead and had the physical, the Pap smear, the pelvic ultrasound, and the mammogram, as well as a breast ultrasound, at the radiologist's suggestion.

"I completed all of those tests," Ann would write to Shortle a year later in connection with an insurance claim, having never seen her again, "except the D and C, which I postponed for work-related reasons."

Eleven

Coming Home

❧

In late November 1994, Ann's driver, Sabaruddin, picked her up from the modest little house on a narrow street in Jakarta where she had been living since returning to Indonesia. In the used car she had bought with the transportation allowance from her new employer, they rumbled south toward Ciloto, a resort town in the highlands an hour and a half outside the city. For three months, Ann and her team of consultants had been preparing for a three-day retreat at which the staff of the State Ministry for the Role of Women was to come to grips with its mission—embedding a commitment to gender equality deep in the government of the fourth most populous country in the world. To some friends, Ann had described her new assignment as a dream job. But it had quickly proved far more frustrating than she had chosen to dwell on in advance. The bureaucracy was sluggish and resistant to change. There was not enough money in the consulting contract to cover all the work Ann felt was needed to do the job properly. Within a month or two, she was exhausted, overworked, and not feeling well. Bruce Harker, who was overseeing the project from the office of Development Alternatives Inc. in Bethesda, had been taken aback, during a visit to Jakarta, when Ann, appealing to him for more money for the project, had broken down in tears. Yet there she was on the first afternoon of the workshop in Ciloto, delivering a paper on international trends in gender and development. Attendance at the workshop was slightly lower than hoped: Even the minister had begged off, sending word that she had been called to the palace for a meeting with President Suharto's wife. By the time Ann left Ciloto a day or two later, her vague feeling of unease about her health had been superseded by a sharp pain in her abdomen, which she was no longer able to push from her mind.

The job in Jakarta had sounded promising enough in New York City the previous spring. With the approach of the United Nations conference in Beijing, the Asian Development Bank, an international development bank with its headquarters in the Philippines, had decided to make a grant to the Indonesian government for the purpose of strengthening and increasing the influence of the State Ministry for the Role of Women. The bank had invited consulting companies to bid on a contract to provide technical assistance—advice on shaping a strategy, training the staff, and setting up databases to measure the ministry's impact. In a joint venture with an Indonesian firm with connections to the Suharto family, Development Alternatives Inc. had bid and won. But in last-minute negotiations, the amount of money available to the team leader for work activities had been reduced, Harker told me. His company had become, in effect, the subcontractor, leaving Ann, the team leader, working for a firm that did not have control over the budget. From the beginning, the going was rocky. In

Jakarta, Ann found herself working out of a dark, dingy office in the Ministry of the Environment without easy access to the ministry she was advising. There were the usual technological aggravations, including cell phone service that seemed not to cover the office where she worked. The ministry staff was inexperienced—and in some cases uninterested—in complex questions involving gender. Recruited from other agencies, many of the staff members needed training—and might move abruptly, without warning, to another ministry at any time. "We found it very frustrating, because there was no interest," Mayling Oey-Gardiner, a demographer who was also a consultant to the ministry, told me. Without a critical mass of support, she said, little could be done. Furthermore, the task was huge. Ann's responsibilities ranged from preparing an assessment of the ministry to working with other ministries on a program to "mainstream" a concern about gender equality into everything from planning and budgeting to evaluation. She was expected to work with local governments on a plan for improving their cooperation with the women's ministry, and she was responsible for preparing a series of reports, including a final one that would give future direction to the ministry and suggest additional projects for the development bank. In Ann's previous jobs, when money had been needed for work activities, it had been found. But this time around, that was not the case. So when Harker arrived in Jakarta a few months into the contract to conduct an interim review, Ann turned to him, in desperation, for help.

"The tears were a surprise," Harker remembered. "Who's accustomed to having a fellow professional start crying in a private meeting over a disagreement about money? It should have told me how much stress she was under. What I took from that experience was what I would take from practically anyone: This is a person who is exhausted, who is extremely frustrated, and who is struggling. To this day, I don't know if there were struggles in her personal life that made her especially concerned about the personal-expenses side of it. That was an issue that led to tears. I don't know what it was anymore—about the housing, the car, not having enough gas money. These are little things that I had long since, in my own life, paid out of my own pocket. I was taken aback by some of it."

Ann had found a small, sparsely furnished house in a *kampung,* a villagelike neighborhood within the city, where her neighbors were largely Indonesian. The street was so narrow, and space so tight, it took geometric precision for Sabaruddin to park Ann's car in its allotted space. The house had a little living room with a bedroom off it, a study, a bathroom, and a kitchen. There was room in the back for the one woman she employed as her *pembantu.* (The Indonesian word means "helper" but is variously translated as house staff, housekeeper, or servant.) Rens Heringa found the place to be "a poky, uncared-for little house" in a neighborhood very different from where Ann had lived earlier. Gillie Brown, a younger British woman whom Development Alternatives Inc. had retained in Jakarta to handle financial management and records, as well as other matters, called the house "an incredibly humble sort of place." But Ann was not like other consultants—those who spoke no Indonesian, lived in "smart houses," and relied on Brown to make arrangements. Brown felt a certain affinity with Ann, though Ann was twenty years her senior. Brown had left the United Kingdom in her mid-twenties with her husband and their three children—a three-year-old, a two-year-old, and a five-week-old baby. They had gone to live in a village in Bangladesh, then on a rice farm in southern Somalia. Trained as an engineer, she had grown accustomed to working in professional settings dominated by men. It seemed to Brown that the humble house was what Ann had wanted—to live surrounded by Indonesians, buying her food on the street. To Brown, Ann seemed to feel she had come home.

Some of Ann's oldest expatriate friends, including Nancy Peluso, had returned to the United States, but she picked up her friendships with Julia Suryakusuma, Yang Suwan, and others where she had left off. Made Suarjana, the young journalist Ann had first met in Yogyakarta in 1988, had moved by himself to Jakarta in February, though he would move with his wife and two children to Bali the following December. He saw Ann occasionally in Jakarta in 1994, he told me. When I asked him if he thought that Ann would have liked to have made a life with him, he told me she knew he was married. Her closest friends, however, did not remember Ann telling them that Suarjana had a wife. They told me they doubted that she knew—or if she did, that she must have believed the marriage was effectively over. Several, including Rens Heringa and Alice Dewey, used almost identical language in describing what Ann had told them about what had become of her relationship with Suarjana. "She told me that she felt that in the end, the difference in their ages was too large," said Heringa, who spent time with Ann in the Netherlands in late 1993 and in Jakarta in late 1994 and early 1995. "They'd had a lovely time, but she didn't want to hold him back from having a full social life in Indonesia. Because she knew she was going to leave, what was going to happen to him? She sent him away. He got married."

Late one night during the last week in November 1994, Bruce Harker, in his bed in Potomac, Maryland, received a telephone call from Ann in Jakarta. Ignoring the time difference, which she well knew, she must have felt the call could not wait. She had been having abdominal pains for some time, she told him, and the pain had become so severe at the workshop in Ciloto that she had returned to Jakarta to see a doctor. The doctor, a gynecologist at a clinic that specialized in treating expatriates, had concluded that Ann had appendicitis and had referred her to a surgeon at Pondok Indah Hospital, a high-end medical center in a wealthy neighborhood of Jakarta. Faced with the prospect of surgery, Ann was trying to decide whether to stay in Jakarta or fly to Singapore. For routine procedures, many longtime expatriates were comfortable with the best Indonesian hospitals. They did not consider themselves foreign enough to automatically mistrust Indonesian doctors. Furthermore, Ann had friends in Jakarta, as well as her *pembantu* and her driver, to help her out if she stayed. But other expatriates, and even some Indonesians, automatically went to Singapore for hospitalization, especially for anything major. Gillie Brown, who had taken her daughter to Singapore for an appendectomy, urged Ann to go there, too. "I thought she was nuts, staying in the country," Brown told me. On the other hand, Harker had once had hip surgery in Singapore, he told Ann, which had been done so badly that it was later redone in the United States. "She wanted to know whether there was airfare and accommodations for her to go to Singapore in the budget," Harker remembered. "I said, 'Look, here's the deal. We didn't budget an appendectomy. You've got health insurance, that's taken care of. We can cover the airfare. We can cover a few hundred dollars.'"

Ann chose to stay in Jakarta. On November 28, 1994, the day before her fifty-second birthday, a surgeon at Pondok Indah removed her appendix. Three days later, she returned home to recuperate in her housekeeper's care. The incision healed promptly, she would tell her insurance company in a letter some months later, but the abdominal pain returned. Her surgeon advised patience, because recovery could take several months. When the pain became too much to bear, she returned twice to the medical clinic, where she saw two internists as well as a gynecologist she had not previously seen. According to her account to the insurance company, doctors at the clinic told her she had an abdominal infection and prescribed an antibiotic. After two and a half weeks on the drug, she felt no better. Meanwhile, she had returned to work after a week of resting at home. To some friends, she said simply that her recovery was going slowly. In e-mails and conversations with Nina Nayar, she seemed unconvinced by the diagnosis. She was lethargic and weak. When she ate, she felt immediately full. A masseuse to whom she had gone for a massage declined to continue, Ann told Dewey. "What is wrong with you is serious," the masseuse warned.

On December 13, Ann met Rens Heringa at a Protestant church guesthouse in Jakarta where Heringa was staying, having arrived six days earlier on a two-month visit from the Netherlands. Ann was more distraught than Heringa had ever seen her. She was in constant pain and barely able to digest food. Weeping, she was certain that the diagnosis of appendicitis was wrong. "She said, 'I have cancer,'" Heringa told me. "I said, 'Ann, how do you know?' She said, 'Well, I feel it.'" She reminded Heringa that her father had died from cancer—as if it was contagious or inherited. Heringa tried to reassure her. She told Ann about her own six-month recovery from an appendectomy in the late 1960s in Surabaya in East Java. She encouraged Ann to get a second opinion, but Heringa tried above all to calm her down. "Listen, this is because your father just died," Heringa recalled saying. "Don't get things in your head. Have yourself diagnosed, absolutely. But try not to be carried away."

On Christmas Day, Heringa told me, she met Ann and Made Suarjana for lunch. The occasion was not festive. Ann, for whom food had always been a source of great pleasure, ate almost nothing. "She clearly was in pain," Heringa remembered. "Made was as concerned as I was. We both felt pretty helpless." Five days later, Ann made an appearance at the birthday party of Ong Hok Ham, the historian. Three weeks later, she and Heringa made a plan for lunch, which Heringa's diary showed was canceled. "Isn't it strange, though, how we continued our regular routine of meeting at restaurants, almost denying what was going on with her?" Heringa said to me, after going back over her datebook. "It looks as if she was of two minds."

In late January, Bruce Harker, in Maryland, received a second late-night call. This time, Ann sounded scared. She had had the appendectomy, she told him, and pain medication had got her through the recuperation. But the pain in her abdomen had returned with ferocity.

"How urgent is it?" Harker asked.

"Urgent," Ann said. "I've got to get out of here and go home to Hawaii."

Ann was afraid to board a flight to Honolulu without knowing that her employer would reimburse her for the cost of the ticket. At fifty-two years old, she did not have what Harker later called "the screw-you resources"—the financial freedom to do what she needed to do and take her chances. When she had asked her younger colleague Gillie Brown if the project had the money to cover the flight, Brown had referred her to Harker. By the time Ann reached him, she seemed to have made up her mind to leave. Harker understood. In that situation, a foreign resident in a place she loved would suddenly feel like she was in a world of strangers—no matter how much affection she had for the culture and the people.

"You have to do what you have to do," Harker remembered telling her. "I can't authorize you to go—that's not something I can do without doing some homework. But just because I can't authorize you to go doesn't mean you shouldn't. Between you and me, two friends talking, I can't authorize you and buy you a ticket, but if you go home, you've made the strongest possible case for being reimbursed. Plus, you'll get the care you want."

Ann slipped out of Indonesia quietly, keeping her fears to herself, for the most part. When she met with Gillie Brown to brief her on how to fill in as team leader, Ann reassured her: "You'll be fine. It'll only be a couple of weeks. I'll be back." She told Julia Suryakusuma, who had postponed a planned birthday party for Ann, that she would be returning quickly. "Don't be long," Suryakusuma said. "You promised to help me with some stuff." Ann called Made Suarjana and told him simply that she was going to Hawaii for a checkup, which seemed reasonable enough. Yang Suwan, who had planned a celebratory birthday meal with Ann, was puzzled by not being able to reach her by phone. From late November on, Yang's calls to Ann's house went unanswered. Once, a man picked up the phone and explained simply that Ann had put off her birthday. On another occasion, he said Ann was very sick, but he did not say with what. A few days after that, Yang heard that Ann was no longer in Jakarta. It seemed unlike Ann not to explain, Yang thought, but Ann had always moved within multiple but separate circles of friends. Perhaps that was how she wanted to live, Yang figured. In which case, she should respect Ann's wishes.

Rens Heringa, however, glimpsed Ann's terror. The two women had been close friends for more than a decade and had many experiences in common. Both had grown up in the West and married Indonesian men whom they had met at university. Both had followed their husbands to Indonesia, raised children there, and eventually divorced. Both were anthropologists with an interest in handicrafts, Heringa specializing in textiles. Each had visited the villages where the other had done her fieldwork. They had circles of friends in common. The afternoon before Ann left Jakarta, in a torrential downpour of the sort that besieged the city during the rainy season, Heringa took a taxi to Ann's house. To Heringa, it seemed as if the world were weeping. The little house seemed bare. There were crates, half packed for shipping. "It was horrible," Heringa told me. "We felt sure we wouldn't see each other again. She was in a bad way. This was just sad, very sad, because we had to say good-bye."

On January 25, 1995, twenty-seven years after first arriving in Indonesia with Barry to join Lolo, Ann left for the last time. Madelyn Dunham met her in Honolulu and arranged for her to be taken to the Straub Clinic and Hospital. Several days later, she was seen by a gastroenterologist, who concluded within a week that her problem was not gastrointestinal. Next, she was referred to an oncologist, who, in the second week in February, diagnosed her illness as third-stage uterine and ovarian cancer. According to her correspondence with her insurance company, the disease appeared to have spread in her abdomen. She underwent a total hysterectomy and was sent home on Valentine's Day to recuperate in Madelyn's apartment, in her care. Once Ann had recovered from the immediate effects of the surgery, she embarked on a series of six monthly chemotherapy treatments intended to, as she described it, eradicate remaining traces of the cancer and prevent further spread.

Maya, who had graduated from the University of Hawai'i with a bachelor's degree, had spent the fall of 1994 traveling in the southwestern United States and in Mexico, largely out of contact. After injuring a knee while hiking, she had spent several days in a bar at the Grand Canyon, drinking coffee and reading novels by William Faulkner, Tony Hillerman, and Ernest J. Gaines. There, in the bar and using a pencil, she had filled out an application to the graduate school of education at New York University. Several months later, in Mexico City, she had telephoned her grandmother in Honolulu and discovered that she had been accepted into a master's degree program. Moving to New York City in late December, she had found a job as a bartender to cover her rent while going to graduate school. After a week on the bartending job, she received a call from Madelyn. Ann had returned from Jakarta, Madelyn told her. The appendicitis had turned out not to be appendicitis. It was cancer.

Barack, meanwhile, was in Chicago, juggling multiple callings. At the time of his mother's diagnosis, he was three years out of law school and an associate in a Chicago law firm that specialized in civil rights cases; he was teaching part-time as a lecturer at the University of Chicago Law School; his memoir, *Dreams from My Father,* which a literary agent had encouraged him to write after the *Harvard Law Review* election, was scheduled for publication in August 1995; and he had begun maneuvering toward possibly running for public office for the first time. The indictment in August 1994 of the congressman from the Second District of Illinois, Mel Reynolds, had prompted the state senator from Obama's district, Alice Palmer, to explore a bid for Reynolds' seat. By the time Palmer announced her candidacy for Congress in June 1995, Obama had already laid the groundwork for his campaign to fill her seat. On September 19, 1995, he announced officially that he was embarking on his first political campaign—a run for election to the Illinois State Senate.

In Honolulu, Ann pressed on gamely. According to her correspondence, Barry helped her with insurance forms and letters in the immediate aftermath of her surgery. After a short time, she moved into an apartment in the same building as her mother and attempted to get back to her life. Her hair fell out, but otherwise she seemed to tolerate the treatment. She attended concerts and seminars at the university, having acquired a collection of colorful turbans and scarves. "She seemed as cheerful as ever," said Michael Dove, the anthropologist Ann had known in Java and Pakistan and who was now at the East-West Center. "She even looked the same as ever, except, I think, she'd lost her hair and was wearing a scarf." She insisted on going to a traditional Hawaiian feast known as a luau with her old friend Pete Vayda and his wife, when they arrived in Hawaii on vacation. She went on walks at Ala Moana Beach Park with the Solyoms—and with Maya when she visited. Georgia McCauley, her friend from Jakarta who was now back in Hawaii, saw her weekly. Madelyn's sister Arlene Payne telephoned regularly from North Carolina and sent books—mostly French authors, at Ann's request, notably Proust and Sartre.

Ann also continued to work. When Alice Dewey dropped by the apartment, she would find Ann at the computer. Gillie Brown sent the progress reports on the project in Jakarta for Ann to edit. Ann dispensed wise advice to Brown. Despite her youth and inexperience, Brown had been thrust by Ann's departure into the role of team leader. She was ambitious to make headway and impatient with the rigid code of female behavior inculcated by the Suharto government. In her first meeting with the state minister for the role of women, Brown received what she would later remember as a lecture on the importance of lipstick—which she was not wearing. As the daughter of a Welsh farmer, she knew that farmers looked after their cows well for a reason: Cows brought in income. It seemed to Brown that Suharto attended to the welfare of Indonesia's women like a farmer tended his herd. That was why the health and education statistics for women in Indonesia looked so good. When she would complain to Ann that nothing in Indonesia was changing, Ann would laugh. "If you can see progress on gender issues over a ten-year period, you're doing well," Ann would say. Ann's advice to the younger woman on dealing with people was unfailingly practical. "She'd always laugh first and say, 'Why don't you do it this way . . . ?'" Brown recalled. With older Indonesian women of high status, Ann suggested Brown try backing off. She could see, in a way that Brown did not, that change would eventually come. "Don't just get frustrated and unhappy," Ann seemed to be saying. Focus on where you can make a difference. Accept that progress takes time.

Quietly, Ann also emboldened Brown to examine the ground rules in her own life. Brown was a married mother of three and the "supplementary income earner" in the family—the role to which married women in Indonesia were consigned by law, Brown told me. Coming from a conservative area in West Wales, Brown felt she had pushed the barriers to their limits. To have claimed even more independence—to have wanted things for herself, such as a career and an identity independent of that of her family—would have felt selfish. Ann inspired Brown, through their telephone and e-mail discussions of the limits on the lives of Indonesian women and through her comments on Brown's reports, to reconsider her own life. "I think Ann was, in the subtlest of ways, trying to say, 'Well, actually, you have these constraints in your own life . . .'" Brown told me. "I think there was a mutual respect in trying to live our lives differently. She was sort of saying, 'There's more: There's you.'"

Ann's compensation for her job in Jakarta had included health insurance, which covered most of the costs of her medical treatment. She had even had a physical in order to qualify—an examination she said had required six separate office visits in Jakarta. Once she was back in Hawaii, the hospital billed her insurance company directly, leaving Ann to pay only the deductible and any uncovered expenses, which, she said, came to several hundred dollars a month. To cover those charges as well as living expenses, she filed a separate claim under her employer's disability insurance policy. That policy, however, contained a clause allowing the company to deny any claim related to a preexisting medical condition. If, during the three months before starting work, a patient had seen a doctor or been treated for the condition that caused the disability for which they later wanted coverage, the insurance company would not compensate the patient for lost pay.

In late April, a representative of the insurance company, CIGNA, notified Ann that the company had begun evaluating her disability claim. (According to CIGNA, the disability policy was underwritten by Life Insurance Company of North America, a subsidiary of CIGNA.) In the meantime, the representative suggested that Ann find out if she was eligible for benefits under the Social Security system. Ann had already been told by Social Security Administration officials in Honolulu that she was not eligible:

She had not earned enough credits in the previous ten years to be eligible for Social Security disability income, and she was ineligible for benefits under the Supplemental Security Income program for disabled people with limited resources because she owned an asset worth more than $2,000, an Individual Retirement Account. In response to the letter from CIGNA, Ann sent back copies of letters from the Social Security Administration and a half-dozen other documents that CIGNA had requested, along with a four-page letter that included a detailed chronology of her illness. "During the three months before joining DAI, the only doctor I consulted was Dr. Barbara Shortle, a New York gynecologist," Ann wrote in the letter. "Dr. Shortle gave me a routine annual examination in May 1994, including pap smear and pelvic exam. She sent me to a laboratory for a mammogram and pelvic ultrasound. On the advice of the radiologist of the laboratory, I also had a breast ultrasound. None of these tests indicated that I had cancer. The pelvic examination indicated that I had an enlarged uterus, but this is a condition which I had had for about five years previously."

Ann's letter did not mention the one procedure, the dilation and curettage, she had omitted to have.

By late June, CIGNA had made no decision on Ann's disability claim. The company was waiting to hear from Shortle, a representative told Ann. Ann faxed a letter to Shortle, whom she had not seen since her appointment thirteen months earlier. She explained that she was being treated for ovarian cancer in Hawaii and that her disability claim had been held up for months while CIGNA investigated whether her cancer was a preexisting condition. She said she had given Shortle's name to CIGNA, which, in turn, had faxed Shortle a request for information. Two weeks later, CIGNA sent another letter to Ann, addressed this time to "Mr." Dunham. Among other things, the letter said, "If we do not receive either the requested information or some communication from you within 30 days from the date of this letter, we will assume you are no longer claiming benefits under your Long Term Disability Plan."

In one of several drafts of a response to CIGNA, Ann coolly leveled a pointed objection.

Since I have sent you a mountain of forms and a lengthy letter dealing with my illness, which is ovarian cancer, I am surprised that you are not aware that I am a woman. I realize that it is unusual for a woman to have a man's first name, but I have signed my correspondence to you with my middle name of Ann. Also we have spoken by phone within the last month. Combined with the fact that my claim has been pending for five months, I am forced to wonder whether it is receiving proper attention.

In mid-August, CIGNA denied Ann's claim on the basis of her visit to the New York gynecologist two and a half months before she started work in Jakarta. Shortle's office notes had indicated that she had formed a working hypothesis of uterine cancer, though Ann said Shortle never discussed that hypothesis with her. When I spoke with Shortle, she said it was quite possible that she had not told Ann of her suspicions. "Whenever you do a D and C on any woman who has bleeding on and off, you're always doing it to rule out uterine cancer," she said. But, she said, the procedure can be therapeutic as well as diagnostic. She might not, at that point, tell a patient her thinking.

Ann requested a review of the denial and informed CIGNA that she was turning over the case to "my son and attorney, Barack Obama." Years later, during the presidential campaign and even after his election, Obama would allude to his mother's experience, albeit in an abbreviated form, when making the case for health care reform. Though he often suggested that she was denied health coverage because of a preexisting condition, it appears from her correspondence that she was only denied disability coverage.

Ann, characteristically, had hoped for the best. If all went well, the chemotherapy would be completed by the end of August, after which it would take two months for the side effects to abate. "Then, assuming that I go into remission and there is no recurrence of the disease, I should be able to return to work in November," she had written to CIGNA in May. Because she would need monitoring and regular blood tests, it would be difficult to take a long-term overseas assignment again. "Instead, I plan to do short-term assignments for DAI which will allow me to return to Hawaii for check-ups in between," she wrote.

When friends called on the telephone, Ann often sidestepped the subject of her illness. In a series of conversations with Madelyn's youngest brother, Jon Payne, they sparred jokingly for the title of black sheep of the family, wondering why they had allowed themselves to fall so far out of touch. To Made Suarjana, calling from Bali, Ann insisted she was fine. He began to notice, however, that her voice sounded different. Slamet Riyadi, a colleague from Bank Rakyat Indonesia, was uncomfortable even asking about her health. Instead, he told her he would pray for her. Dick Patten came away from one telephone conversation believing that Ann had beaten the cancer. Julia Suryakusuma received a letter from Ann, which she allowed herself to understand, only later, had been intended to let her know that her friend was dying. When Rens Heringa called from Los Angeles on a visit from the Netherlands, Ann implored her to fly to Hawaii, but Heringa could not. Ann made it clear to Heringa that she knew she would never get better. Why was she forcing herself to continue with chemotherapy? Heringa wondered. Ann refused to give up hope. "Even when she knew she was seriously ill, it was probably not a matter of denial but really believing she was not ready to die," Suryakusuma said.

Ann Hawkins, whom Ann had first met fifteen years earlier in the mountains above Semarang on the north coast of Java, understood that Ann was extremely ill. With some people, Ann seemed to keep the conversation light so she could think about happier things, Hawkins told me. But she spoke honestly with Hawkins. "She didn't really talk about her life," Hawkins remembered. "Except that I always had the sense that Ann felt very privileged. She felt, yeah, of course her life was cut short. But at the same time she had an extraordinary life. . . . And I think she knew that. I think she *showed* it, in how she treated other people. She felt such abundance—that's the word—in not only her own life but life all around."

Hawkins extended her arms out in front of her, palms turned upward.

"I see Ann sort of like this, with her hands out, giving," she said. It was a gesture, she said, of generosity, perceptiveness, and compassion.

In early September, Ann said good-bye to her friend Georgia McCauley, whom she had known since her days at the Ford Foundation with McCauley's husband, David. In their weekly visits over the previous months, the two women had talked often about their children, rarely about Ann's illness. Now the McCauleys were moving. "It was difficult, because we both sort of knew that we wouldn't be seeing each other," Georgia McCauley remembered. Ann indicated that she believed Barack would be fine: He was happy, and Ann thought Michelle would be a good partner. "She was just worried about Maya," McCauley remembered. "'Will you take care of Maya? Keep an eye out for Maya.'

"She was saying something pretty profound," McCauley told me. "But it was sort of like the end of a conversation, as you're leaving. Nobody wants to face the obvious."

Ann had told McCauley many times that she did not want her children to see her in the state she was in. But in the weeks that followed, McCauley said, "I often wondered, maybe I should have called Barry and bugged him. I asked Maya to talk to him. I said, 'You all need to realize that it's going to happen fairly soon.' But I didn't know him well enough. I just thought it was kind of presumptuous for me to tell him what to do. I know they spoke. It's a difficult issue to deal with."

In mid-September, Ann and Madelyn flew to New York City for a series of appointments at Memorial Sloan-Kettering Cancer Center, widely considered the most respected cancer center in the country. An oncologist at Sloan-Kettering had agreed to give Ann a second opinion. Maya, working full-time as a student teacher while in graduate school, met her mother and grandmother at La-Guardia Airport. Ann emerged from the terminal in a wheelchair, looking dazed and startled. Madelyn, a month away from her seventy-third birthday, was suffering from severe back pain. They were carrying with them Ann's medical records, X-rays, and tumor slides. They settled into the Barbizon Hotel on the East Side of Manhattan, near the hospital. Barack, back from his book tour and one week away from announcing his candidacy for the Illinois

State Senate, arrived from Chicago with Michelle. At the first of two appointments at Sloan-Kettering, Ann was given a physical examination; she turned over the records to the doctor and the tumor slides for reevaluation by the pathology department. Then she returned to the hotel to wait.

Maya and Ann walked in Central Park, bought frozen yogurt, wandered among the glittering displays of smoked fish and cheeses at Zabar's, the legendary food store on Broadway on the Upper West Side. They watched a movie of no particular interest to either one of them, Maya sitting next to her mother, holding her hand. When it was over, Maya asked Ann what she thought of the movie. It was a good distraction, she said, from the turmoil inside. Years later, Maya would remember her uncertainty about how best to help her mother—whether to encourage her to talk about what she was feeling or simply to be with her. If she could just get through the semester at New York University and at the school where she was teaching, Maya thought, she could fly home to Hawaii and stay with her mother as long as she was needed.

On September 15, 1995, the oncologist saw Ann for a second time. On the basis of the reevaluation of the tumor cells and the pattern of the illness, he believed Ann's cancer was uterine, not ovarian, and stage four, not stage three. He recommended that Ann's physician in Honolulu switch to a chemotherapy regimen based on a different drug, Adriamycin, or doxorubicin. The survival rate for women in Ann's condition was poor, he said, and sixty percent of patients did not respond positively to the drug he was suggesting. But if it worked, Ann might hope for a delay in recurrence and a period relatively free of symptoms.

Back in Honolulu, the new treatment proved grueling. Arlene Payne's conversations with her niece became shorter and shorter.

Ann had never been inclined toward regrets. If she regretted anything now, it was not having left Indonesia sooner to get medical
care, Payne told me. "But she fought it for as long as she could.
Then she sort of gave up and just sort of lived out the rest of her
life." The United Nations Fourth World Conference on Women
in Beijing came and went. From the point of view of Women's
World Banking, it had gone well. Much of the language hammered
out in the report of the expert group on women and finance, in
which Ann had played a central role, had been incorporated into
the action plan endorsed by the delegates in Beijing. Hillary Rod-
ham Clinton, then the First Lady, had spoken on a panel on microfinance that Women's World Banking had helped organize. For
the first time, microfinance seemed to have emerged front and center in the world's attention. Nina Nayar, Ann's young protégée
from Women's World Banking, returned from China via India,
then flew to Honolulu to see Ann. Ann's mane of dark hair was
gone. But she was ornamented, as always, for the occasion. "The
turban becomes you," Nayar marvelled affectionately. "I think it's
even more majestic." As Nayar recalled that visit, she and Garrett
Solyom hoisted Ann into a wheelchair and set off on one last field
trip. After all, it was Nayar's first visit to Hawaii. They picnicked
at sunset and tried Ann's favorite Hawaiian foods. At Ann's insistence, they made their way up to the Nuʻuanu Pali State Wayside,
where the trade winds climb the windward cliff of what remains
of the Koʻolau volcano and roar through the Pali Pass as though
through a funnel. There, not far from the tunnels that carry traffic through the mountain and from one side of Oʻahu to the other,
there is a panoramic view of the green Nuʻuanu Valley, Kaneohe
Bay, and the beach town of Kailua. Struggling with the wheelchair
against the wind and trying to keep Ann's headgear from taking

flight, Nayar remembered, she and Solyom maneuvered Ann into the optimal spot. "It was the same feeling as we had on top of the pyramid," Nayar said. "It was probably a parting gift for both of us."

In early November, during a collect call to her mother on a pay phone near the NYU campus, Maya noticed that Ann sounded momentarily confused.

"You know what, Mom?" she later recalled saying. "I'm coming. I'll work it out. I'll do whatever papers I have left. I'm coming. I'll see you there very soon.'

"She said, 'Okay,'" Maya remembered. "And I told her I was scared. And she said, 'Me, too.' And then, 'I love you.'

"And that was it."

On November 7, Maya flew to Honolulu, unsure of what she would find. Ann was unconscious and emaciated. To Maya, she appeared to be starving. But she was alive, as though she had waited. Maya took Madelyn's place by Ann's bed in the hospital room so that her grandmother could go home. Then she talked—about all that Ann had given her, about how she would be remembered with love. Maya had brought with her a book of Creole folktales, which she had been reading with her students as part of a study of origin myths. She began reading aloud. In one story, a person was transformed into a bird. Then the bird took flight.

"I told her finally that she should go, that I didn't want to see her like that," Maya remembered. "And she was gone about fifteen minutes later."

For Barack, not being at his mother's bedside when she died was the biggest mistake he made, he would say later. He was at home in Chicago when he got word. He had last seen Ann in New York City in September, and had last spoken to her, he told me, several days before her death, before she lost consciousness. "She was in Hawaii in a hospital, and we didn't know how fast it was going to take, and I didn't get there in time," he told the *Chicago Sun-Times* in 2004.

Word spread quickly. Dick Patten got the news in Burma, where he was working on a project for the United Nations Development Programme—trying to help the Burmese people, as he would later put it, without helping the Burmese government. Don Johnston, whom Ann had discreetly nudged into domestic happiness, got the news in Indonesia in the field. Made Suarjana, at his typewriter in his office in Bali, wept when Maya called. In a private ceremony, he told me, his family offered prayers to help deliver Ann's spirit to the next world. In Colorado, Jon Payne asked the priest in his church to include his niece in the congregation's prayers. After all, as far as Payne could tell, Ann had been doing what Christians always said saints did—helping people. "She wasn't a particularly religious person, if at all," Payne said. "But she did more things for people than a lot of Christians do."

In Jakarta, Julia Suryakusuma made an impromptu altar out of a table and a Balinese mirror in the living room of Gillie Brown's house on Jalan Gaharu in Cilandak. She placed a photograph of Ann in the center, along with candles, flowers, wood carvings, ikat, and traditional Indonesian cookies and cakes. Like an offering, Suryakusuma told me. She sent around flyers announcing a memorial gathering for Ann. On the afternoon of November 13, two dozen friends turned out. There was a period of silence, followed by a guided meditation, with music, led by an Australian yogi ("a lot of stuff that Ann privately laughed at," Don Johnston told me, chuckling). Wahyono Martowikrido, the archaeologist who had helped introduce Ann to the mysteries and meaning of the patterns in Javanese textiles and the shapes of silver jewelry, and Johnston, the Southern Baptist from Little Rock, Arkansas, were there. So was Ong Hok Ham, the historian, and Yang Suwan, the anthropologist, and several Indonesian women who had tried to start an Indonesian affiliate of Women's World Banking. There were women from Ann's team at the Ministry for the Role of Women. There were messages sent by Bruce Harker; Sabaruddin, Ann's driver; and others. After the guided meditation, Ann's friends regaled one another with memories of and stories about her. When everyone had drifted away, Gillie Brown sat down and wrote a letter to Madelyn, Barack, and Maya in Hawaii, listing everyone who had turned out in Jakarta. "The spirits of all these people will be with you in Hawaii today, as you say your farewells to Ann," she wrote.

In Honolulu, they gathered in the Japanese garden behind the East-West Center, the institution that embodied, more than any other, the spirit of the time in which Ann had come of age and the values by which she had lived. They convened near the stream, whose rambling course beneath the monkeypod trees was intended to signify the progress of a life. The group of several dozen included Madelyn Dunham, Maya and Barack, Michelle, Alice Dewey, the Solyoms, Nancy Peluso, Ann Hawkins, Michael Dove, Benji Bennington, and others—close friends from graduate school, the East-West Center, Jakarta, Yogyakarta, Semarang, Pakistan, and New York. They, too, recounted recollections of Ann. Then they drove east out of Honolulu to the Kalaniana'ole Highway, the road that winds along the wind-whipped southeastern coast of the island of O'ahu. They followed it, past the turnoff for Hanauma Bay, to where the coastline turns wilder and great slabs of rock tilt toward the indigo water. At a scenic lookout, they parked and got out.

Beyond a low wall built of volcanic rock, the ledges descended toward a distant point the shape of an ironing board jutting into the surf. There, gripping each other against the wind, Barack and Maya carried the ashes of their fifty-two-year-old mother across the water-slicked rocks and delivered them into the rough embrace of the sea.

Epilogue

In the aftermath of her death, the heirs of Bu Ann set their sights on the horizon.

Kellee Tsai, who had left Women's World Banking for graduate school with Ann's encouragement, spent two years doing fieldwork in China. She wrote a five-hundred-page dissertation and became a professor of political science and director of East Asian Studies at Johns Hopkins University. But she prided herself on being a closet anthropologist, combining in her work large statistical analyses with hundreds of interviews in the field; she had learned from Ann the impossibility of understanding the numbers before talking to and knowing the people. In China, she met an American whom she married and with whom she now has two children. In her dissertation, she wrote that the memory of Ann, along with that of another friend, "followed me into the field and back. Both would have scrutinized every page, footnote, and table in this dissertation."

For Nina Nayar, Ann's assistant at Women's World Banking, it was time to break out of the role of the good Indian daughter. "Losing Ann was a big moment where you say, 'Well, life is short,'" Nayar remembered. "'You have to do what you want to do now.'" After nearly twenty years abroad, Nayar decided—against the advice of her family, she told me—to base her life in Asia, not in the United States. It was not easy to return to India as a single woman of marrying age with relatives around. "This is the influence that Ann had," Nayar said. "She didn't do the stuff that her parents or community thought was appropriate." Nayar spent two years in Bangladesh, working on building a virtual microfinance network, and much of the next three years in Cambodia as a consultant in microfinance sector development. When she and I first spoke in 2008, Nayar was in Kabul, having turned her attention to the role of microfinance in countries recovering from conflict. By mid-2010, she had worked in nearly thirty countries, mostly in Africa and Asia. She had also abandoned her resolve to remain single. Instead, she had married a man whose values reminded her of Ann's. She was certain, she said, that Ann would have approved.

Gillie Brown, Ann's colleague in Jakarta, was hired by the World Bank in 1996 on the strength of the work she had done as Ann's replacement on the project to strengthen the State Ministry for the Role of Women. By the time Suharto fell in 1998 and the World Bank staff was evacuated from Indonesia, Brown was already planning to resign and rejoin her husband and children, who had returned earlier to Great Britain. But when the bank offered her a job in Washington, she surprised herself by accepting. She left her children in Britain with her husband. She would never have considered a step like that, she told me, if she had not known Ann.

Maybe there was more than one way to be a good mother after all, she thought. Ann's children seemed to have done okay.

Maya, who was twenty-five when her mother died, immersed herself in the profession of her Kansas forebears. She went to work in a new school on the Lower East Side of Manhattan that served a largely poor and Latino population. The staff was young, the work demanding, the learning curve steep. She accompanied her students to museums in upper Manhattan to widen their horizons, and to the city jail on Rikers Island, in a few cases, to visit their parents. Near the end of each pay period, she would rummage through her coat pockets for money to cover her commute. Immediately after Ann's death, Maya had wondered fleetingly if she should remain in Hawaii and help her grandmother. "Then I thought, 'Oh, gosh, Mom wouldn't have wanted that,'" she told me. "'I'm twenty-five years old. It's time for me to really grow up.'"

Several years earlier, Maya had told Ann that she was thinking of getting married. At the time, she was five years older than Ann had been when she had married Barack Obama Sr. Maya was working toward a master's degree, but she had barely begun a career. According to Maya, Ann advised her to wait. If marriage was what she really wanted, she should do it, Ann said. But she should know herself well enough to know who would satisfy her for the duration. Women have choices, Ann reminded her. They had gone through the women's movement, she said, yet they continued to act as if they had no options. They needed to ask themselves what they really wanted, then go out and get it.

"She was reminding me that it was okay to want to do things differently," Maya told me. "Which was, I thought, very enlightened."

In 2002, Maya met her future husband at the East-West Center.

Konrad Ng, a Chinese-Canadian graduate student in political science, shared an office at the center with Maya's martial-arts instructor. Maya, who had moved back to Honolulu several years earlier to help her grandmother, was teaching at a charter school and at the university while working toward a Ph.D. The following year, Maya and Konrad Ng married. After the birth of their first child, Maya dispatched her own dissertation—writing between the hours of ten p.m. and two a.m., she told me—and received her Ph.D. She began teaching history and doing curriculum development at a girls' school, where she developed a class in peace education. She started writing books, including one for children, *Ladder to the Moon*, in which Ann appears one night to Maya's elder daughter, Suhaila, and takes her up a golden ladder to the moon.

"What was Grandma Annie like?" Suhaila asks her mother in the story.

"She was like the moon," her mother replies. "Full, soft, and curious."

Barack, meanwhile, was elected to the Illinois State Senate in November 1996, one year after his mother's death. The original edition of *Dreams from My Father*, which was published in 1995 and sold approximately nine thousand copies in hardcover, came out in paperback the following year and went out of print. Obama ran unsuccessfully for Congress in 2000, then won the Democratic primary for the U.S. Senate in March 2004. Four months later, he gave the keynote speech at the Democratic National Convention in Boston—the speech that laid out, for millions of Americans for the first time, his father and mother's story and made him into a national political sensation almost overnight.

The news traveled swiftly among people who had once known Ann.

"Did you watch the Democratic convention?" a former student of Alice Dewey's wrote in an e-mail to Nancy Cooper, an anthropologist and former Dewey student herself.

"Yes, I did," Cooper answered.

"Did you see that guy who gave the keynote speech?"

"Yes."

"You know who that is?"

"No, I don't."

"It's Barry. Ann's Barry."

Ann's friend from Mercer Island, John Hunt, had happened on the connection years earlier in the frequent-flyer lounge at Los Angeles International Airport on the day the *Los Angeles Times* published its two-thousand-word profile of the first black president of the *Harvard Law Review*. In Yogyakarta, Djaka Waluja and Sumarni, Ann's former field assistants, had no idea what had become of Barry until a photograph of him with Ann, Lolo, and Maya turned up on Indonesian television in a report on Obama during the presidential campaign in 2008. When Linda Wylie, another Mercer Island classmate of Ann's, had the connection pointed out by a friend after the 2004 convention speech, she went looking for a copy of Obama's book. The resemblance between Obama and his mother seemed unmistakable.

"The minute I saw the picture, I felt like crying," Wylie said.

Beyond the physical resemblance, people who had known Ann well were certain they recognized the imprint of her values, her confidence, her intelligence, on her son. There were even traces of her dry humor. Many remembered her pride in him and wished she could have seen his success. Some wondered what she would have made of his choice to go into politics. Nancy Cooper remembered, sometime later, an exchange between herself and Ann during the

1988 presidential election campaign. The Reverend Jesse Jackson, running for the Democratic nomination, had given a speech at the University of Hawai'i —a speech that Cooper had attended. When she and Ann talked about it, Cooper was struck by Ann's excitement about Jackson and his multiracial Rainbow Coalition. Ann seemed, Cooper told me, "to have some sort of insider knowledge." When Cooper asked her about it, Ann told Cooper, for the first time, that her son's father was African. "Then, for me, it was as if a light went on," Cooper told me. "Up till that point, everything I knew about her was associated with Java. . . . In that moment, she was just really enthusiastic about Jackson's campaign. It was almost as if she knew Jesse Jackson."

Two months after Obama's 2004 speech in Boston, the Crown Publishing Group reissued *Dreams from My Father,* and it became an instant bestseller. The editor of the new edition had asked Obama to write a short preface, bringing his story up to date. In it, Obama briskly summarized what had happened in his life and in the world in the years since the book had first appeared in the summer of 1995, while Ann was dying. He ended the preface on the memory of his mother, "the single constant in my life."

> In my daughters I see her every day, her joy, her capacity for wonder. I won't try to describe how deeply I mourn her passing still. I know that she was the kindest, most generous spirit I have ever known, and that what is best in me I owe to her.

When we met in July 2010, Obama was eighteen months into his term as president. It had been a scorching summer. The administration had been taken up with the war in Afghanistan, the biggest oil spill in history, an economic recovery that felt fitful at best. That morning, however, Obama had signed into law a major overhaul of the financial regulatory system, the product of a series of reforms he had proposed thirteen months earlier. By the time he settled into a chair in the Oval Office that afternoon, he seemed downright buoyant. He spoke about his mother with fondness, humor, and a degree of candor that I had not expected. There was also in his tone at times a hint of gentle forbearance. Perhaps it was the tone of someone whose patience had been tested, by a person he loved, to the point where he had stepped back to a safer distance. Or perhaps it was the knowingness of a grown child seeing his parent as irredeemably human.

"She was a very strong person in her own way," Obama said, when I asked about Ann's limitations as a mother. "Resilient, able to bounce back from setbacks, persistent—the fact that she ended up finishing her dissertation. But despite all those strengths, she was not a well-organized person. And that disorganization, you know, spilled over. Had it not been for my grandparents, I think, providing some sort of safety net financially, being able to take me and my sister on at certain spots, I think my mother would have had to make some different decisions. And I think that sometimes she took for granted that, 'Well, it'll all work out and it'll be fine.' But the fact is, it might not always have been fine, had it not been for my grandmother, who was a much more orderly and much more conservative—I don't mean politically but conservative in terms of how you structure your life—a much more conventional person. Had she not been there to provide that floor, I think our young lives could have been much more chaotic than they were."

Disorganized, I observed, could mean almost anything—from a messy house to a messy life.

"All of the above," he said.

As a child, the president went on to say, he did not care that his mother was uninterested in housekeeping or cooking or traditional homemaker activities. In fact, she used to joke about that. But in her handling of financial matters, he said, she put herself in vulnerable positions and was "always at the margins." He ascribed the struggle over her insurance at the end of her life to "the fact that she'd never make a decision about a job based on did it provide health insurance benefits that were stable and secure, or a pension, or savings or things like that." Her neglect of those details was a source of tension between her and her parents, "because they always felt they had to kind of come in and provide assistance to smooth over some of her choices."

But he did not, he said, hold his mother's choices against her. Part of being an adult is seeing your parents in the round, "as people who have their own strengths, weaknesses, quirks, longings." He did not believe, he said, that parents served their children well by being unhappy. If his mother had cramped her spirit, it would not have given him a happier childhood. As it was, she gave him the single most important gift a parent can give—"a sense of unconditional love that was big enough that, with all the surface disturbances of our lives, it sustained me, entirely." People wonder about his calm and even-keeled manner, the president observed. He credited the temperament he was born with and the fact that "from a very early age, I always felt I was loved and that my mother thought I was special."

Looking back, he said, many of his life choices were informed by her example. His decision to go into public service, he said, grew out of values she instilled—"a sense that the greatest thing you can do in the world is to help somebody else, be kind, think about issues like poverty and how can you give people a greater opportunity? . . .

So I have no doubt that a lot of my career choices are rooted in her and what she thought was important." On the other hand, his decision to settle in Chicago, to marry a woman with roots in the city, and to place a premium on giving stability to his children was in part a reaction to "the constant motion that was my childhood. And some of it wasn't necessarily a rejection of her, it was just an observation about me and how I fit in, or didn't fit in, in certain environments.

"My mother lived a classic expatriate life, and there are aspects of that life that are very appealing," Obama said, going on to characterize his mother's life in a way that seemed perhaps to understate the depth and seriousness of her commitment to Indonesia. "Both my sister and I, I think, to one degree or another, wrestle with the fact that it's fun to just take off and live in a new culture and meet interesting people and learn new languages and eat strange foods. You know, it's a life full of adventure. So the appeal of that is very powerful to me. Now, the flip side of that is that you're always a little bit of an outsider, you're always a little bit of an observer. There's an element of you're not fully committed to this place and this thing. It's not so much, I think, me rejecting what she did; I understood the appeal of it, and I still do. But it was a conscious choice, I think, on my part, that the idea of being a citizen of the world, but without any real anchor, had both its benefits but also its own limits.

"Either way, you were giving something up. And I chose to give up this other thing—partly because I'd gotten what my mother had provided when I was young, which was a lot of adventure and a great view of the world."

Was there a moment during the campaign or the election, I wondered, when his mind turned to his mother—the person who had given him the values, the self-confidence, and the life story that became the foundation of his extraordinary political rise?

"I'm sure there were a number of moments," he said. "But there was one. . . ."

It was January 3, 2008, the night of the Iowa caucuses, the first major step in the nominating process for the presidency.

"We had been thirty points down in the national polls," he said. "Everybody was doubting that we could pull something off. And our whole theory in the Iowa caucuses was that we could create this whole new group of caucus-goers—people who hadn't been involved in politics before, people who had become cynical and disaffected about politics. There were doubts, obviously, that an African-American candidate would get the votes in an overwhelmingly white state. And so, caucus night, you go to this caucus site and you see just these people sort of streaming in. And they're all kinds of folks, right? Young, old, black, white, Hispanic—this is Des Moines."

Obama began to chuckle at the memory of that night, his face breaking into a broad smile.

"There was one guy who looked like Gandalf," he continued. "He had a staff. He had installed a little video monitor—I still don't know how he did this—that looped one of my TV commercials on this thing. You know, had a long white beard and stuff? But the mood and the atmosphere was one of hope and this sense that we can overcome a lot of the old baggage. So it was a wonderful moment. At that point, we figured we were going to win that night.

"But I remember driving away from that caucus and thinking not, 'Wouldn't my mother be proud of me,' but rather, 'Wouldn't she have enjoyed *being in* this caucus.' It would have just felt like she was right at home. It was imbued with her spirit in a way that was very touching to me. I teared up at that point, in a way that I didn't in most of the campaign. Because it just seemed to somehow capture something that she had given to me as a young person— and here it was manifest in a really big way. It seemed to vindicate what she had believed in and who she was."

Could he say what it was about that evening that seemed so consistent with her spirit? I asked.

"It was a sense that beneath our surface differences, we're all the same, and that there's more good than bad in each of us. And that, you know, we can reach across the void and touch each other and believe in each other and work together.

"That's precisely the naiveté and idealism that was part of her," he added. "And that's, I suppose, the naive idealism in me."

Acknowledgments

I began working on this book in the late spring of 2008, before Barack Obama was the Democratic presidential nominee. At a time when it might not have seemed reasonable to do so, many people trusted me and gave me the benefit of the doubt. In the text and the endnotes, I've credited the nearly two hundred people who took the time to help me understand my subject. To some of them, I owe an extra debt of gratitude for additional acts of generosity and kindness; there are other people, too, who helped me in different ways. I wish to thank them here.

First and foremost, there is Ann Dunham's family. I could not have begun to understand her childhood and the lives of her parents without the cooperation and openness of Charles Payne, Arlene Payne, Jon Payne, and Ralph Dunham. I do not underestimate the magnitude of what I asked of Maya Soetoro-Ng, whose memories and insights were a gift, bestowed with a graceful balance of candor, loyalty, and discretion. I am indebted, too, to her brother for having made the time to talk with me in the White House and for the frankness and feeling with which he did it.

In Hawaii, Alice Dewey, an inspiration to generations of anthropologists, shared with me her infectious passion for Java, her wide-ranging wisdom, and countless letters and papers. Garrett and Bron Solyom gave me access to Ann's field notebooks and other papers, meticulously archived by Bron. They fed me, gave me a place to work, and explained mysteries of Java that they surely doubted I would ever comprehend. Marguerite Robinson, in Brookline, Massachusetts, gave me a brilliant tutorial in the development of microfinance in Indonesia, as well as invaluable introductions to her former colleagues at Bank Rakyat Indonesia.

In Jakarta, I am especially thankful to Agus Rachmadi of Bank Rakyat Indonesia for serving as my guide to the bank, and to Kamardy Arief, the former chief executive officer. Made Suarjana took time away from his job to travel from East Kalimantan to Yogyakarta and spend several days with me there and in Kajar and other villages where Ann worked. Julia Suryakusuma shared with me her wonderfully illuminating correspondence with Ann. John McGlynn, the American writer and translator of Indonesian literature, took me on an unforgettable walk through one of the last neighborhoods that resemble Jakarta as Ann found it in 1967. Taluki Sasmitarsi accompanied me to villages and markets, and took me all over Yogyakarta on the backseat of her motorbike.

Kris Hartadi, pressed into service at the last minute after another translator was quarantined in Singapore during the H1N1 pandemic, did two consecutive days of simultaneous interpreting in Yogyakarta. Tita Suhartono and Yan Matius in Jakarta helped with research and gave me invaluable practical advice. In the United States, Alan M. Stevens, one of the two coauthors of *A Comprehensive*

Indonesian-English Dictionary, generously translated documents, proofread my manuscript, and enlightened me about such things as Indonesian orthography and honorifics.

At the Ford Foundation in New York, Tony Maloney and Marcy Goldstein made it possible for me to read dozens of grant files in the foundation's archives. In Kansas, Kim Baker combed the public record for clues to the lives of Ann Dunham's forebears. Michael J. Rosenfeld, author of *The Age of Independence: Interracial Unions, Same-Sex Unions, and the Changing American Family* (Harvard University Press, 2007), supplied me with statistics on interracial marriage. In New York, Steven Rattazzi kept my computer running and made my manuscript look flawless. Catherine Talese secured permission to use certain photographs. Jill Bokor and Sandy Smith made available a serene and sunlit aerie in which to write.

At *The New York Times,* Bill Keller, Jill Abramson, and Dick Stevenson gave me the opportunity to write at length about Barack Obama, starting in the spring of 2007, not long after he declared his candidacy, and continuing for a year. Rebecca Corbett, who edited those articles, did not flinch when I proposed a detour to consider the candidate's mom. On the basis of that article, Sarah McGrath at Riverhead Books proposed a book on Ann, and Riverhead gave me the time and the means to research her life in depth. Sarah proved to be as incisive and supportive an editor as one could possibly hope. I am grateful to Geoff Kloske at Riverhead, and to Sarah Stein. Scott Moyers of the Wylie Agency inspired utter confidence that nothing could go awry. Arthur Gelb, the former managing editor of *The New York Times,* encouraged the project from its very beginning.

Mia and Owen Ritter, who have taught me much of what little

I understand about being a mother, tolerated my absences, took an interest in my work, and provided joy and comic relief. As for Joe Lelyveld, to whom I am indebted in too many ways to count, I will say here simply that he gave me unfailingly wise advice, perfectly grilled sardines, great happiness, and best of all, himself.

Notes

Works cited in brief in the Notes are cited in full in the Bibliography.

PROLOGUE

Page

6 *modernized the spelling:* The spelling of certain Indonesian words changed after Indonesia gained its independence from the Dutch in 1949, and again under a 1972 agreement between Indonesia and Malaysia. *Dj,* as in Djakarta, was replaced with *J,* as in Jakarta. The letter *J,* as in Jogjakarta, became *Y,* as in Yogyakarta. Names containing *oe,* such as Soeharto, are now often spelled with a *u,* as in Suharto. However, older spellings are still used in some personal names. Both "Soeharto" and "Suharto" are used for the name of the former president of Indonesia. After her divorce from Lolo Soetoro, Ann Dunham Soetoro kept his last name for a number of years while she was still working in Indonesia, but she changed the spelling to Sutoro. Their daughter, Maya Soetoro-Ng, chose to keep the traditional spelling of her Indonesian surname.

7 *"the single constant":* Barack Obama, *Dreams from My Father,* xii.

7 *put those values to work:* Barack Obama, *The Audacity of Hope,* 205–206.

8 *"I gave you an interesting life":* Interview with President Obama, July 21, 2010.

CHAPTER ONE. DREAMS FROM THE PRAIRIE

For the history of Kansas, I am indebted to Craig Miner, a professor of history at Wichita State University, and to his book, *Kansas: The History of the Sunflower State, 1854–2000.* For the history of Butler County, I received invaluable help from Lisa Cooley, the curator of education at the Butler County History Center and Kansas Oil Museum in El Dorado, and from Jay M. Price, an associate professor of history at Wichita State University and the author of *El Dorado: Legacy of an Oil Boom.* I benefited by reading *Augusta, Kansas 1868–1990*, by Burl Allison Jr., in the Augusta public library, and an unpublished paper, "The Klan in Butler County," by Roxie Olmstead, on file in the Butler County History Center library. Kim Baker, a researcher based in Topeka, combed newspaper archives and public records for the history of the Dunham and Payne families. Most of what I have written about the early lives of Stanley Dunham and Madelyn Payne came from long interviews with his brother, Ralph Dunham, and her siblings, Charles, Arlene, and Jon Payne. A cousin of the Paynes, Margaret McCurry Wolf, also helped me with family history. Clarence Kerns, Mack Gilkeson, and Virginia Ewalt, contemporaries of Stanley Dunham and Madelyn Payne, helped me understand the place and time in which they grew up. Ian Dunham, the grandson of Ralph Dunham, gave me valuable guidance.

18 *grasshoppers blanketed the ground:* Burl Allison Jr., *Augusta, Kansas 1868–1990* (Hillsboro, KS: Multi Business Press, 1993).

18 *planted with kaffir corn:* Jay M. Price, *El Dorado: Legacy of an Oil Boom.*

27 *"dabbling in moonshine, cards, and women":* Barack Obama, *Dreams from My Father,* 14.

31 *campaign weakened the Klan:* Jack Wayne Traylor, "William Allen White's 1924 Gubernatorial Campaign," *Kansas Historical Quarterly,* 42, no. 2, 180–191.

38 *"He looks like a wop'":* Obama, *Dreams from My Father,* 14.

42 *The transformation had begun:* Martin Shingler, "Bette Davis Made Over in Wartime: The Feminization of an Androgynous Star in *Now, Voyager* (1942)," *Film History,* 20 (2008), 269–280.

43 *"One of Gramps's less judicious ideas":* Obama, *Dreams from My Father,* 19.

CHAPTER TWO. COMING OF AGE IN SEATTLE

This chapter is based largely on interviews and correspondence with Marilyn McMeekin Bauer, Susan Botkin Blake, Maxine Hanson Box, Bill Byers, John Hunt, Elaine Bowe Johnson, Stephen McCord, Jane Waddell Morris, Marilyn O'Neill, Raleigh Roark, Iona Stenhouse, Jim Sullivan, Kathy Powell Sullivan, Chip Wall, Jim Wichterman, and Linda Hall Wylie. I also interviewed Thomas Farner and Judy Farner Ware, whose late sister, Jackie Farner, was a friend of Stanley Ann's. On the subject of Madelyn and Stanley Dunham during this period, I am again indebted to their siblings Charles Payne, Arlene Payne, Jon Payne, and Ralph Dunham. The Reverend Dr. Peter J. Luton, senior minister at East Shore Unitarian Church, helped me with the history of the church, as did Judy Ware. The account of the case against John Stenhouse is based on information from his daughter, Iona, and on contemporaneous reporting in *The Seattle Times*.

74 *"my grandfather forbade her"*: Obama, *Dreams from My Father,* 16.

CHAPTER THREE. EAST-WEST

For statistics on Hawaii in 1960, I relied on the *State of Hawaii Data Book,* published in 1967 by the Department of Planning and Economic Development. On the University of Hawai'i and the East-West Center, I read several years' worth of issues of the student newspaper, *Ka Leo O Hawai'i,* and back issues of *Impulse,* a magazine published later by East-West Center grant recipients. At the East-West Center, I received help from Karen Knudsen, director of the Office of External Affairs; Derek Ferrar, a media relations specialist; and Phyllis Tabusa, a research information specialist. Jeannette "Benji" Bennington, now retired from the center, provided invaluable insight and stories. Mia Noguchi, director of public relations for the university, and Stuart Lau, the registrar, helped me with statistics and facts. I benefited from interviews with former students, including Bill Collier, Gerald Krausse, Sylvia Krausse, Jeanette Takamura, Mark Wimbush and Pake Zane. On the subject of the Dunham family, I drew on interviews with Charles, Arlene, and Jon Payne; Ralph Dunham, and Maya Soetoro-Ng. I also used information from interviews with Marilyn Bauer, Maxine Box, Bill Byers, Takeshi Harada, Renske Heringa, Richard Hook, John Hunt, Kay Ikranagara, Kadi Warner, and Linda Hall Wylie. On the subject of Lolo Soetoro, I spoke with Benji Bennington, Bill Collier, Gerald and Sylvia Krausse, Kismardhani S-Roni, Maya Soetoro-Ng, Trisulo, Sonny Trisulo, and Pete Vayda. For the account of the events of September 30, 1965, and afterward in Indonesia, I am indebted to Adam Schwarz's *A Nation in Waiting: Indonesia's Search for Stability* and Adrian Vickers's *A History of Modern Indonesia*.

83 *"Gramps's relationship with my mother"*: Obama, *Dreams from My Father,* 21.
84 *Russian language class:* Ibid., 9.
85 *He had been flown to the United States:* Michael Dobbs, "Obama Overstates Kennedys' Role in Helping His Father," *The Washington Post,* March 30, 2008, A1.
85 *received "invitations to campus":* Ka Leo O Hawai'i, October 8, 1959, 3.
85 *interview in the* Honolulu Star-Bulletin: *Honolulu Star-Bulletin,* November 28, 1959, 5.
86 *"If the people cannot rule themselves":* "First African Enrolled in Hawaii Studied Two Years by Mail," *Ka Leo O Hawai'i,* October 8, 1959, 3.

88 *"many things I didn't understand"*: Obama, *Dreams from My Father,* 10.

89 *"There's no record of a real wedding"*: Ibid., 22.

90 *left in late June: Honolulu Star-Bulletin,* June 20, 1962, 7.

90 *"No mention is made"*: Obama, *Dreams from My Father,* 26–27.

93 *little thought to black people:* Ibid., 18.

93 *encountered race hatred:* Ibid., 19–20.

93 *"the condition of the black race"*: Ibid., 21.

94 *Obama only imagines their reaction:* Ibid., 17–18.

94 *"I am a little dubious"*: David Mendell, *Obama: From Promise to Power* (New York: Amistad, 2007), 29.

95 *"weren't happy with the idea"*: Obama, *Dreams from My Father,* 125.

95 *"he didn't want the Obama blood sullied"*: Ibid., 126.

97 *"grande dame of escrow"*: Dan Nakaso, "Obama's Tutu a Hawaii Banking Female Pioneer," *Honolulu Advertiser,* March 30, 2008.

103 *Like some Javanese:* Indonesians are addressed by their first name, usually preceded by a title—never by their last name, if they have one. The Indonesian equivalent of *Mr.* is *Bapak,* meaning "father," or its abbreviated form, *Pak,* as in Pak Soetoro. The title is an expression of respect for age, position, and other attributes. Sometimes the name is shortened, as in Pak Harto for Soeharto. The equivalent of *Mrs.* is *Ibu,* meaning "mother" or "married woman," or *Bu,* as in Bu Ann. However, because I have written this book in English and many of the names are Western, I have tended to use, for consistency's sake and where possible, surnames on subsequent references. For family members of Ann Dunham, I have often used first names.

104 *"beyond her parents' reach"*: Obama, *Dreams from My Father,* 42.

106 *"choked with bodies"*: Adam Schwarz, *A Nation in Waiting,* 21.

106 *"one of the worst mass murders"*: Ibid., 20.

106 *married on March 5, 1964:* Date given on passport application filled out by Ann Dunham in early 1980s, from her personal papers.

CHAPTER FOUR. INITIATION IN JAVA

The description of Jakarta and Indonesia in the late 1960s and early 1970s and details of Ann's life there come from interviews with Halimah Bellows, Halimah Brugger, Elizabeth Bryant, Bill Collier, Stephen des Tombes, Michael Dove, Rens Heringa, Ikranagara, Kay Ikranagara, Samardal Manan, Wahyono Martowikrido, John McGlynn, Saman, Garrett and Bronwen Solyom, Sumastuti Sumukti, and Yang Suwan. I also relied on *A History of Modern Indonesia* by Adrian Vickers and *A Nation in Waiting* by Adam Schwarz. On the subject of Ann's employment, I am indebted to Irwan Holmes, Kay Ikranagara, Trusti Jarwadi, Leonard Kibble, Samardal Manan, Felina Pramono, Joseph Sigit, Sudibyo Siyam, and

Stephen des Tombes. Information on the Institute for Management Education and Development also came from the archives of the Ford Foundation. For the facts of Lolo's work, I relied on his brother-in-law, Trisulo, and on Sonny Trisulo, Lolo's nephew. Insight into Ann as a parent came from her children as well as from Richard Hook, Kay Ikranagara, Don Johnston, Saman, Julia Suryakusuma, and Kadi Warner, among others.

111 *"join in the killings"*: Adrian Vickers, *A History of Modern Indonesia,* 158.

115 *Indonesia's Prague Spring:* Schwarz, *A Nation in Waiting,* 33.

119 *"The Indonesian businessmen"*: Obama, *Dreams from My Father*, 43.

127 *"They are not my people"*: Ibid., 47.

128 *Ann's loneliness was a constant:* Ibid., 42–43.

129 *"power had taken Lolo"*: Ibid., 45.

132 *"She loved to take children"*: Obama, *The Audacity of Hope,* 205.

132 *"you're going to need some values"*: Obama, *Dreams from My Father,* 49.

133 *ideal human virtues:* Koentjaraningrat, *Javanese Culture,* 122.

137 *"I was an American, she decided"*: Obama, *Dreams from My Father,* 47.

137 *"no picnic for me either, buster"*: Ibid., 48.

138 *"in Hawaii very soon—a year, tops"*: Ibid., 54.

138 *"never would have made the trip"*: Obama, *The Audacity of Hope,* 273.

CHAPTER FIVE. TRESPASSERS WILL BE EATEN

For the details of Ann's 1973 bus trip, I relied on her letter to Bill Byers and interviews with Jon Payne and Arlene Payne. The information on Ann's life as a graduate student came from Benji Bennington, Evelyn Caballero, Alice Dewey, Mendl Djunaidy, Ben Finney, Jean Kennedy, John Raintree, Garrett and Bronwen Solyom, Kadi Warner, and Brent Watanabe. For the sections on her experiences in Jakarta and Yogyakarta in the mid-1970s, I spoke with Rens Heringa, Terence Hull, Kay Ikranagara, Wahyono Martowikrido, Nancy Peluso, and Maya Soetoro-Ng. I also had access to some of Ann's academic records and correspondence with Alice Dewey.

146 *"'You two will become great friends'"*: Obama, *Dreams from My Father,* 64.

146 *Obama's account of his father's Christmas visit:* Ibid., 67–69.

149 *baking cookies was not at the top:* Ibid., 75.

152 *Her most important market informants:* Alice G. Dewey, *Peasant Marketing in Java,* xiv.

153 *"the best and most comprehensive study"*: Koentjaraningrat, *Javanese Culture,* 176.

158 *Her interest was function:* Bronwen Solyom, Symposium on Ann Dunham, University of Hawai'i at Mānoa, September 12, 2008.

158 *"was interested in the place where vision meets execution"*: Maya Soetoro-Ng, foreword to S. Ann Dunham, *Surviving Against the Odds: Village Industry in Indonesia,* ix–x.

160 *course in entrepreneurship:* Interview with Mendl W. Djunaidy, associate dean, East-West Center, October 7, 2008.

160 *"I immediately said no"*: Obama, *Dreams from My Father,* 76–77.

CHAPTER SIX. IN THE FIELD

Most of the material in this chapter comes from Ann Dunham's field notes, proposals, papers, and drafts, and the unpublished version of her dissertation, "Peasant Blacksmithing in Indonesia: Surviving and Thriving Against All Odds." I also drew on Garrett and Bronwen Solyom's writings on the Javanese kris; correspondence between Ann Dunham and Alice Dewey, and a 1974 edition of *Guide to Java* by Peter Hutton and Hans Hoefer. I used material from interviews with Clare Blenkinsop, Nancy Cooper, Alice Dewey, Michael Dove, Maggie Norobangun, President Obama, John Raintree, Khismardani S-Roni, Taluki Sasmitarsi, Maya Soetoro-Ng, the Solyoms, Sumarni and Djaka Waluja, and from e-mails written by Haryo Soetendro.

175 *Clifford Geertz confessed:* Richard Bernstein, "Anthropologist, Retracing Steps After 3 Decades, Is Shocked by Change," *The New York Times,* May 11, 1988.

176 *part-time unpaid cottage-industry workers:* S. Ann Dunham, "Women's Work in Village Industries on Java," unpublished paper from the 1980s.

178 *But Ann intended to expand the concept:* Ann Dunham, "Occupational Multiplicity as a Peasant Strategy," early draft of dissertation.

179 *sounds of forging:* S. Ann Dunham, "Peasant Blacksmithing in Indonesia: Surviving and Thriving Against All Odds," unpublished dissertation, 1992, 499.

187 *One scene of Pak Sastro and his wife:* Ibid., 556–560.

188 *"men of Kajar are fated"*: Ibid., 495.

188 *"Whenever villagers have a problem"*: Ibid., 533.

189 *"There are numerous stories of kerises rattling about"*: Dunham, "Women's Work in Village Industries on Java," 41.

191 *In the acknowledgments:* Dunham, unpublished dissertation, vii–viii.

197 *In a haunting scene:* Obama, *Dreams from My Father,* 94–96.

CHAPTER SEVEN. COMMUNITY ORGANIZING

The account of Ann's years in Semarang and her work on the Provincial Development Project is based on interviews with Clare Blenkinsop, Alice Dewey, Carl

Dutto, Don Flickinger, Bruce Harker, Ann Hawkins, Richard Holloway, Sidney Jones, Dick Patten, Nancy Peluso, John Raintree, Jerry Mark Silverman, Maya Soetoro-Ng, Kadi Warner, and Glen Williams. For the brief history of early credit programs, I also drew on *The Microfinance Revolution: Lessons from Indonesia* by Marguerite S. Robinson and on *Progress with Profits: The Development of Rural Banking in Indonesia* by Richard H. Patten and Jay K. Rosengard. The final paragraph, about the Ford Foundation, is based on documents in the Ford Foundation archives.

214 *"they believed that poor village women":* Letter from Ann Sutoro to Hanna Papanek, July 2, 1981.

216 *one-third of the 486 units:* Robinson, *The Microfinance Revolution: Lessons from Indonesia*, 115–118; Patten and Rosengard, *Progress with Profits*, 22–30.

217 *providing not only capital but training:* Ibid., 31–35.

220 *"Many hours of my childhood":* Maya Soetoro-Ng, foreword to S. Ann Dunham, *Surviving Against the Odds: Village Industry in Indonesia*, ix.

222 *"would be superb":* Memorandum to the File from Sidney Jones, March 10, 1980, PA 800-0893, Ford Foundation Archives.

CHAPTER EIGHT. THE FOUNDATION

This chapter draws heavily on information from grant files in the Ford Foundation archives. In addition, I had access to some of Ann Sutoro's personal papers, field notes, and correspondence from this period. I've also relied on interviews with Terry Bigalke, Halimah Brugger, Bill Carmichael, Carol Colfer, Bill Collier, Alice Dewey, Michael Dove, Jim Fox, Adrienne Germain, Ann Hawkins, Rens Heringa, Richard Holloway, Kay Ikranagara, Tim Jessup, Sidney Jones, Tom Kessinger, David Korten, Frances Korten, David McCauley, Georgia McCauley, John McGlynn, Paschetta Sarmidi, Adi Sasono, Suzanne Siskel, Maya Soetoro-Ng, Saraswati Sunindyo, Julia Suryakusuma, Frank Thomas, Pete Vayda, Yang Suwan, and Mary Zurbuchen. Some information on the history of the Ford office in Jakarta came from *Celebrating Indonesia: Fifty Years with the Ford Foundation 1953–2003,* published by the Ford Foundation in 2003.

226 *"Life in the bubble":* Interview with Mary Zurbuchen, September 30, 2008.

231 *William Carmichael, Ford's vice president:* "Recommendation for Grant Action," April 18, 1985, PA 800-0893, Ford Foundation Archives, 4–5.

232 *Ann wrote in 1981 to Carol Colfer:* Letter from Ann Sutoro to Carol Colfer, February 2, 1981, PA 800-0893, Ford Foundation Archives.

233 *"With all this complexity":* Memorandum to the files from Ann D. Sutoro, November 3, 1981, PA 800-0893, Ford Foundation Archives.

235 *"a country of 'smiling' or gentle oppression":* Memorandum to participants, Delhi Conference on Women's Programming, from Ann Dunham Soetoro, April 18, 1982, PA 809-0878, Ford Foundation Archives.

236 *"our best reference on the condition":* Memorandum to the files from Ann D. Sutoro, March 16, 1984, PA 835-0145, Ford Foundation Archives, 2.

237 *"Okay, sport":* Interview with Sidney Jones, July 1, 2009.

237 *"How do you think she felt?":* Interview with Saraswati Sunindyo, February 17, 2009.

237 *"a lonely witness for secular humanism":* Obama, *Dreams from My Father,* 50.

237 *her chin trembles:* Ibid., 126.

237–238 *"the unreflective heart of her youth":* Ibid., 124.

238 *"helping women buy a sewing machine":* Ibid., xi.

260 *"looked like a black ball surrounded by a brilliant white light":* Ward Keeler, "Sharp Rays: Javanese Responses to a Solar Eclipse," *Indonesia,* 46 (October 1988), 91–101.

267 *helped shift the government's focus:* Memorandum to the files from Mary S. Zurbuchen, October 29, 1998, PA 800-0893, Ford Foundation Archives, 6.

CHAPTER NINE. "SURVIVING AND THRIVING AGAINST ALL ODDS"

Material in this chapter came from interviews with Jim Boomgard, Alice Dewey, Michael Dove, Ralph Dunham, Ben Finney, Jim Fox, Rens Heringa, Dick Hook, Mary Houghton, John Hunt, Don Johnston, Nina Nayar, Barack Obama, Dick Patten, Sarah Patten, Marguerite Robinson, Sabaruddin, Maya Soetoro-Ng, Garrett and Bronwen Solyom, Eric Stone, Made Suarjana, Julia Suryakusuma, Trisulo, Sonny Trisulo, and Yang Suwan. In connection with Bank Rakyat Indonesia, I spoke with Sulaiman Arif Arianto, Kamardy Arief, Ch. Oktiva Susi E., Cut Indriani, Sriwiyono Joyomartono, Agus Rachmadi, Slamet Riyadi,Tomy Sugianto, Flora Sugondo, and Widayanti and Retno Wijayanti. I also drew on personal papers and field notes of Ann Dunham's, her letters to Dewey and Suryakusuma, her reports to the bank, her unpublished dissertation, and her curriculum vitae.

271 *helped make up the difference:* Interview with Maya Soetoro-Ng.

273 *"spir. develop (ilmu batin)":* This appears to refer to spiritual development. *Ilmu batin* is an Indonesian phrase referring to esoteric learning or mysticism.

275 *Madelyn would rent a hotel room:* Interview with Adi Sasono, January 22, 2009.

278 *first credit project for women and artisan-caste members:* Ann Dunham, curriculum vitae, 1993.

278 *In the Punjab:* Dunham, "Peasant Blacksmithing in Indonesia: Surviving and Thriving Against All Odds," 877–879.

281 *"in many ways the most spiritually awakened person":* Obama, *The Audacity of Hope,* 205.

281 *Though Ann had been led to believe:* Interviews with Alice Dewey.

283 *a rate of 120,000 a month:* James J. Fox, "Banking on the People: The Creation of General Rural Credit in Indonesia," in Sandy Toussaint and Jim Taylor, eds., *Applied Anthropology in Australasia* (Perth: University of Western Australia Press, 1999).

284 *"probably the single largest and most successful credit program":* For the history of the microfinance program of Bank Rakyat Indonesia, I have relied on *The Microfinance Revolution,* vol. 2: *Lessons from Indonesia,* by Marguerite S. Robinson; "Banking on the People," by James J. Fox; and *Progress with Profits: The Development of Rural Banking in Indonesia,* by Richard H. Patten and Jay K. Rosengard. Additional information came from a long interview with Kamardy Arief, the former chief executive officer of Bank Rakyat Indonesia.

286 *115,000 loans a month:* James J. Boomgard and Kenneth J. Angell, "Bank Rakyat Indonesia's Unit Desa System: Achievements and Replicability," in Maria Otero and Elisabeth Rhyne, eds., *The New World of Microenterprise Finance: Building Healthy Financial Institutions for the Poor* (West Hartford, CT: Kumarian Press, 1994).

286 *helped the bank weather the crisis:* Richard H. Patten, Jay K. Rosengard, and Don E. Johnston Jr., "Microfinance Success Amidst Macroeconomic Failure: The Experience of Bank Rakyat Indonesia During the East Asian Crisis," *World Development,* 29, no. 6 (2001), 1057–1069.

286 *more than four thousand microbanking outlets:* Interview with Sulaiman Arif Arianto, managing director, Bank Rakyat Indonesia, January 14, 2009.

287 *"the finest development worker":* Interview with Mary Houghton, November 14, 2008.

291 *"a little of his magical power had managed to rub off":* Dunham, unpublished dissertation, 285.

302 *"is one of the richest ethnographic studies":* Michael R. Dove, *Anthropological Quarterly,* 83, no. 2 (Spring 2010), 449–454.

CHAPTER TEN. MANHATTAN CHILL

This chapter is based largely on interviews with Niki Armacost, Nancy Barry, Brinley Bruton, Donald Creedon, Susan Davis, Sri R. Dwianto, Ruth Goodwin Groen, Dewiany Gunawan, Sarita Gupta, Bruce Harker, Mary Houghton, Don Johnston, Celina Kawas, Dinny Jusuf, Wanjiku Kibui, Nina Nayar, Brigitta Rahayoe, Barbara Shortle, Maya Soetoro-Ng, Garrett and Bronwen Solyom, Made

Suarjana, Monica Tanuhandaru, Kellee Tsai, Pete Vayda, and Lawrence Yano-vitch. I also had access to some of Ann Dunham's correspondence and personal papers dating from this period. Amy Rosmarin made available to me a videotape of a professional presentation made by Ann.

319 *microfinance institutions were reaching only a tiny fraction: What's New in Women's World Banking,* 2, no. 2 (May 1994).
326 *"I am now going further into credit card debt":* Memo from Ann Dunham Sutoro to Nancy Barry, September 8, 1993.
331 *"except the D and C, which I postponed":* Letter from Ann Sutoro to Barbara E. Shortle, July 18, 1995.

CHAPTER ELEVEN. COMING HOME

This chapter relies on interviews with James Boomgard, Gillie Brown, Alice Dewey, Michael Dove, Bruce Harker, Ann Hawkins, Rens Heringa, Don John-ston, Georgia McCauley, Ferne Mele, Nina Nayar, Mayling Oey-Gardiner, Dick Patten, Arlene Payne, Jon Payne, Nancy Peluso, Slamet Riyadi, Sabaruddin, Bar-bara Shortle, Maya Soetoro-Ng, Garrett and Bronwen Solyom, Made Suarjana, Julia Suryakusuma, Tanya Torres, Pete Vayda, and Yang Suwan. I also had access to some of Ann Dunham's personal papers and correspondence.

353 *biggest mistake he made:* Scott Fornek, "Stanley Ann Dunham: 'Most Gener-ous Spirit,'" *Chicago Sun Times,* Sept. 9, 2007. In response to a question from me, President Obama, through a spokesman on Dec. 16, 2010, confirmed the *Sun-Times* account and said he had last spoken with his mother several days before her death.

EPILOGUE

This epilogue includes material from conversations with Gillie Brown, Nancy Cooper, John Hunt, Nina Nayar, President Obama, Maya Soetoro-Ng, Sumarni, Kellee Tsai, Djaka Waluja, and Linda Wylie.

360 *approximately nine thousand copies:* Interview with Peter Osnos, former pub-lisher of Times Books, March 2, 2008.
360 *in paperback the following year:* Interview with Philip Turner, former editor in chief of *Kodansha Globe,* March 4, 2008.
362 *"best in me I owe to her":* Obama, *Dreams from My Father,* xii.

Bibliography

Bresnan, John. *At Home Abroad: A Memoir of the Ford Foundation in Indonesia, 1953–1973*. Jakarta: Equinox, 2006.

Dewey, Alice G. *Peasant Marketing in Java*. New York: Free Press of Glencoe, 1962.

Dunham, S. Ann. *Peasant Blacksmithing in Indonesia: Surviving and Thriving Against All Odds*. Honolulu: University of Hawai'i, 1992.

Dunham, S. Ann. *Surviving Against the Odds: Village Industry in Indonesia*. Durham, NC: Duke University Press, 2009.

Ford Foundation. *Celebrating Indonesia: Fifty Years with the Ford Foundation 1953–2003*. New York: Ford Foundation, 2003.

Hutton, Peter, and Hans Hoefer. *Guide to Java*. Hong Kong: Apa Productions, 1974.

Koentjaraningrat. *Javanese Culture*. Oxford: Oxford University Press, 1985.

Miner, Craig. *Kansas: The History of the Sunflower State, 1854–2000*. Lawrence: University Press of Kansas, 2002.

Obama, Barack. *The Audacity of Hope*. New York: Crown, 2006.

———. *Dreams from My Father*. New York: Three Rivers Press, 1995.

Patten, Richard H., and Jay K. Rosengard. *Progress with Profits: The Development of Rural Banking in Indonesia*. San Francisco: ICS Press for the International Center for Economic Growth and the Harvard Institute for International Development, 1991.

Price, Jay M. *El Dorado: Legacy of an Oil Boom*. Charleston, SC: Arcadia, 2005.

Robinson, Marguerite S. *The Microfinance Revolution,* vol. 2: *Lessons from Indonesia*. Washington, DC: The World Bank, 2002.

Schwarz, Adam. *A Nation in Waiting: Indonesia's Search for Stability*. Oxford: Westview Press, 2000.

Solyom, Garrett, and Bronwen Solyom. *The World of the Javanese Keris*. Honolulu: Asian Arts Press, 1988.

Vickers, Adrian. *A History of Modern Indonesia*. Cambridge, England: Cambridge University Press, 2005.

A Note on Photos

Over the past three years, people surprised me repeatedly with photographs of Ann Dunham. There was the photo of Ann, at forty-four, on a Manhattan rooftop—the photo that left me wondering about her in the first place. There was the photo of Ann, in a borrowed sarong and *kebaya,* at the University of Hawaiʻi at age twenty-one. Over a dish of crisp fried cow's lung in a Jakarta restaurant in 2009, Samardal Manan pulled out a black-and-white snapshot dating back to 1969. When I met Bill Byers, he showed me a photo, of Ann in a dashiki, which he had held on to for thirty-five years. Classmates, colleagues, field assistants, a driver, a professor, protégées, family members, and friends unearthed images in old albums, stuffed in envelopes, bent at the corners. Ann kept photos, too. For years, she documented in photographs as well as writing the working lives of the blacksmiths and other craftspeople she studied. She took her camera on field trips with teams of younger colleagues to places like Sulawesi and Bali. Some of those pictures became part of her dissertation. After her death, many were kept by her close friends. Some of the images in this book were made public during the 2008 presidential campaign by Obama for America, the campaign organization. But most were made available to me by family members and friends of Ann Dunham, some of whom chose not to be credited by name.

Photo Credits

Page 28: Courtesy Margaret McCurry Wolf
Page 56: Linnet Dunden Botkin
Page 64; photo insert page 5: Polaris
Pages 99, 147, 148; photo insert page 2, middle: AP Photo/Obama for America
Page 102: Gerald and Sylvia Krausse

Page 139: AP Photo/Obama Presidential Campaign
Page 144: Bill Byers
Pages 167, 170: Nancy Peluso
Page 254: Collection of Julia Suryakusuma, reproduced with permission of Julia
   Suryakusuma